The craft's vibration increased exponentially and the ship's hull screamed in protest as the pilot slapped a single button. The pilot yelled out, "I am ejecting the sleep modules under protocol 37-4279, sending them to remote locations to prevent contact with the fairly primitive society on the planet below!"

The pilot locked its gaze on a monitor with a collection of icons, which ranged from reddish-orange to green. As each red one turned green, cylindrical pods rocketed out of the ship. After ejecting, the pods fired up their engines and careened off towards the planet below. Many of the icons changed to a flashing red as their ejection failed. Only about fifty of the escape vehicles were able to eject, leaving a hundred still on board.

A giant lurch knocked the pilot out of its couch, sending it careening off to the side of the cabin. Its head collided with a bulkhead on the side, stunning it. It pushed itself back to its feet and shook its head, trying to shrug off the pain. With a final head shake, it scrambled back into the couch and started keying in a sequence.

Barely visible in the shaking and stuttering camera, the pilot screamed one last time, "If anyone gets this message, I am transmitting the corrupted course logs to aid in rescue. Please send help......" Then, it pressed a final button on the console. The pilot's couch immediately sunk into the floor and disappeared from view.

A Novel by
G.A.PINKLEY

The world of Anthropia was created by G.A.Pinkley and Edward Gorgen

Anthropia Origins: Of Wolf and Men

is the first novel in the Anthropia saga.

Anthropia

an·throw·pee·ah [an(t)-thrō-ˈpē-ə]

The word Anthropia is derived from a blending of:

Anthropomorphic: described or thought of as having a human form
or human attributes.
and

Lycanthropy: the assumption of the form and characteristics of a wolf
held to be possible by witchcraft or magic.

Foreword from the author.

The world of Anthropia takes place in a reality that is similar to the Earth you know, but with many differences. Tectonic forces shaped the world differently than our earth. Its continents formed closer together and with no immensely large oceans splitting the world, so people were more exposed to other cultures they share the planet with. Countries, religions and politics developed differently from your Earth, but will feel familiar. The most comforting, or frustrating, aspect will be human nature ... that's hard to change.

Anthropia Origins: Of Wolf and Men is a work of speculative fiction that explores how the population of Earth would develop if an alien race crashed on the planet during the middle ages. It melds science fiction, fictional politics and anthropomorphism together with a slice of hard science fiction. It wraps it all up in an entertaining story of struggle, scientific discovery and triumph over human nature that defines the future of Earth.

This book explores several themes in some capacity: mild violence, politics, religious discussion and speciesism.

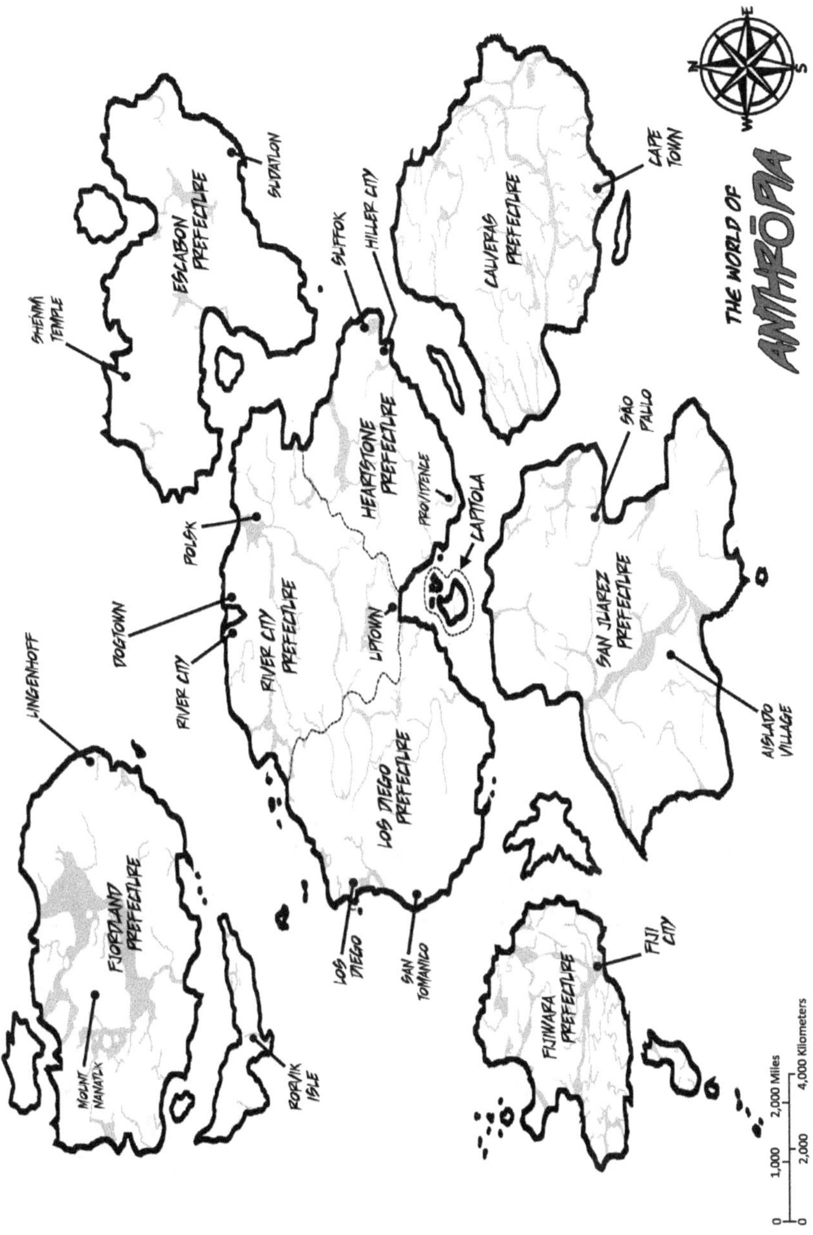
SUDATLON
ESLABON PREFECTURE
SHENMÄ TEMPLE
HILLER CITY
SUFFOK
CALIVERAS PREFECTURE
CAPE TOWN
THE WORLD OF ANTHRŌPIA
HEARTSTONE PREFECTURE
PROVIDENCE
SÃO PALLO
POLSK
CAPTIOLA
DOGTOWN
RIVER CITY
LIPTOWN
SAN JUAREZ PREFECTURE
RIVER CITY PREFECTURE
LINGENHOFF
AISLADO VILLAGE
LOS NEGO PREFECTURE
FJORDLAND PREFECTURE
LOS NEGO
SAN TOMANICO
FIJI CITY
MOUNT NANATIX
RORNIK ISLE
FIJINARA PREFECTURE
1,000   2,000 Miles
0   2,000   4,000 Kilometers
0

Chapter 1
Year 1357 – Rain of Fire

Video status: <u>Declassified</u>.

Black Box recording from Alien mother ship wreckage.

Mothership recording device located in the wreckage discovered July 25th, 1957.

Due to technological limits, data was previously unrecoverable until 2024.

Original voice translation completed March 27th, 2026 by the Talon Intelligent Computer (TIC) manufactured by Dres-Tek.

Subsequent High Resolution footage recovered December 21st, 2027.

VIDEO METADATA: ALIEN CRASH INCIDENT.
VIDEO DATA RECOVERED FROM ALIEN CRAFT.
CRYSTAL STORAGE DEVICE.
BLACK BOX RECORDING.
OVERDUB ENABLED.

————

"Mayday, Mayday!"

The pilot was laying on its belly while furiously clawing at the control panel in front of them. The creature's appearance was eerily similar to one of Earth's four-legged canines. Its face was completely covered in jet-black fur and was clothed in, what appeared to be, a pilot jumpsuit with a slim, white fur collar. Smoke and sparks were pouring out of the panels behind it and the video was cutting in and out.

"Pilot, Rank One," the translation was interrupted, as its name was an untranslatable series of whuffs and squeaks. "...of the Explorer Class ship, Wandering Mist." The pilot yelled over the horrendous sounds the ship was making.

"We were dispatched to the newly discovered, uninhabited remote planet Delta-2279675 to survey it for the..." the translator again failed on a name. "...Alliance." A violent explosion rocked the ship, making the pilot scramble to hold itself in its couch. The caninoid tapped madly at the console, trying to get the ship to respond.

"During Interspace-Compression-Transit, the ship sustained heavy damage. The damage also corrupted the main computer and the navigation ..." The ship lurched heavily mid-sentence, causing the camera to cut out. "... system. There is no record of what caused the damage in the logs, but it must have been catastrophic. We stayed in cold sleep for an estimated 350 extra cycles due to the corruption and are now in uncharted space."

The pilot paused while it looked over at a display nearby and then returned to its monologue, "The ship woke me from sleep as we approached what it thought was the correct destination, but we came out of jump too close to an unknown inhabited planet." It looked over at the cockpit recording camera. "Due to the damage in transit, the ship's autopilot is offline, manual controls are marginally functional and we are on a collision course with the world below. The ship has been unable to wake anyone else in the crew due to system corruption and I have been working alone to try to save the ship." The cabin suddenly groaned, causing the pilot to look up at the grating sound. "For the past 2 cycles, I have been trying to regain control of systems with very little luck."

The ship shuddered, rolled to the side and back again as the pilot quickly tapped at the control panel, trying to get the ship to respond to any input. "I managed to manually access some of the life support systems and have gained extremely limited control over them." The pilot reached over to the side console to tap a button. "We are entering the atmosphere at high velocity and the ship is starting to break up." Suddenly, it yelled loudly, "We have to abandon ship!"

The canine worked at the console with fury and focus to key in a sequence. The ship was beginning to shudder violently, making the camera image stutter and jump. Smoke and sparks in the cabin intensified and the pilot furiously hammered away at the keys on its console. "I have managed to nudge the guidance systems to crash the ship into the middle of a large ocean, hopefully to minimize the impact to the planet below."

The craft's vibration increased exponentially and the ship's hull screamed in protest as the pilot slapped a single button. The pilot yelled out, "I am ejecting the sleep modules under protocol 37-4279, sending them to remote locations to prevent contact with the fairly primitive society on the planet below!"

The pilot locked its gaze on a monitor with a collection of icons, which ranged from reddish-orange to green. As each red one turned green, cylindrical pods rocketed out of the ship. After ejecting, the pods fired up their engines and careened off towards the planet below. Many of the icons changed to a flashing red as their ejection failed. Only about fifty of the escape vehicles were able to eject, leaving a hundred still on board.

A giant lurch knocked the pilot out of its couch, sending it careening off to the side of the cabin. Its head collided with a bulkhead on the side, stunning it. It pushed itself back to its feet and shook its head, trying to shrug off the pain. With a final head shake, it scrambled back into the couch and started keying in a sequence.

Barely visible in the shaking and stuttering camera, the pilot screamed one last time, "If anyone gets this message, I am transmitting the corrupted course logs to aid in rescue. Please send help......" Then, it pressed a final button on the console. The pilot's couch immediately sunk into the floor and disappeared from view.

The rescue pod shot out the front of the ship and out into space, away from the planet below. The flight recording switched to an external video feed from the escape pod that focused on the large spacecraft careening towards the planet. The ship was bellowing smoke and fire as a series of explosions erupted from its hull. Large chunks of the ship started breaking away from the craft, each blossoming into orange and yellow fireballs, streaking down toward the planet below. As the escape ship accelerated away, the view of the main ship receded before abruptly cutting out.

[End video]

<u>Chapter 2</u>
Year 1357 – The Wrath of God

Angus Perrault stepped out onto the smoothed out dirt patch in front of his home near the southern coast of Rorvik Isle in the prefecture of Fjordland. He had worked hard for years to be able to buy a plot of good farmland that he could call his own. His house wasn't much to speak of, but he was proud of it. He had labored to build a two-room shelter over the years, which was still too small with a wife, two children and a third on the way. The sun was rising over his land as the world was waking up. Fields of grain were waving in the light, early autumn breeze with the golds of the wheat dancing in sync to the tall cornstalks in the adjacent field. Beyond his fields, he could see the southern horizon and the ocean was just visible over top of the plants.

Harvest time had descended on the region. Good fortune has smiled upon their family this year: the weather had cooperated with just enough rain to produce a strong, healthy crop. The corn was at its perfect sweetness and would bring his family a good amount of money.

"Well," speaking out loud to the dog that was sniffing around the horse's watering trough, "we should get to work." Grabbing the horse from the barn, he walked her to a small wagon and hitched her up. Satisfied she was secured properly, he guided the horse down towards the cornfield so he could get to work on the harvest.

Angus had been toiling away for hours, breaking off corn cobs and placing them into the wagon. His leathery, tanned face was glistening from the sweat beading upon his brow, the cart nearly half full from his day's labor. Reaching up for another cob to break off, he froze as an explosive boom erupted from all around him. The earth then lurched up from under him, propelling him over a meter upward in the air. He flailed as he flew upwards, before crashing down on his face. He rolled over onto his back. "What in god's name was that?"

***

The earthquake had caused a lot of destruction in the area. The lowland farms were decimated by a series of tidal waves coming in off the ocean. Angus' farm was higher in elevation, so his crops were spared, but his home was now in need of some repairs. The earthquake had cracked a wall and shattered a few windows. Marissa returned from town with the children on the day of the earthquake to help out for the next couple of days. He spent the following day shoring up the house and boarding over the broken windows to keep the weather out. The house was now darker inside, but at least it was stable and weather-tight.

Now they really needed to get his crop to the market and sold. Angus really wanted to get new windows for the cottage before winter set in. He thought to himself, *"Should be a good year for us and we really need the cash now for these darn repairs."* They had collected nearly a wagon load of the corn two days ago. With the additional cost of the repairs, they really wanted it full before they headed to the market. Angus would have to be in the field early to top it off before they headed into town.

***

"Good morning my dear." Marissa leaned over to give her husband a kiss on the cheek. "I hope you're not too tired from yesterday's work on the house?"

Angus rolled over to face his lovely red-haired wife. "Not too bad, honestly. We'll have a lot of corn to sell today since we lost two days." The man swung himself upright and proceeded to pull on some work clothes.

Angus and their dog stepped outside his cottage and started to hitch up the horse to the wagon. Now that the house was fixed, he needed to get back to the field to pick more corn. Picking up a basket he needed, he rounded the back of the wagon to throw it in the back. Suddenly, the skies erupted with a series of explosions. The noise was deafening and nearly knocked him over with its ferocity. As he jerked his head up to the heavens, a large, orange fireball bloomed in the sky over the nearby ocean. Fire streaks started spilling from the main fireball and kept appearing one after the other. The sky soon became filled with them, glowing orange trailed by black smoke, as they rained down upon the horizon way off in the distance.

"God..." He dropped the basket he was a carrying and stood silently, watching the heavens pour out their anger at the world, *"Hath wrought fury down upon the land. What has angered you so?"* he wondered silently to himself, as he watched the fury until it ended.

***

It seemed like yesterday to Angus, but it had been over a week since the fireballs streaked across the sky. Since the event, he and his family had harvested three wagonloads of corn and were down in the town's market today to sell them.

"Hey Angus and Marissa." A short, stocky, elderly woman named Heather stepped up to the cart and proclaimed, "I'll take a dozen ears."

"Morning Heather!" Angus said as he turned to the woman. Marissa had already moved around the front to help fill up her beat-up little market wagon. "How are you and Peter?"

"Oh, you know." She smiled a little bit and continued, "as good as can be. We're just getting older by the minute and fixing the house after the earthquake was tough. What do you think about the earthquake and fiery skies last week? Peter and I were out gardening both times when that happened. Frightened the devil out of us when it happened."

"I was outside hitching up the wagon and all I could do was watch in awe," he replied. "I hope it's not the end of the world...however, it doesn't seem to be." He emphasized his comment by looking around the market. "Sure does look like the gods are angry about something."

Heather paid Marissa for the corn. "Well, only time will tell. Thankfully our house didn't have much damage. I feel sorry for those who lost their crops due to the flooding. People will be telling stories about this for ages. It was a hell of a sight to see when the fireballs came." A grin crept across her face. "At least Peter will never stop telling it," she said as she rolled her eyes in a joking manner. "Well, have a great day, you two!" she said as she walked away from their stall.

***

"Come on, get moving." Angus ushered his kids into the wagon shouting, "We're going to be late". It was Sunday and they always went into town to hear the pastor's sermon.

They arrived at the small church building that served the small community as a gathering place for social events. It was evident by the singing, they were indeed late to the sermon. Having missed the normal praises and prayer, Angus, Marissa and the kids slipped into the back row just as the pastor was beginning his sermon.

"We have sinned," the pastor said aloud to the congregation on the first sermon after the fireball's appearance. "Something we have done has angered our gods...their fury was cast down upon the ocean as a warning to us ALL. Each one of us should look inside, to meditate on our past actions and atone for the wrongs we may have wrung upon others, lest God rain down his wrath directly upon us!" His intensity grew throughout his address.

Waves of muttering assent rolled over the thirty or so people in attendance at the morning sermon.

"I ask ALL of you to go home...think about your lives...think about your loved ones," he said as he slowly worked his gaze over everyone in the group, "Think about how you can better please the gods, lest they unleash heaven's fire directly upon us again." He walked slowly around the lectern to face the group. "Honor thy gods and spirits." Then, the priest dismissed his parishioners. In a hushed silence, everyone slowly got up and filed out of the room.

<u>*Part 1 – The Chicken Coup*</u>

Mists were hanging over the farmland early in the morning, as Tarkhan Ganbaatar pulled on his clothes. He was proud to have his own little slice of prime pasture in southern Escabon and worked very hard to keep on top of it. He needed to move the sheep to a new pasture, as the one he had them in was getting a bit thin. The grass in his second plot was getting overgrown and ripe for trimming. He splashed some water from a bowl on his face and rubbed it as clean as he could before heading outside.

Before he could move the herd, he needed to attend to the chickens he was keeping for fresh eggs and meat. Stepping out of his dwelling, he swung to the left toward the coop and into the fenced area around the shed. "What the ... ?" he muttered to himself. The building door was closed and secured with a large wooden hinged bar to keep out predators. Something wasn't right. He couldn't put a finger on it but something was off. He ran his hands down the length of the board and stopped when he saw a deep gouge, as if a tool made the damage.

"That wasn't there last night when I locked them up," Tarkhan said aloud. A puzzled look crept across his face. *These look like claw or teeth marks, like something was digging at or biting on the board,* he thought.

Slowly, he raised one end of it to open the door and let the chickens out. When he opened it, the nesting birds all began to drop to the ground and started walking outside. "1. 2. 3...." He counted the birds as they passed by him. *"That's odd, I am one short."*

Slowly, he checked around the interior and couldn't find the missing bird, nor did he see any holes it could have escaped through. *"I'll have to keep my eye out for what happened,"* he thought. Once outside, he looked for tracks, feathers, anything that would give him a clue.

***

Over the course of the next month, he kept counting. His bird count was dropping by one every few days with no signs of what or who may be stealing his poultry.

This morning was different. Tarkhan went to the coup and noticed a couple of feathers laying about and there were tracks in the fresh mud. He bent down to examine one. "Fox," he abruptly said aloud. "How has it been getting in there?" His gaze shifted to the bar across the door.

That day he was going into town anyway, so he stopped into the blacksmith's shop. Hopefully he had better metal latches to better secure the door. "Morning, Sangpo," Tarkhan said, as he opened the door to the blacksmith's shop.

"Good morning, Tarkhan. What can I do for you this fine morning?" the smithy said as he put down a tool he was holding.

"Well, it's a morning. Not a 'fine' morning," Tarhan said emphasizing the fine part of his reply. "I have a fox problem. Somehow it is getting into the coop, despite the hinged bar on the door." He rubbed at his face. "I mean, the bar is still on the door and there's a chicken missing every three or five days. It's perplexing. You have anything that would positively lock the bar?"

"Let me look to see what I have laying around that might work," said the smithy, as he started rummaging in a box on the shelf. "Aha, I was hoping to still have one. Here." Sangpo handed a metal hook and screw to Tarkhan. "Just screw that in and the hook latches." He pushed on a hinge that self-locked when it was latched. "That should keep out unwanted pests."

"Thanks." He reached out to take the hook from the man. "I still can't figure out why the bar is back on the door though." Tarkhan started to reach into a pouch on his belt and asked, "What do you need for this?"

"Oh, nothing today. Just bring in some eggs next time you come by," he said as he smiled at Tarkhan warmly.

"Sure thing!" And with that, Tarkhan walked out of the shop back into the bright sunshine.

***

Tarkhan installed the latch after he returned to his farm and went about his daily chores. With the end of the day approaching, he walked back into the fenced chicken area and started shooing the birds towards the building. "Twenty-seven," he stated positively to himself after a count of the poultry. He barred, latched and double-checked the door on his way out that night.

The next morning, he awoke and immediately went out to see if his new locks had worked. "*Hmm, everything looks latched,*" he thought, as he looked around to see if the visitor came by overnight. "Well, I see no tracks."

He proceeded to open the latch to let the chickens out. Slowly, the birds made their way out of the shed, being counted, "Two short?!?" he exclaimed. "How the hell can that be?" He walked around the pen, recounting twice. "Damn it, two are indeed missing."

That night, he decided to stay up and watch. Tomorrow would be rough, but damn it, he was going to see how this is happening. It was summer, so the days were quite hot. Just before dusk, he quickly made some stairs out of crates, so he could climb onto his roof. Maybe he could catch the burglar in its tracks.

For three nights, he had camped out on the roof...to no avail. The thief never made an appearance. "*I wonder if the fox saw me up there? Maybe he could smell me and stayed away?*" He sat down on a log in the chicken pen, staring at the door bar and latch. "*There's no way it should be getting in there. Maybe if I pop a hole in the corner room of the house, I can watch from inside?*" He wondered and decided that was just what he was going to do.

Dusk had just settled over the farm and Tarkhan set himself in a chair by the porthole. Luckily the moon was nearly full, making things a lot more visible outside. He extinguished his reading lamp to reduce any extra light that could alert the fox to his presence.

Four hours went by and he found his eyes heavy, even nodding off a few times before he caught something moving at the corner of the chicken pen. Moving silently, so he could see better through his hastily-made porthole, he stuck his face right up to the wall. The shadow moved along the fence before using a rock to jump into the pen. The red fox landed softly and looked around, scanning for anything nearby for a few minutes. Padding up to the door, the fox arched up to land his paws on the side of the building and nosed at the bar trying to lift it up. The latch was working, so he flopped back down onto his paws. Soon the animal arched back up, this time right at the end of the bar and stared intently at the end. He moved a paw over and started clumsily poking at the latch, working it with a claw. With an almost inaudible snick sound, the latch came undone. The fox then nosed the bar up, unbarring the door. Then, he went inside, pulling the door closed behind him somehow.

After a few minutes, the door pushed open a little and the canine emerged with a chicken in his maw. The animal put the carcass down and proceeded to very quietly lower the bar back down. Jumping back up on its hind legs, the fox nosed and clawed the latch back into place.

"GRAWWWWW!!" Tarkhan burst out of the house, running full speed at the coop, trying to scare away the thief. The fox quickly grabbed the hen and jumped back over the back fence. The animal then darted out and started running down the road, before stopping suddenly. Swiftly, it turned its head back to his pursuer and just stared back at the man. The animal kept his gaze trained on Tarkhan for a few moments, before twisting its mouth into a smile. The fox then turned away and trotted down the path away from the farm.

"*Did that fox just smirk at me?*" He was certain the animal was mocking him somehow.

***

Tarkhan went back into town the next morning to pay the black-smith another visit. "Hey, Sangpo, I need some more help," he said, as the smithy turned from his work to face the visitor.

"Is something wrong with the latch I gave you the other day?" Sangpo inquired.

"No, the latch works just fine," he paused. "This is going to sound crazy, but I finally caught the fox in the act. Some...somehow it opened the latch." He scratched at his temple. "The damn thief unlatched it, raised the bar and stole a chicken," Tarhan replied, twisting his mouth to the side. "The weirdest thing was before the fox left, it closed the door and locked it all up."

The smith rubbed his balding head in thought for a moment. "Locked it up? What do you mean?"

"Locked it up!" Tarkhan looked a bit frustrated. "As in, the fox closed the door, lowered the bar, *very quietly mind you*, and relatched the hook before making off with another chicken. I have never seen or heard of a fox that smart."

"Interesting." Sangpo sat down on a stool. "I heard a few other stories about seemingly smart and bold actions by foxes and wolves lately." He began rummaging under the small desk in front. "This is all the way from across the prefecture." He pulled out a lock and key and handed it to Tarkhan, "I think you're going to need this."

Part 2 – Pandora's Box

"Constable, thanks for coming out here." Jeremiah Crossier, who ran a small sheep farm in the northern region of Heartstone, reached out a hand in greeting. "I have a problem that I hope you can help with."

Constable Derby Markus shook his hand. "What seems to be the problem?"

"I have a lamb thief." Jeremiah wasn't much for small talk. "Those damn wolves are at it again. I have lost three ewes this month." He looked over at the field where the sheep were grazing. "I am at my wit's end and I need assistance, as I am just one man."

Derby turned his gaze to the sheep as well. "You're not the only one complaining about the wolves. They are getting bolder."

"Yeah, smarter too," Jeremiah said as he shook his head. "I have tried everything, trapping, poisons, hunting, etc. They used to be able to be controlled, but they are evading all my traps. Before you ask, yes, I have moved them all over the place, but they just seem too damn smart. I haven't caught or killed one in over a year."

The constable removed his hat so he could wipe the sweat from his brow before speaking. "Yes, every farmer in the area has been saying the same thing: 'Damn wolves.' So, here are my thoughts: I will wrangle up the hunters in the town. We will set new traps, track them and eradicate them. We can't have our livelihoods interrupted like this."

"Sounds good Derby. Let me know when you get things all set and I will help as much as I can." Jeremiah patted the constable on the shoulder.

"We'll get them!" Derby said as he climbed onto his horse to head back into town.

***

Three weeks later, the townsfolk started their hunt. The first thing they did was to send the best trackers out to survey the hills, in order to locate where the packs are. Notoriously, wolves were hard to find, since their territories were large and the terrain in the forests made their movements hard to follow. Thankfully it was spring, so the wolves should be closer to a den while the pups are young.

"Alright everyone, quiet down." Derby waved everyone into their chairs. "Okay, what have we found?"

A sandy-haired man with a ruddy colored beard stood up. Leif Kroker was one of the top trackers and became the unofficial leader of the team. "We have located three different dens, all in the remote edges of the valley. One pack is in the north, one in the west and one in the southeast."

"Good, have you come up with any plan to get at them?" the constable asked the man quickly.

"Yeah, I think we can set up some traps along certain paths we think they have been taking. We can give that a few days to see if we catch anything. We can hunt them if those don't work," Leif stated.

"Really?" A farmer in the back stood and spoke up. "We haven't caught any in traps for over a year now. We should just go hunt them right now!" He sat back down on his chair with a thump.

A murmur of assent ushered forth from most of the people gathered in the room.

Derby stated, "Okay, sounds to me like a majority want to get on with it. Let's make this official: all those in favor say, 'Aye'." Everyone in the crowd was in agreement. "Okay, Leif, let's go get them."

***

Two days later, Leif and the small group of hunters returned on horseback, arriving at the constable's office in the small town hall that the village had erected about ten years before. "Constable," Leif greeted Derby. "Well, we got one wolf. He's a big one and it took about four shots to bring him down." He sat down on the chair. "We found something odd too. He's abnormally large and his front paws are really weird."

The constable leaned forward. "Weird? Forgive me, you are more familiar with wild animals than I am. What's 'odd' about them?"

"Their front toes," Leif held up his own hand to illustrate, "They are longer than normal and it looks like they might just be long enough to hold a tool. It's really baffling." He put his hand back down on his lap. "We have the wolf's body with us if you would like to see for yourself."

"Yes, please," the constable paused, "bring it around back to the horse stable."

Leif's men brought the wolf carcass around the back to the stable and placed the body on the table. "This ... is what I am talking about." He pulled the paw up to show it. "See. They are almost as long as ours," He placed his own open palm up to the wolf's. "The outer toes also curl inward. They look almost like our own thumbs."

Derby bent down to look closer "Yeah, I see what you mean." He touched one of the blunt claws before continuing, "Where did these wolves come from? They can't be from the local region."

"Who knows? All I know is they are dangerous and we need to be rid of them." The tracker looked sternly at Derby. "We will head back out in a day to see if we can get one from another pack."

The constable nodded. "Yes, please do. Also, please bury this somewhere," he said as he pointed at the dead wolf on the table.

***

It was three days before Leif and three other men headed out to the east to check out another pack of wolves. When they got deep into the forest, the path disappeared, so they dismounted and tied up their horses, continuing on foot.

The forest was very thick, so they had to walk very carefully to avoid making noises, lest they spook the pack. Leif knelt down to check out a track in the mud saying, "These are fresh," he said aloud while pointing to the track. "They were here not too long ago."

The expert tracker stood up and looked around, surveying the area to find any telltale signs of which way the beasts went. He unshouldered his musket and motioned for the others to prep them. Leif started slowly walking through the tall ferns, following what he thought was the trail.

Leif reached forward and parted a thick grouping of ferns revealing a clearing ahead of them. "They must have went through here," he said, while pointing to a fresh track in front of him. The tracker took a couple of steps forward and just when he stepped past the last visible wolf track, his foot went through the leaves and sticks.

"AAAHHH!" Leif exclaimed as the loss of footing caused him to fall face-first into what should have been a pile of leaves, but was actually a 6-foot deep pit. He dropped his gun as he tumbled and landed with a sharp 'crack' as he hit the bottom of the hole. "Dammit," he said as he cradled his wrist and the pain shot up his arm.

The others rushed forward to see what happened after hearing the shrill scream from Leif. The pit below was intentionally dug out, every surface of the hole was covered with wolf claw marks. The bottom of the pit was littered with a bunch of long sticks, piles of leaves and plant debris. "This looks like a trap," one of the other men exclaimed.

Two men hastily climbed down to help Leif out of the pit. Once they got him out, one of the men took a closer look at the sticks that were holding up the covering of leaves. He pulled one out with him, "Look at this. These sticks aren't cut with a knife, they are chewed. Look at all these teeth marks."

A third man started wrapping Leif's hand and wrist in a splint, "We should get him back to the village. Davan, grab some of those sticks so we can show the others."

***

Once back in town, they took Leif to the local doctor to look at his wrist. After that, they paid a visit to the constable. "Constable Markus," Leif said, as the four of them entered the Constable's office.

"Sit, sit." Markus motioned to the seats near his desk. "Tell me," he paused, noticing Leif's wrist in a splint. "What happened?"

"I fell into a hole." Leif looked down at his wrist and then continued, "And I broke my wrist. That wasn't the worst thing though. That hole was actually a hastily dug pit trap." He moved his wrist to lay it on the desk. "That trap wasn't dug by us. It was covered by long sticks with a layer of leaves and plant debris to hide it. We were following a fresh set of wolf tracks and I fell into it. It was very, very well hidden."

"Hmm. Do you know who set it?" Derby asked.

"Yes, we do ... or are at least pretty sure. Davan, show him the sticks." Leif looked over at one of the other trackers.

Davan stepped outside for a second and returned with four long sticks. He set them down on the desk in front of Derby. "These were under the leaves. They aren't cut with a tool. These have been chewed into sticks." He picked one up and showed the end to the constable. "This is going to sound really strange, but we all think the wolves dug this trap for us."

The constable's face contorted in a frown, "Are you joking? That sounds crazy."

"No, we're not crazy. These chew marks are not what you see from, say a beaver. These are decidedly canine bites." Davan's face was serious. "These are not normal wolves we are dealing with."

<u>*Part 3 – Harp of Blue*</u>

It was a lazy Sunday afternoon in the mountains above River City for the Cazkov family. Eliza was busy in the kitchen corner making dough to bake some bread. Sunday's were always the best day of the week for Eliza. She always enjoyed making the family's bread for the week while her daughter Kalina practiced her harp. Kalina was actually getting quite good at it, so the money they had spent on her birthday was worth it. The soft, peaceful music she played made the day ever more relaxing for the family.

Jakub was over in the other corner with a leather strap, working to sharpen the knives he was going to need for the week. Their family's farm dog was snoring peacefully in the corner on the little bed they made her. There was a funny reason they had named the dog Blue. When she was just a small puppy, she knocked some blue pigment off a table onto herself. Her cream fur was dyed blue all summer, until she shed it away in the fall.

"Jakub, how many sheep need shearing?" Eliza asked him.

"Oh, probably a dozen this week. You need some extra for yarn?" He got up to look outside and froze. "Damn it, I think something is out there," he said, just as all the fenced sheep starting bleating loudly and running around inside the enclosure.

"Blue!" he yelled at the dog, snapping it out of its nap. "Go get 'em!" Grabbing a shiv, he opened the door and the dog sprinted out towards the sheep pen and cleared the fence in one quick bound. Jakub hustled down there to see Blue was facing off with a wolf. Snarling at the intruder, they traded fanged snaps at each other before she attacked. As she lunged, both her and the wolf sank each other's teeth into their opponents neck, causing both animals to whine and pull back.

They circled each other, blood forming at the bites in their necks. Blue lunged again, this time getting slapped down by the slightly larger animal and it sank its teeth deep into her haunch. Jacob jumped into the pen, blade first. He ran forward and impaled the wolf in the shoulder causing a spray of blood to drop all over the pinned dog. The wolf reared back snarling at the man, the fresh knife wound made it back away from him. The wolf turned, jumped over the fence and bounded back into the forest.

"GET OUT OF HERE VARMINT!" Jakub shouted as he yelled after the predator. "Oh Blue," he reached down to carefully pick up the dog to carry her into the house, so he could tend to her wounds.

"Oh Jakub," Eliza said as she moved a side table into the middle of the room so he had a place to put the injured dog. As he put Blue down, she brought over a bag of supplies for tending to the dog's wounds. Blue must have been in shock from the blood loss as she laid quietly on the table, so he got to work tending the wounds as quickly as he could. Jakub immediately applied a clear salve to the wounds. The blood was clotting up nicely, so he wrapped the cuts with some strips of white cloth. "Well, that will do," he said as he carried her over to a blanket in the corner to let her rest.

***

Blue's condition didn't really improve for a long time. The family was worried she wouldn't make it, the wounds were obviously more serious than they previously thought. For nearly eight weeks, the dog did little more than sleep, eat, drink and take short trips outside.

As Jakub tended to her, he slowly noticed that her eyes had become a much more vibrant amber color and her front paws were disfigured. He was sure they hadn't been broken during the fight, but he couldn't be sure. They looked similar to a dog's paws. He pressed them in the middle and the toes splayed apart. *Are they longer?* he thought to himself while examining them. The outer two looked a little more thumb-like and could rotate inwards. He examined them with one hand, rolling the thumb inwards towards her pawpads and mimicking the movement of his own thumbs.

***

Over the next few weeks, Blue began to drastically improve and life returned to normal for the family. The wretched wolf never came back to try to get more sheep. Jakub was really happy about that, but he also idly wondered what happened to it after it's altercation with Blue.

Another Sunday rolled around and the family was doing their normal activities. On this particular day, Blue decided to sit next to Kalina, who was playing the harp, being absolutely enthralled while watching every finger stroke on the strings as she played.

Kalina got up to go into the kitchen to get a piece of freshly baked bread her mother just brought in from the outside oven. Mom handed a piece to Kalina just as a harp string was plucked. At first, it was a single string, then a few notes in a row.

The family all looked at each other when they realized that no one was playing the harp. They simultaneously turned their heads to look over towards the instrument. Blue was sitting on her hindquarters, front paws up in the air plucking at the strings with purpose. It wasn't complex to start, but Blue was working out some of the patterns that Kalina had been playing earlier. Soon, the notes started to coalesce into a simple, beautiful, melody.

Eliza dropped her bread knife as the reality of what Blue was doing sunk in.

First meeting of the Eight Orthodoxies Council, September 8th of the
year 1500.

Brief notes taken by Cedric DeAngelo.

Council members present:

Dharmasha Samsara – Temple of Dharkna, Escabon
Reverend Booker Garrison – National Church of Heartstone
Apostik Rüdiger Berge – Fjordland Neopagan Mission
Pastor Lee Vasquale – San Juarez Mesomeric Church
Shinshoku Taadaki Yamada – Shinto Templars of Fijiwara
Bishop Alejandro Diaz – Luther-Perez Church of the Lagi Coast in
Los Diego
Ensi Asim Osari – Calveras Sumarina
Cardinal Quinn McCarthy – River City 9th Order of Light

Today, the great leaders of the eight major religious orthodoxies
gathered in the coastal town of Providence in the southern Heartstone
region. Their topics of discussion revolved around improving relations among the regions, but most importantly, to discuss the growing
threat of the intelligent canine infestation throughout the lands.

As human settlement is pushing into the wilderness, they all noted
increasing attacks on their followers by the wild canines in their
provinces. Some of the leaders detailed accounts that show attacks
were getting more frequent and more intricate in their execution.
Their followers have expressed worry about their safety and would
like some official help in containing the canines. Many local leaders
are suggesting that they should perform 'culling' to reduce the population, but are looking to their religious leaders for guidance.

Discussions went back and forth on the morality of what the people are asking them to agree to. Six of the eight leaders are of the opinion that humans are their God's children and animals are theirs to do with as they please. To them, humans are special in God's eyes and that protecting his children through a culling of these animals would be acceptable, even pleasing to their gods. Dharmasha and Shinshoku have expressed their dissent, believing that all creatures are to be respected. They suggest studying the population to better understand them, but are unable to convince the other six council members of the wisdom in their words.

In the end, the council voted six to two to give their blessing to allow provinces to do what they feel is right for them and their region. They drafted a general proclamation of assent, but did not dictate how this was to be done. They felt each province can decide the appropriate method to reduce the canine population.

"Hi Constable younger, what brings you up here?" Geoffrey Rousseau had just opened the door to his remote cabin after a knock on the door. The man at the door was middle aged, the hair above his ears and his beard starting to gray. Personal visits were unusual, people usually left him alone. Geoff was a fur trapper by trade and lived in the very remote wilds of Fjordland to be closer to his game and very few came up here.

"Sorry to surprise you, but I am here on official business." Samuel Younger smiled and extended a hand in greeting. "The province is in need of your services."

"Oh? Interesting." He shook the man's hand and gestured him inside. "I was just about to knock off for the day. Would you like a drink? I just opened a bottle of wine."

"Oh, sure. I will have a small one. It's still a long ride back to town." The constable sat down at the chair that Geoff motioned to. "Thanks," he said as the man poured him a small glass. "So I just got a letter from the prefecture's magistrate. They would like to offer a serious bounty for hunters, like you, to bring in ANY wolf you can. With no limit."

Geoff put the bottle of wine back down on the table and asked, "The magistrate has declared war on the wolves?" The trapper then took a sip of his own glass of wine. "That's something I usually leave alone. I mostly get smaller animals for fur." He placed his glass back on the table. "Wolves are extremely smart. I almost never see them and when I do, it's just on a very far away ridge."

"Yeah, I know." Sam idly scratched at the bridge of his nose. "There have a been a lot of problems with the local wolf population, as of late. They are getting really bold and causing a lot of farmers to lose livestock. Some have reported that many children have been threatened."

"I have heard complaints, but isn't that just because we keep moving in the wilderness?" He glanced up at Sam. "I mean, aren't we going to see more conflict, as we start to farm the land more?"

"Yeah, but we can't stop progress. Here." Sam pulled out a piece of paper and handed it to Geoff. "This is the bounty they are willing to pay."

Geoff whistled to express his amazement, then said, "That is a large sum. Is that for a dozen wolves?" He put the paper down on the table.

"No, that is for *each* wolf." Sam drank the last swig in his glass. "They are very, very serious about this."

"I see." He nodded to the constable. "That is very apparent. What's the time frame?"

"No time frame, they just asked for as many as you can." Sam put his empty glass back down on the table. "Just bring in any you get to me and I will get you paid." Sam stood up and said, "I need to get moving, lots of other people to talk to today. Good to see you Geoff." He shook his hand and departed the cabin.

***

Over the course of the next few weeks, Geoffrey worked very hard to try to catch one of the wolves. He tried every trap he could think of and none of them worked. Upon every trap inspection, he could always see wolf tracks all around them, but it seemed that they knew where they were and avoided them. One of them even defecated on one of his traps. *"It's like they were taunting me."* he thought to himself as he recalled that day.

That night, he was going to try something different. There was recently a small forest fire, so the area was still a bit smokey. He had taken a set of clothes and hung them in the smoke over his fire to give them a heavy smirched scent. He knew one of the paths they used, so he was hoping to get into a nearby tree in order to finally shoot one.

Geoffrey got his clothes on, hiked out to the tree he had chosen and climbed high up in the branches to wait. As dusk approached, he finally saw a wolf wandering its way slowly through the trees, staying very hidden. As the wolf rounded a tree, he slowly raised his firearm and steadied his breathing. The wolf paused as it sniffed at the air, while Geoff simultaneously squeezed the trigger. The wolf yelped and immediately dropped to the ground, as his shot appeared to paralyze the animal.

Before he climbed down, he reloaded his musket in case the animal got aggressive and attacked. Once down, he readied the gun to his shoulder and approached the clearing where the wolf was laying with its back to him. The gray coated animal was still breathing, so he approached cautiously.

He heard a twig crack off to his side and he froze. Suddenly, out of the scrub brush, three wolves charged him. The one that came from the left jumped and clamped its jaws over the barrel of his gun, ripping it out of his grip. The other two came from behind and lunged, knocking him slightly off balance. Then, he quickly reached for a large knife hanging from his belt and held it out in front of him, as the three new wolves circled around.

The wolf he shot had gotten up and was slowly padding towards him, its face wrinkled up in a snarl. He saw only a little wound where his bullet grazed the wolf. "You faker!" He shouted at the wolf. It relaxed its face, almost seemingly laughing at him with its expression. He pointed the knife at the leader, calling it out. "Your move dog," the fur trapper stated firmly. The other three wolves moved around behind him, encircling and almost herding him at the wounded wolf.

The wolf quickly dropped its head down and snarled in a challenge. "Oh yeah, come at me!" Geoff used his free hand to gesture at the animal. Just as he finished yelling, the wolf charged forward and then jumped high, aiming at his head. The weight of the wolf came crashing into him, as it bit down on his knifeless forearm. Geoff instinctively slashed at the wolf, cutting it across the shoulder as he twisted, deflecting the animal off to crash on the ground.

He scrambled back to his feet and squared off to the wolf and warned the beast, "You want more? Come on." The wolf circled for a little bit before lunging. The wolf came in low this time. Geoff stabbed, but the wolf twisted sideways and sunk a full set of teeth into his thigh. He grabbed the wolf's mouth with his free hand and pulled at it, trying to get it to release. The animal wasn't letting go, so he stabbed a few times at the animal's haunches, landing a few small hits.

The wolf released, backed up and lunged at his face with its full force. The attack knocked the hunter backward onto the ground, while the animal snapped furiously at him. The wolf was in full fury, trying to land a solid bite on the man. He stabbed upward, plunging the knife up to its hilt in the shoulder of the wolf. It snarled in a near howl. The wolf redoubled its attack, landing a solid bite into Geoff, digging its teeth deep into his shoulder. He stabbed again, this time plunging the knife in deeper. Then, the wolf back-pedaled and faced off with him. The animal's snarl softened while it assessed the man. The wolf took a moment and glanced past the trapper, nodded and then turned to limp off into the brush.

Geoff turned to look at the three remaining wolves. They were just standing back, watching him. One of them moved to pick up the hunting rifle in his mouth. Then, they all moved off into the brush and disappeared, taking the rifle with them.

He looked over his dripping wounds. He was covered in a lot of blood and his clothes were getting blood-soaked. He limped back up the trail to retrieve his hidden bag and bandaged his wounds. Once done, he slowly limped back home.

***

At home, he tended to himself. "That wolf got me pretty good," he said muttering to himself. He had deep bites in his thigh, his shoulder, a variety of little cuts on his face and torso. Geoff spread an herbal salve on the open wounds, wrapped himself in bandages, and went to sleep.

Geoff awoke very early and pain shot through his head from the bright light. He laid there for a little bit, trying to get the motivation to sit up in bed. As he sat up, all he could do was utter an exasperated "Ugh" to himself. Slowly, Geoff swiveled off the bed, stood up and limped over to the cistern. He scooped himself a large glass of water and downed it in one go.

Geoff laid in bed most of the day, dozing in and out of consciousness. As the day carried on, his body began to get more and more uncomfortable. Sweat was pouring from him profusely, body aching deep down in every joint and his head was swimming with dizziness and pain. He knew he needed energy, so he limped himself over to his food cabinet and ate a batch of dried meat. Finishing his quick meal, he drank a big mug of water before collapsing back into bed.

***

Milo Stefanik awoke in the middle of the night to the sounds of his sheep bleating very loudly. He had been farming here in the Fjordland mountains for ten years and had never been woken up in the middle of the night by such a racket from the flock. He swiveled off the bed and plunked his feet into his boots. He grabbed his coat, lit a lantern and grabbed his musket as he went out the door to see what was all the fuss.

As he approached the pen, all of the sheep were crowded off to the side, staring at the other side, bleating in terror. Milo lifted the lantern up to shine more light at where they were looking. A large gray mass was hunched over a bloody sheep. As he raised the lantern, a pair of shiny yellow eyes looked up at him, causing him to freeze in his tracks. The beast's bloody face had sharp fangs protruding from its short muzzle. It turned its head away from the man, letting Milo get a better look. The animal was covered in short gray fur, had pointed ears and wore an elongated face with a mouth full of fangs.

He broke himself free from shock and raised his musket to take aim at the monster. "Get out of here you foul beast!" he yelled, just before pulling the trigger. The musket ball struck the beast in the shoulder, knocking the animal backwards. It immediately growled at him, turned quickly and ran off like a man. The beast cleared the fence in one giant leap and disappeared.

Milo turned to look over at the murdered sheep and wondered what kind of animal he just saw. "I haven't ever seen one like that before, that was not a normal wolf" He rubbed his chin before dragging the carcass outside the pen. "I'll deal with this in the morning." he said to himself and went back inside the house.

***

Early in the morning, Milo cleaned up the remaining mess inside the pen and put the sheep into a burlap sack. He hoisted the body up onto his saddled horse and turned towards the house. "Jenna, I'm going into town to talk to the constable!" He yelled to his wife. She came outside to hear him better. "He is not going to believe me ... I don't either really," and he climbed on the horse and headed off into town.

When he got to town, he made a beeline to the constable's house. He tethered his horse to a tree and went to the door, knocking loudly. Constable Younger answered the door. "Hi Milo, what brings you here?"

"Good morning Sam. My sheep flock was attacked last night." He ran a hand through his messy hair "It wasn't a normal attack."

The constable's face wrinkled into a scowl. "There's been a lot of that over the past few weeks," he sighed.

"Yeah, something got to the flock and killed, no, *tore* apart one of my sheep," Milo stated. "I got out there in time to see it in the lantern light. This wasn't a regular predator," he paused, pondering what to say. "It was a monster. It looked more like a half man, half wolf. The face was almost a man and his face was stretched a little like this." He illustrated it with his hands. "It had fangs, yellow eyes, pointy ears and partially covered in fur. The sight made me almost soil myself," he sighed. "I must sound crazy."

"Normally, I would say yes," Sam said as he smiled. "But you are not the first one to say the exact same thing to me."

"I brought the sheep with me if you would like to examine it. That thing pretty much mutilated my animal," Milo paused. "That was a murderous monster."

"Yeah, people are dubbing it 'Le Loup Garou'. People are claiming it is a man who is cursed to don the shape of the wolf to murder and maim the innocent," the constable said. "Bring the sheep carcass around back, and I will look at it."

***

Geoffrey slowly awoke. His head was thumping, the room was bright and it stunk with unfamiliar smells. He could hear every droplet of rain pattering on the roof above him. He rolled his head to the side. His cabin was a mess. It looked like a tornado had went through it. Everything was broken with debris strewn all over the place. His door was half off its hinges hanging open and moving slightly with the breeze coming into the house.

He closed his eyes to shield himself from the light and swung his legs over the side of the bed. "How long was I asleep?" he muttered, his voice sounding a little gravely. He tried to stand up, but stepped on a piece of debris, which caused him to immediately lose his balance, fall over over and land squarely on his back. "Oof."

He reached his hand up to rub at his face, but swatted himself solidly on the chin with his hand. "Wha..." he began to say, before he realized that his face was visible in his vision. Quickly, he reached up and put a hand on his face, only to find a muzzle there instead. He sat up quickly and brought his hands up to look at them. "*Oh my god, what are these...paws?*" he thought as he looked at the back of his hands. They were covered in a light gray fur and his fingernails were now short stubby claws.

"No no no no no...." He gasped and scooted backwards away from his hands, until backing himself against the wall. Geoff silently stared at his legs and feet for several minutes. They looked like a wolf's: Long, slender and weirdly shaped. "What nightmare is this? I must be hallucinating," he stated in a disbelieving tone, and remained there silently staring at his deformed legs and hands for nearly 15 minutes.

He slowly got to his feet. He had trouble walking and slowly made his way over to the one little mirror he had in the kitchen and looked at his face. "Oh my god. I look like that wolf I shot," he said to the monster in the mirror, who was staring back at him with amber eyes.

"God must be angry with me for trying to kill that wolf and this is his punishment," he told himself aloud. He looked himself over in full since his shock wore off a little. He had a wolf's set of teeth, wolf's ears, wolf's claws and a wolf's tail, but walked upright like a man. "This is going to take a while to get used to," he added.

At this point, he started to notice some bones in the debris scattered around his humble house. "How long has it been since I was conscious?" he said, as he walked over to the door and gazed up at the drizzling sky, before looking over at the grasses in the field nearby. The green grasses were starting to get a golden sheen, a sign of the fall approaching. "Months," he said quietly. "What do I do now?"

As he stood there puzzling over the last few months, he heard the faint sound of horses plodding up the path. He couldn't see them, but guessed they were still a few minutes from arriving at his house. Geoff started to freak out. He couldn't be seen this way, so Geoff ran quickly around to the side of the building and off in to the dense undergrowth nearby. He wanted to hide himself from the view of the approaching men.

***

There was a group of three riders who came to a stop in front of the cabin. The riders were scanning around, surveying the area. Thankfully, Geoff was hidden completely from their view. His hearing was dramatically better now and he could hear everything, including the heavy breathing of an overweight man in the group.

"Well, this is Geoff's place." The lead rider was Constable Younger and he climbed down off of his horse. "Hopefully we can figure out why we haven't seen him in months," he added, as the other two climbed down and pulled muskets and pistols off the saddle bags.

Jeffrey, the eldest son of the Constable, looked around the homestead. The area was overgrown with weeds and Geoff's horse was nowhere to be seen. "I don't think anyone has been here for quite a long while." He pointed to the front door that was hanging askew, nearly off its hinges. "Look at the door."

Samuel slowly walked up to the door and ran a finger over a bunch of claw marks dug into its face. "Be ready, the beast might be here." He readied his pistol and slowly walked inside with the gun raised. As he stepped into the room, his boot kicked some of the debris and made a clanking noise. "This place is a mess. No one is in here, but it sure smells like a dog."

The remaining two men walked inside and they all just stood there, looking around the room. The entire cabin's contents were broken and scattered about. Samuel pushed a cloth off some debris with his boot to expose some bones. He bent down to get a closer look. "Horse," he stated emphatically. "This is a leg bone from a horse." He raised his head to look around at the room, noticing a lot more bones.

The third man, Ezikiel Oberright, was a bit overweight and made the floor in the cabin strain when he stepped inside. He walked over to the bed and saw it was covered in soft gray fur. Pulling out a little pouch, he collected some of the fur to take back with them. Then, the man bent down next to the bed to pick up a tooth saying, "This is human." He started rummaging around in the debris for a little bit. "There's a whole mouth full of teeth down here, but no jaw. What beast would have pulled out someone's teeth?"

Constable Younger stood back up after surveying the bones and the disaster inside the cabin. "This is where the beast has been hiding, that's for sure." He turned to face the other two. "I'd say poor Geoff is dead. We need to head back to town to get a team up here to hunt the beast down."

***

Geoffrey remained hidden until the constable and the other two were well out of earshot, before softly walking back to his cabin. *"I have to get out of here, I am no longer safe,"* he thought to himself and quickly began putting a few small belongings into a leather satchel. Digging through what was left of his clothes, he tried to find things that would fit his new body and cover up his nakedness. He ripped the lower legs off some trousers and made a hole in the back with a knife for his tail. Thankfully, he found that a normal shirt and jacket still fit his physique, so at least he had some clothes. Lastly, he put a knife, a pistol and some coins he had stashed away into his bag, before stepping out through the doorway.

He paused in the doorway, turning his head to look back into the cabin that sheltered him for all these years, and sighed softly to himself. "Goodbye old friend," he said to the cabin and then turned to run down the road away from his home.

The scientific community has widely agreed that the programs to eradicate the intelligent canines, in the 15th and 16th centuries, led to the rise of the human-like canines. Religious leadership, once pro-eradication of the smart canine species, have now shifted their stance that these beasts were created as god's wrath for human sin. They believe that their gods allowed the minions of hell to release these hybrid monsters among the humans as punishment for humanity's misdeeds and moral crimes. Rather than wait for the afterlife to punish the sinners, the gods are now cursing them to a new life as a mindless, blood-thirsty beast. They didn't deserve to be human anymore.

By the late 16th century, most prefecture governments had passed laws or guidance authorizing the extermination of werewolf kind. This effort only put humans into more conflicts with the growing population, unknowingly accelerating the growth of the canine population.

Once scientists studied and understood that canids were sentient creatures and not mindless beasts, the humans in control of the governments felt heavy public pressure to step up their eradication efforts. They began seeing them as a true threat to the human dominance of Earth. During the attempted purges, the local canine settlements viciously fought back to protect themselves and their children, showing the humans they weren't going to quietly accept genocide.

This increasing resistance led prefecture governments to collaborate in a more formal way. On June 21st of the year 1656, the governments of the eight prefectures held a summit to address the rise of

the werewolves as a recognized species. This was also the first time
that all governments around the world put aside their differences to
cooperate with a concerted, coordinated effort.

This newfound cooperative spirit lead to a historic event in 1682,
which brought all human civilian governments together in a summit.
United in their fear and hatred of the canines, they agreed to form one
cohesive government to combat this rising threat. They created Capitola as the head of the global government. The civilian governments
agreed it would be an independent state located in the central part of
the world. This would serve as the location of the global government
until further notice.

Chapter 7

Year 1827 – Werewolf Physiology

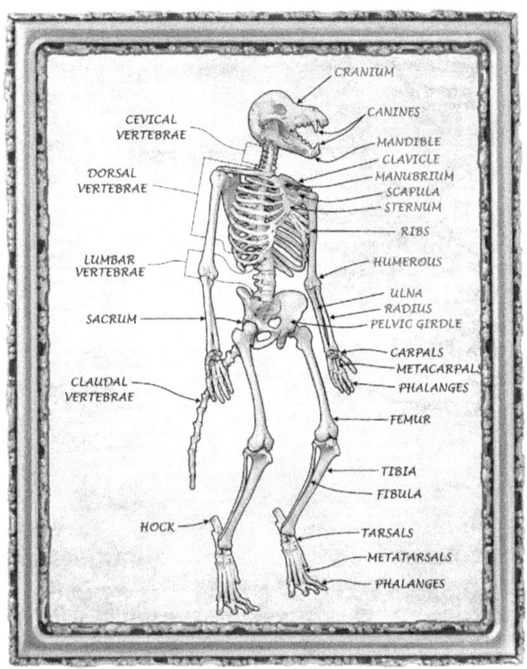

Quick Notes and Outline for Research Paper
Montague Brexton
Afferton Medical Institute
Werewolf Physiology

During my research, I examined nearly five hundred living individuals of different species, sub-species, races and colors. I surveyed them for height, weight and general physique.

I was also given access to six cadavers during the project. Please note that all of these individuals donated their bodies with full consent.

The cadavers evaluated during the research were as follows:
a) 1 male human
b) 1 female human
c) 1 male werewolf, sub species gray wolf – first generation
d) 1 female werewolf, sub species fox – first generation
e) 1 male werewolf, sub species gray wolf – second generation
f) 1 female werewolf, sub species fox – second generation

<u>General physique and appearance</u>

There are some obvious differences, but they also have a lot of similarities between the species.

a) FUR vs HAIR
b) TAIL
c) EAR POSITION and SHAPE
d) LEGS
e) JAW
f) NOSE
g) CLAWS
h) ORGANS
i) SKELETAL STRUCTURE
j) REPRODUCTION
k) HEIGHT and WEIGHT
l) STRENGTH and AGILITY
m) INTELLIGENCE

a) One of the most obvious differences is a werewolf will have a full coat of fur versus the small amount of hair a human has. The werewolf is similar to a terrestrial canine in that they will grow winter coats and shed them in the spring. Colors of the werewolf can vary widely depending on what sub-species they are.

b) The werewolf also has a tail similar to a feral quadrupedal canine. Tail lengths will vary, but all tend to hang between the knee and ankle of the individual. Tail length also seems to be correlated to the sub-species of the animal. Foxes tend to have long bushy tails, whereas the Calaveran wild dogs tend to have the shortest tails. The other sub-species fall in between, with various sizes and bushiness.

c) Ears on a werewolf are much higher on the skull than a human. Most ears are triangular shaped with the notable exception of a wild dog's ears. They are large, round saucer-like shapes. A werewolf's hearing is vastly better than a human's. Again, these traits share similarities to the region's four-legged counterparts.

d) Legs are fairly similar between a human and a werewolf. The largest difference is the length of the metatarsals. A human can walk using the balls of their feet, i.e. using the metatarsals and phalanges. A werewolf walks using the phalanges (basically, they walk on their toes). This shows in their walking cadence. Alternately, humans walk in a more smooth shuffle, while a werewolf will bounce a little while walking. Canines pick up their toes in a more perpendicular fashion and carefully place them down vertically while in stride. Werewolves also use their tail to enhance balance while walking. While in stride, their tail is held out horizontally. This allows them to keep very good balance while walking on their toes.

e) Jaw structure is radically different. Humans have a very short mandible with flat teeth. A canine has a much longer, extended mandible with long pointed teeth. Human's teeth are meant for chewing and grinding, where a werewolf's jaw will be better at tearing.

f) Noses are much different between humans and werewolf-kind. A werewolf nose is usually black and damp. They also have nearly 14 times the nasal cavity than a human does. This makes their smell vastly more sensitive.

g) A werewolf has long pointed claws, unlike a human nail. A closer examination shows that they are actually similar and are both made with a Keratin protein. A wolf's claw has a hard outer shell and a softer inner portion. Also, their claws are anchored directly to the finger bones, unlike a human nail that just resides on the surface of the skin. This makes a werewolf much better at digging without tools.

h) Organs: There are no real differences between the organs of a human versus the canines.

i) Humans and werewolves share very similar skeletal structures with each other. Additionally, if you put aside the tail in this discussion, the bone count between the species are the same. The human frame has 206 bones and canines have the exact same number, despite the difference in their structural appearance.

j) Reproduction in canines is very similar to humans with a couple of notable exceptions. A female werewolf's reproductive system is very similar to a human female. They only menstruate once in a year, as opposed to a human, who can conceive children once a month. Males are very similar to their feral counterparts in the structure of their genitals.

k) When looking at height and weight, we see a lot of variation. It really depends on what generation a werewolf is. A first generation (a transformed human) wolf will generally be taller than their human counterpart. This mainly has to do with the modification to the length of their metatarsals and walking on their toes. A post transformation-recovery werewolf will weigh very similar to what their human form did.

When you look at a second generation (born a werewolf), you will see a wide variation in heights and weights. This seems directly linked to the sub-species they came from. Wild canines all vary in sizes. Coyotes and wild dogs tend to be medium sized at 1.8 meters tall (on average). Foxes are the smallest of the canine species, averaging about 1.5 meters tall. San Juarezian Maned Wolves tend to be tall, lanky with very long legs and arms. Average height for the maned wolves is just under two meters. Wolves are the largest both in height and stature, just like their feral counterparts. Depending on the sub-breed of wolf, they can range from 2 to 2.2 meters in height. Of course, an individual's height will be dependent on nutrition during childhood, just like in humans.

l) All canines are extremely athletic with great endurance. Typical canines are stronger and faster than a simi-lar-sized human and will outmatch them in any sporting event.

m) From what I have observed in my research, were-wolves are equally as smart and clever as any human.

Bumping along slowly in his seat, Joseph Cunningham guided his horse and wagon down a rutted, bumpy road. In this area, it had been taking him an average of a day to get from town to town, but with the recent heavy rain, this section was taking him a long time. *"Hope I get to town before nightfall,"* he thought to himself.

He was getting tired and the rhythmic undulations in the road were not helping him keep awake. As the horse crested the long hill he was climbing, the small town ahead of him came into view. "Finally," he said aloud, as he reached the outskirts of the village. "Hey there good friend!" he said to a fellow walking out of town. "Where can a weary traveler park his wagon?"

The expression the man wore on his face really said to leave him alone, but he responded. "Over that way," he gruffed at Joseph and pointed toward the west side of town. "There's a clearing over that way."

Joe thanked him and shook the reins making his wagon lurch out of the mud when the horse started pulling. Slowly, they moved off to the side of town the man had pointed him toward. The clearing was rutted from heavy travel, but no one was there on this day. He pulled back on the reins and stopped his horse in the middle of the clearing. Climbing down off the driver's seat, he began making preparations for the night. He unhitched the horse, walked it to the side of the wagon and tied it up before going around back to get food for them both. After putting a good meal in his belly, he doused the fire and crawled into the back to get some sleep.

***

He awoke to a very clear morning with an almost deafening amount of song birds singing in the light morning breeze. He made some coffee to drink along with some dried jerky for breakfast, while listening to the sounds of the town waking up. After dumping the last of the coffee down his gullet, he hitched up the horse and headed into town.

In the center of town, there was plenty of space in the market area, so he stopped his wagon at the edge of the square. He climbed down and began setting up his wagon to hock what he was selling. The town was still waking up, so he had plenty of time to set up. He flipped down the side of his wagon, creating a platform where he could stand above the people, where he could be seen.

Over the next hour, many more people came to set up and sell their goods. Looking around, Joseph noted they were mostly farmers with corn, carrots and the like. There were a few women setting up to sell handmade clothing.

"LADIES AND GENTLEMAN!" he barked out over the crowd, many turning to look up at the man yelling at them. "I am Doctor Joe." Not that he had much education, but he loved using the title. He paused to see how many moved toward him.

"We live in troubling times," he began. "Lurking around every shadowy corner are evils." He pointed at a woman. "You Ma'am, what do you think is out there?" He watched her shrug her head noncommittally. "You sir, what keeps you up at night?" The man folded his arms and didn't respond at all."

"Werewolves," he said aloud. "Werewolves are everywhere." He waved his arm from left to right, gesturing across the entire crowd building in front of him. "There are monsters out there in the night. Those murderous, drooling, hungry beasts lurk around every tree ... every forest and they are looking to get you!"

"What can you do to keep yourselves from being turned into a mindless beast, you might ask yourself!" He smiled and placed his hands open palmed on the rickety table he erected on his stage. "What

would you say if I told you that you CAN do something about them?"
He paused for twenty seconds for dramatic effect. "I have a way." He
reached down to pick up a brown-tinted, medicinal style bottle. "I
have invented a medicine that will help you help yourselves." He held
it up so most of the crowd could see it.

"This elixir is scientifically formulated to repel werewolves." He
smiled down at a little girl holding her mother's hand nearby and
sai, "You don't want to get bitten, right?" His face twisted into a
concerned smile.

"I call this miracle product 'Werewolf-B-Gone' and I guarantee you
will love this." He opened up his bottle and smelled at it. "You
take one tablespoon per day and your troubles with werewolves will
be gone!" He moved his gaze across the audience, seeing many of
them engrossed in what he was saying. "It works in two ways. First,
drinking it will repel the werewolves."

He took a swig of his bottle, though it was only whiskey. The
salesman grinned inside and thought, "*what they don't know doesn't hurt
them.*" "I use it daily myself, as I travel a lot and I am always afraid I
will be taken in the night by those beasts." He put the cork back in
his bottle and set it down on the table. "I formulated it to taste good,
unlike a lot of the medicines out there. You will NOT hate drinking
it!"

"Second, if you ARE attacked and bitten by a werewolf, the healing
properties of my elixir will prevent you from turning into one of
them!" He looked back down at the little girl, "We definitely don't
want that, now do we?" Again, he let his face twist into a concerned
smile, though a little less genuine-looking this time.

"One bottle of my Werewolf-B-Gone will last a person one month
and I guarantee that it will keep you safe from the werewolves!" He
had them. Everyone was fixated on his every word. "For the low price
of two dollars per bottle, you are guaranteeing protection for you AND
your family."

"I'm selling this elixir at this low price because I want to protect you
AND your family from the werewolf scourge." He looked through the
audience, adding, "you can't put a price on the safety of your family,
now can you?"

Many of the people were buying way more than they could afford,
but he was laughing all the way to the bank. By midday, the town
square was emptying. He decided now was a good time to leave, so he
packed up his wagon. Once finished, Joseph climbed up on his wagon,
whipped the reins and trundled out of town. "*Demand is way stronger*

than I thought," he thought, giggling a little to himself. *"If demand is that high in every town, I'll have to make four times the stock next time!"*

***

Dr. How made decent time, despite the bad roads, but he wasn't going to make it too far before dark. He directed the horse to pull off to a clearing in the forest so he could camp for the night.

Joseph climbed down and started to walk around the back to start his nightly camping routine. He opened the back covering to his wagon and was startled by three sets of amber eyes staring at him. He stood there, paralyzed in fear, as three gray and brown wolves jumped out of the wagon. All of them were clothed in what seemed to be normalish farmer style clothes. Two of them moved around behind him and put heavy paws on his shoulders.

"Nice to meet you, DOCTOR Joe," the wolf in front of him said, with a toothy grin. The wolf stepped forward, slowly moving his face nose-to-nose with Joe's. "We are not monsters, you shyster." He looked over at one of the other wolves proclaiming, "Dusty, hold him." The one wolf stood behind him and locked Joe's arms behind his back.

The lead wolf went to the back of the wagon and brought out a bottle. "So, just what are you hocking, huh?" The wolf opened the bottle, waved it around in front of his nose and gave it a good sniff. "Whiskey, molasses and....is that a hint of vinegar?" He wrinkled up his nose and then smashed the bottle on the ground.

"It's bad enough you are selling people bogus medicine and conning them out of their hard-earned money, but using their distrust of wolves to do it?"

"What do you care?" Joe was finally able to speak. "They don't like your kind."

"That may be true for most of them, yes. But we will not tolerate this. You are preying on those villagers fears and stoking hatred for my kind." He motioned to the third wolf. "Let's take care of this," he said as he nodded toward the wagon. The smaller wolf went inside and started handing crates of Joe's elixir to the larger wolf. Raising the bottles up, he started smashing them on the ground one by one, until the whole wagonload was destroyed.

The smaller wolf in the back of the wagon threw a large bag into the hands of the larger wolf. As he caught it, it made the telltale sound of a jingling coins.

"You bastards, I am just trying to make a living." Joe started to struggle to break his arms free when they took his money away from him, but was failing miserably, as the wolf was obviously stronger than he was.

The large wolf stepped up nose-to-nose with Joe and wrinkled his nose menacingly. "Go make an honest living," he said as he punched Joe hard in the gut, dropping him to his knees. "Get out of here. I might not like how some of the townsfolk treat us, but people like you are scum."

The other two turned and started walking back toward the forest. The large wolf reached down with his paw, putting a claw right under Joe's chin. "I am going to give this to the town constable," he said as he held the bag of coins by the top, dangling it in front of Joe. "If we see you back this way trying to con these people again, you're going to wish I only smashed your bottles." With that said, he turned to walk with his pack into the forest.

"GET BACK TO WORK YOU MUTTS!" The foreman screamed as he came out of his office to overlook the factory floor. "I don't pay you to yammer to each other."

Janos looked up from the piece of metal he was hammering and scrunched up his nose at the bellowing fat man looking out from his balcony. "*Hmph!*" he thought, "*that man wouldn't know hard work if it jumped out of his brandy and smacked him in the face. Besides, he DOESN'T pay us.*" Silently sighing, he looked over the cadre of others trapped here ... all chained, some wearing chained collars, even a few muzzled. As he started to shake his head, he felt a solid *PHWAP* on the back of his head, making his nose hit the hammer he was holding.

"Can you understand words, you smelly dog?" The sweaty, pale line manager stared at him. "Boss says shut your trap and hammer on that steel!"

Janos put his ears back and hurriedly went back to his forge work, lest he suffer more severe abuse. Yet he felt that someday, he would break free of this dungeon.

"Yeah, that's a good doggy, obey your master." He then spat on the floor next to him. "Don't start thinking you're smart. Know your place or you'll get worse than that!"

Angrily looking away, he began hammering again. As he pounded away, the anger receded to a numbness in the back of his mind. This is the only part of this life he enjoyed. The feel of the metal, the artistry he could create with just a mallet.

Bang.

Bang.

Bang.

Hours had passed while Janos hammered away on the metal parts before him. The room was getting very hot and sweat was dripping heavily off his muzzle from his exertion. As he paused to admire his work, the shift bell went off, snapping him suddenly into the here and now.

"Alright dogs, back to your cages!" the shift manager yelled at the whole floor. Soon, ten or so guards started moving around the room, unlocking each canid from their station and shoving them toward the exit.

Janos was one of the last ones unlocked and pushed almost hard enough to make him fall over, "C'mon, get your ass moving!" As he was shuffling to the door, he started passing the next group being brought in to keep the plant working. All of them were here under similar circumstances and subtly nodded to each other as they pass in the hallway.

***

Janos was shoved into his room and sat down on the floor resting his back against the cage wall. The room that held the canines was filled with literal animal cages, bars for walls and ceiling, straw mats to sleep on and their food in bowls. Their captors didn't even have the decency to remove the chains and collars. Glumly, he reached over and grabbed the bowl of food that was left for him. It was sort of a sloppy mix of water, gravy and something that reeked of expired meat. Sniffing at it to figure out what is was, his nose instinctively wrinkled up, as it was pretty rancid. "Smells like horse again," and slowly started to eat it.

The whole place stank. Nothing was ever cleaned and with fifty or more unwashed, ungroomed wolves living in close quarters, there was almost a fog of mixed musty scents hanging in the air. The only light in this place was a solitary skylight. Since he was a dayshifter, it was dark in the room for most of his time in the cage. *"At least I have good night vision,"* Janos thought to himself, as he glumly finished his rancid meat.

A few nights ago, he noticed that Batu, a white wolf, (though in this place, more of a dirty gray) was missing. Sighing, he spoke out loud to no one in particular, "Well, Batu must be dead." Not surprising, this place wore everyone down and Batu wasn't the toughest one out there. He was sharp as a whip, but not the most physical wolf. Janos wasn't surprised that he couldn't keep up with the hard labor they had to do each day. Worst yet, rumors had always circulated around that some of them had been taken away for sadistic games to entertain the wicked humans.

The room softly rang with the sound of keys and a clang of a door being unbarred. Light filtered in as the door opened and two big, dumb guards were dragging in a black wolf. They came to the empty cage next to Janos, threw the new wolf in and locked the door. Once the guards left, he got a good look at the fellow, who was pretty beat up. By the scent alone, Janos knew he was beaten and bloody.

About 20 minutes later, the guy rolled over onto his back. "Where am I?" he said aloud, in a weak voice.

"Well, if there is a hell, that's where you are," gruffed Janos. "You're somewhere on the south side of Polsk, captive in a factory." Janos turned an ear to the door and listened for a bit to see if the guards were still there. After a couple of minutes, he could only hear the sound of the other captives breathing. He continued his conversation with the new wolf. "Where were you before today?"

"I ...," he started coughing a bit, obviously his chest was a bit bruised. "I ... was out at the market in Dogtown getting food. As I walked in the market, I just saw a flash, then woke here." He slowly rolled over to look to see who was talking to him.

"What's your name, kid?"

"Zakh."

"Well Zakh, most of us here have a similar story. Me, I was trying to find a place to grab a drink and just walked into the wrong place. I tried to leave when I realized it, but it was too late." he paused for a minute, "I hope you like metal work."

***

Months went by with the droll, abusive, mundane routine of forced labor. A few inmates disappear and new ones replace them swiftly.

Thankfully, during the evenings, the guards pretty much leave the prisoners alone. While they 'supervised', the goons were usually busy playing cards and drinking, which left the prisoners to quietly talk. "These lunkheads," Janos started saying as he turned to Zakh, then continued, "Don't know that the dumbest of us canines are way smarter than THEY are. Take Rikoh, for example. He's huge, really intimidating and every guard thinks he's just a big dumb dog. Before landing here, he was studying physics while he was working on the railroad."

"We need to do something," Zakh (or Smokey as we have been calling him, as he was forces to tend the wood-fired kiln) offered up. "We can't live like this. I can't live like this." He flickered his ears in frustration and anger.

"Well, before you landed, we started working on a plan, but it's very slow going." Janos lowered his voice a little. "We make metal parts for them, but there's only a dozen of them in total. Many days on the floor, there are very few guards, let alone many of them paying any real attention to us. As long as those wagon parts keep flowing, they mostly ignore us unless they need to beat up someone for the thrill." Looking over at the door to listen for any guard activities, he continued, "Fritz over there is a genius with detail and has been slowly making keys for these shackles." He tugged at his collar to get at an itch, which revealed worn away patches of fur. "Fritz needs to make enough so the floor team can all free themselves at the same time. Thankfully, the guards are too stupid or lazy and one key works on everything in here."

Zakh's ears perked up a bit and whispered, "How close are we?"

"Maybe another month, Smokey. Fritz does not tell anyone much, so it can't be beat out of us." Janos continued, "Don't worry, ALL of us are getting out of here one way or another. These pricks don't know how strong of a pack we are. The reckoning WILL come." His muzzle opened up in a large toothy grin as he winked, showing the younger wolf he meant it.

***

Janos was banging away on a fender, doing his usual masterful job of shaping it. His head snapped up when the towering wolf, Igor, in the back of the room, let out a sharp bark. Then, he stood up swiftly, grabbing the nearest human guard and began to headbutt him. Janos always wondered how anyone managed to capture him, as he has to be the largest wolf on the planet. "*It's time,*" he thought to himself.

Over the past month, they were all given keys to hide within reach at their workstations. Other than the keys, they were told nothing much else. Some of them were given specific tasks, but no one knew everything in order to keep the plan secret. Once Igor started his fight, Janos's assignment was to take twenty canines and head up to the second floor cages to free the other prisoners.

The room soon erupted with humans running in, trying to subdue Igor. There had to be ten humans trying to stop him and it was a bit hilarious seeing how ineffective they were against him. All the guards' attention was on the back of the room. Everyone immediately went for their keys to unshackle themselves. Very soon, there were fifty freed canines all moving with a purpose. Ten leaped in to subdue the guards attacking Ivan, though he probably didn't need the help. Another small group went for the entry to secure it before it could be locked by the guards. Everyone else grabbed whatever item nearby that could be used as a weapon and started fighting.

"*What a sight to behold!*" Janos thought to himself. "Okay everyone!" he yelled out, "second floor with me!" They all charged down the hallway, toward the front of the building. Some ran ahead to over-power the remaining guards at the security doors, as well as unlock the entrance of the building. Twenty or so canids ran up the stairs. Janos was the first to reach the cell block and pulled the heavy security bar off, while another canine unlocked the main latch with a key.

Bursting into the room, there were only two guards to deal with. The guards were pretty quick to give up and dropped their clubs immediately. Everyone went around to unlock the cages and unshackle the night shift crew. Once freed, all of the prisoners ran for the stairs to escape.

As the group came back down the stairs, another group was returning from the factory floor. "Everyone is freed, get out of here, we'll take care of this!" said Damian, the only fox on the crew, said with his lips curled up in a grin. "I've been waiting so long for this!" In his paws, he had what looked like a matchbox.

One thing they knew was that there wouldn't be any constables coming, as this human operation was run by criminals. "Once we are were outside, we'll be safe," Damian said out loud to the other canines nearby.

Everyone streamed out into the streets, with Janos being one of the last out of the building. He stopped and took a moment to smell the fresh air. He turned his gaze back at the nondescript brick building that was his prison for the last year. As he did so, Damian jogged out of the building.

Damian came up to him and grabbed Janos by the shoulders and shook him in happiness, "Now, watch this!" He turned back toward the building, just as thunder started to erupt deep inside the factory. As the explosions reached the front of the building, the windows began to blow out one-by one, followed by jets of yellow, orange and purple fire. The glorious cacophony of sound and color heralding his freedom was something Janos would never forget.

June 15th, 1907

Today, we reached a milestone in our expedition. We located a plateau on Mount Nunatak that we deemed a good place to create a base camp for the remainder of the exploration of the region. David Karuk, the leader of the expedition, is directing the camp setup and shelter construction. And it should be complete in a day or two.

The past few weeks have been tough and even though we are in summer, the weather has been absolutely uncooperative up here in these remote mountains. Between the icy rain, winds and even snow, it has made our progress to this point very slow and arduous.

June 21st, 1907

Base camp is finally complete, though behind our original timeline. David's team really did a fantastic job overcoming adversity and I commend his drive and survival knowledge. A windstorm kicked up a few days ago, blowing over some of our camp structures and covering us with a couple feet of snow.

This location is uniquely positioned for us to reach a lot of the local area within a day's hike, so we should be able to make some really good progress on the survey in the nearby area.

July 1st, 1907

Scouting surveys of the area have revealed a lot of interesting-looking features in this mountain range. I am really looking forward to tomorrow as we are starting a journey to nearby Piniartoq Peak. Through my telescope, I can see some strange rock formations peeking out from under the snow that look absolutely intriguing, almost alien. I've never seen anything like this when I was surveying around the Aleutian Range.

July 15th, 1907

I haven't updated my log much, even though we have been back in camp for two days. I had to formulate my thoughts since what we found is almost beyond comprehension. I needed a couple days to digest this in order to put it into words.

When we reached our destination, of what we now call the Piniartoq Puzzle, we found what looked like a pointed metal rock formation jutting out over a cliff. From a distance, the structure looked absolutely foreign, unlike anything I have ever seen before.

As the chief geologist, I really needed to put my hands on it, to touch it. There HAD to be something special about this and an explanation to its strangeness. I became obsessed with it and had several spirited debates with my colleagues. I eventually convinced David to let me take Hans Klifur with me on a special trip to investigate the anomaly, as he is the best rigger and climber out of the group.

The outcropping was a few hundred meters up a sheer cliff face with really tough-looking terrain. Breaking out the climbing gear, Hans slowly started his climb, securing anchors and cabling as he went. It took us hours, but we slowly made vertical progress towards the ledge.

Even though it was cold, we were both sweating and out of breath as we climbed up onto the ledge. Hans remarked on how difficult that face was to climb. After a few moments of rest, I began breaking out what little inspection tools I was able to bring on the climb with me. The formations were all but invisible from atop the ledge due to the snow cover. The portions sticking out over the ledge were only visible from the ravine below and hidden from us. Hans broke out a tiny shovel and began to dig into the snow mound.

After 30 minutes of digging a small tunnel deep into the snow, his shovel hit something solid with a clink. It was oddly metallic sounding for a rock. I could hear Hans rustling around in the hole. Whatever he was doing was making metallic scraping and clanking noises. Soon, Hans emerged from the hole carrying a small, golden and silver, jagged-shaped object and handed it to me.

I stood there in stunned silence, as this was clearly a metal object, but extremely light for its size. There were burn marks all over it and the edges appeared to be melted. Whatever happened to this piece, it was clearly violent. The plate was so strange, as no machinery I have seen has a metal like it. How did it get here?

Hans pulled a few more chunks out of the hole. There was a lot more debris buried in the mound, but we didn't have the ability to bring much back with us. We made the decision to head right back to camp with the parts to show the crew. Once back in camp, no one could believe what they saw. So the next day, the entire crew went to excavate more of the site, as this discovery was the most excitement we have had so far on this expedition.

We unearthed a lot more parts, but we were a survey crew, not heavy excavators. All in all, we brought back dozens of pieces from the wreckage. There were some fabric remnants, a glass panel fragment with unknown laminated parts on the back. The most curious piece was a weird sculpted handle with multiple buttons, but made from a lightweight material that was clearly not metal.

Once back to base camp, David and I made the decision that this was too important to wait until our scheduled return in a few months and we immediately started the trek back to our headquarters in Lyngen to put together an excavation and retrieval crew. This cannot be lost to the weather.

Chapter 11
Year 1941 – Discovery

"Let's see what is in there." Andreas Maliksaid spoke aloud to himself, as he put a new slide in the electron microscope. He was attending the prestigious Ichanchi Medical school in Fjordland working on his PhD. He was using the latest electron microscope technology developed by another researcher at the school. His previous two college degrees were in medicine and he was currently working on his PhD. His thesis was focused exclusively on blood research. He had been trying to figure out what caused leukemia and he had been scanning various blood types to get a good look at the cells.

Rosalind Apgar was working in the same lab as him, studying material science. She came from Calveras and was as smart as a whip. She had been using the microscope for her PhD as well, and the two had struck up a good friendship.

Later that morning, Andreas and Rosalind were sitting in the cafe near the university while taking a break from the lab. They were having a casual conversation talking about his research project.

Rosalind was looking off into space while thinking. "You know, canines are very healthy. They don't seem to have major diseases, like leukemia. Maybe you should also look at some of their blood. It might give you some inspiration or new avenues to explore."

Andreas took a sip of coffee while she finished talking. "You know, that's a good idea. I think they have some samples in the blood closet. I'll see if I can use some."

***

Later that day, he inquired about the canine blood samples and was given a vial to use. Once back at the lab, he prepped a slide for the blood and slid it into the machine. Then he loaded the film and closed the cabinet. They kept it enclosed to keep the dust out of the sensitive equipment. He reached around the side and hit the button to fire up the machine. The process was nearly instantaneous, but the film still needed to be developed, which would take the lab a couple days to process. He rolled the film into its protective case and removed it from the machine. There were about a dozen other film plates he needed to develop as well. He grabbed them all and walked down two flights of stairs to the film lab.

***

Two days later, he got a call that his photos were ready. Andreas made a detour on his way to his office so he could review them.

Unlocking his door, he opened it and put his coat and hat on the rack before sitting down at his desk. He slid the photos out of the envelope and began to thumb through them, looking for anything anomalous. When he got to the canine blood sample, he paused. He put down all the rest and stood to hang the photo up in order to assess it better.

"What are those?" He squinted at something funny on the surface of one of the blood cells. "Is that a mite?" The object was so tiny he couldn't really see much. There were a few in the picture, but not on every cell. "Hmm...," he said as he rubbed his chin. "I need a higher resolution photo."

Andreas sat back down at his desk, grabbed the phone and dialed a number. "Professor Donkar? Andreas Malik here. I think I found something interesting, but I need to use the high resolution microscope." He listened for a few moments as the other party spoke. "Yeah, I just need to get better magnification. Can I book it for today?" He listened again. "Great. I'll be there at 1 pm."

***

Two days went by after he used the better microscope to re-shoot pictures of his canine blood and the lab had the photo ready earlier that morning. He had picked it up on his way to his office and hung up the photo right next to the previous one, so he could compare them side-by-side. He could now see the 'mite' better and it sure did look like a mite or a tick; but very, very, VERY tiny. It was nano-scaled and had a teardrop-shape body with ten legs. The mite didn't look natural, but mechanical, bearing a striking resemblance of a tiny machine. He could see segmentation on the legs, but they had way too many joints when compared to a real tick or mite. They looked like they had way significantly more articulation than an insect leg. They looked like they could could easily manipulate objects. The mouth area was interesting too. Instead of pincers for biting the mouth was pointed, almost needle-like.

"This doesn't look like anything that looks natural. Someone else needs to see this to make sure I am not hallucinating." Andreas said as he grabbed the phone to call Professor Donkar. He really wanted to get a second set of eyes on this unusual discovery.

HONK, HONK.

"*Sigh.*" Traffic had come to a standstill on the 405 freeway again. He was getting tired of this commute. "We need to move closer to the shop," Saul Rogov muttered aloud to his family in the car. He had moved himself and his family down to Los Diego with an idea and a hope ... and the weather. Life here was so much more pleasant than the run down dives that made up most of Dogtown over in River City, and he hoped this was their ticket out of the poor house.

"Well, we should have rented in downtown San Tomanico before prices started going up," his wife replied. "Someday, if your new business venture works, we can stop renting that dive of an apartment and move by the beach."

They fell silent as there wasn't much to say. He kept creeping forward, the constant yo-yoing of the car was making him grumpy. Some random surf-pop song was playing on the radio as his mind wandered toward his business enterprise. He couldn't get his mind off all the things he and his partners had to do to really get the business going.

"Oh hey honey, it's your ad!" His wife turned up the radio as he swiveled his ears toward the car speaker.

The commercial opened up with a catchy surf-rock song that quickly built up to a crescendo before settling into a softer version of itself as Saul's voice came on.

"Hey there fellow canines. Do you love your old car, but hate that it wasn't designed for you?"

"Come down to Saul's Auto Specialties on the scenic Highway 1 in San Tomonico and we can help! We can make your car work for you!"

"All of us hate having to sit on our tails in seats designed for humans. We can take that uncomfortable seat and give your tail the room it needs by opening up the back for your comfort."

"We offer all sorts of upholstery options from breathable mesh to the finest leather in a huge array of colors. Our talented team can customize any car for you!"

The voice-over switched to a deeper voice of another canine.

"Air conditioning not cutting it? Feel like you want to shave yourself to cool off? Saul's can help! We can upgrade that subpar air conditioning in your car or completely add it if it wasn't built with it. Stop panting today!"

"We have all kinds of car accessories too!"

"Saul's Auto Specialties can help you get more enjoyment out of your car. Stop panting and get down here! Call 555-WOLF today. That's 555-9653."

"Call today and we will strive to make you happy!"

Saul turned down the radio a bit as it transitioned to another ad.

"Well, let's keep our claws crossed." Saul looked over at his wife with a pleasant smile.

"Daddah?" Little Anya looked up at her father while stacking some wooden, lettered blocks on the carpeted floor and asked, "Daddah, why do they hate us?"

Viktor put down the newspaper he was reading onto his lap and looked down at his daughter gazing up at him, with her fuzzy little face scrunched up a bit. "Who hates us?" the father asked with a slight tilt to his head.

"The hairless monkeys." Looking down at her blocks, stacking another one and completing the word 'mean' and continued. "Why do they hate us?"

"*Oh boy,*" he thought to himself, "*this is going to be a tough one.*"

"First thing my dear, it's not nice to call people 'Hairless Monkeys'. That is also mean, just like what you spelled in your blocks. Did something happen at school today?" dad asked.

Pushing over the block tower, watching the top three scatter softly on the rug, "Rrrick." She was rolling her R's as she spoke. Anya sometimes did that when her emotions got the better of her. "Rick called me a lousy, mangy, flea bitten, smelly mongrel who shouldn't be at school with them." She started sniffling a little bit. "He was being mean."

"Hmm." He idly scratched at his chin with a claw, while he thought for a moment. Viktor moved his paper from his lap to the coffee table, before getting to his feet and moving over to sit down next to her. He reached his arm around her and pulled her sniffling face to his side. "After he said that, what did you do?"

Choking up a little bit, Anya muttered, "I got mad, rrrreally mad," and then buried her eyes in her father's arm fur. She sobbed for a little into her father's arm then looked up at him. "I stood up and snarrrled at him. Then, I pushed him over and ran outside." Her voice trailed off as she looked down at her hands, adding, "The other kids were saying mean things too." She buried her face back in her dad's chest and cried some more.

Vik knew it was going to be a little rough for her growing up in a mostly human community. The job offer and the promise of making a good, safe life for his family was too lucrative to pass up. He stood, picking her up to hold her in his arms, resting her muzzle on his shoulder. Making his way back to his chair, he sat and placed her down next to him.

Reaching down to pull her face up towards his to look into her eyes, he asked, "Did you know, our kind were once like them?" He pulled his lips into a small smirk. "Yes, our ancestors were once humans like them. Very little hair, no claws and without our wonderful smiles." He pulled his lips back into a very toothy grin and then smooched her between her eyes.

Wiping her teary eyes with the back of her hand, she whispered, "How is that possible?" She paused for a second before adding, "Is that why they hate us?"

"Well, they hate us for a variety of reasons, but mostly they fear us. That's hard to believe given our astonishingly good looks." That made her giggle a little bit, which made him happy. "Let me tell you a story." He sat Anya next to him on the couch and began his anecdote.

"Long ago, the world was just humans living alongside nature. Most people lived rural lives in small communities and most people were farmers, ranchers, hunters and the like."

"Our history books tell us of a great skyfall back in the 1300's. The heavens opened up and streaks of fire rained down all over the world. This scared many of the humans, leading many great writers and poets to write of the end of the world, to write of *The End Times*." Viktor gazed down at his daughter, his lips curled up into a smile as Anya's attention was fixed on his words. "Well, the end of the world didn't happen and it faded into stories told to their grandchildren. Some 50 years after the great fireballs, rural folk started noticing that wild dogs all over the planet were getting smarter. They were easily avoiding the traps hunters had set and in fact, some were smart enough to turn those traps on the hunters, much to the humans' dismay."

Viktor continued, "This newfound intelligence caused great fear amongst the humans and their leaders. So much so, all the world's leaders came together to declare that the best thing humans could do to protect their communities was to exterminate the canids. This was barbaric, even in those times, but it was thought to be the righteous path towards the protection of humans." Before carrying on, he looked carefully at Anya to make sure he wasn't upsetting her. Viktor was relieved that she was still listening and not frightened by his story. Reaching over to the table, he grabbed a water glass and took a sip before pressing on with the story.

"They tasked their best hunters, sending them out all over the world to do their bidding. When cornered or caught, the canines would ferociously defend themselves. With intelligence close to the humans, they were pretty effective in keeping the hunters at bay. Over the years, many hunters were hurt and some lost their lives. Unbeknownst to anyone at the time, these encounters would lead to the creation of our people."

"Many of the survivors soon fell very sick. Months would go by where these people slowly changed...changed into beings like us." He watched her face wrinkle in thought, but it was more quizzical rather than fear. "Religious faithful all over the world labeled these changed people as monsters and born of evil."

Anya placed her hand on her father's arm, "Why do they think we are evil? I'm not evil."

"Well, I know that, how could anything so cute be evil?" He smirked and ruffled her ears and she giggled. "Most of our people are naturally born canines now, but old stories speak of the changed. It is said that the changed couldn't remember anything during their change, that their memories returned to them after a time." He reached up and rubbed his chin, hoping this next bit doesn't scare her. "During the madness of the change the early ones wandered off in severe hunger. Mindlessly hunting prey and even attacking humans during their time of insanity. I guess this led human kind to believe we were bloodthirsty killers and must be evil. Centuries later, many humans still believe we are monsters and are a threat to them. I'm sure your classmate Rick has been told by his parents that very same thing."

Anya wrinkled her face, "I guess that's why they hate us."

"Naw, they mostly are jealous of our beautiful fur coats." Viktor stuck out his tongue in jest and then gave his daughter a big hug.

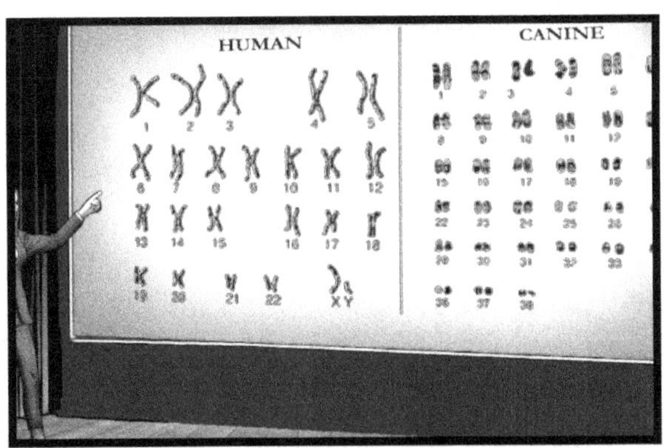

"Wow, that's a lot of people out there," Rachael remarked to Edward, as they stood just offstage to present their paper to the scientific community. Low incoherent murmuring could be heard from the audience by the two waiting, until they were called upon to speak.

"Yeah, our paper has garnered a lot of attention, both good and bad. A lot of those folks out there are highly skeptical, especially the religious parties." Edward smirked and gestured to the audience. "So many are dubious because they still believe," he raised his hands and did an air quote to punctuate his words, "that 'they' are made by the devil, demons or whatever evil forces they believe in. That's an utterly ridiculous notion. We triple checked and have validation from three top level research groups around the world."

"Yeah, I know. I'm still really nervous speaking in front of large groups...especially with listeners who basically hate what I'm saying and will demean me … I mean us … just to 'prove' they are right. Utterly mind blowing how closed off some people can be." Rachael sighed internally before steeling herself mentally by taking a very, very deep breath.

A hush slowly fell across the crowd as Professor Abhijeed Vascale from the Calveras Science Academy walked on stage and settled behind the podium. "Distinguished guests," he spoke a little far away from the mic, so it wasn't well heard over the PA. Then, he stepped a little closer so he could be heard. "Sorry about that. Distinguished guests, journalists and congress members. Thank you for traveling from around the world for this presentation. Rachael Thomas and Edward Nordmann have joined us to present the findings of their research into the Werewolf phenomenon. I will say, their work is groundbreaking and has been vetted by top scientific minds from around the world. In the modern history of our world, I don't think there has been a higher level of scrutiny and exhaustive peer review performed on a body of work. So without further ado, please welcome them to the podium."

As they walked out from behind the curtain, a muted applause ushered from about half the crowd. Skeptics of the work looked at the stage with disdain, scowls and outright disgust, many remaining seated with their arms crossed.

Ed motioned for Rachael to step up to the mic to start their presentation. Nervously, she stepped behind the podium, reaching her hands out to grip the back rail to calm her nerves. Taking a deep breath, she began, "Thank you everyone for coming. We at the San Juarez Research Institute would like to thank the Calveras Science Academy for inviting us here to present ... I mean ... speak to you about our work and what discoveries we have made."

Looking a bit pale, she looked over at Ed for a confidence boost. He motioned to her to take a breath and continue. "Over the past 20 years, we have been researching how the werewolf races came into being. When comparing their development and growth to the fundamentals of evolutionary theory, the evidence didn't fit neatly within those theories." She paused for a moment while Ed brought up the first slide.

Rachel continued when the slide came up, "Normal evolution takes millennia to show any appreciable change in a species." She gestured to the graph, showing a timeline illustrating the evolution of the canines on the planet, prior to the 1300's. "Everyone on the planet was astounded, and frightened, when canines went from a stable form to rapidly getting smarter in the space of a hundred years. That defied all scientific evidence, as well as all logic."

"It wasn't long before these smart canines, normally shy creatures who avoided human contact, increasingly came into conflict with humans. As humans pushed further into wild areas, attacks on humans by canines drastically increased in frequency." Rachel glanced over the audience for a moment before continuing, "In the early 1500s, local governments asked people to stop keeping canines as pets. That guidance was codified into law when the global government was formed."

She paused while glancing down at her notes. "It wasn't long after the first 'werewolves' appeared on Earth. Once it became widely known that humans somehow could be transformed into a hybrid of canine and human, it was postulated by the scientific community that some outside force was acting to accelerate the evolution of both canines and human-canine hybrids."

Rachel gestured to Ed to go to the next slide. "Here we see an overlay of the timing of canine development and werewolf appearances. This shows the rapid evolution and subsequent arrival of the first were-wolves. This should not be possible ... but there it is."

"Early stories were passed down through generations before be-ing written down, so early data is a bit speculative or inaccurate at best. Early transformations were attributed to intervention by gods or demons. Contrary to that popular assessment, there is a logical, scientific explanation for the rise of the humanoid canines. Ed is our resident science historian and will cover some the recent history of werewolves."

Swapping places, Ed settled up to the podium and began, "Early in the discovery of the werewolf phenomenon, someone who was 'turned' usually fell ill for weeks at a time while their body changed. They would be in a state of delirium, barely conscious through the fevers and hallucinations. This illness took its toll on both the victim and those around them. Depending on the health of the individual, some did not make it through the process and died. Most do not remember anything during the period of illness, only awaking weeks or months later with a different body. Many others were murdered, thought to be possessed by demons." He paused for moment to let that last sentence resonate in the minds of the audience. "These were dark times, where fear of them overruled our love and compassion for family members and friends."

"In 1907, an expedition crew was tasked with surveying a remote and snow-covered mountain range in Fjordland. During that trip," pausing to wait for a slide to change, "the survey crew happened upon mysterious wreckage. Photography wasn't portable enough at this point to be included, but I am showing a photo from a later trip. The crew couldn't carry much back, but what they did carry back baffled the science institutes around the globe. The metals, the construction and what we now know as electronics, were not created here. It was not of this world."

Murmurs rumbled through some of the crowd at that last statement. Rachael watched Ed grin a little bit. Ed continued, "In the late 1930's, the first commercial electron microscopes were released and allowed us a closer look into the canines and werewolf inner workings. In 1941 Andreas Maliksaid looked at a variety of blood samples from human, canines and werewolves. He discovered very tiny, nanoscale-sized structures in both the canine and werewolf samples. Human samples sometimes had these same structures, but only in a small percentage of the specimens." Looking up at the slide, he said, "This structure was not thought to be a naturally occurring. It was mechanical in appearance, looking like a tiny machine. Many dismissed his discovery as pure coincidence or a complete fabrication, since this was the first period we could see structures this small."

Ed looked back to the audience in order to know when to continue, "Not much was known for many years what the presence of this nano device had to do with the rise of werewolf kind, if anything, but there were many theories."

"Skipping forward to the 1950's, independent developments by Ferndando Vasques and Hitori Suzuka discovered the Double Helix DNA strand, which was postulated to be the building blocks of life."

"Researchers refined their technique for 20 years, culminating in genome sequencing in 1977 by Magnus Salvatore." He drew in a breath before continuing, "After a few years of refinement, David Schwartz of the Heartstone Medical Institute applied these techniques and started looking at the genetics of humans, canines and werewolves. What he found was the werewolf is truly a hybrid of canine and human. What he did not know was how they managed to become hybridized."

Pausing for a moment to let that settle, he concluded his remarks by saying, "and this is where Rachael's work comes in." He gestured for Rachael to retake the podium.

Rachael looked back over the crowd to gauge them, some enthralled, some bored and others wearing dour expressions. She certainly knew who was going to be a thorn in her side during the Q&A session. Glancing over to her side, she added, "Thank you, Ed." before unpacking the main reason why they were there.

"Ed had uncovered some deeply buried, but declassified, military experiments that got me curious." That comment elicited a few murmurs from different parts of the auditorium. "The ethics of some of those experiments are very questionable, but here goes."

Steeling herself for this difficult topic, she said, "It turns out that one group figured out how to extract these nano-scaled machines and started injecting soldiers with them to see what happened. This was done without their knowledge or permission. Thankfully, nothing happened to them except for one notable exception. Months after his injection, one soldier fell sick and slipped into delirium as his subsequent transformation into a canid was well documented."

The air in the room was smotherlingly thick with silence. "This report never stated why the transformation happened so long after the introduction of the machines into this individual. I had Ed do some more digging and he even interviewed the gentleman about the incident."

"Nothing about this man's life was different, except for one thing. Despite the long-standing laws banning individuals from keeping canines as pets, this soldier had kept a dog as a companion. That newly-revealed detail inspired me to procure a supply of the machines, along with various types of human and canine blood to start testing."

Rachael's nervousness finally gave way to the excitement her research always brought her, as she said, "I started with pristine human blood samples, added some nano machines and observed what happened." Glancing over to the picture on the slide she continued, "What you can see here is the regular human blood with the machines in close proximity to the human cells. There is absolutely no effect of the machines on human cells. Nothing happened in all these trials."

"My next step was to obtain cells from what I call the 'original' dog. There are small populations of genetically unmodified canines in isolation. They never developed the high level of intelligence seen in the developed canines and their DNA was perfect for me to start with. I sequenced the genes before I started the experiments for reference. Then, I mixed a sample of the original dog cells with the machines and immediately could see some activity. The machines touched the dog cells and then quickly entered that cell. I couldn't see what was going on internally, but eventually the machine would leave the cell and enter a different cell. This happened over and over, until every cell in the sample had been invaded."

After pausing for a new slide to appear, she continued, "This is the original DNA sequence for the unmodified dog." She nodded to Ed to advance the slide. "And this is the DNA sequence after the machines did their work. You can clearly see the sequencing is very similar, but with modifications to certain areas."

"I repeated the experiment, but using werewolf cells instead of the dog DNA." A side by side of the pre- and post-experiment werewolf DNA flashed on the overhead. "What I observed was the machines would enter the cell and then leave. The DNA was the same pre- and post-test, so the machine clearly identified the werewolf cell, but didn't affect any changes."

"These machines are clearly attracted to the canine cell, so there must have been some trigger that caused them to jump into action like they thought something was in need of repair in the dog cell."

Rachael paused for a moment to gauge the audience and figure out how she wanted to proceed.

"Next, I really wanted to know why the machines identify only dog cells, so I started looking at the cell's outer structure." The next picture appeared of a microscope image of a dog and human cell, side by side. "I wondered if it was sort of like our white blood cells that attack the foreign bodies to prevent infections. During one late night, unbeknownst to me, I accidentally contaminated a human cell culture with dog cells, before I added the machines. I expected nothing to happen as I was planning to repeat the human cell test."

Inhaling deeply, she continued, "I was completely taken aback when I viewed the sample under the microscope. The machines appeared to go into a dog cell. After leaving the cell, the machines appeared to attack the human cell." Turning to look at the new image on the overhead, she continued, "but not destroying it. It seemed to go in and out of the cell, manipulating the inner working and exterior composition of the cell." Looking back at the audience, she could see that more people were listening to her intently.

A new slide appeared that showed the human DNA sequence next to a werewolf sequence. "After the test, DNA of the human cells showed a new DNA structure. It was just like the werewolf DNA that I sequenced earlier." She took a breath. "What I think is going on," she paused briefly, "is the machines require a canine cell to reference or 'check' the DNA. If there are human blood cells nearby, it sees them as damaged and 'heals' them."

Looking up at the a slide again, she said, "This is pretty conclusive. How does this work? We don't understand any of the tech used to make these machines. They appear to have only a limited amount of information storage and need a reference to tell if it's a cell it should be maintaining or ignoring.

"What I couldn't explain is what causes the person's illness and subsequent, permanent transformation into a canid. Historical reports almost always involve some sort of trauma, so that got me thinking." The slide changed to just a list of medical compounds. "During trauma, our bodies release norepinephrine, which is adrenaline. Concurrently, the body releases cortisol, prolactin, HGH otherwise known as growth hormone and other hormones. I wondered if that wasn't the trigger, so I prepped another experiment."

She continued, "I put human cells, canine cells, the nano-machines and a concoction of these hormones together. The results were extreme. The machines went into overdrive and transformed the human cells into canids in rapid fashion." She flipped to an image of a human, half metamorphized, laying in a hospital bed. "Ed had found the records of a case where someone was in a fight with a canine. During that fight, they were both seriously injured." She pointed up at the screen. "This man's body rapidly turned canine. The process took about eight weeks. During that time, the doctors kept the patient sedated for everyone's safety."

She motioned for the next slide. "This is another case study we found. This man was accidentally exposed to canine blood due to a blood transfusion, but didn't really have any injuries, so nothing happened to him. Genetic testing six months after the incident showed his DNA was indeed changed to a canid's, but physically there was no immediate transformation." Ed clicked to the next slide for her. "For nearly 40 years, he slowly took on more characteristics of a canine. Over his lifetime, he exhibited increased body hair that was the color of a wolf. His human teeth fell out and were replaced by canine teeth. His fingernails slowly grew out into claws, but no major skeletal changes happened."

"What I suspect happens is this: these nano-machines see the canine DNA, combined with presence of trauma hormones and kick the body's system into overdrive. Since they see 'widespread' damage to the cells, i.e. the human cells, it tricks the body into releasing massive amounts of growth hormones. This growth spurt would be similar to puberty, where the patient goes into an accelerated maturation phase of development. In this case, it effects significant physical changes in a short amount of time."

Rachael looked out at the audience for a moment, then placed her hands on the podium, "I'm going to interject a bit of information here that could explain where these machines came from." A new slide with a photo appeared on the overhead screen. "During our investigation into the military experiments, we obtained some government reports detailing some of the items recovered from the various alien spaceship crash sites. When I was reading through documents, I found references to alien artifacts that looked like medical devices. Photos of the devices made them look like high-tech syringes, but the reports didn't state what was inside. I suspected they were filled with these machines." She paused for a few moments when some of the audience started murmuring. "I think the machines arrived with the spaceship crash are were used during medical emergencies. The aliens who made these 'Nano-Docs' must have had similar-enough DNA markers to our native canids for them to work. It's pure happenstance that their crashing on our planet would have such wide ranging effects."

"All of our experimental work has been duplicated by organizations around the globe and all of the experimenting has shown the same results. These machines can and do transform humans when canine blood is entered into the mix." She turned to face the audience. "That is all for our presentation today. Thank you for your time. " She motioned to Ed to flip to a slide with the San Juarez Research Institute logo.

She sighed in relief as presentation came to an end. *"They are going to assault us with questions, not all of them will be pleasant,"* she thought to herself, pausing internally before another thought crossed her mind. *"Researchers all around the world are studying the alien artifacts that have been retrieved from around the globe. Hopefully we will learn a lot from them and understand who they were and why they were here. Human technology has a long way to go before we can decipher it all."*

Abhijeed stepped back onto the stage to address the audience, "Thank you Rachael and Ed for that wonderful presentation. They will now take some questions."

The old van came to a trundling stop in front of a dingy building deep in the San Juarez Mountains. "Okay, we're here," the driver said aloud to Olivia Morales, whom he picked up at the tiny, regional airport.

Olivia thanked the driver as she stepped out of the vehicle and closed the door. Although the outside of the building looked run down, she was excited to work with the state-of-the-art ground telescope nearby. The telescope was finally commissioned after a ten-year delay and much-politicized construction. Many of the local residents fought the telescope's installation, as they believed it would destroy the area around it. "*Hmmph,*" she thought to herself, "*There would only be handfuls of people at the site at any one time and would barely be noticed after it was up and running.*"

The driver opened up the back of the van and handed Olivia her two bags. "The van leaves for the facility four times a day: 7 am, 1 pm, 7 pm and again at 1 am. So if you miss it, you're stuck for a bit," the driver said as he smiled as he closed the door.

This was the apartment building where all the visiting scientists and staff were housed. Olivia had managed to get funding for a two-year assignment to study and map asteroids that came near the planet and was really excited to begin her work. She had already been given the keys to her apartment. Hefting her suitcases up three flights of stairs, she unlocked the door to her room. It was small, decently appointed, but thankfully warm.

After grabbing a quick shower, Olivia left the apartment to take a walk in the village attached to the apartments. It was small, but the roads were actually paved (she was glad for not having to trudge through mud to get some food). Most of the buildings were in need of some paint, but overall the town was tidy. The package she received at the airport had a list of recommended eating establishments. She soon found herself in front of a small place named 'Buddy's' that served local San Juarezian cuisine, despite the non-local name.

Stepping inside, it was just an ordinary looking place, with bright colored paint indicative of the area.

"Dr. Morales!" shouted a gentleman with a mustache in a white suit who got up from a table and made his way over to her. "I am Dr. Franklin Hernandez, the administrator of the San Juarez Experimental Telescope Array." He extended his hand, "Nice to meet you in person. Please, won't you join me? I just sat down."

Olivia shook his hand, "Nice to meet you too and thank you." She smiled and followed him over to the table where two other people were seated.

"These are Dr. Becken and Dr. Tibayan." She greeted them and sat down in the empty chair. "Dr. Morales just arrived today and will be mapping out asteroids in near-earth orbit. Hopefully keeping us from impending doom," he chuckled, finding his own words humorous. "Why don't I order for you? Do you like chicken? Spicy? Their chicken dishes are the best."

She nodded and they talked away throughout the whole dinner about the telescope, and about what the other two scientists were working on. Eventually their meal came to a close. "Okay," she said as she patted her mouth with the napkin she had and got up, "I should get some sleep, it has been a long day of travel and I am beat." The others also stood up to say their goodbyes.

"Grab the morning van to the facility and I will give you the tour." He reached out and shook her hand. "See you about eight o'clock."

***

Olivia had settled into her work routine pretty quickly over the past few months. She was doing most of her work at night, since the light blocked out much of what she was trying to see during the daylight. Her work involved using data from a combination of spectrometers, radio waves, and light-based telescopes. During her allocated time, the instruments hummed away while she plowed through a ton of data in the following days.

She had already managed to catalog nearly thirty new objects in orbit around the earth. Most were uninteresting rocks, but one stuck out in particular. It showed an extremely high concentration of metal, even though it was no bigger than a typical van. Olivia had decided to spend her next twelve sessions focusing all the instruments on the one object to really get an understanding of what it was, which would take about two months due to telescope priorities. Thankfully, the grant foundation was extremely interested and gave her the go ahead to focus on one.

***

After a couple months of observations and data crunching, she finally had some concrete findings she could present. She flew back to São Paulo to meet with members of the San Juarez 'Science & Technology Bureau', who had provided the funds for her research.

"Thanks everyone for joining me," Olivia said with a smile to the dozen or so people in the room. "As you have been briefed, I found something very exciting." She turned on a slide projector that flickered to life.

"Over the past six months, I have been tracking and cataloging asteroids and other Near-Earth-Orbit objects." She pressed a button flipping to a slide showing the Earth overlaid with elliptical orbits of the objects she had found. "Most of these were uninteresting rocks and icy bodies. Nothing about these were exciting, nor pose any danger to us here on Earth." Olivia flipped the slide again. "Except for NEO-7298." The next slide showed the Earth with only one elliptical track. "This one is nearly ninety degrees out of plane with almost all the naturally occurring asteroids and comets." She flipped the slide to add some numbers to the graph. "This object is roughly the size of a large van, cylindrical in shape, and has metal spectrometer readings like no other object identified to date."

She looked over the room to gauge a response, but the there were only bored faces at the table. "This object is on a roughly 30-year short orbit around the planet and is moving relatively slow for a normal celestial body. Normal asteroids are moving from 17 to 25 kilometers per second, whereas this is moving at about a tenth of that."

"During my observation window, the object was passing at its closest point to the planet in its orbit. I directed the team to aim our best telescope at it during this window and they were able to get these photographs." Olivia clicked over the next slide. "This is the object in question." Several people in the room gasped a little. "This is a bit blurry due to the resolution we can get from the San Juarez Experimental Telescope Array cameras, but the object is a perfect cylinder and appears to be whole."

"Based on the off-the-chart metal reading from the spectrometer, I believe this object is not of natural origins." She clicked over to another slide. "We know much alien technology has been found on the planet and we have used that as a basis for many scientific discoveries. The spectrometer readings on this object match the metals composition in samples found across the planet." She clicked back to the photograph of the object, adding, "What we are looking at here is the most intact example of alien technology found."

A gentleman in a suit stood up. "I'm sorry to cut you off a bit early Dr. Morales. From what I have seen here, and in the reports you sent, our experts believe you are absolutely right. As of this point, this information is now classified at top-secret. Our office will be in touch with you on continuing to lead this work, but I must stress this is now classified."

Canine Consumer Products Expo 2012

The mostly-canine crowd erupted in applause after a young, nicely dressed fox walked onto the stage. "Hello CCPE 2012! I am Ailani Ludo." He let the crowd's applause die down. "I hope you have seen a lot of cool tech so far here at the show. We have a lot of great product debuts lined up this week but I am really excited for the next presentation." Ailani glanced off the side of the stage and then returned his gaze back to the audience. "Please give a warm welcome to Kamilla Teller, CEO and founder of Canid Customs, Inc." Ailani walked toward her and shook her hand before heading backstage.

"Good evening everyone!" Kamilla stepped to the front of the stage as the Canid Customs, Inc. logo floated above her on the screen. "As you know, I founded CCI in 2002 with one goal: To make exceptional bath products for Canines. For far too long the major manufacturers refused to pay attention to the special needs of my canine brethren."

"Over the years, we have developed better and better products to help us, well, get a better bath," she joked, as the audience chuckled. "That brings me to this." She looked up and gestured at the screen before looking back to the audience. "I want to introduce you to the new Animax Shower Module." An animation started playing, panning through all the features inside. "This is a state-of-the-art, fully computer-controlled shower and drying module engineered to give you, my canine friends, the best and quickest bath experience possible."

The overhead screen zoomed in. "It has two separate rain showers for those who prefer the natural feel of rainfall." The screen showed an animation of a canine silhouette standing under the rain heads. "For those who prefer a more vigorous shower, the Animax has 24 programmable body sprayers to give you an all-body simultaneous wash covering every square millimeter of your body."

"The true innovation that sets this model apart from its predecessors is we have now fully integrated our shower and drying modules into one sleek, easily-installed unit. The unit has 6 blowers that will get you dry in about 10 minutes without requiring you to get out of the shower and making your whole bathroom wet." Kamilla looked out towards the audience.

"The last truly impressive innovation I want to talk about is our brand new Cygnus X-1 Control System. The controller is fully programmable, allowing the entire family to have their own settings." The overhead screen showed an animation of the controller being assembled. Slowly, the device came to life on the screen and began scrolling through the user interface. "The water pressure, number of shower heads in use, temperature and drying speed can be independently customized to your taste, giving you the ultimate control in your bath experience with the touch of a button. It is completely water-proof and claw touch friendly, so the control unit will last the lifetime of the shower."

The screen above her zoomed out to show the entire shower and the product name. "But I have another surprise," she said as she smiled. "We have been able to optimize the design, manufacturing and supply chain so much that we will be able offer the Animax Shower for an MSRP of $2999.99. If you add the cost of our premium shower and drying modules in our current lineup, you will see you can get even more value for the same money, stretching those hard earned dollars farther. The Animax Shower Module will be available at all major retailers and distributors by the end of the month."

"I am fully confident the Animax will give you the ultimate in cleanliness that you want...that you deserve." She waved at the crowd. "And remember, we at CCI make the best products for you. Made for Canines, BY Canines. Thank you and have a great expo!" Kamilla waved as she walked off the stage while the audience applauded.

<u>Part 2 – Biographies</u>

Chapter 17
Tyler Dresden

(Narrator)

Michael Dresden, founder of Dresden Industries, would become a household name as he built his company on the back of pioneering efforts in space exploration and communications. Founded in 1962, Dresden Industries would go on to develop the first compact computer guidance systems for rockets and satellites in the late 1960s.

Dresden's company would go on to be a juggernaut, opening up global communications and creating a near-global monopoly.

In 1970, Dresden married a brilliant scientist named Maria Glover and the marriage was deemed the 'most important social event of the century'.

In 1980, Michael's greatest achievement would turn out to be nothing business or science related. In August of that year, they gave birth to Tyler. Tyler quickly be proved to be a genius.

By age three, he was able to read at the level of a ten year old. By nine, he was reading high-school level science text books. His teachers claimed he was even smarter than either of his parents and would someday prove to be the smartest person on the planet.

By age twelve, he was taking apart engines, fixing computers and wrote his first piece of software, a game he called 'T-Shock'.

He also had a wild side, turning some of his youthful energy towards surfing and skateboarding. Tyler proved to be an outstanding athlete, winning several championships in both activities.

At sixteen, he graduated Summa Cum Laude from the preeminent Los Diego Tech. After university, Tyler's dad helped him set up a division of their company that would soon develop home entertainment systems. His video game system started to dominate the market,and ended up in just about every home around the globe by the end of the 1990s.

Three years later, in 2003, tragedy would strike the Dresden family. Michael was killed by an explosion while working on an experimental rocket design in his laboratory. His global empire would be passed over to Tyler, making him the youngest ever CEO of a multinational corporation at the age of twenty-three years old.

Tyler's brilliance proved to be just what his father's company needed, as over the next fifteen plus years, he would conceive of and push forward massive leaps in computing and connected communication tech. In a bold move, he renamed the company to Dres-Tek to 'better reflect the mission of the company'. Dres-Tek would be the first company to create consumer grade touch screen and mobile technology to serve the growing canine population of the world. He is on record stating, 'Canines have the right to be treated like the rest of us humans. The government and industry needs to treat them as equals. They love, they have families and are just as smart as you or I'.

He became known as a maverick and eccentric tech magnate. His eccentricity made him prone to run off on spur-of-the-moment adventures around the world. Many close friends and colleagues worried that his need for constant adventure and adrenaline would prove his undoing.

For all his brilliance, Tyler couldn't control everything. In early 2020, Tyler abruptly disappeared without a trace. According to rumors, he went off on one of his solo midnight surf trips and did not come back. Many fear he was killed in a shark attack on the coast of San Tomanico. Tyler was also a longtime canine rights activist and many suspect foul play in his disappearance, but no evidence has turned up to substantiate those claims.

Swiftly after Tyler's disappearance, stockholders seized control of Dres-Tek. Many wonder that without the brilliance of Tyler, would it remain a dominant player in the world or would it stagnate into irrelevance? Many fear they will never know the answer to Tyler's disappearance.

***

"Ahh, what a beautiful night." Tyler thought to himself as he stepped out of his car on the ridge overlooking the white sands of his favorite surf spot. The moon was bright and one could make out the tops of the perfect waves crashing down. "Not too big, not to small," he said aloud as he assessed the waves on the beach below.

After about ten minutes carefully putting on his wet suit, he walked down the meandering rocky path to the beach. Shoving his surfboard into the sand to stand it up, he surveyed the beach.

"Hey Tyler my man!"

The words came from his left and he turned to see who said it. "Mateo!" he shouted and walked over to the coyote that had become his best surfing buddy over the years. "Glad to see you got my message!" As he gave Mateo a great big bro-hug, he said, "Ready for this?"

"Yeah man," Mateo quipped, "I wish your messages weren't so cryptic. I hate having to work out what you are up to."

"Yeah, unfortunately I'm too famous these days and too important to soooo many people. I can't even get time to myself, so I have to sneak away," he said as he was shaking his head. "Last thing we need is paparazzi following us here."

Mateo responded with a chuckle. "Last thing I, or my family, needs is to be a target for your 'friends' in the government or the press, but I'm glad to see you. Shall we?" he said while motioning to the zen-like rhythmic waves at the end of the beach.

"Most definitely!" They both grabbed their boards and walked towards the ocean.

Tyler envied his buddy living a much simpler life than his. His was all meetings, more meetings, press conferences, tech conferences, government inquiries, etc. These 'outings' were about all he managed these days and they were getting harder and harder to squeeze in. And now, at 42 years old, his body definitely didn't recover from his adventures like he used to. "Tomorrow's going to be rough at the tower."

Hitting the waves was such a peaceful thing of beauty that the two guys truly treasured, since it was just their boards and the waves. They both caught three or four nice waves, but nothing special. Paddling out for their fifth go, Tyler looked out on the horizon and noticed something, "Hey man, there's a great wave coming in a couple, let's try to catch it!" he yelled to his friend.

"Awesome!" was Mateo's reply.

Paddling through the first small wave, they crested over it and both of their mouths dropped. "Oh man, that's way bigger than it should be," Tyler said in a gasp. They looked at each other and immediately turned to start paddling hurriedly towards the beach. As the wave approached, it grew in size and the water dropped out from under them.

The wave picked them up with such force that they both tumbled off their boards and were carried by the wave. It was so large they were hurled onto the rocks, way above the base of the cliff. The last thing Tyler remembered that night was the sharp pain in his head.

***

Tyler woke in a daze, his entire body on fire with pain and fever. He was so hungry, weak and couldn't focus. *What's that smell and why can I hear so much?*" he questioned to himself. He rolled over onto his side to see where he was. Uttering a loud painful groan as he turned, he asked to no one in particular, "Where am I?".

Slowly a curtain parted and a female coyote came in. "Take it easy," she ordered. "You need food and rest. You aren't through this yet." She sat down on the bed next to him and proffered up a plate of food, the scents dazzling in his nose.

"That's what I was smelling," he stated emphatically. Tyler grabbed the plate and shoveled the meat into his mouth as fast as he could, though he found it really difficult to chew.

"Rest Tyler, you need rest. Mateo will be back later tonight and when you are awake again, we'll talk through what happened. Now, go to sleep," she said, with a stern look on her face.

***

It was a few more days before Tyler woke again, he was still not feeling any better. In fact, he felt hotter than before and he still couldn't see very well.

"Hello there, miss, umm, coyote?" he spoke, but kind of weak.

Again, the curtain parted around the bed and she came in with a similar plate as before. "I am Micah, Mateo's *better* half. Here, you need protein," she said as she handed the plate to him, gesturing to the food with her eyes. "Eat up. Mateo had just run out for some supplies and will be back any moment."

Tyler focused on eating. He was still having a really hard time chewing, everything just felt off. After finishing, he placed the plate on the nightstand and dozed off.

About an hour later, Tyler was awoken by the clunk of a door shutting. He heard a quiet conversation between Micah and Mateo go on for some time before the curtain parted. Mateo stuck his big face through the gap.

"Hey buddy," Mateo said with a smile, but also a worried look, "you want to talk?"

"Yeah, what the hell is going on? I can't see very well, it's dark in here and I'm burning up. I can hear and smell EVERYTHING," Tyler said a bit exasperatedly.

"Well, umm." He thought for a moment before sitting down in the chair that was at the foot of the bed. "You, umm ... You're at my house." His facial expression told Tyler he obviously didn't want to have this conversation. "Let's go back to the surfing," Mateo paused for a moment, adding. "You remember anything from that night?"

"Yeah, it was a wonderful night of surfing until that giant wave hit." Tyler thought hard for moment, then mentioned, "but I don't remember anything after falling off the board."

Mateo began, "Yeah, I'm not surprised, you hit your head on the rocks really hard and I thought you were dead." He paused a little before continuing, "I gashed open my head and chest on the rocks, too." He opened up his shirt, showing nearly a foot long scar, the almost white stubble of fur growing around it.

"I awoke dripping with blood. It took me about ten minutes to find you and it was very lucky I did. I carried you over my shoulder up the rocky path to your car. It's a good thing I knew where you always hid the keys to your car and I brought you here. My vet is just down the road, so I called her over and she treated us."

Tyler squinted at Mateo's chest. "Wait, why is the fur already growing around your scar?" Tyler questioned.

"Well, umm, well you have been here for 4 weeks. You were alive, but not waking up." Mateo went silent for a few moments. "You remember that little book of contacts and bank accounts you gave me if I ever had an emergency? Well, that came in really handy." He fell silent again trying to figure out what to say next.

After a minute of silence, Mateo again started speaking. "I called some of the contacts and they were extremely worried, but ALL of them said to keep this very, very quiet. They encouraged me to use those accounts I had to hire some confidential help." He paused to take a breath. "Yeah, so we did. I kept having Sandy, my vet, come by to check on you. After about 2 weeks, it became apparent this was even more serious than we thought, so we brought in a specialist." He coughed, rubbed his nose and thought carefully, "No one has seen this in a hundred years in our community."

Tyler just laid there silently listening to his friend. "I'm just a humble mechanic, so it wasn't exactly clear what was going on when the doctor told me. I had to do some reading to understand and I ..." He pursed his lips. "Umm ... remember I said I carried you out? Well, I was bleeding and so were you. I guess, enough of my blood got on your wounds also ..." Mateo's voice trailed off.

Tyler was taking in what he said, but not quite catching the implication through his foggy mind, so he piped up, "What do you mean, 'also'?"

The coyote put both his index fingers to his lower lip trying to come up with the right phrasing. "Well, when one of our kind's blood gets mixed into humans, the human becomes one of us. We were told as kids and that's how our species began all those years ago. None of us really put much thought into those stories our parents told. I just wrote it off as folklore." With a bit of a sad face, he continued, "I'm afraid you have been infected."

Tyler's eyes opened wide and some vague memory was surfacing, "Infected? Like infected with what?"

"Well, in my research I learned that those alien artifacts they've been discovering had a medical machine that worked on a microscopic level. Those machines would fix them up in case of an accident. I'm sure you read about them since you ARE the smartest guy on the planet." Mateo's lip curled back into a smirk. "Well, I guess one of us had the dormant machines in our blood. When my canine blood made contact with your wounds ... " Mateo's speech tapered off.

Tyler's face went expressionless as his foggy mind was having trouble processing a memory. He hadn't really paid attention to medical technology, but some of his high school science class memories started surfacing. He steeled himself and stoically replied, "Give me a mirror."

Mateo looked off to his side and spoke through the curtain, "Micah, can you bring a hand mirror over here for us?"

The curtains around the bed parted and Micah came in and sat down on the edge of the bed, handing him the mirror. "You sure you want to see right now?" she asked Tyler.

"Yes, I do," he said and grabbed the mirror. Steeling himself while holding the mirror away from him, he awaited the moment his face was visible. His new appearance was slightly shocking. "I look like a monkey!" Though his vision was still pretty awful, his face was getting hairy, his jaw was pushed out and he could see that his teeth looked different, yet very monkey-like.

Micah began, "Yeah, you are only partway through the change. The specialist brought some old records and they say you will end up looking like us." She motioned to Mateo and herself, "not like you are now."

Mateo spoke up, "The specialist and your emergency contacts all emphatically said don't tell anyone about and contact your lawyers." He took a moment before continuing. "I have some more bad news. Your board of directors seized control of the company while you've been missing. I used some of that money you gave me to pay some canine activist lawyers while you've been out to see how to handle this moving forward. Now that you're awake, you can pick up where I left off. You're probably better suited to fight this more intellectually than I ever could."

"Well damn," Tyler grunted and looked down at his hands, turning them over to look at the fur stubble growing and how his nails were growing thicker into claws. "How do I reclaim my identity? I guess that's the biggest question."

"Your lawyer friends did say there's a way to do that and having my vet attending you will help in that regard. The activist group instruct-ed her to document the changes with photos and DNA samples and will continue to do so till you're finished." He smiled, saying, "At least you'll get most of my good looks." He smirked and squeezed Tyler's shoulder.

"Har-Har," Tyler added, "always the self-proclaimed pretty boy you are."

"I will say one thing," Mateo bemused, "your black hair is making your fur tone darker than mine. Not many dark-furred coyotes out there. Though we'll see when it all is done, it's likely you'll be pretty much my twin."

"Mateo," Micah added, "we should probably let him rest, he's got four weeks to get things in place to take back his life, but he needs to recover."

"Okay, okay, you're right." Mateo looked over at Tyler. "You get better, you hear? You're truly family now, brother."

***

'5...4...3...2...'

"Good evening from the UBN 10 news desk. I am Jordan Helmsey and I have some breaking news. Just a few hours ago, Tyler Dresden, the presumed-dead CEO of Dres-Tek, has miraculously risen from the dead and reappeared on the world stage after 20 weeks missing. In a press conference held in front of San Tomanico City Hall in southern Los Diego, the heart of the canine Ethnotropolis, Tyler shocked the world once he stepped up to the podium. For the first time ever he showed the world his new face. The face was now that of a canine. His looks are now similar the local coyote population in the area. We now go to footage from that press conference."

The television camera switched over to city hall as Tyler stepped onto the stage from behind a curtain to a loud collective gasp from the crowd.

"Late on the night I disappeared, I went for a moonlit surfing trip to the secluded Graphico beach with a long-time canine friend, as I have done many times in the past."

"While out on the ocean, a freak tsunami struck and flung us both onto the rocky beach. Both my friend and I were seriously injured and I was knocked unconscious."

"My friend carried me to the car and took us to his home where his family, some close friends, and trusted medical professionals nursed me back to health."

"During that rescue, enough of his blood must have entered my wounds causing the transformation you see before you."

"First, I would like to thank my loyal friend and his family for my rescue. Per his request, I have not publicly revealed his name and I ask all of you to respect his wish to remain ... anonymous."

"I know there will be lots of talk that I am not really Tyler

and that this is all fake. Now that I am back, I would like
to emphasize I am the same person I was before, just with
a few 'enhancements'. Think of it like I had very heavy
cosmetic surgery." Tyler smiled, showing his new canine
grin.

"The board of directors of Dres-Tek have seized control
and are not recognizing my ownership claim. I will be
using all legal avenues to reclaim my company and ensure
it continues into the future as my father envisioned."

"Thank you for your time, I will not be answering any
questions tonight."

The television returned to the studio with a stunned look on anchor
Jordan's face.

"What a bombshell. Tyler Dresden...is now a canine. I don't think
anyone could have seen this coming. What will happen now? Will
Tyler regain control of his company? What will be the global fall-out
from the world's most influential man not being human anymore?"

"Stay tuned to UBN 10 with Jesse, Rami and Martinez for this and
other news analysis on 'Global Politics Today' after the break."

"Hey Ivan, sit down and we'll deal you in," Francisco yelled as Ivan walked into the room.

"Sure thing." Ivan sat down on the creaking chair at the poker table. He didn't used to get invited to this room, since it was only reserved for the boss's best guys. "Deal me in," he said as he plunked down some money.

"So, we're playing 5 card stud," Thor said. His real name is Nikolus, but everyone calls him Thor because he's loud and packs a lightning quick and thunderous punch.

Just as Thor was dealing, the door opened and Markus peeked in. "Hey Ivan, Francisco, boss wants to see you two."

"Dammit, I was just about to take all your money," Ivan smirked as he got up.

"Yeah, yeah, just like last time you 'won'. I still have that nice token of your loss around my neck." Thor pointed at the gold chain dangling over his shirt.

"Oh, don't worry. I will get that back." Ivan grinned at Thor, as he grabbed his cash and departed the room.

The two of them walked up the stairs to the boss's office. David was standing guard at the door and waved them in. Ivan opened the door and let Francisco enter first, then closed the door behind them. The boss always wanted the door shut and Ivan never forgot that.

"What's up Dorian?" Francisco asked.

"I have a late job for you two tonight." Dorian Wolinzki motioned for them to sit down in front of his ornate walnut desk. "I hear that old Gregor down on 7th has been holding back, claiming booze sales are slow." He tapped a matchbox on the desk to slide one out and then lit up a cigarette in one smooth motion. "Go down there at closing and have a 'look' at his books. A little pigeon told me he's cooking them."

"Okay boss, sure thing. We'll have a look." Ivan nodded at the boss. Before he made a move to get up, he added, "Any other jobs you need done while we're out?"

"No, just this one tonight. You two have been doing a good job keeping your sheep herded. Keep doing it."

***

Ivan and Francisco headed down the stairs and out the front door. "I'll drive," Ivan remarked as they stepped up to an old 1950s sporty red car.

"Why do you keep this hunk of junk? You can afford a better one." Francisco scowled at Ivan's car.

"This? This is a classic. They don't make them like this anymore. New ones have no personality, no soul, man. There's nothing like the rumble of an old V8." Ivan tossed his keys up in the air and caught them in his other hand.

"Yeah, new ones don't stink like they used to." Francisco lightly punched Ivan's shoulder. "Come on Hot Rod, let's get moving."

They got in and the old car sputtered to life with a twist of his key as he patted the dashboard, "This is the first car I ever bought. I will be buried in it."

As they drove, Francisco pulled out his silver handgun and gave it a wipe down with a rag. It was only twenty blocks or so before they pulled up in front of Gregor's liquor shop. Both of them got out and walked in.

"Fellas!" Gregor greeted them from behind the dingy counter. "To what do I owe the pleasure of your visit at this late hour?"

"Well, the boss asked us to come down here and check your books. He heard you were skimming off the top," Francisco said, as Ivan leaned heavily on the counter, making it creak a little. He then locked eyes with Gregor's. "That's not true, is it?"

"No, no, my books are all above the table," Gregor said a bit nervously. "Business has been down since that new DA has been cracking down with those new alcohol laws they just passed. Plus, this area has been getting rougher."

"Hmm," Ivan thought for a moment, "so you're saying we're not doing good enough at protection? Are your customers scared to come down here?"

"I'm not sayin' that at all." Gregor paused before continuing, "It's just a lot of people have been leaving Dogtown for the suburbs. Business ain't what it used to be."

Franciso looked old Gregor in the eye. "Well, let's look at the books, the real books, not those 'government' ones."

Ivan walked over to the front door, clicked off the 'Open' sign and locked the front door. "You're now closed for the night," Ivan gruffed at the old man. "We haven't got all night."

Francisco grabbed Gregor and dragged him to the small office behind the counter. "Alright, show me."

Ivan prowled around the liquor store while Francisco sat with the old man. Seeing the wall of whiskey, he started towards it. "That's what I need right now." As he reached the shelf, he started to notice that most of the bottles were dusty. Many rows were empty with just as much dust on them. "Hmmph." It looked like he hadn't been restocking. Grabbing a choice vintage 1992 River City Distillery bottle, he wiped the dust off and opened it letting the aroma fill his nose. "Very good stuff," then took a swig.

Ivan kept walking around, noticing the same patterns of dust on every shelf. "Sure looks like not much has moved through here, maybe the codger is telling the truth," he muttered as he took another gulp of whiskey.

Bored of inspecting the place, he flopped down into the old rickety chair behind the counter. Leaning back, he propped up his feet on some dusty crates and amused himself with the tabloid newspaper Gregor was reading. "Tyler Dresden turned Coyote by Illicit Sex Cartel!" printed boldly on the cover with a photo of a trashy Coyote female poorly edited into the shot. "Such trash. Why does this paper exist?"

After randomly flipping through a few more pages and chuckling to himself, Francisco came out of the room with the old man.

"Okay, our friend here is good." He gave Gregor a strong pat on the shoulder, "Let's get out of here Ivan and let the man get back to...umm, business."

Climbing into the car, Ivan turned the key, roaring his old car to life. Dropping the gear lever into drive, they moved off. "I had a good look around while you were looking at the books," Ivan began. "He hasn't sold much lately, everything had a coat of dust on it." He paused as he made a left turn. "Not much has moved off his shelves. Wonder who has it out for the old man that they would accuse him of stealing from us?"

"No idea, his books were fine." Franciso replied. "He might not clean up his shop that often, but he keeps meticulous track of people coming through the door and what they bought. There hasn't been a lot coming through that old, creaky door."

***

They returned back to the bosses' place after having a good look around Gregor's place. It sure looked like he was being honest about the slowdown in business. In hindsight, Ivan reflected that it had been a lot emptier in Dogtown for the past year.

Heading back upstairs, David was still sitting on the red velvet couch and only nodded to them as they knocked and entered Dorian's office.

"So, what did you find at Gregor's?" Dorian again motioned for them to sit.

Francisco nodded to Ivan, "Well, we found nothing." Ivan said. "His books were clean and there were a lot of dusty crates of unsold liquor plus a lot of bottles on the shelf were dusty. I'd say he was being truthful with us."

Dorian thought for a moment, "Well, that old codger hasn't lied before, so that tracks. I'll send someone to have a chat with our pigeon to find out whose trying to mess with him." He paused for a moment, "Francisco, you can head out for the night. Ivan, please stay here for a minute, I have special request for you."

Francisco got up, nodded to the boss and Ivan as he headed out, making sure the door was closed as he left.

"Now," Dorian began, "you've been a loyal man all these years, save for that little incident all those years ago."

Ivan internally winced as he thought about his life on the street and when he got caught by Dorian's guys. He tried to steal some cash from their car when he was fourteen.

"I saw potential and decided to bring you in. You're like a son to me now, so that's why this job I have for you is crucial." Pausing for minute and shifting forward in his chair, he continued, "I have been asked a favor by the big boss from Uptown."

That perked Ican's interest. *"Why would Pierce be asking for a favor?"* he thought to himself.

Dorian continued, "It seems Pierce wants to broaden our horizons. He wants all The Five Families to go legit, like he has. He wants to help us take our business interests global." He smirked, continuing, "I'm a bit suspicious of his motives, but I can see the writing on the wall with the global push to stamp out organizations like ours. His first request is to send over one of my best guys to work for him and he will do the same. You're loyal to me and would do this no matter what, yes?"

"Of course Dorian. You're the only family I have," Ivan stated emphatically.

"Good. You go over there and be my eyes and ears. All I ask is that you do what he asks. Just keep me informed if there's anything underhanded going on." Dorian leaned back in his chair making it creak.

"Of course, you have my word," Ivan nodded.

"Good, I know Uptown is halfway across the prefecture, but this could turn into something great. Pack your stuff and head that way tomorrow. Pierce's men will let me know when you arrived." Dorian stood up and clasped Ivan's shoulders before sending him on his way.

***

Ivan packed up all of the belongings he cared about into his old car and headed west. The drive took him about two days to cross the mountains. He hadn't ever been out of the Dogtown metro before, so he spent a lot of time taking in the scenery. Snow was just starting to fall on the mountain tops as winter was headed their way soon. Thankfully it wasn't sticking to the roads. *That would really be a handful in this car,* he thought to himself, imagining driving this old car on a freezing mountainous freeway.

After coming out of the mountains, it was still a day's drive to get to Uptown metro. Once in the metro, he followed the handwritten directions he made for himself. The route took him through down-town with its sparkling high-rises that were in stark contrast to the rundown, crumbling industrial feel of Dogtown. Toward the far edge of downtown, he made a left into a less imposing, but even more architecturally upscale business district. He soon pulled in front of NP Financial, Pierce's financial arm of Pierce Industries. Stepping out of the car in front of a very modern looking office building, he whistled to himself. "Impressive." The building had a full glass front and almost looked like a church, with its peak of the roof falling off dramatically on both sides. Right about the time his gaze came down from the peak of the building, a man came out to greet him.

"Mr. Grecov, welcome. Mr. Pierce's office is on the third floor. I'll park that for you," he said gesturing to his car. "Just have Gillian at the desk call for your car when you're ready to go."

"Oh sure thing," Ivan said as he handed the fellow his keys and entered the building.

The office lobby was gorgeous. *"Neville Pierce must be doing very, very well for himself. All the decor is top notch."* Ivan thought to himself. He saw the elevators, entered an open one and pressed the third floor button.

Upon arrival on the third floor, there was no mistaking the wealth this guy had. The whole floor was open with a beautifully lit lobby area that had the latest modern designer furniture. In front of the elevator was a desk with a redheaded woman sitting behind it, while on the phone.

"I'll be with you in one minute," she gestured to a chair nearby and finished up her phone call. "You must be Ivan from Dogtown?"

"Yes ma'am," Ivan replied.

"Nice to meet you and welcome to the team," she smiled. "Mr. Pierce is unfortunately delayed but I'll ring Jean St. Claire and tell him you have arrived."

Once off the phone she ushered him up, "Follow me please." She led him to a giant wall of opaque glass, opened the door for him and closed it behind him.

"Welcome Ivan. I am Jean St. Claire, please sit down," he gestured to a really comfortable chair to sit in. "Dorian has a lot of positive things to say about you: He is proud of your loyalty. You're forceful when needed, subtle when necessary and utterly trustworthy." He leaned forward towards Ivan, "We have been building a financial empire over here for the past fifty years and have moved beyond petty things like liquor, drugs and general thuggery," he remarked. "But, we are not without our needs for solid, trustworthy men like yourself. We need people that won't hesitate to take the necessary actions and are comfortable handling things a little unorthodoxically."

Mr. St. Claire stood up and turned to look out of the commanding view he had from the wall of glass in his office proclaiming, "We have a vision of taking our network and our associates to greater heights. Propelling us from just the River City Prefecture and onto the global stage." He turned back to look at Ivan while gesturing outward with a hand. "We have moved ourselves into banking, finance, insurance, etc. in our development throughout the region via buyouts and ac-quisitions. We have approached all of the families in River City and convinced them all to join up, pool our resources and influence to turn us into a global powerhouse. Dorian is fully on board and aware of everything we are trying to do." He let Ivan think about that for a few moments.

"That's an ambitious plan." Ivan choosing his words carefully.

"Times are changing Ivan," his face turned serious. "The old ways Dorian and the others use will not work for very much longer. We have changed our business model considerably and I was brought on board about twenty years ago to facilitate that transition." His face softened up. "Dorian has always been our ally over in Dogtown. He and the other families have held control of their territories for a long time. All of us made sure to never step on each other's toes and that's the mutual trust we have built over the decades. Which is why we think tightening our alliances will benefit us all."

St. Claire sat down and made eye contact with Ivan. "Well, do I have your trust? Are you willing to do what it takes to help make us all very rich and powerful?"

"Are all the families doing what Dorian is, exchanging loyal people?" Ivan was curious to how comprehensive the integration was.

"Yes. This way we all have eyes and ears in everyone's houses to keep us all honest with each other. Once we get the greater corporation all set up, everyone has a seat on the board."

"Okay. Then yes, I am in," Ivan nodded to the man.

"Great!" A booming voice said from behind Ivan that made him jump. "I needed to make sure I could trust you."

Ivan turned and then stood up immediately, nearly stumbling over his own feet in his haste. His face definitely gave away the shock at seeing the large black wolf standing behind him.

"I am Neville Pierce. Jean is the face of our corporation. A lot of people around the world are still scared of my kind and we all thought it's better to have a human be seen at the head of our organization when you start expanding globally." He extended his hand out towards Ivan, "Pleased to meet you, Ivan."

Ivan steeled his nerves. He was always uncomfortable around canines as he could never read them from their faces. Extending his hand out the wolf grabbed his hand with both paws and firmly shook it. "I have only seen," he glanced over at the man still sitting at the desk. "... Mr. St. Claire on television. I didn't realize you were actually a werewolf."

"We don't like to call ourselves werewolves. We don't transform like in the myths. That's a leftover, derogatory, old word. We prefer canines or canids. Welcome to the team Ivan," he said with what Ivan thought was a smile. "There's only one more thing to make sure you're fully on board."

Suddenly he was grabbed by two other canines he didn't notice. One of them stuck a very, very large syringe into his arm and injected him with a silvery, blood red serum.

"What are you doing?" Ivan's face flashed with anger and he tried to jerk his arm away while they injected him. The wolves were stronger than he was and he couldn't pull free.

"Dorian is fully aware of the plans and said you would do anything for him. We need loyal people on all sides of the political and species spectrum willing to do what it takes." Neville showed Ivan a toothy grin to emphasize his statement.

Ivan started to get a little dizzy and sat down on the chair again.

"To be global, we need people to make this work. Besides, I think you'll like the benefits this will offer you." Neville's lips curled up into a smile.

Ivan could barely hear what the wolf was saying as he went limp in the canid's grasp and passed out.

***

Ivan groggily opened his eyes. Everything around him smelled strongly of antiseptic. *"Why was the room extremely loud?"* Ivan thought to himself.

As his eyes came into focus after adjusting to the bright room, there were a dozen people...all canines, some on beds, some with a digital tablets and some monitoring equipment around the other beds.

Ivan tried to raise his arms, but found his wrists cuffed to the bed. "Can someone tell me what is going on?" he said loudly and began to pull fiercely at the arm restraints. When they didn't give an answer, Ivan pulled even harder, making the equipment attached to the bed shudder.

"Hi Ivan, we are glad you are awake." A while clothed canine turned from the tablet she was looking over. "All of us here are excited to help you transition to your new role."

Ivan began to look at himself more carefully. His arms were furred and his hands were now claw-tipped. "What the hell did you do to me?" He began to get angry and his lips curled up in a snarl.

"Please calm down, Mr. Grecov," she said, adding, "I know this all is disorienting but you will get used to it swiftly. You are going to be faster, stronger and smarter than you ever were before. If you promise to relax I will take off those arm cuffs." She walked over to take a look at one monitor near his bed before she undid the wrist restraints. "These enhancements will greatly improve your physique and will give you more tools that will benefit our enterprise and mission. Trust me, you will really enjoy being the new you. I speak directly from experience."

"What are you talking about?" he nearly spat out the words, stumbling over his tongue a little bit as Ivan growled at her.

"When I first came to this place, I was a mess," she glanced over at him before writing some numbers on her tablet. "I was a hopeless drug addict. My body was nearly destroyed by my addiction to methamphetamines and I was going to die soon." She put the tablet down on the table and came over to him.

"Pierce Industries has many divisions. This one is called N-Bio-medics," she pointed around. "We help people who can't help themselves, like me." She grabbed a stethoscope and started listening to his heartbeat, "I was offered an alternate treatment in order to live. Maybe you remember hearing about the origins of us canines? The alien tech that initially turned humans into beings like me?" She moved the scope down to listen to his breathing.

Ivan scrunched up his face still a little puzzled at what she was saying.

"Well, those machines, or 'Nano-Docs', were emergency doctors for their species. We are using them to give people the opportunity to live on whether terminally ill or disabled. Though, they have to make one life changing decision ... to choose to not be human anymore." She smiled pleasantly, "There wasn't any other option for my illnesses so I chose this."

The doctor looked Ivan directly in the eyes while she snapped her claws to watch his ear reactions, "I went on to get a medical degree and landed a job here helping other people, like me, recover and survive."

"Mr. Pierce is making sure this organization includes everyone, especially the growing minority canine population. We are growing at a fast pace and ... umm," she puzzled at how to phrase it. "Your background, isn't exactly ... umm ... squeaky clean. He has needs for your specialist skills to help grow this empire and your new physique gives you unmatched strength, agility, hearing, smell and intelligence." She grinned a little slyly at Ivan, "We selectively chose the donor's blood to make you one of his best men." Her grin pulled into a large smile, "You could say, you're one of Mr. Pierce's sons."

"When you're ready," she held up a mirror to show him his new face. "Mr. Pierce would like to greet his new head of security and fully discuss your new role in the greater organization."

Chapter 19
Ingrid Sjöberg

"Yes. Mmhmm. Yeah, we can do it for that price." Ingrid Sjöberg said into her phone. "Delivery time? I believe we can fill that order in about eight to ten weeks." She continued to listen for a couple of more minutes. "Yes, that sounds great. I will email over the contract and we will get this going ... You're welcome. Bye now."

Ingrid sat back into her chair with a very pleased expression on her face. She had been working really hard to land that contract. "That will really help fund the new laser cutting division," she quietly said aloud.

Ingrid's family has been building this trade and manufacturing empire for four generations. Great-Grandfather Erik started metal-working in a barn to keep himself busy during the harsh winters in Fjordland. His talent with metals soon forged him a great reputation and he starting making custom iron works for the local wealthy families. His success soon found him expanding quickly become the leading iron works establishment in the city.

His two sons, Erik Junior and Gunnar took the reins after their father passed away at sixty-two. They already had proven their worth by working alongside their dad, becoming metalworking masters in their own right. They also began to expand into wood products and soon combined furniture with their metal craftsmanship to create a new line of upscale home goods that were sought after all over the region.

At thirty-eight, Gunnar died of pneumonia without having any children so Erik Jr. carried on running the business. He eventually had one child, Jarl, who grew up in the factory alongside his father.

Once he inherited control of the growing empire, Jarl took the business global by setting up retail stores in every major metropolis which sold their exclusive line of furniture. Jarl eventually married Rota, who was the major of the Jorvik City. They soon gave birth to Ingrid, a blonde little firecracker. During the birth of their second child, Rota had a miscarriage and died during childbirth leaving Jarl with only his daughter, Ingrid, as the sole heir.

When Ingrid was only twenty-two years old and in college, Jarl suddenly became ill during a particularly cold winter and passed away. This left Ingrid as the new owner of 'Sjöberg Fine Furnishings'. She left college to take over the empire.

***

The windows were gradually dimming as Ingrid leaned back in her chair to stretch. She finished reaching out and then looked at her watch, "It's getting late." Ingrid had been too inexperienced when her father passed away to run the entire business so she appointed the vice president of operations to the CEO position and took over the manufacturing division to cut her teeth on running such a large, global company. That was 15 years ago. In that time she had completed her law degree on the side and was now running the sales and supply chain teams. She felt she was well on track to run the company in about three years.

RING Ingrid picked up her phone to see who was calling. The caller ID said 'Rory' and she smiled. She had been seeing him on and off for the last seven years but her company kept her very busy. There wasn't a lot of time beyond the occasional dinner and a club night with him, "Hey you. What is going on?"

"Are you STILL at work?" Rory asked her.

"Yeah, I still am. I just finished up and was going to head home."
She said, slightly yawing during that last word.

"Oh no...you are NOT going home on a Friday night," he said with
a serious but joking tone. "You need to meet me at Vertigo."

"For you, sure. Meet you at," she looked at her watch. "I can be
there about ten. Sound good?"

"Sure! I'll meet you there!" and he hung up.

Vertigo was a Techno-Industrial dance club in downtown Lingenhoff that was loud, dark and smokey. This was hardly a good place for
a quiet time together. *"Okay, I'll stay till midnight,"* she said internally
to herself. *"I am getting too old for these clubs."*

***

She had deposited her car at home so she could take a taxi to the
club. It was really tough to find parking in downtown so a cab was
vastly easier to deal with. The taxi lurched to a halt on the bumpy,
cobblestone streets outside the club. She handed the cabbie some
cash and got out of the car. Once the door was closed, she turned
around towards the club entrance and its bright neon sign. It had just
rained so the air was thick with moisture. The rain gave the club's
neon sign a beautiful and serene halo around it.

On the way out the door she had grabbed her favorite coat: a stylish,
abstract patterned, embossed purple leather jacket. It was one of her
favorite ones and always felt most like herself when wearing it. She
strode up the steps to the club doors as a dozen or so people having a
smoke outside eyed her.

The bouncer nodded and opened the door to let her inside and
out of the rain. The interior was exactly the same as it was the last
time that Rory took her to this club and it was a comforting sight
to know some things didn't change. Tonight was a particularly busy
night at the club, the place was packed wall to wall with people.
She meandered through the dancing crowd, the scent of alcohol and
smoke hung in the air as she weaved her way over to the side where
the tables were. Rory and her always met over there to make it easier
to find themselves. She eyed him already seated in the third booth
and headed over that way.

Rory got up when he saw her and gave her a big hug, "Glad you made it," he had to yell as the club was really, really loud tonight. Looking at his watch, "I was worried you were going to bail. Do you want something to drink?"

Moving to talk in his ear, "No, I'm fine." She did not drink much at all, "Shall we dance?" and she pulled him toward the dance floor.

They danced for what seemed like hours to her. Ingrid suddenly felt a bit light headed. "I need a break!" she yelled over the thumping techno song that was playing and started leading him back over to the seats. The stage lights and the booming bass were making her head hurt so much that she stumbled.

Rory caught her, "You okay?" he looked a bit concerned.

"I am just a little dizzy." Ingrid managed to get the words out as she again led him off the dance floor. They almost got to an open booth and her head started spinning so she quickly sat down on the floor. "I think I need to go."

"Okay, let's go." Rory put an arm around her and headed to the door. He signaled to a person at the door and the staff guy waved a taxi forward.

Rory helped her inside and she flumped down into the tatty back-seat of the cab. Her vision was getting very blurry. "I guess I am working too hard."

Rory sat down next to her and leaned over to look at her face, "Yeah, you have been. Let's get you home." He gave the address to the cab driver and the cab nosily moved forward.

Ingrid fell asleep five minutes into the ride.

***

"Miss Sjöberg," a soft spoken request came with a light knock on the door. "Miss Sjöberg, Rory is here to see you," Ingrid's housekeeper, Alicia, said.

Ingrid opened her eyes but everything was too bright, "Thank you, let him in."

Rory walked into the room and half sat down on the nightstand next to her bed. "How are you feeling this morning?"

"Tired and still dizzy." She looked over to the other night stand to notice a glass of water left by her housekeeper. She reached over for it and pulled it to her lips and took a nice long drink.

"I would say you had one hell of a hangover, but I know you don't drink." Rory frowned. "You might need to get to the doctor. This doesn't sound like just a case of '*the workaholic.*'"

"Yeah, I will have Alicia call them and set up an appointment." She squeezed her eyes closed, "My head is pounding, I think I am going to try and sleep some more."

"I will talk to Alicia on the way out. You rest, I'll check in later." He ran a hand through her hair and quietly left the room.

***

Over the next few months, Ingrid's headaches and dizziness got worse. It was so bad, she took a leave of absence from her company and had been to many clinics for test after test.

"Miss Sjöberg, I am Doctor Sanderson," as he sat down behind the desk in front of Ingrid and Rory.

Rory has been kind enough to be her support during the past months. "*I'm glad he is here.*" she silently said to herself.

"Thank you for coming in to see us in person." He looked down at the chart in his hands. "We have received the latest test results. I am afraid I have some bad news." He looked up from the chart, looking into her eyes.

Ingrid sunk into here chair a little deeper and frowned, "What is the bad news?"

The doctor cleared his throat a little bit, "I am afraid that what is causing your headaches and dizzy spells is a brain tumor." Pausing a little before going on, "The tests, the X-rays, the MRI scans all are conclusive. The tumor is malignant and has spread to sixty percent of your brain." He closed the chart and put it on the desk. "It is in-operable and there isn't anything we can do."

She started to immediately cry and put her face into Rory's shirt. She stayed that way for a couple of minutes before looking up to the doctor.

"We can try chemotherapy, but at this late stage of the cancer, the odds of it working are very, very low," the doctor said with a very sad expression on his face.

Ingrid pulled her face from Rory's wet shirt, "How long?"

"We estimate four to six months," the doctor closed the file in front of him.

***

Over the next few months, Ingrid explored every treatment, every specialist to no avail. The answer always came up the same. She even reached out to non-traditional treatment clinics around the globe but they were either crack-pots, or just would alleviate some of the symptoms rather than a cure.

RING Ingrid was sitting silently in a chair looking out a window when her mobile rang. The phone ID'ed the caller as Pierce Indus-tries. "Hmm, that is interesting." She knew of that company. They were mostly in the financial sector and she had turned over the day to day operations to someone else. Ingrid thought to herself, "*Why would they be calling her directly?*"

She pressed the phone to accept the call, "Hello, this is Ingrid Sjöberg."

"Good afternoon Miss Sjöberg, I am Neville Pierce head of Pierce Industries." The unfamiliar voice on the phone said.

"Good afternoon to you to Mr. Pierce." She was a little surprised. Usually calls from a company rep, not the head. "What can I do for you?"

"I apologize if this call is bit out of left field. I have a proposition for you." He said to her. His voice had a deep, gruff and bassy quality to it. "Pierce Industries is a very diverse company. We started off in banking and finance, but now have branched out into insurance, legal services and the latest acquisition is a medium sized pharmaceutical company called N-Biomedics."

"I had a meeting with your acting CEO about our financial and insurance services and I heard of the unfortunate news about your health." Neville paused briefly before continuing. "The new company we acquired has a ground breaking new treatment that will cure your cancer. It is a non-traditional treatment and was designed as a last resort for terminal patients. People just like yourself."

Ingrid stayed quiet for a moment thinking about what he said, "I researched every treatment, every 'cure' and every clinic around the globe and found nothing that could cure me. I have never heard of this company, why is that?" She queried as this sounded fishy.

"I know you are skeptical. This is bleeding edge science. We have worked very hard to keep it out of the press. It is fully legal and I have personally seen to that, but not widely known since it is very non-traditional. If it was not legal and didn't work, I would not have bought the company."

She just sat there on the phone, silently wondering if this is too good to be true.

"Since my company is now under contract with yours I would like to offer this treatment to you, as an offer of goodwill. I would like you to fly out to our labs in Uptown City in the River City Prefecture to meet directly with me and our medical staff to go through the procedure." She heard a slightly guttural throat clearing before he continued, "I hope you will. Your family's history is in that company and I would hate to see it lose its soul. Would you be interested in finding out more?"

Thinking about it for a moment, *what have I got to lose?* she thought to herself. "Sure, I will be happy to come see what this treatment is about."

"Splendid!" he said excitedly.

She pulled the phone away from her ear because Neville's voice was pretty intimidating when he was excited.

"Your CEO said you had taken a leave of absence due to your illness, so I am guessing you have availability to fly this week, yes?"

"Yes, I have nothing on your schedule this week."

"I will have my staff make all the arrangements with your assistant. Feel free to bring someone along for support. I look forward to meeting you in person," he said before hanging up.

***

The six seat private jet smoothly touched down on the tarmac at the Uptown Metro airport. She was really glad that Rory agreed to come along with her. Since her diagnosis Rory has been her bedrock, keeping her from slipping into depression and making her life much more enjoyable.

Upon walking down the exit steps a driver stepped out of the black limousine and walked over to them. "I have to apologize, but Mr. Pierce was tied up with a conflict and couldn't personally get away. He will meet you at the clinic." He reached out with a hand towards their suitcases, "I can take those," and motioned them to the open rear door.

It took about 20 minutes for the limo to pull up to a non-descript white building with a small 'N-Biomedics' sign over the door. Their driver opened the door for them and spoke, "They are expecting you inside."

Upon entering the building, they were greeted by a black-haired female receptionist and guided them to a small lounge. "There is coffee, tea and water if you would like. Mr. Pierce is just finishing up a meeting and will join you here shortly."

"I am so nervous, but excited...but mostly nervous." Ingrid glanced at Rory as she sat down on the couch.

Rory plopped down next to her, "Well, remember, you are not committed to anything so you can always walk away if any part of this procedure makes you nervous." He grabbed her hand and gave it a little squeeze.

The door to the room was opaque but they could see a figure approaching. As the door swung open they were faced with a large black wolf, though he did look quite dapper in the blue business suit he was wearing.

"Ingrid!" He reached out a massive hand (paw?) and extended it out in greeting. "I am Neville Pierce. You look a little surprised at my appearance," he chuckled deeply and his ears flickered.

"Umm ... yes, a little surprised." She stammered a little, finally saying, "I thought the head of the company was.."

"Human?" his lips curved up into a smile, "We know it would be much more difficult to navigate the global political landscape with this face," he waved a hand in front of his own muzzle to add to his point. "Many are intimidated by us canines so one of my partners is the public face of the company." His head swiveled over to face Rory, "You must be Rory, welcome."

"Pleasure." Rory shook his hand.

"Please," he gestured back to the couch. "Have a seat. I will walk you through what they are doing here. It is really exciting."

Neville reached out his claw and tapped a button on the shiny white wall, which then lit up with the logo of the company. "First thing, I do want to stress that this is a very cutting edge treatment but it works one-hundred percent." He clicked a remote and the slide changed. "I don't know how much you know of the history of us canines but," he clicked to a microscopic photo and it enlarged to reveal a tiny oval with even smaller appendages. "This is what we refer to as a 'Nano-Doc'. These are not a human creation, but machines acciden- tally released by an alien species upon the globe." He clicked and the slide changed to a collage of eight different wild canines. "Sometime in the 1300s, they were accidentally released into our atmosphere. Scientists theorize that the aliens must have been genetically close enough to our world's canine population that these machines were able to infect the native dog species. These Nano-Docs 'repaired' the local canids making them as smart as the human population."

Ingrid had heard a little of this, but science was not her specialty so she forgot most of it.

"Let me know how much of this you know and we can skip forward." Neville inquired.

Rory spoke up, "Not much for me." He looked over at Ingrid, who shook her head no.

"Okay. We want to make sure all the clients who use this service are fully aware of this piece of history." He looked down and clicked the slide button. "How us canines came into being was through contami- nation of a human body through a cut or injury with that of one of the 'smart' canine's blood. The Nano-Docs read the DNA of the canine blood. They decide the human cells are injured and begin working to 'repair' the body. That resulted in an irreversible transformation into beings like me, which have a hybrid DNA structure somewhere between human and canine."

"I'm sorry Neville, but what does this have to do with curing my cancer?" Ingrid asked.

Neville looked back from the screen. "I was just coming to that," he smiled then clicked to another slide. "What the team here figured out is how to 'cultivate' the Nano-Docs outside a body. We do not have the science or technology to be able to engineer anything like them, so by cultivating them we can use them to treat patients."

"So, they can cure a human body?" Rory spoke up. "It doesn't sound like it from your history lesson." Rory furrowed his brow.

"Yes, you are correct. They do not work on human DNA. They just don't react to it by itself. These machines must have some sort of basic programming that identifies key DNA sequences and then takes a reference cell and gets to work repairing." Neville looked over at Ingrid seeing her facial expression change as she was connecting the dots.

"Wait." She put her hand up to rub gently under her nose. "When you say 'reference cell,' what are you using?"

"The machines only do their job in the presence of feral or humanoid canine cells." Neville looked between them. "Yes, I can see what you both are thinking. The only way this works is the patient becomes like me, a canid." He waited for a moment because he could see they were still processing the information. "A cell's DNA gets morphed into this human-wolf hybrid but the real key trigger is an injury. When the body receive trauma it releases hormones: Adrenaline, growth hormones and the like. When the devices detect that it triggers the body to go into a rapid growth phase, changing the physical characteristics in a short period. Without the hormones, it would take a lifetime by themselves. Also, the machines won't cure the cancer in time without said trigger."

Silence fell between them and Ingrid retreated into her thoughts pondering the reality of what he was saying. Would she have to change herself to live? Could she live with that? Be in a new body? She sank deeper into the sofa with the weight of what was just presented.

"What is the morality of this? One might ask oneself." The black canine gestured to himself. "My feeling is if there was a god out there he guided the aliens to our planet to bring us into existence." He smiled softly at her, "No one wants their life cut short and this is a way to extend your life. I am not immortal so it's not cheating death, just prolonging it. The Nano-Docs eventually cease working after a while on their own. We are just using the science gifted to us to make the most of our lives."

"I..I," She stuttered a little bit before pausing to think for a little bit more. "I need to think about it...hard."

The wolf sat down onto a chair next to the couch. "I fully understand. What I am offering you is a second chance. But ultimately, that decision is yours to make, not mine." He went to the door and motioned to someone nearby.

"One more thing I would like to point out. The legality of the procedure will be handled through our legal division. They will make sure that you are legally protected throughout the process." He glanced between the two. "You will remain yourself: mentally and legally after it is all done. They will handle the government documents: identification changes, assets, etc. Nothing will be taken away from you by anyone. We have iron clad legal documents that have been proven in many court proceedings."

Neville let them think for a little while before adding, "What I suggest you do is go the hotel tonight, have a meal together and discuss things." He smiled. "I will call you in the morning. If you want to see more the car will bring you back and we can tour the lab, talk to some of the staff and some of the former patients. That way you can really be sure you are making the right choice for yourself. I called for the car. It will be waiting for you outside."

After saying their goodbyes to Neville, they left the building and both climbed into the limo. They remained silent for a while and the car accelerated away.

***

When they arrived at the hotel, the driver looked into his mirror. "If you want to go to a restaurant I can take you there," he said.

"No thanks, I think I need a simple meal." Ingrid wasn't that hungry as the presentation was gnawing on something in her stomach.

"There's a good burger place a block away if you want a walk." The driver pointed down the street. "Mr. Pierce has taken care of everything at the hotel. I will take your bags in and they will be waiting in your room. Just let the front desk know when you return and they will give you the key to your room."

"Thanks," Rory said, as they exited the car.

The two of them slowly walked down the street with neither one of them really saying much to each other. Rory was looking ahead and Ingrid was paying more attention to the sidewalk directly in front of her.

"That ... was a lot to take in," her friend finally said and Ingrid silently nodded as they walked. The walk to the restaurant only took about five minutes. Rory pushed the glass door to let Ingrid enter before him. The place was nice enough. Woody with so much vintage nostalgia plastered all over the walls they could barely see what color the wall was. The sign by the door said 'Please Seat Yourself' so they took a booth in the far corner.

Slinging themselves into the booth, they just looked at each other while the waiter took their order for food. When he left Rory began, "I never imagined that the medical treatment was going to be that. The thought of using alien tech to change your whole body into something else. My mind is officially blown." He put his hands up to his head and used them to emote his head exploding.

She sighed, "Yeah it is certainly out in left field. Is it right? Is it wrong? Some part of my brain recoils from the thought. Would I be cheating death?" She paused as the waiter brought her the cola she asked for. "I want to live, I'm not done with life. I wanted to have a husband, have children." Pointing a finger at her head, "But this tumor says otherwise." Nervously, she returned her hands to the table and intertwined her fingers as thoughts furiously bounced around in her head.

He reached across the table and cupped her hands in his. "I am not religious so there is no moral dilemma for me, but this would be your choice." He reached over and put a finger under her chin and lifted her face up to look at him. "I will support you whatever you choose. I do want you to remain in my life."

She looked back down in contemplation, "Yeah the thought of it makes me feel guilty deep inside. But maybe that's me feeling sad for all the life...and you...that I'd miss if I didn't take this option."

He doubled his grip on her hands, "Look. The time we have spent together in the past few months despite your illness ... have been the best part of my life so far." A tear rolled down from the corner of his eye. "I wanted to be that husband. I wanted to be the father of your children." He pulled a hand to wipe his face. "You know, we can still have that if you choose the treatment."

Ingrid looked up, "Well the husband part, yes."

A smirk grew across his face. "Well...If I'm going to propose to you I will have to do something drastic, because I want children too. Might as well be a couple of little fur-balls instead of none."

She half closed an eye and tilted her head. "Are you proposing to me?" She thought a little more. "Wait...fur-balls??"

"If you choose go through with it I will join you." Rory said emphatically. I want you to be with me no matter what and I want to be there at your side. You, me and a couple of our own pups."

***

"Welcome Ingrid and Rory," the female fox doctor walked into the room. "I am Tina and I will be your guide in this new chapter of your lives. We don't get many couples in here." She looked at Rory. "I am so proud that you have chosen to take this journey with her. That is so romantic!" the doctor said with a sincere look on her face. Rory blushed at the doctor's comment and looked over at Ingrid with a smile.

She sat down in the chair across the coffee table with a couple of tablets. "Here you go," as handed each one of them a tablet. "This is the most exciting part. These are your donors."

Ingrid started flipping through the images on the tablet. "Donors?"

"Yes, when each one of us are born we never get to choose our faces. We get what we get." She smiled. "Today, you get to choose who you want to be physically. We have canine donors from all species, colors and markings. Take a look through them. Choosing a new face is incredibly personal so take your time."

"Couple of things to note," Tina added. "You can ignore the weights, your body can't gain mass. That would violate physics. You will weigh slightly less than you do now as the process is very energy intensive. We do our best to keep the body fed, but nothing beats a good amount of protein and you won't be eating solid food while you are under sedation."

"Second, your coloring might be slightly different from the picture. When the Nano-Docs do their thing, it's not always a one-for-one copy, but you'll *mostly* look like the donor. I will leave to let you study these." She said while getting up and leaving the room.

After flipping through dozens and dozens of images, one stuck Ingrid's fancy. She looked at Rory, "Is it shallow that I think one of them would look good in my favorite purple jacket?" Ingrid had settled on a coppery-brown colored female wolf with bright green eyes.

"Yes...INCREDIBLY shallow," as he pulled a big goofy face. "Let me see," as he pulled her tablet to face him. "Ooh, that's SASSY. I wouldn't mind waking up to her ... I mean you."

"Okay goofball, what have you picked?"

"I kept going back and forth between a couple. This one here," he turned the tablet to show her. "But I'm not sure I would even fit in my car with his body. He's a big dude at 275 pounds of all muscle. Just imagine what I would look like after working out." He flexed a bicep, "Check out these guns."

She smacked his arm, "Like I said, goofball. I don't want you to become a narcissistic, body obsessed jock." Ingrid stuck out her tongue at Rory.

He pulled the tablet back and swiped to a different one and showed her. "Now this is good. Decently slim build and a pretty face." He slid the tablet back to her for her to review.

"Yeah, that one fits you sly, goofy dog." She just shook her head at her fiancé.

The doctor returned and sat down across them. "Tina, I think we have chosen," they both slid the tablets over to her. "Great! I will send in the med techs that will get you ready." She turned and smiled before she left the room. "Neville Pierce said he will be here personally to welcome you when you are finished. See you in about 8 weeks." Tina turned and left the room.

Rory reached for her hands and gave her last human kiss they would ever have.

***

The strong scent of antiseptic pulled Ingrid out of the darkness. She could feel her ears turning towards each and every noise and beep in the room. She tried opening her eyes but it was way too bright and she shut them again.

"Doctor, it looks like Ingrid is stirring." The human technician across the room said to Doctor Tina.

The fox walked over to Ingrid and put a hand on her wrist and said, "Keep your eyes closed for a little bit. I will dim the lights until you get adjusted." She reached over to the console and turned a knob slowly dimming the lights. "There, that should be much better."

Ingrid opened her eyes, blinking a bunch of times because they were very dry. She looked up at the doctor standing over her. "Is it all done?"

"Yes, it sure is. Here," she proffered up some eye drops. "Let me get some drops in your eyes." The doctor put a few drips in each one.

She knew the doctor was a fox when she met her the first time but now it was different. She could not only see the fox, but she could smell her. She could not pick up the slight musk before but now it was very distinctive. It wasn't unpleasant but definitely identifiable.

"Who turned on the damn sun?" She heard a voice from inside the room. Ingrid looked over and realized that was Rory in the other bed. His voice sounded similar but a lot deeper and gruff.

Tina walked over to Rory and dialed down the light that was hanging over his bed. "Sorry about that Rory, I didn't think you would be quite awake yet. Welcome back to the land of the living. Let me get some eye drops in your eyes as well." Rory opened up his brilliant green eyes and let the doctor put some drops in.

"Pfffft" Rory made a funny sound, "I feel like my tongue is swollen. This is so weird."

Chuckling out loud at Rory's noise Ingrid added, "I see your sense of humor is still there."

The door opened into to the room and Neville walked in. "Greetings and welcome back! I promised I would be here when you awoke."

The two med-techs in the room began doing a bunch of checks on each of them as Neville pulled over a rolling chair in between their beds. He set his large frame down on the chair making it creak and pop.

"I am glad to see you both awake." He looked over at Rory, "Chose a coyote, eh?" He then turned over to Ingrid and smiled, "How do you feel?"

"Other than groggy, I feel great. I never knew there were so many smells and sounds in a room. Its slightly overwhelming." she remarked to his question.

"Well, you will get used to it." He looked at his watch and frowned, "I wish I could spend more time, but duty calls." He walked over to Rory and shook his hand. "Congratulations! if you thought you were clever before, you will amaze yourself now. Coyotes are widely known to be extremely smart...and troublesome too." Neville winked at Rory as he said that.

Turning around to Ingrid, "I am glad you chose to live on, you won't regret your decision. I look forward to our blossoming working relationship. Keep an eye on this one,." he thumbed at Rory with a smirk. "Oh, and thank your wood smiths when you get back to the factory. I love the magnificent desks they crafted. I have them in all my offices." He smiled and walked out of the room.

Doctor Tina finished reviewing the charts. "Okay everything looks good. Rest up tonight and we will get started tomorrow on the physical therapy. You have a lot of new things to get used to... walking, tails, bathing, grooming... to mention just a few."

Chapter 20
Hiro Adachi

"Good evening and welcome to 'Focus on Fijiwara' for Wednesday, September 16th 2015. I am Tadao Kanemoto."

"And I am Leilani Xu. Our first story tonight is on the increasing popularity of the canine species in Fijiwara by its residents."

Tadao continued, "We will also discuss the particular cultural significance of the fox in religion in the bustling region and what impact this has on public perceptions." Pausing momentarily, "Leilani and I are pleased to bring on our first guest. Please give a warm welcome to Doctor Diah Teodoro. She is a university professor of Anthropology and an expert in modern Human-Canine social studies at Kembro University in Taichung Province."

"Welcome to the show, Diah." Lei said with a smile.

"Thank you for having me on the show." Diah smiled back at the two presenters.

"Let's jump right into the subject," Lei began. "Throughout most of modern history starting from their appearance in the 14th century, the canine population has been shunned, persecuted and even subjected to attempted genocide. World wide, over the last 50 years, that sentiment has softened significantly. Here in the Fijiwara prefecture, negative perception of the canine population really started a positive shift in the 16th century but seemed to really take hold in the 1800s. Why do you think that is?"

Diah smiled. "Well, here in this continent the population has been heavily influenced by both religion and secular studies. The most influential religion on the continent, as most know, comes from the teachings of Jun'ichi Shinto. In his teachings he said: 'Everything has its own divinity' which means that the gods or spirits can be anything. This spiritual essence is everywhere. It lives in and manifests itself in objects and most importantly living things." Diah took a moment to sip water that was provided on the coffee table.

Tadao took the pause as an opportunity to continue the questions. "So, do people think the canine fox community are somehow gods or deities?"

Putting the water glass down and continuing. "Well, back in the days before the rise of the canines ... animals, and especially foxes held a special place in the hearts of the religious in Fijiwara: foxes were extremely shy and elusive and it was a rarity to see one. Most of the sightings were at night. Gradually fox mythology morphed from them as an animal, to spirits placed here by the gods to watch over us. If you encountered one you were considered blessed by the gods."

So," Leilani conjectured, "Are there people who think the humanoid foxes are spirits that bless us by walking around amongst us?"

"Oh, a few," Diah added. "There actually has been a resurgence in that belief mostly amongst the older, more religious of our continent. Some even have formed new Shinto sects, worshiping them as being sent here by the gods to watch over us and protect us." Pausing to take another sip of water, "Most of the younger people have grown up around them just treat them as another person. Though there is always some older, less tolerant people out there who still hold a hatred toward them. So the fox community always has to be a little cautious."

"That's most interesting," Tadeo offered up. "That's all our time we have for this segment, but thank you for coming on the show Diah." Reaching down to the coffee table and holding a book up to the camera, "If you would like to read more on the subject of Humans and

Canines, make sure you pick up Doctor Diah's new book, 'Canines, our Human Counterparts'. Now available everywhere."

"Up next," Leilani began, "Night markets and Night Culture. We will go to our youth correspondent Hiro Adachi."

The screen switched over to show Hiro standing in the middle of a bustling market. "Thank you Leilani and Tadeo." Hiro began his podcast style segment. "I am here at the Keelung Night Market in Fiji City and we're going to do some exploring!" he exclaimed as he looked behind him at the bustling scene behind him. It was wall-to-wall people walking past different stalls to look at what's on offer.

"Keelung is probably my favorite Night Market in all of Fijiwara. First, look at all the classic neon lighting down here. It makes for a dazzling feast for your eyes with all the vibrant colors, making for a wonderful evening out with your friends. This spot is a favorite among young adults as there's a ton do to here."

"Food," Hiro remarked. "Keelung is the place you want to go to sample every kind of cuisine from around the world and this makes it a foodie's paradise. You can spend all night just going from vendor-to-vendor to sample just about anything your stomach desires."

Hiro and his camera buddy Niko began walking down a particular alley. "This is Tailung Alley and this is the place to get your eats on. You have everything." The camera panned down along the row and settled on a stall with a fox family serving up some smoked meat on a stick. "Now this looks tasty." Hiro stepped up to the stall and reached out his hand to the fox behind the counter, "I am Hiro Adachi with Focus on Fijiwara. Tell us a little about yourselves."

The fox reached out his hand to shake Hiro's. "I am Makoa Kalawai'a."

Hiro continued, "So, where are you from and how long have you been making these tasty looking treats?"

"Well, my family is originally from the island of Nā Mokulua. Our family has been making selling food here in the market for three generations with the fourth coming along soon." Makoa reached his arm around his pregnant wife. Returning his gaze back to Hiro, "We are selling an old family dish: smoked fish skewer. The fish is smoked Marlin made with spices and a smoking technique is a family secret."

"It looks delicious." Hiro said as Niko panned the camera across the counter. "I will have stop by here later to give this a try." Looking back at the camera Hiro exclaimed, "Let's keep going, there's lots more to see here in Keelung."

Continuing forth, they started walking past another alleyway as Niko panned the camera down its entire length, making it look like it goes on forever.

"Now here's Ifuku Alley. You want clothes? Then hit this place up. There's loads of variety and many of these folk will help create your perfect custom outfit. In fact, this is where I get all of my clothes!" Hiro ran a hand down his sleeve to show off his pinstriped jacket. "You too, can look this good and for a fair price to boot!"

"Down this way is where all the night life is." Hiro was gesturing towards the end of the crowded alleyway. "Naitokurabu Way. That's where you go if you want to hit up the clubs. There's drink and dancing till all hours of the night down here."

Hiro stopped and faced the camera, while Niko widened the shot to show the bustling scene behind him, "Alright, that's only a small sampling of this place. You need to get yourself down here to experience it even if it's just once in your life. Now back to Leilanin and Tadeo over at the 'Focus on Fijiwara' studio. Good night everyone!"

***

As Niko aimed the camera down to the ground while he powered it off, Hiro smiled, "Well, think that was good?" This was Hiro's first gig as the first youth correspondent for the network and he really wanted to make an impression. This paid so much better than the online podcasting he had been doing for the past four years while trying to get noticed.

Niko looked up from his camera, "Yeah, that was excellent. Informal, entertaining and that's just what they were looking for in a new style segment. Now, let's get some of that smoked stick meat." Niko grinned.

"Definitely!" Hiro said while Niko was putting his camera equipment way. "That stuff smelled so good." Once the camera gear was stowed, they leisurely walked back the way they came.

Occasionally they grabbed a snack from this or that vendor, while moving along the alley before finally coming to the one stall they remembered. "Oh man, I hope this is as tasty as it looks." Hiro caught the attention of the taller fox in the booth, "Two sticks please!" He then watched as the fox put the sticks over the fire to warm them up before handing it to Hiro. "Thank you," he then paid him for the food.

"Here we go," Hiro said as he started to bite into the fish but stopping mid-bite as the ground started rumbling. Before he could even remove the stick from his mouth the building behind the stall erupted in an explosion. Flames and shrapnel bellowed forth. The force of the explosion propelled them and the vendor stall ten meters back, landing in large pile of people and debris.

The entire alley was in chaos from smoke, burning buildings, and the shrapnel scattered about. People were fleeing the alley as the sirens of the fire crews and ambulances arrived on the scene.

Hiro, Niko and one of the foxes were rescued from under a pile of rubble while the fire crews worked on putting out the burning building. All three were unconscious, but breathing, so they were whisked from the scene to the hospital.

***

"We interrupt our normal News at Ten program here at FNN to bring you a breaking story." The news anchor at the desk stated, "In the night market of Keelung, an explosion rocked Tailung Alley destroying a building and tearing through multiple market shops. Reports say that four people are dead and dozens more injured. The police on the scene say it appears to be an accident and a failure of a gas line. FNN reached out to the public works department and according to a spokesperson there, the Keelung Night Market area had been slated for infrastructure upgrade early next year.

"It is also being reported that two of FNN's staff on assignment in the area, youth correspondent Hiro Adachi and cameraman Niko Takahashi were injured in the blast and have been taken to a nearby hospital and reports say they are in critical condition but are expected to survive. We will continue to monitor events and will give you updates, as we receive them."

***

Hiro slowly opened his eyes and immediately shut them as the room was really bright. "Ouch, someone please dim those lights," he quietly said, before reopening his eyes slightly. Letting them adjust to the brightness for a few moments, he looked around the room. It appeared to be a non-descript hospital room with various pieces of equipment hooked up to him, beeping slowly with his heartbeat. *"Where the heck am I?"* Continuing to scan the room he noticed another bed with what appeared to be a fox hooked up to similar equipment to his.

At that moment, a male attendant walked into the room. "Oh, you're finally awake," the man quietly said. "Your friend should be waking up soon. I'll go get the doctor." He then walked out of the room.

About that time, Hiro started to notice how weird his vision was. "Why is my nose so large?" he wondered as he reached up to rub it. When his hand got half way up, he opened his eyes fully because he thought his own vision MUST be playing tricks on him. He rolled his hand around which looked like paws covered in short black fur with wisps of white around the fingernails. He looked again and noticed they were not a shadow of his imagination but that this was happening. For real. Then he moved his hand up to his face to feel his nose. Except, it wasn't a nose. His entire face was elongated and covered in reddish orange fur.

About that time a blonde headed doctor and three other attendants came into the room, "Hi there, I am Reyna Estrella. You are at a recovery clinic specializing in people who have your condition and I'm here to help council and support you through all this." She sat down on a chair next to him with one attendant checking the equipment next to his bed. The other two went over to the fox in the bed nearby.

Still in a bit of a daze, Hiro asked, "What happened?" He looked a little bit puzzled.

"Well, you were the victim of an explosion down in the market," she offered up. "In the aftermath, you and your friend Niko over there were found buried under some rubble. You two were also found with one of the canine vendors who happened to be knocked down on top of you. His blood dripped onto both your wounds," she paused, waiting to see if Hiro wanted to say or ask anything before continuing.

When Hiro remained silent, she continued, "I don't know how much of scientific history you happen to know, but alien nano machines are found in most canine's blood. When the fox's blood contaminated your wounds, your body was turned into a canine by the tiny alien machines during recovery. You are now a fox." She reached over and grabbed his paw.

A loud groan came from the other chair in the room before Niko sat straight up, "What are you doing to me?" he exclaimed while the two attendants tried to keep him from flailing.

Hiro looked at his friend and said, "Calm down Niko!" He then turned his head back to Reyna and thought, "*This is a dream ... this HAS to be a dream,*" and he poked at his arm hard enough to make him yipe. "Okay, not a dream," his ears laid flat at that realization, "What am I going to do?"

"Well, you both are through the hard part of this. We specialize in taking care of people who are affected, like you were. It's a very, very painful process during the change. Once the regular hospital identified what was happening they called us in." She paused for a moment. "We flew you to our treatment center where you were then kept sedated. We did that because you would have been in severe pain or even dangerous. During the change, sometimes the patient does quite literally go mad and get violent. We did that for your protection and the safety of our staff."

Hiro looked at her and then down at his new legs, "What happens now?"

"What comes next is physical therapy to get you used to your new body as it works a little different now." She smiled at him. "Rest assured, you are being taken care of. Since you were on assignment your employer, surprisingly, had insurance that would cover this. Even if that wasn't the case there's a global foundation that helps out, too. Your network has also committed, in writing, that you'll both still be okay to return to your jobs after a full recovery."

"Now Sven here will remove the sensors and help you get some real food." She again smiled, "Don't worry, we're here to help. These three will take you both to rooms with some full mirrors so you can get a good look at yourselves. Tomorrow, we'll get you into regular rooms and start the physical therapy."

***

Returning to work was a relief since the both of them were getting quite bored. Hiro and Niko were humbled by the warm welcome back with lots of supportive and inquisitive coworkers. It wasn't all roses as there were a few people that were bothered by them and didn't want to work with them. Thankfully, the network accommodated by shuffling the staff around to give them a more friendly team.

Hiro began to take classes in Political Science and Sociology on the side to help propel himself into a better career. Eventually those choices really paid off. After three years of working his way to a Senior Correspondent role at the network, he was given his big break to get behind a desk.

"Welcome to 'State of Politics' on FNN, I am Jeo Seong." The female anchor began, "Tonight, I would like to welcome the newest member of our political analyst team, Hiro Adachi." She paused, "Hiro started his career as a youth correspondent at FNN and has proven himself a clever, astute political scientist and will bring his great insights and analysis to our team. Welcome Hiro."

"Thank you Jeo, I am humbled and excited to be part of this team."

Chapter 21
Maya Metta

Haoqi Din opened the door, stepped out of the car and reached around to rub his lower back. "That was a long, long road trip." His journey had brought him almost all the way across the prefecture from Sudatlon.

Hao had been traveling all over the prefecture to gain insight into the religions of the Escabonian people for his book. His latest trip brought him to Zhangmi, the center of the Shénmì Zōngjiào religion. This faith was more commonly known as Shenism and this temple was located in a very northern region of Escabon.

The main temple was at the base of a mountain range at the top of the prefecture, nearly 200 kilometers outside of the nearest decent sized population center. The road was unpaved, rough and muddy and his poor little car would need some repair work when it got back home from the abuse.

The temple was ornate, which at one point had vivid red beams, but was weathered from the harsh climate of the northern regions. The temple was at the center surrounded by small structures that mostly looked like homes and some barns, which he presumed were for livestock. "This village feels like it is stuck back in the Fourteen Hundreds," Haoqi said quietly. It was virtually untouched by the rampant capitalism and development that was happening in the southern region.

He had been in a few Shen temples before and from the outside this looked similar, but slightly larger. Pushing open the main doors, his nose inhaled the heavy scents of incense used in their religious prayer. The room had about 30 worshipers in the midst of prayers. Interspersed amongst them were Shen monks adorned in their signature white tunics decorated with reds and purples.

As he walked forward one of the priests noticed him and approached. "Welcome traveler, how may I help you?" He bowed respectfully, as he asked the question.

Haoqi bowed, matching the depth of the monks bow. "I am looking for Sensei Norbu, I contacted him about my visit."

"Yes, yes. Right this way." The monk turned towards the back of the temple and started walking.

Following behind him at a few paces they walked slowly through the center of the temple. Haoqi had made arrangements to speak to the Sensei in order to gain more knowledge of the Shen religion. The room was filled mostly with humans, except for one young-looking white wolf dressed in the archetypal clothing of the Shen.

Passing through one of the many characteristic red doors in the temple, it opened into a well lit room. In front of him, was an amorphous short table where a man was sitting cross-legged with his eyes closed in a meditating pose.

"Sensei, a traveler is here and was asking for you." He gestured to the pillow on the floor.

Nodding at the guide, Hao went to sit down on the pillow and tried his best to cross his legs. Now that he was closer, he could see the weathering on the man's face. His complexion was covered in deep wrinkles and looked like old weathered leather.

"Hello Mr. Din." The Sensei opened his eyes as he spoke. "I hope your travel here was not too difficult?"

"Sensei Norbu, thank you for asking," Haoqi replied to the man softly. "The weather was not too bad,. I'm glad I wasn't trying this trip in the winter."

"Yes, yes. We are isolated for a long part of the year." He glanced towards the window before resetting his gaze on Haoqi. "Your letter indicated you would like to know more about us and our ways, yes?" The man replied in a very polite and concise matter.

"That is correct Sensei. I am writing a book on the region's religions and would like to know a lot more about Shénmì Zōngjiào." He pulled a notepad out of his jacket pocket. "Any objections to me taking notes?"

"No, not at all. Where would you like to start?" Norbu asked.

Over the course of the next few hours, the Sensei walked him through the history of their faith and the philosophy behind it. Hao scribbled furiously, asking a few questions when he wanted more detail on a subject.

"So Mr. Din, that is our philosophy, albeit a bit of a condensed form." Norbu stated, and then added, "Understanding for our people takes a lifetime."

"Hmm." Hao rubbed his chin, stating, "I do have one more question. It seems that Shénmì is mostly a human-based religion, at least from what I have seen over the years."

"Ahh yes, the canines. It is our belief that the spirits saw that humanity was leaving behind their connection to the earth and thus themselves." The man rubbed his chin. "The spirits gifted us with a reminder of our past and created a more wild version of ourselves to help us rediscover who we are."

"If that is the case why isn't there more canids among your followers?" Hao asked out of curiosity.

"We have many canines amongst our flock though not many choose the life I, and my fellow monks, have chosen. They are," he paused to think about the words, "'too energetic' is a good way to put it. The nature of the canines is one of activity. They are so full of life that they are unable to obtain the meditative states we normally achieve. Thus, they grow restless in the pursuit of enlightenment. They are happier with physical work. Farming, herding, building and often choose paths that align with their energetic nature."

"Most interesting. I haven't spent much time with anyone of their species so I couldn't have imagined." Hao thought that is a unique perspective to follow in his research.

"We do have one woman here who is a canine amongst the temple staff. Her name is Maya Metta. She was abandoned at the temple at a very young age and grew up here. She is now a young adult and sadly, is also getting restless." The Sensei paused while being in thought for a few moments. "You should talk to her to get her insights."

***

After exchanging parting pleasantries, he left the Sensei's study and started walking through the temple. Hao slowly walked around the perimeter looking at all the ornate architecture and the beautiful scroll work that adorned nearly every square millimeter of the interior. Hao started sketching what he thought was a particularly beautiful dragon themed ornament when he was startled by a voice.

"Hello Mr. Din."

Hao turned around to see the white wolf that he noticed on the way in, "Oh, hello."

She bowed, "Sensei said your were interested in learning a bit more about me and my kind." Din bowed back in respect, "Would you like to take a walk so we can talk more?"

Haoqi and Maya walked along a dirt path near the temple that was bordering a field where farmers were tending a field of barley. "So Maya, how did you come to be at the Zhangmi temple?"

She took about a half dozen more steps as they walked before speaking. "I was an infant when I arrived. The Sensei said a human couple surrendered me to a monk working in a field. He said they silently handed him a basket with a white furred canine child in it and walked away."

"Do you remember anything about your parents?" Hao inquired.

Silently, she kept walking for another minute before speaking, "No, I don't really. A random memory occasionally surfaces but they are mostly vague impressions." She looked over into the field at a worker chopping at a weed in the field and then continued, "Most of my memories are of this place, the kindness shown to me, but..." she trailed off.

"But?" Hao inquired.

"No one knows where I am from. Was I born this way or was I a human before I became me?" She walked along staring forward. "I feel something missing. Family, I think. Everyone who is here at the temple came from somewhere and at least remembers that."

"Do you find peace during your prayers? Does the mediation help?" asked Hao.

"I do somewhat. I really believe in the spiritual connection to the world around us and I hold those thoughts dear to me and close to my heart." She said looking over at Hao. "Some part of me is longing for something more...deep?" Her face wrinkled up, as she looked back forward. "I mean, some deep connection to other people, some sort of bond outside the confines of the ordered life of a Shen monk."

As they walked they kept talking. the topics ranges around: day to day life at the temple, spirituality and the canine relationship to it. They were just finishing up with what activities she really enjoyed as they arrived back at the temple.

"Maya and Mr. Din!" Another monk announced an important tone as they approached them, "Sensei Norbu would like to speak with you both."

***

It was getting late in the day, so the room with Norbu was a bit dimmer since the window was facing southeast.

"Please sit down, both of you." Then, the Sensei looked at them both, "While you were out walking I have been thinking." He then looked at Maya and pointedly asked, "Maya, I sense a growing unrest in you, am I right?"

"Yes, the daily life here, the meditation and the prayers are all fine, but over the past few years they haven't been as fulfilling as they used to be." Looking down into her hands, she added, "I feel there's something missing."

Norbu nodded, "Yes, I have sensed that." He looked over at Haoqi, "Sharing the stories and what our religion means to us is always given freely. Your presence here gives me an opportunity to give Maya a chance to find her way in the world." He idly turned over a paper on his desk, "I would like you to take Maya with you back to the southern region."

Maya looked from Sensei to Hao and back again. She was nervously interlocking her fingers together contemplating what was being said.

"Take her to the Xi'An Temple located in the city there. I would like to send her there to broaden her wisdom." He looked directly at Maya. "I do not know what more we can teach you here will help progress you spiritually. The staff at the temple there will help you find your way, help you in whatever education you want to pursue and ultimately bring you the inner peace you are still searching for."

The old man then looked at Haoqi, "Can you do this for us...for me?"

"Well, I am headed to another province first for another interview." He looked towards Maya. "If she would like to, I would be more than happy to pay back your kindness in speaking with me." Haoqi added, "I do need to leave tonight though if you decide to join me."

Her ears perked up a bit, as she looked over to Hao and then toward Norbu. "I will. Thank you, Sensei." She got up and bowed to the only father figure she had ever known.

***

"So," Haoqi sat down at the other side of the cafe booth with Maya. After not seeing her for three years she felt better, "How are you finding life now?"

"It has been wonderful. After arriving here, the wonderful people at the temple got me in touch with a local specialist in education and found a program I was interested in." She sipped at the cup of tea that the waiter brought over to her before Hao had arrived.

"That's good to hear," he said as he motioned to the waiter to get him a coffee. "What did you chose to study?"

"Well, they found me a school that had a reputable religious studies program with a modernized version of Shénmì Zōngjiào. It blends the old teachings with the modern world and reconciles all of this."

She waved around the cafe. "I also took a minor in political science, because after seeing more of this world the dynamics of political theater started to fascinate me."

"Fantastic! Where did you end up after finishing your schooling?" Haoqi inquired right before taking a sip of his coffee.

"I joined a community outreach program helping teach religion to underprivileged youth, who are primarily canines in the South Downtown district," she said with a warm smile on her face. Her ears flicked towards the kitchen as a pot banged back in the kitchen. Then the white wolf asked, "How did writing your book go?"

"Oh, it came out pretty good. It wasn't a best seller, but at least it gave me some legitimacy in the literature world." He took another sip of his coffee. "Currently, I'm working on one that talks about the modern political landscape and how the growing canine population is having substantial effects on it."

"That sounds neat." She leaned back into her chair and brought her cup up to her nose to inhale the soothing scent of the tea.

"Yeah, I actually got funding from some group called 'NP Philanthropy'. They are a huge outreach group helping the canine communities around the world." He put his empty cup on the table. "We'll see how that goes."

"It sure is a small world." Maya looked over at him before continuing. "After I finished the university course, I started looking around for what I wanted to do. That job I took happens to be with your sponsor as well."

He motioned to the staff about getting a coffee refill and turned back to Maya. "That's cool. NP Philanthropy is a wing of Pierce Industries and they have been branching out a lot." He nodded to the man who delivered the coffee refill. "They seem to be taking canine equality very seriously so that will ultimately be great for you." Maya was looked up at Haoqi inquisitively.

"Yeah, I really am enjoying working with the youngsters. They are so smart and curious." She sipped at the last of her tea. "I think this is exactly what I was missing when growing up at the temple. Directly working with people and helping them discover their place in the world. It's like having a surrogate family. I'm really happy they gave me this chance."

Haoqi downed his second coffee. "Well, I need to get to a meeting. I am supposed to be meeting with Neville Pierce directly on what he wants out of this book. He's in town for some other business." Haoqi stood up and offered his hand, "Great to see you again, we should do this again since we live so close."

She stood up and instead of shaking his hand, she gave him a big hug. "I can't thank you enough for what you did all those years ago. I am so much happier now!" She pulled back from the embrace saying, "And yes, we will need to get together again."

"Yeah, I can meet at that time," Zuri remarked to the caller on the phone. "Text me the address and we will be there."

Zuri hung up the phone and looked excitedly at it for a moment. *"I've been trying to get this meeting for a year now."* Her own inner voice whispered to her. Three years ago she heard rumblings about 'safe houses' around the globe trying to hide and protect werewolves. Over the centuries, canines have been exploited, enslaved, driven away, beaten, murdered and hunted for sport. No one deserves this kind of treatment and she really wanted to meet the people doing this nearly impossible work.

Taking a deep breath to calm her excitement she sat back in her old, creaking chair. Her gaze lingered at the corner of her desk where a photo of her and her mom stood. Slowly she shifted her gaze to the bookcase. Scattered around the shelves were knickknacks, books, photos and several awards. Her gaze stopped on her most prized item, a crystal plaque from the Calveras Foundation for Truth's prestigious Excellence in Journalism for her work on exposing a government bribery and corruption scandal. Zuri couldn't help but say aloud, "That certainly didn't make everyone in the government happy."

"What did you say?" Jamin Baloyi looked over at her from his current task of cleaning some camera equipment.

"Oh, sorry. I was just reminiscing a little bit," she looked at him and her lips curled into a big smile, "I have some good news." She paused letting him look at her giant smile.

"Oh, don't keep me waiting, tell!" he remarked.

"My contacts finally were able to get me in touch with someone in the werewolf sanctuary group. We have a meeting!" She elatedly said, adding, "They are going to meet us tonight so we can talk about doing a story on them."

He carefully put down the rag and a tool he was holding. "Alright! That's awesome!" his face started grinning and he issued a thumbs up to her and then mentioning, "Do we know what they are willing to talk about or show us?"

"Yes, he is going to send me an address to meet at at 7 pm tonight. He can't give me more details until we talk in person." Her phone made a buzz on her desk. "Just a sec," Reaching for the phone and unlocking it, she continued her thought, "He just texted, we are to meet at the Pretoria Tavern over in Marklin."

Jamin grabbed his computer and looked up the place. "Well, that's certainly an out of the way place. It's in the industrial district on the other side of Cape Town so we should be prepared." Opening his desk, he pulled out his handgun and placed it on his desk to illustrate his meaning.

***

Zuri and Jamin pulled up along the curb across from the tavern. The road was unlit except for a small lit up 'Pretoria Tavern' sign in the window that gave them any clue it was there. "Boy, I'm glad I brought the beater tonight." Jamin chuckled a little bit. "Not the nicest area at all."

They both got out of the old car, the doors making horrible squeaks followed by a rattling thunk as they closed them. Jamin pulled his small bag of camera gear out of the back seat and closed it again. The area was absolutely empty so they just walked across the street to the tavern door.

The door was really thick and had very worn mahogany wood with old brass knobs. The door had evidence of a couple bullet holes hastily patched up at some point in the past. Jamin pulled it open, "Let me go in first," and he stepped up into the building.

Once inside the place was actually pretty decent. It was clean, decently lit, but absolutely empty except for a couple of really large men sitting in a booth. They proceeded to head up to the bar to talk to the bearded man cleaning the counter-top. "Hi there, I am looking for Esraa," Zuri asked of the barkeep.

"I don't know anyone by that name," he quietly replied.

"He also said that the sun rises in the north." Zuri added, "Heard of him now?"

The barkeep nodded at the men in the corner. One of them walked over and deadbolted the door while the other turning off the outside bar sign.

"Oh that Esraa, come with me and leave your car keys on the counter. We'll take care of hiding it for you. Don't want it getting stolen. This way." He pushed back a curtain over the door and gestured for them to go through.

In the back of the place was a dingy garage area where a low-profile delivery van with worn lettering of 'Dallie's Flowers' emblazoned on the sides. The bar keep stepped up to the van and opened the side door. "Here you go. Sorry there's no windows but you know the drill." One of the guys from the front was following them and jumped into the driver's seat. The barkeep opened the garage door and the van backed out and left.

***

During the drive, they changed vehicles three times. "Obviously, they aren't taking any chances." Zuri remarked out loud to Jamin.

Soon, they slowed down and went into the garage of another building. The driver shut off the van. "Okay, this is the final stop."

Then, the van door opened and they were greeted by a multicolored canine. The face looked masculine, but it's not always easy to tell what their sex was from the face. He was wearing fairly plain clothes, just an unbuttoned short-sleeve shirt and cargo shorts that showed off the radically different leg structure all canids have. His fur was a dizzying pattern of yellow, black and whites with the signature large, round ears of the native hunting dogs in the region.

"Welcome Zuri and Jamin. My name isn't Esraa, that's a fake. I am Ruhiu, but just keep calling me 'Esraa'. Sorry about all the spy stuff, but we HAVE to be careful so our sanctuaries stay hidden. There's a lot of people who don't agree with what we do here."

Zuri reached out offering her hand in greeting and Esraa embraced it with both his hands in return, "Thank you for allowing us the priv-eledge of seeing behind the scenes. The work you do is so important. What has happened to your people over the centuries is so awful and we want to help. We really want to help change people's minds so I really, really appreciate the chance you are taking." She added, "I'll call you by Esraa during the interview so don't worry, that secret is safe."

"Just to be clear, you are welcome to record, but please don't film and humans for their safety or anything that might give a clue to the location. Are you ready?" Esraa said with a smile.

"Understood," Zuri said as Jamin handed her the audio recorder.

After Jamin had the camera ready, they started to walk out of the room. They entered into what looked like a lunchroom and lounge area. There were about a dozen or so canines around, mostly all multicolored hunting dogs, but a few smaller gray ones with much smaller ears.

Stepping in front of Jamin and facing the camera, he motioned to Zuri that he was recording, "I am Zuri Mandla and I am bringing you into a deep dive into the hidden world of werewolf sanctuaries. For years, the canine population on our planet has been the subject of discrimination, hate and outright murder. Behind the scenes for a century, many people have helped out the canids, sheltering them, freeing enslaved ones and hiding ones that are under threat."

She continued, "I have been given unprecedented access to one of these facilities to see what goes on, to meet one of the key people of this organization and to tell the real story. Hopefully, we can help make life better for them and everyone in the world."

"Tonight, we are going to be talking to the organizer of this sanctuary, Esraa." Jamin widened the camera to frame both of them. "Esraa. First thing, thank you for letting us in, to show the world what you really are doing here. Can you tell me about what you do and why you are doing this?"

"Thank you Zuri. There is a lot of misinformation out there on canines and also on what our group does. First thing, we are NOT a terrorist organization. We don't have an army, we don't attack people or the government. Nor do we 'force' transformations on humans." He paused to let his statement absorb in people's minds before continuing, "What we do is help out canines in need."

Zuri questioned, "What reasons do most of the canines here need help?"

"As you said, we are discriminated against, beaten, held hostage, and murdered. A lot of the folks here have fallen afoul of any one of those reasons and many countless more. We get them out of the situation and give them shelter, placement assistance, medical help, pretty much whatever we can do to get them on their feet and someplace safe." Esraa paused for Zuri's next question.

"I don't understand why, after centuries, we still cannot get along. All the canines I have met were just as easy to talk to as any human. They have families, jobs and are just as smart as anybody." Zuri stated.

"The sheer amount of vitriol spewed at us is almost incomprehensible." Esraa continued, "By nature we are extremely family oriented, loyal and will sacrifice anything for each other. We are not frightening and we're not monsters. We love like humans do, we get frightened, we get sad, we have joy and we have pride. We have all the same strengths and weaknesses as any human does." His eyes shifted as a little sadness flashed across his face, "And just like humans, we have bad apples, but that does not make us any less worthy. Just because we have teeth and claws doesn't automatically make us homicidal maniacs."

Just as Zuri was getting ready to ask a few questions more before touring the rest of the facility, a thundering boom erupted that blew open the door to the room. Human mercenaries poured through the door and started shooting multiple rounds. Everyone inside immediately ran away or ducked for cover. Jamin dodged behind a storage rack and continued filming. During the chaos, Esraa had turned and as he did so, stepped in front of Zuri just as a bullet hit his side. He reached for his side as he fell back onto Zuri.

***

Zuri woke up in an unfamiliar bed, stiff and weak. "What, what happened?" She sat up and looked around the room. As she panned to the side, she saw a mirror with a female canine reflected in it and asked her, "Hey, what happened....." She trailed off as the image perfectly matched her lip movements simultaneously with her and then gasped as she realized that she was alone in the room. She had nothing to say for a minute before everything clicked together in her mind all at once. She exclaimed, "WHAT THE HELL?!?"

Getting up to run over to the mirror she immediately tripped and fell flat on the ground. Lying there for a minute and getting her bearings, she rolled over and sat up to look at her legs. Their shape was absolutely different, joints in different places and thin with a completely unfamiliar paw shaped foot. Carefully, she got up and shuffled to the mirror slowly to work out how her new legs worked. At the mirror, she gazed into her new green eyes first before exploring the foreign shape of her face. It was the face of a hunting dog, the gold, brown, black and white markings all swirled around in an almost dizzying pattern. Opening her mouth she inspected her new teeth. While she was poking at her tongue with a hand claw, Esraa walked in. "Oh hey," he said, "You're awake."

"What happened? Why am I like this?" She walked over to him. "What happened the other night?"

He looked her in the eyes. "Let's sit down," gesturing to a chair. Sitting himself down in front of he, he took her hands, "It has actually been eight weeks since our interview."

Zuri was shocked, "EIGHT WEEKS?" she exclaimed. "How has it been eight weeks?"

"That night, one of the hate groups, the Humans First Coalition, coincidentally found and invaded our sanctuary. During the chaos I was shot. That same bullet went through me and into you. I fell backwards onto you and we both passed out. Our own security forces managed to disable and or drive off most of the terrorists. I guess while we were incapacitated, enough of my blood got on your wounds to cause this." He turned over her hands to look at them. "I never, ever wanted this to happen and I am so sorry."

Sitting quietly contemplating her own new hands, curling them and looking at the claws, "I have heard of this, but I didn't think it happened anymore." She paused, while holding up a hand to look at the back side, "I smell and hear everything, this is unnerving."

He sat silently for a bit, thinking of what to say next, "Well you will get used to it. We have helped a few people who had this happen and they all got through it. The reason you were out eight weeks was we have found it much easier if the patient isn't conscious during the change. It's quite painful and the person can go entirely mad during that time. So we kept you sedated until your body was mostly done changing. I hope you're not mad. It's going to be a little emotional for a while, but rest assured, we are taking care of you.

"I, uh..." she stammered a bit, "How do I go on with life?" A worried look spread across her face.

"Well, we do have some positive news. Your camera man, Jamin, caught it all on tape and all the big networks aired the video. The response has been outrage and sympathy across the world, so your plan to raise awareness for our kind has worked in a round-about way." He held her hands again, "I'm still very sorry this happened. I know you didn't choose this."

"Well, do people know I survived? Jamin? My mother?" She looked worriedly at Esraa.

"Yes, they know. They know what happened to you. Both have been here regularly in support. Jamin will bring your mother down now that you're awake." That made her smile a little bit, "Don't worry, our team of lawyers has done this before. Everything that has happened has been fully documented, so you'll still be able to be yourself." He grinned pleasantly, "You'll just have to get used to that tail and the proper way to bathe now."

"This has been one heck of a game Bob!" one of the television announcers exclaimed.

"I know Hal, it's truly a nail biter. Just to recap, we are at 25 seconds left in the Heartstone Championship game and the Saint Hood College Falcons lead the Suffok University Jaguars 21 to 20. The Jaguars took their last time out and will have the ball on 4th down at the Falcon's 45 yard line."

"The Falcons were expected to dominate the Jags but that hasn't happened. The real MVP of this game is running back and wide receiver, Brennan Clark. His year started out really slow with three fumbles in the opening game. Everyone thought Coach Germaine would kick him off the starting team. Germaine gave him another shot and he miraculously pulled it out, getting over fifty yards rushing and over a hundred yards on catches in the next game. Coach took a gamble and it certainly paid off!" Hal finished.

Bob chimed in, "Yeah, and his year after that has been stronger and stronger. He now leads the league in rushing yards and touchdowns and will take home the prestigious Jackson Mann trophy for most yards in a season." Bob paused to look at a monitor, "Alright Hal, let's return to the game, the Jaguar's are lining up in the Wildcat formation with the Falcon's in mixed man-zone coverage. Brennan is lined up wide right. Do they go with Brennan? That's probably their strongest play here, but the Falcons have man-to-man coverage on him. That man is Rekman Walker, the toughest one-on-one defender in the league."

The Jaguar's quarterback, Rami Herkov, looked around, giving his count, then yelling 'HUT' and the play was underway. Brennan surged forward and then immediately cut back inside, leaving his coverage out of place to his outside. The quarterback rifled a ball through the coverage hitting Brennan perfectly on the numbers.

"OH MY, that was a perfect throw to Clark!" the Hal yelled.

Brennan turned up field, but the Falcon's coverage was closing in on him, with the prefecture's best outside linebacker coming full steam at him. Clark dropped his shoulder, hitting the defender off balance and then spun free.

Bob's exclaimed, "What a move, can he do it?"

Brennan broke free from the linebacker and glanced to his left seeing the secondary coverage closing in. He turned right and put on the steam.

Hal started verbally following the play, "He's at the 20.....the 10...AND HE'S IN!. THE JAGUARS COME FROM BEHIND TO CINCH THE CHAMPIONSHIP!"

"What a run Hal, those moves by Clark proves he has the stuff for the GFL. He's going to be a top pick in the draft in the spring. Let's go to Liz, down at the sidelines." The camera switched to a sideline camera.

"Thanks Hal and Bob, I'm Liz Markham down here with Brennan Clark. So Brennan, did you think you could do it?"

Still out of breath Brennan responded, "Well Liz, we knew this was going to be a tough one tonight. I wasn't sure I could get past Rekman on that last play, but I managed to get inside of him and Rami nailed that pass."

"Well congratulations Brennan on a great season!" Liz said loudly over the roar of the crowd. "Look forward to your first season in the GFL."

"Thanks, I couldn't be more happy for our team. Thank you Coach Germaine for having faith in me."

***

"They are demons sent forth to destroy humanity. To take our place. To conquer us." Senator Joseph Clark stood at the podium and said his words forcefully into the microphone in the senate chamber as a representative of Heartland Prefecture. "God has allowed these 'werewolves' to flourish, to punish us for our own sins and transgressions." He slapped his palm on the podium." We must not allow that anymore. They are animals. They are monsters and should be treated as such." His face was turning a little bit red at his anger.

"Today, I am introducing a bill to curb this threat to our humanity." He looked out into the chamber, settling his gaze on a small grouping of canine representatives. "We must not allow their kind to make decisions for us, decisions for our future, decisions for our children's future." Joseph paused, letting his anger reverberate in the room. "This world belongs to humans. This bill will restrict these werewolves, these dogs, these MONSTERS, from holding any seat in the office regardless of how 'human' they seem. They are not human and can never, EVER be allowed to be anything more than animals." His brow was glistening with perspiration as he stared out over the other senators, many of whom were muttering and some of them outright booing him. "Speaker, I yield the podium."

***

"Wow. Did you catch Senator Clark's speech today?" a young man named Amos was shaking his head at the thought. "That guy is way off his rocker"

Sitting around the table in a back room of a dingy, empty pub in the downtown area of Hiller City in Heartstone, were five young men. Amos, Nigel, Rurik, Cristopher and Rodrigo were sitting in a circular booth having some drinks.

"That man is dangerous." Nigel responded to Amos. "You would think, that by now that sort of talk would be gone."

"I know, but he has been sucking in a lot of people in with all his 'wrath of god' crap and all he will do is set us all back a hundred years with his hate." Rodrigo said while twirling his empty pint in his hand. "If he manages to pass this law, what's next? People from San Juarez aren't good enough? Fijiwara?"

Rurik scoffed, "Politicians. They think they know what's 'best' for us all. I don't live in fear of the canines. Every one of them I have met have been nice enough. Those suits are so disconnected from real life. Clark only keeps his job because he riles them up with fear, so they keep voting for him."

Cristopher was silently listening to the others banter back and forth for a while before Cris spoke up, "I know someone," pausing for a moment to make sure he got their attention. "I have an idea on how to stick it to that guy. We'll see if he changes his mind or not but we can maybe stir people up enough to realize who he really, really is. Though that's already pretty obvious if you have any sense about you."

Cristopher then went on to lay out his plan to his friends.

"That could work, I'm in." Rurik agreed.

"I think we're all in." Amos added while everyone else nodded. "Let's do this."

***

Brennan was ecstatic with their victory the other night and was really looking forward to letting loose this evening. He really didn't drink much due to his focus on his workouts and games. His fraternity was throwing a huge, all campus party in his honor tonight. Brennan was eating a morning snack in the common room when his buddy Kenji, a fellow frat brother studying here from Fijiwara, brought a tray holding a breakfast sandwich, and sat down across from him.

"What would his father think if he knew Brennan's best friend was a fox?" Brennan just shook his head at the thought. *"He would disown me."*

"Mate, I just saw the speech your dad gave yesterday. Glad you didn't see that before the game, that would have been a downer. How do you cope with that?" Kenji inquired.

Brennan stabbed a sausage with a fork. Hard. "I guess I just tune him out. Not that he was ever around due to being in the Capital so much. I mostly was raised by mom and our au pair. Neither one of them ever said much about politics, so thankfully I turned out okay."

"Huh, weird that you went onto studying law and minoring in political science." Kenji smirked and then let out a chuckle.

"Well, I guess it wasn't hard to pick up things about government growing up, so I thought it would be an easy minor to add." He smirked back at Kenji before stuffing the last of his food into his mouth. "Well man, I have a few classes to get to before the party. See you tonight!"

Brennan was up in his room reading the last of the day's assignment when someone banged on his door.

"Hey, it's nearly 10." The thumping of the music volume tripled when Karl stuck his head in the door. "Got lost in that exciting law book again, I see. Come on Mr. Famous. Everyone's looking for the 'Stud'. Get your butt down there."

Brennan threw on some party clothes quickly. He was hoping that Alicia would show tonight, so he splashed on a little cologne even though the smell of booze would probably mask that. "Okay, let's do this." he said, as he walked out the door and downstairs to the party room.

As he cleared the stairs, everyone in the room suddenly started cheering loudly.

"There he is!" Kenji screamed into the mic at the DJ turn tables. "The man of the hour. Get that boy a drink!" There had to be a hundred people crammed in the room with more on the upper balcony level. Friends jammed drinks into each of his hands and two girls pulled him out onto the dance floor.

***

Parking their beat up old sedan blocks away from the frat, the five young guys from Hiller City got out of their car. They all had dressed up to try and fit in with the preppy kids at the University.

"Okay, everyone knows the plan." Cristopher looked at his watch and noted that it was about 11:30. The party should be roaring and crowded. "This is an open party so just act like you belong there."

They all entered through the front door, nodding to everyone on the way in like they knew everyone. Slowly, they scouted around the dance floor. They were looking for Brennan, the football son of who many considered to be an asshole senator. Rurik spotted him over in the back leaning up on the wall chatting with some friends by some bar tables.

"Okay, Rurik, we'll go towards the bathroom area in the back. You hang out nearby him and when he puts his drink down, put this stuff in there." Cristopher handed him a vial with some clear liquid in it and nodded towards Brennan. "Once he feels sick and makes a run for the toilet, we'll do the rest."

Making sure that his pals were in position, Rurik grabbed a beer so not to look out of place and sat down at the table right by Brennan. Brennan was really engaged with the ladies talking to him so it didn't take long for him to put down his drink and turn back around to the girls. Once he was not paying attention, Rurik dumped the small vial of liquid into his drink and then made his way towards the front door to leave.

***

Brennan was really glad Alicia and her friend came as he really wanted to get to know her better. But with his football training and studies he never really had the time. He kept talking with them, meanwhile he had grabbed his drink and kept sipping on it. Twenty minutes went by and he was starting to feel dizzy and disoriented, "*I must have had too much tonight,*" he thought to himself.

"Excuse me ladies, I need to leave for a minute," and he dashed towards the restroom.

As he ran past, the four hanging out at a table near the restroom slowly got up and followed Brennan. One of them stood outside to keep watch.

Brennan burst into the restroom and wanted to sit down on the toilet because he could barely stand. His head was spinning, his vision was blurry and was on the verge of passing out.

Once inside, the three found the football champion slumped in the stall. The sedative they slipped into his drink was working as he didn't even acknowledge their entry to the bathroom. Nigel pulled out a large syringe with a silvery red liquid and pushed out the air bubble in prep. Amos snapped his fingers in front of Brennan's face to get a reaction.

"He's oblivious, stick him." Amos said as Nigel jabbed his arm with the needle and pushed all the liquid into Brennan.

"Say hi to your dad for us," Cristopher said defiantly while Nigel pocketed the syringe and left the bathroom.

On the way out Cristopher told some random frat guy that there was someone passed out in the bathroom and they quickly fled the area.

***

Brennan woke to a splitting headache and he was feeling feverish. *Say hi to your dad for us* kept echoing in his head and he could barely open his eyes from the shooting pain behind his eyes. "Ugh. What did I do last night?" He sat up and put his head into his hands.

A soft knocking at the door made him wince. Undeterred, he answered, "Come in."

"Hey buddy, how are you feeling this morning?" Kenji walked in with two large bottles of water. "You seemed to party a little too hard last night, drink up." He handed Brennan the water and sat down on the sofa nearby, "You look bad."

"I feel worse," Brennan quietly spoke. "I just remember getting dizzy and running for the bathroom."

"Yeah, someone found you passed out and we carried you up to your room." Kenji clasped his hands together, "Rest. You let me know if you need anything."

"Thanks man," and the young athlete fell instantly back asleep.

***

The next morning, Brennan awoke feeling even worse. His head hurt, everything was on fire, aching and he was sweating profusely. Barely able to move, he grabbed his phone and rang Kenji. "Hey man, I must have picked up a virus or something. This isn't right, I can barely move."

"Oh man, I think the Charlene is over there in the kitchen. I'll ring her and she'll get you to the hospital somehow."

About 10 minutes later, two of his fraternity brothers led two paramedics into his room. "This is not a hangover," one of the medics said after examining him before adding, "we need to get him over to the ER."

Returning in a few minutes, they rolled a stretcher into the room and carefully lifted him onto it. One of the paramedics then said, "Okay, we're off to St. Guinevere." On the way out, they instructed Charlene to contact his parents to let them know.

***

Brennan's dad stood by a window looking into his son's room, hands behind his back with a dour expression on his face. A doctor knocked and opened the door, then came in.

"Hello Mr. Clark, I am Doctor Hassan. I am looking after your son."

Joseph turned to the doctor, "What is wrong with him?" he demanded from the doctor.

"Well, what we do know is this isn't a regular illness, this is...this is something different. A specialist is testing his blood right now and hopefully we will know more in an hour or two."

"What happened to him was..." Another voice spoke up and the two of them turned to see a man in a suit walk into the room. "Was done on purpose. My name is Dexter Van Graoff. I am a special investigator with Capital Security." He extended his hand out to Joseph to shake his hand. "Dr. Hassan was getting to this, but they found traces of a hallucinogenic sedative called Ketamine in his system, a heavy dose. Someone slipped it into his drink at the party. What is more worrying was the staff also found a needle puncture in his arm. Someone administered your son some sort of shot and we're testing to find out what that is right now."

"What do you mean 'administered'? Forcefully?" Joseph's face scowled.

"Yes, forcefully," the investigator replied dourly. "We think someone is trying to get to you through your son. You seem to have very polarizing views on a lot of topics so there is a good chance this is a politically motivated attack."

"Mr Clark," Dr. Hassan added. "Your son is in good hands and the agent was kindly able to post men throughout the building. I suggest you go home and get some rest. I will call you when we find out what this is."

***

"Welcome to Heartstone Tonight, I'm Troy Alvarez. Tonight's top story is Brennan Clark, winning running back for the Suffok University Jaguars in this year's collegiate football championship, has been hospitalized."

"Our investigative news division has uncovered that his hospitalization is the result of an attack during a fraternity party in his honor. We do not know the nature of the attack, nor are there any leads to who was responsible."

"Brennan was extremely popular with the student body and his team. There seems to be no motivation to attack Brennan himself, which has led many to speculate that this is a political attack given his father's recent rhetoric as seen here in this clip."

"This world belongs to humans. This bill will restrict these werewolves, these MONSTERS, from holding any office regardless of how 'human' they seem."

"Capital officials have declined to comment."

***

A week went by before the doctors called Joseph Clark, and Brennan's mother, Melissa, in to speak to them about Brennan.

Joseph again found himself staring blankly at the window to his son's room, his hands stuffed in his pockets. A scowl grew on his face as he noticed Brennan's face was looking odd. He turns around when he hears a knock. Dr. Hassan, another doctor and Agent Dexter filed into the room.

"So, is he better? Has he been awake? Is there any prognosis?" He demanded.

Hassan cleared his throat, "Mr. Clark, we have identified what your son was subjected to. This is going to be difficult to process, but your son will never be the same." He looked over to Brennan's mother's face to see she was extremely worried. "He was injected with an experimental substance by someone."

"Doctor, let me explain this," Agent Dexter put a hand on the doctor's shoulder. "We had to bring in a specialist to figure out what this was. The substance your son was given was an experimental serum that was developed for treatment for terminally ill patients, a last resort cure. A lab in Hiller City was broken into the night before the incident and one vile of the treatment was stolen from their supply. Their security is absurdly tight so it looks like the thieves had help from someone to get in."

Joseph stepped up to the agent. "What 'kind' of serum?" his fists clenched as he asked that question.

"It was a mixture of steroids, growth hormones, adrenaline, canine blood and a batch of cultivated alien nano 'doctors'." The agent took a deep breath because this wasn't going to be easy. "Like I said before, this was developed as a last resort option for people who are dying. This serum allows the machines to heal the body but there is one. Big. Side effect."

Melissa stood up and came over and asked, "What side effect?" She put a hand on her husband's sleeve looking very, very worried.

"The machines heal the body and the patient makes a full recovery, but at a cost. The body becomes a canine." Dexter said solemnly.

"WHAT?" roared Joseph. "You have to be joking. This is one sick joke." He slammed a fist onto the table nearby and Melissa just sat down as tears rolled down her face.

"No joke sir, this is very real." Dexter said bluntly.

"Excuse me agent," Doctor Hassan spoke up and then turned to Joseph. "According to the experts we brought in your son will make a full recovery, but there is nothing we can do to stop it. The process is extremely painful so we have to keep Brennan sedated during this. He will remain so for months."

"GOD DAMMIT!" Joseph yelled. "Who the fuck did this, I want them locked up!" furiously saying to the agent. He turned to look through the glass at his son. When the red flash of anger drained from his face he commented softly, "Who turned my son into a monster?"

"Mr. Clark," the doctor added, "Your son's mind will still remain the same after..."

"NO!" Joseph's face turned red again as he shouted. "That is NOT my son anymore!"

"Oh Joseph," Melissa finally spoke grabbing her husband's hand. "You can't mean that?"

Angrily the senator pulled his hand from his wife's and stared coldly at Dexter, "Someone killed my son to get to me. You WILL find them and punish them and I will make sure this can't happen again."

***

"Good evening, I am Troy Alvarez and you are watching Heartstone Tonight. It has been 4 weeks since the attack on Brennan Clark. Sources say that the award winning running back was infected by a stolen medical treatment for terminal cancer patients. This treatment uses the alien 'Nano-Docs' or nano-scale machines that have been linked to the creation of the canine population across the globe. The treatment is used to cure terminally ill people who have no other options left."

"Two weeks ago, Senator Clark, Brennan's father held a press con-ference to speak about it." a news clip flashed on the screen.

"My son was brutally attacked by political opponents and was murdered. I will use all avenues at my disposal to make sure this cannot, and WILL not EVER happen again."

"Contrary to his statements, our sources say that Brennan is still alive and that this treatment cures anyone who takes it, but with one serious side effect. Unfortunately there is no reversal to this treatment and Brennan Clark will be transformed into one of the canine species as a result of this attack on him."

"Heartstone Tonight's Correspondent Sandra Williams was able to speak with Melissa Clark, Brennan's mother briefly today." A clip of Melissa and Sandra in the studio flashed on the screen.

"Mrs. Clark," Sandra looked over at Melissa, "Reports say your son is still alive and not dead, contrary to what your husband has been telling the press. Is that true?"

Melissa looked over to Sandra, "Yes, yes that is true. Brennan is alive."

"What about the reports of his condition? That he has been infected and is turning into a canine?"

Brennan's mother looked down at her interlocked fingers on her lap for a moment before looking back to Sandra, "Yes. That is true."

"Then why is the Senator saying he is dead?"

"Joseph believes his son is truly dead. He can't...won't acknowledge that inside he will still be the same little Brennan that we raised. He absolutely believes he is now a monster." A sad expression fell across Melissa's face.

"So, you disagree with him?" Sandra said, with a concerned look on her face.

"Yes I do. Joseph's hatred for the growing canine population has got the best of him." She frowned while saying that. "I have kept quiet for too long, not that he would listen to me anyway. I do NOT agree with him at all and as a result, I have filed for divorce this morning."

"Shocking development in the Brennan Clark case. We will let you know when we have more information. I am Troy Alvarez for Heartstone Tonight."

***

"Hi Ms. Brennan," Doctor Hassan said when coming into the room. "We stopped the sedation about an hour ago, so your son should be coming out of it soon. He will need a familiar face there when he wakes up."

"Thank you doctor." She got up from the waiting room chair and followed the man into Brennan's room.

Doctor Hassan motioned to a chair next to his bed. This was the first time she was able to get to see him up close and in person. She paused standing next to his bed. His face was so unfamiliar now. They tell her that his fur pattern was that of a typical timberwolf from the region. The grayish-brown of his upper face contrasted by an off white lower half. She reached up to run her hand over his forehead and felt the strange shape underneath. A soft, but sad smile crept across her face as she reached down to hold his hand. Sitting down slowly she whispered, "My little Bren."

Twenty or so minutes went by before he started to stir. He rolled his head to the side, as he opened his eyes a little bit before focusing on Melissa. "Mom?" Brennan said, the words struggled to form a little and sounded more gruff than before. "Mom, where are we?"

Melissa stood up and held his hand and looked lovingly at him. "We have a lot to talk about."

***

It was another 2 years before Brennan was able to recover and graduate with his degree. He was sad that he couldn't continue his football career as the GFL had never allowed canines to compete due to the significant physiological differences. The human players would have been completely outclassed by their canine counterparts. Thankfully the university had honored his scholarships as that would have been a public relations nightmare for them. He was such a popular person and there was huge outpouring of sympathy from the community over his plight.

Brennan began to get dressed in his new suit. His mother had gifted him with a bespoke red pinstriped suit tailored for his new physique. He could no longer could wear full pants. His legs were too shapely to make that work so his new business suit pants were just shorts that came to his knees. He ran the jacket material between his fingers. It was made with a micro mesh material that was developed specially for canines as it breathed a whole lot better so he could stay cool.

He stood up in front of the full length mirror to see himself. "I do look good in this," he said as he hand-brushed some of the fur on his face to straighten it. Brennan grabbed his briefcase with his laptop and snagged his keys on his way out of the apartment turning to lock the door on his way out. When he was walking down the stairs he could see the black car that way waiting for him.

Once outside the driver opened the back door and gestured to sit down, "Mr. Clark, Mr. Pierce is excited to meet you."

As Brennan ducked into the car and sat down before realizing that someone was in the car with him.

"Greetings, world famous Brennan Clark," the large black wolf next to him in the car extended a hand with a smile.

Brennan reached back and shook it, "Thank you, nice to meet you."

"Pierce, Neville Pierce," he leaned back into the seat in front of Brennan. "I have a lot of meetings today unfortunately, so I thought I would speak with you on the way to one. Hope you don't mind."

"No, not at all." Brennan had already been to Pierce Industries' local office for a dozen different interviews.

"Good! My people tell me you are a great candidate for the position. We picked you out of the hundreds of graduates because of what happened to you." He paused for a moment. "Our company has expanded into a lot of areas over the past years but our lobbying arm really needs competent lawyers who understand different...perspectives." Neville smiled at him.

"I trust my team implicitly and they all say that you are the one for us. I would like to formally offer you a position at NP Legal, our lobbyist division." He handed Brennan a spiral bound document. "That position comes with great pay and a lot of perks."

Brennan flipped it open and thumbed through the pages. His ears perking up seeing the salary offer and had to steel himself from getting too excited. "The offer is very generous, Mr. Pierce."

"The job will be tough, there are a lot of people who hate canids as you know very, very well." He looked over Brennan's face to see if he could read him. "Oh, here we are," as the car came to a stop.

As they got out of the car Pierce turned towards Brennan, "So, what do you think?"

"The work sounds exciting, getting to help make the world better is a great cause." He smiled and said, "I will take it."

"Great!" He motioned to the person standing in the door, who then went inside. "Come inside and we will make it official."

Another large black wolf in a black suit walked up to them, "This is Quenton Fedeyosev, he will be your personal security. "Come inside. I have taken the liberty to get you into a bigger apartment that's nearby. Welcome to the team."

Chapter 24
Renata Alonso

Renata banged her head on the interior trim of the four wheel drive vehicle, as it dropped sideways into a large rut, "Ouch, that hurt!"

"Sorry ma'am, this road is barely a horse trail and with all this rain it's a muddy mess." Juan Muñoz exclaimed over the loud exhaust noise. "We have probably another hour at least before we get to the village. This is going to be very, very slow going."

Renata rubbed the side of her head and thought, "*I don't think that will be a bruise, thankfully.*" She settled into her thoughts as the vehicle lurched to and fro in tune with the ruts and undulations in the road. She still couldn't believe that there were still prominent ruins that hadn't been discovered yet. "*Somehow, this jungle is very, very overgrown, and that must be why it has remained hidden, even from the air,*" she theorized. That was a lingering thought that was poking at her constantly throughout her journey thus far.

She thought about all she had explored: the ruins of ancient civilizations, the lost cultures. It's still hard to believe how advanced these people were thousands of years ago. She had been studying the ancient sites for the better part of 20 years now and was never ceased to be amazed at the sites she was able to visit.

About a month ago, she was contacted by Juan. He had found out about a man that knew of some undisturbed ruins in a remote southern region of San Juarez in the Tacuarembó Province. They had spoken with a nearby administrator, who helped arrange for a visit to this newly found archaeological site.

***

Arriving at Aislado Village, Renata stepped out of the vehicle. She raised her arms over her head and stretched them back after the long, bumpy journey. This village was tiny, maybe a dozen or so buildings and many of which needed repair. Rainwater runoff was flowing and twisting down along the paths between the buildings to eventually snake its way down to the valley below. The local valley had been cleared at some point in the last century and was being used by the locals for agriculture.

Juan came around to her side of the truck, "Well, here is our contact's village." Just as he said that a man came out from one of the buildings nearby and headed over to them. "Are you Damião?" he said, as the man approached.

"Yes, I am Damião Ramirez and welcome to Aislado," he said as he extended his hand to greet him. "I hope the rain didn't make your journey too rough."

"The roads were definitely soggy, but it's nothing we can't handle. This is Renata Alonso." Juan gestured over to her.

"Pleased to meet you and thank you in advance for this opportunity." she replied, extended her hand in greeting.

"You are most welcome! So come with me now. We have a places for you to stay tonight. It's too late to head out tonight so we'll go first thing in the morning." Damião gestured to the buildings.

***

Early the next morning, Juan, Damião, Renata and a fellow named Lucio loaded up into the truck and started a bumpy ride further into the mountains. Lucio jumped into the driver's seat, turned the ignition and brought the old truck to life.

"We will only be able to go part way in the truck," Damião said loudly over the truck exhaust. "That area hasn't seen people for a century or more so there are no roads. We will have to hike for the last couple of hours."

About four hours in to the rough journey Lucio pulled off into what could only be loosely described as a shoulder. "Okay, time for that cardio work you wanted." He grinned at Renata and then stepped out of the truck and headed around back to the tailgate.

Juan pulled out backpacks and started doling them out to everyone. After putting his own on he reached into the back and slung a rifle over his shoulder.

Renata looked at Juan with a puzzled look. "What's that for?"

"Oh, I was warned by the local administers that there are a lot of púmas out here and they DO NOT like us. Or, should I say they DO like us...for lunch." He chuckled, "Mostly just for assurances."

***

Hiking through the jungle was a slow going affair. The ancient path was severely overgrown on top of it being very steep and wet. It had to have been at least two hours of hiking before they came to the first sign of the ruins.

Renata stepped up to the rubble and ran a hand over some of the fragments. "This used to be the entry stones that let travelers know they were entering the city." She ran a finger through the intricate carvings while clearing out the dirt and debris. "These carvings are amazingly preserved."

Damião and Lucio were up ahead hacking away at the ferns and vines to make the path passable. As they chopped down a huge swath they opened up a view of a large, moss covered, pyramidal structure. It was remarkably intact despite the thick canopy of trees that obscured the sunlight.

As they walked forward they tread on what used to be a stone paved courtyard, though many trees had uprooted the stones. Renata and Juan set their packs down so they could take the structure in better.

"We're losing the light," Juan casually mentioned. "We should probably set up camp for the night and get an early start in the morning."

***

After camp was set up, Lucio gathered some wood to make a fire. Due to all the rain, it took him a while to get the fire lit and it brought some much needed warmth to the crew. In the meantime, Juan and Damião pulled out and prepped some food to cook for them all.

"So," Renata asked of Damião, "What interesting stories do you know about this place?" She pulled out a notebook so she could take notes.

"There are only fragments of stories told by the local elders. These people built a huge empire that stretched all the way to the southern coast. They believed in a sun god that ruled over all of them and the animals were an extension of their gods. They built this temple as high as they could as they wanted to be closer to god." Damião said. "The stories say they angered the gods by building so high that the gods cursed them with disease and brought down their empire." He though deeply for a moment, "That's about all I remember from the old stories. No one wrote anything down so much has disappeared like this place.." His voice trailed off on his last comment as he gestured to the temple.

Lucio spoke up, "Well, I remember another story that my great grandmother told me. Before their downfall the most powerful of them were gifted with abilities that allowed them to transform into their spirit animal forms. This gift would help them hunt and better rule the world." He squinted one eye in thought and noted, "I think they were called 'Nagual' by the peasants."

Renata kept scribbling notes as they kept talking about local myths and traditions before closing the book, "Well, I am beat. We'll pick this up in the morning. Goodnight, everyone."

She crawled into her tent and fell asleep quickly as the day was thoroughly exhausting.

***

Renata woke to the sounds of chirping birds and millions of insects singing their morning songs. Changing her clothes into a fresh set, she unzipped the tent and crawled out to see Juan heating some coffee over the fire. "Good morning!"

"Morning sunshine," Juan smiled as he handed her a cup. "Ready for this?" The morning sunshine lit the area with foggy means giving the whole place a peaceful, spiritual feel.

She sipped at the warm liquid, "Yeah, I can't wait. This place looks beautiful, but haunting in the morning light."

After eating some energy bars and finishing the coffee, the two explorers unpacked the cameras so they could document the collapsed and fallen empire of rain-soaked debris.

"Okay Renata, should we start with the main temple building here?" Juan asked.

"Yeah seems like a good place to begin," replying to him with a smile.

They spent about four hours photographing, measuring and documenting the main building. "This will take years to study," she mentioned to Juan working nearby. "Should we scout around the area to map out the rest to figure out the plan?"

Juan agreed with her and they started hiking around the area. They identified about a dozen different buildings but most of them were crumbling. "It's amazing that the temple is so intact when everything else has deteriorated so much." Juan spoke out loud to no one in particular.

Renata and Juan were exploring around the backside of an outbuilding when she froze. She heard a growling and looked over to her left. There, she saw a native wolf brilliant red-orange fur with a black mane of spikey fur on its head and back. The animal looked very lanky with legs that were impossibly long.

Juan saw her freeze and looked in the direction she had turned towards. "Don't move. That's a maned wolf and it's not happy with you," he said as he slowly reached down for the rifle in his pile of gear.

Unfortunately, Renata didn't heed his warning. In a panic she tried to move behind a boulder causing the wolf to lunge at her, snarling and biting at her arm. Juan quickly shouldered the rifle and waited for it to back away. He fired a shot to try and scare away the animal with an intentional miss. However, the animal lunged again directly into the path of the bullet, hitting it in the shoulder. The momentum of the lunge carried the animal forward to fall on top of Renata. She pushed the animal off her and scooted backwards away from the wolf who had fallen limp from the wound.

Juan, Damião and Lucio rushed to her. "Oh, that bite is deep," Juan stated in monotone, "Let's get you away from here." He helped Renata to her feet and hiked away to the camp while Damião and Lucio remained near the animal.

***

Back at their camp Juan attended to her arm. "This is going to sting," he cautioned as he sprayed her arm down with a disinfectant he pulled out of the first aid supplies.

Renata winced as he sprayed, "Ouch."

Juan cleaned most of the blood off and continued the triage by wrapping the wound with a gauze. "We will need to get you off the mountain for proper treatment."

Damião and Lucio returned to the camp soon there after. "It looks like the wolf was a female just protecting her young." Damião said as he rubbed his head. "I took a good look at her. She was still alive, just unconscious so I sedated her and treated her wound. Lucio looked around and found her den 20 meters away. She wasn't rabid, she just looked like she was just protecting her pups." He paused for a little bit, "Those maned wolves are usually on the plains, so I don't know why she was up here. Maybe she was pushed into the hills by farm development."

"All right, you're okay for now," he smiled a little at Renata. "We still need to get you out of here." Juan dug into his pack and pulled out a satellite phone to call for an evac.

***

"Welcome to the 7 o'clock News on UBN 4 in San Juarez, I am Matias Pérez."

"Top story tonight is world renowned Anthropologist and Archaeologist Renata Alonso was injured by an animal attack while on an expedition to explore a recently discovered ruin in the mountains of Tacuarembó Province about 4 months ago. Reports say that she was attacked by a local wild canine species known as the Maned Wolf. Locals claim she has become what they call a 'Nagual', which is derived from ancient myths of humans who could transform themselves into animals. What we know today is that she was infected with the alien 'doctor' microscopic machines which led to her hospitalization."

"We now go live to a press conference, where Renata will be appearing for the first time in public, since this incident."

***

Renata quietly walked up the stairs to the podium amidst the camera flashes and a soft murmuring of the crowd. Approaching the podium she slowly put her hands onto it, steeling herself to speak. Her new body was similar to the San Juarezian maned wolf that bit her in the attack. The blazing orange fur a sharp contrast to the dark hands, ears and long mane on the top of her head. As she looked out over the crowd the sunlight made her violet eyes sparkle.

"Thank you all for coming out today to listen to me talk about the events of four months ago." She paused while the cameras flickered away. Renata was still not wonderfully used to speaking with her new mouth but she continued, "Four months ago I was exploring newly discovered ancient ruins in the mountains of southern San Juarez. During that expedition, I happened upon a wild canine mother who was threatened by my presence." Her nerves were still jittery so she paused for a moment. "She attacked me as she thought I was a threat to her family. During that engagement the animal was shot and I was exposed to her blood through an open wound I received from her bite during that attack."

Murmurs rustled through the audience so she let that die down before continuing. "As you probably already know, my blood was contaminated with hers and it also carried the alien nanomachines with it. Those machines 'repaired' my body into what you see today."

She paused again, then replied, "I will answer some questions now."

"Ms. Alonso, David Brinn from FNN news. Do you hold any resentment towards the animal who bit you?"

"No," she remarked, "she was just doing what any mother would do when her children were threatened."

"Kathy Schmidt of the Calveras Times. Was the wolf in question a feral canine or a humanoid canine?"

"This was a wild canine, not one of the humanoid species of wolves. She was just following her protective animal instincts." Renata answered.

"Vladimir Cristov from River City News 10, how hard is this on you and your family?"

"That's a good question, Vladimir." She steeled herself for a moment. "This transition has been really rough on me mentally and physically. I would like to thank the medical staff at La Plata Medicalla for all their support through this. The physical change was long, painful and arduous and I cannot stress how much their staff assisted me. I would not wish the pain on anyone." Continuing on that question, "My family has been extremely supportive and has been there for me throughout this ordeal."

"Sven Jansen of the Fjordland Gazette, how hard was it to get used to the physical differences from your human body?"

"I have gone through months of physical therapy to learn to walk and balance properly. Speaking took some time to figure out. Eating was pretty easy to get used to but my diet has had to change somewhat. Bathing is a lot more involved with all this fur. Next question," she added.

"Patrick Steel of Heartstone News. Do you find people outside the medical field and family are treating you differently?"

Her ears flickered a little bit and she frowned, but quickly pulled her face back to a pleasant expression. "Yes, a lot of people treat me differently. A bit like I'm diseased and as if they don't want to engage with me. Some have shown outright hatred for me now. I feel like that's a symptom of misinformation and fear. I am still the same Renata that I was before."

"Luis Gonzalez of SJBN, what's next for you?"

"For me?" she though for a moment, "I am going to keep doing what I was doing before. I am still the same person inside, despite my changed outward appearance. I love discovering and exploring. I fully intend to return to the site down in Tacuarembó and I'm excited to continue my work there. I also plan to be more involved in hopefully changing public perceptions of the community that I now find myself a part of."

Then, she concluded with, "That's all the time I have today. Thank everyone for your questions and thanks again to everyone that helped me through this trying time." Renata smiled at everyone and turned and walked carefully off the stage.

It took Tyler Dresden about six months to finally wrest back control of his company from the board of directors who locked him out of his own company while he was missing. The board tried every legal maneuver to keep him out. First, by denying he was really Tyler and then by saying he was unfit to lead the company due to his 'condition'.

He was happy to be in charge of his global telecommunications empire again but sometimes it just didn't feel like enough anymore. *"Cell phones? Tablets? Is that my destiny, my legacy?"* he thought quietly as he sat in his office at the top of the Dresden building. Tyler got up and began pacing back and forth on the giant glass wall that overlooked the city.

The phone on his desk beeped. He padded over to the desk, flopped down into the chair and hit the speaker button. "Hello Amanda, what is it?" he asked of his assistant.

"Sorry to bother you but someone named Neville Pierce from Pierce Industries would like to speak with you." She paused, then continued. "He says he has an offer that should peak your interests."

Tyler thought for a moment to remember where he heard that name before. *"Oh, that's right. Pierce Industries."* They were heavy into finance, legal and scientific investment up in the River City prefecture. "Sure Amanda, put him through and we'll see what he's offering."

"Hello, this is Tyler Dresden."

"Hello Mr. Dresden," a deep rumbling voice said in response to Tyler. "I am Neville Pierce from Pierce Industries. I have been trying to connect with you for a couple of months, but I guess my requests never got through due to your legal battle with your investors." The voice on the phone paused for a moment. "The reason I am calling, is our scientific research division has been investigating some alien artifacts. I'm sure you're aware of them, being a brilliant tech minded guy. Quite frankly, my team isn't as smart as you are and have hit a wall in the research."

"Well I'm not a genius, I just make great cell phones but I appreciate the compliment." Tyler said frankly.

"Oh come on Tyler. Graduating Summa Cum Laude from Los Diego Tech at the age of sixteen, revolutionizing the home video game industry, creating modern cell phones like the one I'm talking to you on. Give yourself the credit where its due." He paused before speaking. "I know you have been through a lot over the past year, so I'll get straight to the point. We need your brain and I suspect you love challenges."

"Intriguing," Tyler thought for a moment. "Alien technology you say?" Tyler smiled to himself. He had acquired a few of these artifacts himself and they led to some of the newest tech in the mobile devices he released last year.

"Yes. We are trying to do some very important work and I think you are just the man that can crack it." Neville dropped his voice a little. "Are you interested? Want to give that big brain of yours some exercise?"

"Sure. That sounds interesting. Sure beats figuring out how to make better software on our phones." Tyler replied.

"Great!" the voice boomed really loudly through the phone. "Why don't you come down to Uptown. We will sit down and talk through my proposal in person. I'll have my staff coordinate with yours and get all the logistics, NDA, etc. taken care of. How about two weeks from now?"

"I should be able to make that work. Look forward to meeting you Mr. Pierce."

"No need to be so formal, just call me Neville. I'll be seeing you soon."

***

Tyler's plane landed at Uptown Metro Airport two weeks after his call with Neville. When he stepped down the stairs onto the tarmac there was a large black car waiting for him with its driver standing by it.

The driver greeted Tyler and opened the door to let him inside. The car slowly drove to the far end of the airport to a private gate which opened as the car approached. Once inside the gate, the car moved into a heavily guarded area. There had to be 30 guards of mixed company around each corner as they needled their way through the compound. Tyler noted that more than half of them were large canines, whose size was impressive on their own, ignoring the fact there was a small army of them. However, with the giant rifles in their hands were even more intimidating.

They approached a closed hanger door and parked next to the personnel door to the side. The driver opened the car door to let Tyler out. As he was climbing out of the car a human in a business suit came out to greet him. "I am Dr. Havastein. I am the manager of Pierce Industries' Industrial Division here. Please," he gestured to the door. "Please follow me."

Upon entering the door Tyler walked into a well lit, spotlessly clean hanger. Residing in the middle of the hanger was a sleek, modern looking version of an old Space Shuttle used in the 1980s by the space agency. Tyler thought it was was most likely an recent mothballed prototype. "That's a pretty slick looking aircraft," Tyler said aloud to no one in particular.

He was admiring the perfectly smooth, white hull when Havastein guided him to a side door. "Neville just arrived and is waiting for you in here." The man opened the door and let Tyler walk through it, then closed the door behind him.

The room inside was a small cozy conference room that was very quiet, he couldn't even hear the air system running. The air was fresh inside so it appeared to be working just fine. A large black wolf got up from a couch and crossed the room. The wolf extended a paw, "Welcome Tyler, I am Neville Pierce."

Tyler reached his paw out and was absolutely dwarfed by the canine's paw size. "I didn't know you were..."

"A canine?" Neville chuckled. "That has been a well kept secret. Welcome to our industrial division. The subsection here is where we are researching the alien technology that has been found across the world." He motioned for Tyler to sit down.

"Your company seems to have a lot of 'divisions'. It seems you've got your fingers in everything." Tyler smirked at the wolf. "Where did you get the spacecraft outside?"

"A couple of years ago we bought out the assets of a failed aerospace company," Neville glanced over at the door when Tyler had just come in. "That prototype was one they built, but never landed the contract with the Earth Aerospace Administration to finish it so they folded."

"Ahh, I see," stated Tyler. "What is your plan for that?"

The wolf sat back into the couch. "Since I was a boy, I always wondered where my kind came from. I was a natural born wolf of two great parents but we were very, very poor. They were unfortunately murdered when I was very young, so I grew up on the streets doing whatever I could to survive. I am ashamed of some of the things I had to do but life was different for us back then. I worked very hard to get myself to the point where I can now use some of my resources to understand where we came from and this subsection is the culmination of that desire."

Neville reached down to his phone to tap the screen and an image appeared on the wall screen. "Do you know what that is?" he asked.

"Hmm." Tyler studied the blurry image for a little bit. "Cylindrical object, looks like a piece of a rocket booster or something. Is that photo taken in space?"

"Close." Neville leaned forward. "This object was discovered in 1997 and is in a near earth orbit around the planet." He touched his phone again. "Spectrometer readings show this object is made of the same metals that we have found in the spacecraft wreckage found scattered around the globe." The business man clicked the phone again to return the image of the object. "This object is clearly of alien origin and I intend to retrieve it."

"Retrieve it? Won't the government be trying to do that if it is so valuable?" Tyler tilted his head when he said that. "I know if I had known about it, I would want to get it to study it."

"I obtained the files on the object from a source about 10 years ago. Back in '97, the government classified it as Top Secret, shut down the program down and buried the discovery. My contacts discovered it and passed the reports along to me. I think the government is too worried about terrestrial problems to deal with the likes of this. We haven't had much of a space program since the early 90s." The wolf closed the image on the screen. He then turned back to the coyote. "Tyler, I have been dreaming of finding out who we are," he pointed to himself, "and who you are now, my entire life. Over the years, I have been funding expeditions and obtaining all alien technology I can get my hands on. You need to see this."

The wolf got to his feet and walked over to what appeared to be a blank wall. He put a palm to a panel and the wall slid up. As it opened, lights turned on, illuminating a series of objects. "This...is only a small portion of what I have procured."

Tyler got up and started looking at the rows. Obviously this was a curated exhibit as the objects were encased in their own clear cases. "I am familiar with some of these objects, I have some like them in our research labs. The latest generation of my phones use that new signal type reverse engineered from one of these." He pointed at a little wristwatch-like item.

"And that is why I need you." Neville smiled at Tyler. "My team has been working long and hard but they just couldn't crack most of the secrets in the devices on this wall. When someone took apart one of your latest phones they realized you had cracked some of those secrets."

"Yeah, I just had a brilliant flash one late night when poking at the electronics inside." Tyler looked around. "So, where's the big stuff?"

Neville chuckled deeply, "Sharp and astute deduction. Tyler." He walked over and palmed another spot, which made a door open with a hiss. They went inside and Tyler was looking at another hanger sized room with groupings of large spacecraft debris. "Our team has been exploring the remote mountains and the deepest seas. That alien ship must have been large as hell as there is a lot of large debris that is impossible to get off of the sea floor. Our team has been sifting through the salvaged wreckage and they think they have related systems grouped together. I think that's where you come in. You'll be able to find what they are missing. You are smarter than almost everyone on my team combined."

"I know its flattery, but I must admit I kind of like it," Tyler thought to himself. He walked over to one of them and touched the metal. It should have been cold and metallic but it had a strange texture, almost as if it was grown. "And that spaceship is your beginning of this journey?"

"Yes, it's only a prototype, but we have all the engineering we need from it to make it vastly better," the wolf leaned forward. "It's only the first step. I need your brain, your intuition to get this off the ground. Your father was a leading scientist in space exploration before his unfortunate accident. Seeing what you have done with the company after you took over, I KNOW you can leap way beyond what he did."

Tyler moved over to a table that had remnants of what appeared to be a computer console. Idly, he picked up one chunk and turned it around to get a look at it.

"What I am proposing is a partnership." Neville continued, "I would like to set up a joint venture between our companies. We will properly reverse engineer the alien technology and power private, not government controlled, space exploration. We can develop new technology to help this world before we destroy ourselves." He walked up to Tyler. "I have already purchased the entire airport here, as well as some coastline in southern Los Diego for the launch site. But, I need your brilliance at the head of all this. You are the right leader for this team. I have a business brain, so I am not the right wolf for that job."

Tyler's brain was buzzing with thought, *"Maybe this is the legacy I have been looking for."* He continued, "I have all the archives from his work back then, but maybe with inspiration from all this," Tyler pointed to the piles of debris scattered about the hanger. "We can really eclipse what has been done before."

"What do you say?" The large wolf smiled at the smaller coyote. "I think your company can run just fine without your watchful eye."

Tyler reached out a paw, "I am in."

***

"Welcome to High Tech on the Global News Network, I am Victor Simonoff." A ruddy haired presenter sat behind a desk in a blue casual suit. "Tonight's big story is Tyler Dresden, of Dres-Tek, has announced a new joint venture with Pierce Industries."

The screen switched over to a press conference in front of Dres-Tek. Tyler and Neville were standing out in the sunlight behind a wall of microphones on the podium erected in front of an awe inspiring piece of stainless steel corporate art in a pond.

"Today, I would like to formally announce that I am personally teaming up with Neville Pierce of Pierce Industries in a new venture that, I promise, will reshape the world as we know it." Tyler paused, listening to the camera flashes clicking away. "We are forming a joint venture company together and this will be Dresden-Pierce Aerospace and Exploration."

Tyler continued, "Over the past sixty years, people around the globe have tried to conquer space but have not made a lot of progress. My father was at the forefront of that research and unfortunately his life was cut tragically short in the pursuit of that dream. I have decided to continue my father's passion in pursuit of knowledge and advancement of all the people of Earth. We intend to revolutionize the whole industry with new technologies that will build upon my father's work and new technologies will be developed by our new company." He paused again. "We are bringing on the best and brightest engineers and scientists for this endeavor. With the combined technologies and financial resources that Dres-Tek and Pierce Industries bring to the table we have the resources to accomplish this."

Glancing for a moment over the crowd to see their reaction, Tyler continued. "I will personally be heading up the scientific operations while Neville will deal with the business aspects. That will free me up to put my whole attention to make this happen quickly, accurately and most importantly, safely."

For all those Dres-Tek investors that may have concerns over me changing my focus, I have already made arrangements for my Senior Vice President to take over the day-to-day operations and it will be in very, very good hands." Tyler smiled, "Don't worry, what we learn, discover and invent will be licensed allowing development of consumer tech that will be useful for the entire world."

The screen switched back to the studio desk.

"What an incredible development." Victor stated enthusiastically. "I am personally excited to see what comes out of the joint venture of these two powerhouses. The stock market took well to the news, as Dres-Tek stock jumped nearly 40% on the news. Pierce Industries is a completely private company so we have no real information other than they have very, very deep pockets."

The screen popped up a closeup image of Neville Pierce. "A bit of a shocker today was the public appearance of Neville Pierce. Pierce has been the never seen, secretive figure behind the world's largest and wealthiest private company. Jean St. Claire has always been the on-camera identity we all are familiar with. There has been much speculation over the years on just who Normal Pierce was but today we know for sure that the black wolf standing next to Tyler was indeed the man himself. Why Neville Pierce chose today's event to make his first public appearance and reveal the man behind the curtain has yet to be seen."

"We will keep bringing you up-to-date news, as more information on this historic event unfolds."

Chapter 26

Ingrid Sjöberg – Part 2

Within six months of returning back home Ingrid had taken complete control of her family's company. Many of the executives she had in place to run the business couldn't deal with her life choices quit or she removed them due to insubordination. With the new financial resources she had access to (thanks in no small part to the deal she made with NP Financial) she expanded the company into the largest high-tech industrial manufacturer on the planet over the next few years. Moreover, they had spread into automotive, aerospace and electronic manufacturing under a series of subsidiary companies focused on the different markets.

Rory joined Ingrid in running the company after they had got married. He seemed to have a real knack for people, probably from his time working at a bank as a loan manager. "Here's that contract with Dres-Tek for you to have a last look at." Rory had printed it out for her to read at home this morning. Ingrid preferred to read them in physical form, rather than digital. "All the details should have been revised."

"Thank you, dear," Ingrid kissed him on the nose, as she took the papers. "That is some radical new machinery they want us to make. I wonder what Tyler Dresden is cooking up that needs such precision work."

"Yeah, who knows. That guy is an absolute genius. Just like all coyotes," he gave her a really goofy, tongue lolling out the side of his muzzle expression.

"Do I need to get a rolled up newspaper?" She pretended to swat at his butt as he walked out of the kitchen on his way to the shower.

***

After reading through the contract and then heading into the office for the day, she plopped down into her office chair. She grabbed a pen from the drawer, signed the contract and then pressed the intercom, "Alicia, come and take this contract down to legal so they can process it. Thanks." Moments later, her assistant came in and took the signed document.

Ingrid turned her head to the computer and started going through the emails. "Garbage, garbage, garbage, Tyler Dresden ... well, there's something that is possibly interesting." She opened the email.

> 'Mrs Sjöberg, I want to speak directly with you about a new contract. I have sent off a fresh mutual NDA to your assistant for you. This project is for my new joint venture, Dresden-Pierce Aerospace and Exploration, and I would like to stress just how important is that this is kept strictly confidential.'

"Huh," came out of her mouth. She reached over to the intercom. "Alicia, did we get a letter from Dresden-Pierce Aerospace and Exploration?"

The box squawked back, "Let me check." There was a minute of silence, as she could hear her assistant shuffling through the documents on her desk. "Yes, a courier, or maybe private security, delivered it this morning. The black wolf was huge so probably security. I will bring it to you."

"Bring your notary stamp when you come in," Ingrid mentioned.

Ingrid thanked Alicia, then opened it and read through the document. It was pretty much boilerplate top security NDA language and just like anything she had for Dres-Tek. She signed it and her assistant notarized it. The package came with pretty explicit instructions about calling the person who made the delivery and they would come and pick it up personally.

***

The rest of the day was pretty much routine: contracts, review meetings, production meetings and the like. At about five in the afternoon, Alicia buzzed in.

"A Mr. Dresden is on the phone. He wants to have a video conference with you. Can you take one right now?" Alicia asked.

"Yes, give him my mobile number and have him call me."

Ingrid moved over to a couch that she had in her office and set her phone up on a stand. Just as she finished, the video call came in. "Hello, this is Ingrid Sjöberg."

The phone screen popped up with Tyler Dresden in a white, unremarkable looking conference room. "Good afternoon Mrs Sjöberg. Happy to get to speak with you in person."

"Same here, Mr Dresden," she affirmed back to Tyler. "What can I do for you?"

"I only have a few minutes right now, but I have a proposition for you." He reached a claw up to the phone and the camera reversed to show the room. "We are working on a really exciting project here at Dresden-Pierce Aerospace and Exploration, I'll call it DPEA for short."

The screen moved as he started walking to a wall of items standing in well-lit shelves. Inside, there were rows of clear acrylic cases just like one would see in a museum. "These. These are alien artifacts that have been collected from around the world. They all are pieces of technology that we are working to reverse engineer. We want to understand their technology and bring these advancements to the world."

Ingrid grabbed her phone so she could have a better look at the objects.

As he panned the camera across the rows of them, he continued speaking, "These are only small pieces of the puzzle. They are key to what we are doing but not the biggest piece." He walked out through a door into a very white, brightly lit location. His phone panned across the room revealing a large aircraft hanger. There were large groupings of wreckage arranged on the floor. "These are parts of the alien spacecraft that Mr. Pierce has spent years and a small fortune acquiring. Many of these were rescued from deep within the ocean at great expense and difficulty."

He flipped the camera back to himself. "We are going to learn from all this tech and get serious about space exploration again." He slowly walked back into the conference room and sat down in a chair. "We are putting all of the puzzle pieces together: scientists, astrophysicists, engineers and the like, but we need to find a strategic partner to help us build and manufacture the parts."

The coyote settled his phone on a holder on the desk. "You have made a lot of excellent equipment for Dres-Tek and I want your company to be that strategic partner as I know your quality and business ethics."

Ingrid leaned forward, "I would be most interested in being that partner."

"Excellent," he smiled. "I'll get the contracts over to your legal team. They will be non-specific as I only want you and your husband to know the details of what we are working on." He paused, "Oh, one little more detail! All of the manufacturing needs to be onsite so you will need to set up new operations here locally. Is that a problem?"

She thought about it. "No, we already have been setting up operations globally so it would be all up to the contract."

Tyler flickered his ears, "No doubt. This will be a very lucrative contract Ingrid. Your company will be extremely well paid for this top secret work. Now, I have to jump off. Look forward to meeting you in person."

She said goodbye and Tyler ended the call.

"This sounds like the most exciting thing going on ANYWHERE on the planet," she thought to herself.

"This rain is driving me nuts," Renata said out loud to Damião, her dig partner. They were back at the excavation site at the Aislado temple. Her fur was soaked, cheek fur dripping and was making her uncomfortably damp all over. They were trying to excavate one of the collapsed entrances but all the rain was making everything really slow going. They have been working on the site for about two years now and last month they identified the entrance to the lower level on the back side on the building.

"Yeah," Damião said showing his arms covered in mud up to his elbows. "It's a pain for me to clean up this clay, I can't imagine how much 'fun' it would be for you now." He smirked at her, when he finished his words.

Renata wrinkled up her face, "Yeah yeah, laugh it up. Though I do have a new appreciation for full body showers now."

They had slowly revealed stone steps down into the lower building after removing a ton of dirt and building stones that had filled up the stairway. Once they had reached the passage into the interior the carpenters have been making progress in reinforcing the ceiling, but that had really slowed their progress to about 10 meters per day. The team was really excited to find out what secrets lie within the temple. *"Was it a tomb of a leader? What kind of artifacts will be found? What will we learn about these people?"* she couldn't help keep thinking to herself.

The grant they received allowed them to have a half dozen laborers on their crew. They were very hard workers and she was very glad to have them as they couldn't make much progress on the dig without them. None of them seemed to be bothered by her appearance which was a blessing. She ran across so many people in rural areas who were clearly uncomfortable around her.

"Okay fellas," Damião said aloud to the group. "Time to head back down the hill before we lose the light." They all spent about 10 minutes putting away their tools before hiking down the grade to their trucks. They were camping at the site for five to seven days at a time and today was the day to head back down the mountain to take a break. When they got approval to start excavations, they had opened up a larger path so they could bring their vehicles a lot closer to the site.

"Good thing these seats are waterproof." Her soggy fur and clothes made a soppy splat noise when she sat down in the truck. "I will be happy if we get a few days of uninterrupted sunlight next week." The engine of the truck sputtered to life and Damião put it in drive to begin their rough four hour ride back to the village.

***

The shower was a god send as she had to get a week's worth of dirt and grime out of her fur. It had been an especially wet week and she looked forward to a nice sleep in a dry bed. The excavation team had constructed a few new small houses in the village for the dig team so they had a place to stay that wasn't just borrowing a room from the locals.

The next day, Renata climbed out of bed and could see the clear sky from the single window in the hut. *"Well, where was that this past week?"* she chuckled to herself while putting on some clothes to head outside to meet up with the team for some breakfast.

She greeted Damião and they started walking down to the supply building in order to get some food. Off in the distance, a rhythmic chopping sound started growing in intensity and they both turned to look. Over one of the hills a helicopter came into view and started circling the valley. Soon, it settled onto the road down by the fields where it was open enough to land. "Curious," Damião remarked. "That must be for us. No choppers come out this way just for the farmers."

She nodded in agreement and they walked down the road towards the helicopter. As they approached, the pilot shut off the engines and the passenger door opened. A man stepped out wearing a business suit and looked completely out of place here in the mountain valley. He peeked his head inside to say something to the pilot before shutting the door.

The man then turned and saw the two approaching him. "Ms. Alonso and Mr. Ramirez?" the man questioned at them. "I am David Coppernick." He extended a hand to them in greeting. After shaking their hands he added, "I am glad I caught you here at the village. I'm sorry to surprise you like this but I represent the Pierce Foundation, which provided the grant for your work here."

"Nice to meet you." Renata spoke, "What brings you all the way out here to the Tacuarembó province? Must be important."

"Yes, I came out here at the personal request of Neville Pierce." David paused for a moment and then continued. "Mr. Pierce has been actively keeping up with your findings out here but I come with an unrelated request for you personally, Renata."

"Oh?" She was intrigued of what he could want that would warrant sending out an office guy to meet with her in the remote wilderness. "Sure, would you like to head up to the village so we can sit down?

"Yes, please," he remarked, as they began walking up the path to her bungalow. Once they got up to here cabin, Damião excused himself. David and Renata sat down in the simple chairs she had inside her room. He opened up his briefcase and pulled out a manila envelope and handed it to Renata. "Take a look at these."

She opened up the envelope, slid a battery of photos out and started thumbing through them. "What are these?" she asked David.

"Those," he paused, then said, "Those are alien artifacts that Mr. Pierce has been collecting for a long time and he wants your assistance. Your anthropological knowledge will be invaluable to his work. He asked me to invite you to São Paulo to meet in person to discuss what he needs."

"I don't know. This discovery has just revealed a new chamber and I don't know if I can just fly off and not be here." she said.

"I understand. This request is a bit out of the ordinary." David nodded his head in acknowledgment. "I am also here to offer 10 more years of funding for this project. Plus the annual support will be triple what it is so you can increase the scope of the work here. This offer is regardless of whether or not you can assist on his new endeavor, no strings attached. The trip would only be a few days and I assure you it's a worthwhile project.

Renata mulled it over for a few minutes. *"What's a couple of days?"* she thought to herself. "Sure, I'll go and speak with Mr. Pierce."

"Good, Neville was pretty sure you would be interested." He paused, then smiled at her, "I am pretty sure the dig will be in good hands with Damião in your absence. Shall we head out then?"

"Sounds good. I will meet you down at the helicopter. I need to put some clothes together for a few day's stay and let Damião know I will be gone for a few days."

After David got up and headed down the hill, she knocked on Damião's door, "Neville Pierce has tripled the annual budget for the dig and extended it to 10 years, no strings attached. He also wants me to head to São Paulo for a personal meeting. I will be back in a couple of days when it's time to go back up the hill. It must be nice to have such deep pockets that he can just throw cash at this dig with no promise of anything in return."

Damião nodded at her not showing much emotion, but being genuinely pleased for her. Then he said, "Great news on the funding. Hopefully it's an interesting discussion. I'll see you in a few days."

***

Renata was nervous, as she had never ridden in a helicopter before. The trip took about an hour and half to get to São Paulo and she spent most of the trip looking out the window at the wonderful scenery below. The helicopter descended down to a small airport and landed near a white industrial building.

Once down on the ground with the engines shut down, they both got out and walked over to a door that had a very plain sign that said 'Pierce Industries'. David opened the personnel door for her. Once inside the structure she was met with a hanger containing a private jet being serviced by a couple of technicians who looked at her idly as they walked past them. They headed over to a small office placed at the back of the hanger. David opened the door for her and they went inside.

"Welcome!" A large black canine looked up from a stack of files, stood up and walked over to her. "Ms. Alonso," he greeted her with a giant paw, "I am Neville Pierce. Please," he waved an arm towards the conference table. "Have a seat." After she and David sat down, he joined them. His chair creaked in protest as his large frame sat down on the dainty chair.

Renata looked at him, "It is a pleasure to meet you, Mr. Pierce. That was a pretty unusual way to get me to a meeting." She smiled at him.

"Yeah, I have such a busy schedule and most of my time is completely booked. I was down this way for other business. I really wanted to talk to you about a project that could really use your expertise." He poked at his phone with a claw and the images she saw in the photos appeared on a wall. "These...as David mentioned, are alien artifacts." The images started cycling through close-ups of different artifacts. "I know you aren't an expert in alien tech, so this may seem a little out of your wheelhouse but I assure you that you'll understand why I brought you here."

He looked over to her to speak. "I have been collecting every artifact that I can get my hands on. I have been fascinated by how my species came into existence and I have devoted a lot of financial resources to obtaining them. You may have heard, but I just recently formed a partnership with the tech magnate Tyler Dresden to help me find out who they were and how their technology works." He paused for a second. "You probably wonder why I would like an anthropologist, specializing in primitive earth cultures, to help us in space exploration? Well, I hope to extract data from these items and I will need help deciphering their language and culture from their recordings in order to understand them."

"That sounds like a tough job. How much of this data has been recovered?" she asked bluntly.

"We are close to cracking their recording technology thanks to the genius of Tyler Dresden. He had cracked some of their communication tech previously which you will find in all Dres-tek mobile phones," he lifted up his own phone to illustrate his point. "Currently, we haven't gotten any useful data because so much of it was destroyed, but I have a plan to get more data."

Renata pulled out her phone and mulled things over in her head. "How am I going to offer any more insight than Mr. Dresden can? I know nothing about tech. I just know about old temples, ancient carvings and civilizations."

"What you do is completely relevant to our mission. I want someone that understands ancient cultures and can use that same line of
thinking to build a picture of who these aliens were. Someone who
can weave together an entire culture's thinking, just in the way you
have done for ancient humans civilizations." He pulled out one of
her books she wrote five years ago on a minor southern San Juarezian
society. "Someone just like you. Not everyone can do that and you
have a gift for it."

She looked back over to the view screen while it was still cycling
through the artifact photos. "Well, most humans are...well...human,
so that always came easy to me. What's to say these aliens think
anything remotely like humans do?"

"I don't have any idea," he nodded. "I do think I have a way though."
He tapped at his phone again and a new image popped up on the
viewer. "This. This is the key that unlocks the future."

Renata got up to go stand in front of the screen to get a closer look.
"What am I looking at here?"

Neville got up and came over to stand by her. "This is the key.
This was spotted back in the 90's, but has been largely ignored by the
scientific community and the global government since its discovery."
He clicked his phone again and the image zoomed in and more detail
became apparent. "This, I believe, is a piece of the original spacecraft
that crashed here on Earth and is in a long orbit around the planet.
Just like a comet around the sun. It appears to be pretty intact and we
are going to retrieve it next time it comes close. If it's what I think it
is, we should have a treasure trove of intact data and technology. Your
work will help us decipher it and to learn who they were and why they
came here."

"That's a lot to take in," she gazed directly into Neville's yellow
eyes.

"I am 100% sure you can help crack this and to show you how
serious I am," he looked over at David and nodded. David stood up
and handed her a bound document. "Take a look at this."

She took the document that David handed her and started thumbing
through it.

"You will be paid handsomely for your work. This is the most
exciting project I can think of in all of history and I am pouring
enormous amounts of capital and resources into it." He turned to
look at the alien artifact image still showing on his phone screen and
put his arms behind his back while thinking. "This will change the

course of history." Neville turned to look at her. "You can help do that. Interested?"

She began parsing all this information in her head, while flipping through the details of the contract. This would set her for life and she wouldn't ever need to worry about money or grants ever again. Several moments went by when she looked up, her violet eyes sparkling with excitement. "Yes. Yes I am."

"Haoqi!" Maya jumped up into a full-body hug with her friend.

"OOF!" Haoqi made a noise pretending to be tackled by her. "I didn't know I was a tackling dummy. Training for football?" He grinned at her as he put her back down on her feet. "Shall we go inside?" He pointed to the same café where they reunited six months ago.

They walked inside and proceeded to the counter. "It seems so long ago that we came to this place. Still the same here." She looked to the barista behind the counter, "I will take a rose tea, please."

Haoqi ordered his usual coffee and they both went to sit down at the same table they had before. They had met up about twice a month after getting back in touch with each other a few years ago. "So, the book went on sale last Monday."

"Ooo...how are sales looking?" Maya looked up as the server brought them their drinks.

"Well, first day sales seem alright. It's not on track to be a best seller but better than the first one." He took a sip of coffee, wrinkled his nose and put a scoop of sugar in it. "It has a lot of positive reviews from legitimate reviewers but you do NOT want to read the comments on the book seller's pages. So many angry people out there spouting unjustified hatred for the subject. They hadn't even read it and were giving it one star reviews," he just shook his head after sayin that aloud. "There are twice as many bad reviews than the number that have actually sold. They should not let people put in a review without having purchased the book."

Maya reached across the table and grabbed his hands, "I'm sorry."

"Well, either way my sponsor was really happy with the book and I got paid plenty enough, even without sales." He smiled. "Besides, I have another meeting with Mr. Pierce later today for a new project."

"Oh, do tell me my dear Haoqi!" She lifted her cup of tea and took a sip.

Haoqi smiled when she said that. "Oh, they haven't told me anything of what the project is. I have to get the non-disclosure agreement in place first." He furrowed his brow and his eyes darted back and forth. "It's TOP-SECRET," he whispered.

Maya swatted at his shoulder, "Silly man." She sat back in her chair cradling her tea cup with both paws.

"Oh, how did your presentation at the university go last week?" he asked her.

"Great, the auditorium was packed. Seems like there are a lot of canids who are struggling for spiritual identity in this world and I'm glad to be able to offer them a way to feel like they belong in this world. It's great to feel needed by the community." About 3 months ago Maya had taken a teaching position and her first semester had started a few weeks ago.

***

Maya parted with Haoqi outside the cafe and headed back to the university to get some more work done. Her office was on the second floor of the Religious Studies building and while she was climbing the last flight of steps she pulled out her keys from her pocket. She flipped through them and found the key to open her office door at the university.

Just as she opened the door she heard, "Miss Maya Metta?" She turned to look at who said her name.

"Hi there, yes I am Maya. How may I help you?" She flickered her ears as a flash of worry crossed her mind. There was a large black wolf in a green leather jacket obviously following her up the stairs.

"I am sorry to startle you. I am Ivan Grecov and I am personal security for Mr. Neville Pierce," he said in a deep rumbling voice. "Mr. Pierce would like to speak with you. He is in the car outside and would like just a few minutes of your time to discuss an opportunity."

"Huh. Neville Pierce is here to see me personally?" That's odd," Maya thought to herself wondering if this was a ruse to abduct her. "Umm. Calling for an appointment would have been a little bit better," she said nervously looking past him down the stairs.

Sensing and hearing the apprehension in her voice, Ivan spoke in a reassuring tone "Mr. Pierce would be happy to come up and discuss this in your office, if you prefer?"

"That would be great," she smiled and turned back to Ivan, "Give me a few minutes to get these papers in their place," she said nodding towards her office.

A few minutes passed by as she nervously filed her student's papers. She had left the door open so she could see them approach. Ivan and another equally large black wolf, who was sharply dressed in an obviously very expensive tailored suit, approached the open door. *"That one would obviously be Mr. Pierce, I kind of recognized him from the recent news,"* Maya thought.

"May I come in?" he asked as he approached the door.

"Sure, have a seat." The wolf turned his head to the door and nodded to Ivan as he shut the door closed behind him. Then, he had a seat in her office.

"I am sorry for not giving you any warning for my visit. I am Neville Pierce. I have a very tight schedule and through some luck had a cancellation in my schedule. I really wanted to stop by with a proposal for you. I had called your department and the person I spoke with said you had office hours so I took a gamble and came to meet with you."

"Nice to meet you," she was still wondering what such a powerful figure would want with a young professor like her.

"I know you have work to get to so I will get straight to the point." He handed her an envelope with a bunch of photos. "I have been acquiring artifacts from the extraterrestrial crashed ship for many years. You might have heard of the partnership that my company and

Tyler Dresden have formed called 'Dresden-Pierce Aerospace and Exploration', or DPEA for short. Our purpose is to figure out who these aliens were and unlock the secrets their technology holds."

Maya shuffled through the pictures and stopped at one that looks like a picture taken in outer space of a beat up cylindrical object. "How can I help? I'm not a technologist, engineer or scientist, I am a theologist."

"Ahh, but there's more to it than figuring out the technology." He pointed to the pictures she was holding, "We are working on extracting data from their tech that we can use to decipher their language and piece together what their civilization must be like."

"Again, I'm not a linguist either so how would I help?" she said, with a slightly negative tone.

"We have world renowned anthropologist Renata Alonso on the project team, and I want you to work with her to decipher their culture. I think to properly figure out who they were, we need to have more than just a scientific approach to figure them out. Do you think if someone was trying to figure out this planet that scientists alone could properly write our history?" Neville sat back in his chair.

She crinkled up her face thinking about it. "I don't know. That's a lot to think about."

"I know. Have a think about it." He reached down and packed up the pictures into the envelope. "I need to keep these pictures for security unfortunately, but.." he placed another envelope on the desk. "This is the contract I am offering and it has details about the salary. Think about it and call my office next Friday. You wouldn't be needed until after this semester is over anyway so you can finish out with your students, regardless. I can guarantee you will find this to be intellectually satisfying and exciting."

***

"Excuse me, your tea, ma'am," the server said casually as they server placed the cup down in front of Maya.

She was dreading the conversion she was about to have with Haoqi as she had become quite fond of spending time with him over the past six months. She wanted to accept it but was having second thoughts about leaving the university and her friend so soon. She stared out the window of the café in contemplation, watching the rain softly fall on the street outside. The café door rang as it opened and Haoqi came inside waving to her. He closed his umbrella and stowed it by the door, before sitting in the booth seat across from her.

"Man, it's wet outside." He smiled. He then turned to the server signaling he wanted his usual coffee.

She looked at his neatly trimmed head of hair. "You got a new haircut. You look all respectable now."

"It was time for a change. Lots of change," he smiled over at her. From her expression, he could sense that something was troubling her, "Something's up. What's going on?" He reached over and placed his hand over hers.

"Well...change," she looked down at his hand. "I ..." she couldn't speak for a moment before looking up at him. "I have been offered a once-in-a-lifetime opportunity that will require me to move to Up-town over in River City." She sniffled a little as she started to get sad.

"Oh, do tell," he reached out and squeezed her hand.

"I...can't say much as it's a secret project, but I would be working for Dresden-Pierce Aerospace and Exploration," smiling at him meekly then looking back down. "I fought long and hard with myself on this decision. I love this city, I love what I do at the university but I just can't pass this up."

Haoqi reached his hand up to her chin and applied a little pressure to raise her face back up to his. "Well, I think I know what's really bothering you," he let his mouth twist into a lopsided smirk. "You won't be doing this alone. I have an offer in my hands from them as well."

Maya looked up at him with tearing eyes, "Really?" she sniffled.

"Yes, and now I know I won't be breaking your heart if I accepted my offer." They both stood up and gave each other a long hug.

***

"Alright, time for me to head to the airport." Haoqi had sold most of his apartment furnishings before shipping out the few things he cared to keep. "I will see you in a few months when your semester is over and are able to join me out there," he said before giving her a smooch on her nose before giving her a tight hug.

"Bye for now." Maya smiled at him.

"Oh, one more thing," his lips curled into a huge grin, "I will have a great surprise for you when you arrive."

"Ooo....that's evil. Making me wait three months for the reveal," she poked a claw at his sternum. "Truly, truly evil."

They heard a honk from a car horn outside. "Okay, that's my ride. See you in three months!"

***

The semester had ended uneventfully and without much drama before she flew out for her new job. The past three months were really tough due to the excitement of the new job. Without Haoqi to meet up with, she grew a little restless. He had initially called her during the first week but unfortunately would not be able to speak with her for a couple of months due to some training. She got to briefly chat with him after the training but his voice was wrecked. It was as if he had a nasty cold so he couldn't talk for very long.

She had never been on a plane before and Mr. Pierce had graciously sent a private jet to pick her up which was quite a luxury. The plane softly touched down at a small airfield outside of Uptown and it taxied over to a building where she would be working. A person on the ground opened up the stairs on the plane and she walked down them slowly.

The plane's engines fully throttled down as a small group came out to greet her. There was Neville Pierce, a coyote that she recognized as Tyler Dresden and a white wolf dressed in a casual suit.

"Ms. Metta." Tyler walked up to her and offered a hand, "Welcome to the team."

"Looking forward to this, it's exciting!" She smiled at Tyler. "Mr. Pierce, good to see you again." She then looked over at the third canid standing there, "I haven't met you yet." She extended a hand and instead of shaking her hand, the wolf gave her a big, tight hug.

"Welcome, my darling!" and he gave her a quiet smooch on the nose.

"Wait a minute..." She recognized the voice, although a little deeper than before. "Haoqi? Is that you? How?"

"Yes!" he exclaimed. "I am going to be the documentarian for the company. I'll be filming, interviewing and eventually producing a film." He reached down and took both her hands in his, "I always felt awkward that I fell for you since I was human and you weren't."

He nodded over in Neville's direction, "Pierce industries has a subsidiary that has a treatment for terminal patients that 100% cures them, but the side effects are this," he pointed at himself. "I initially told them that I wouldn't take the job if you didn't accept yours as I couldn't be without you. He was moved by my dedication to you so he offered me an option to become like you. So damn right I said yes." He gave a toothy grin. "Two months of training was actually the treatment."

Maya stepped back with a concerned expression on her face, "Wait ... were you sick?"

Haoqi realized what she must have thought, "No, no, no, I wasn't sick. The treatment works for any human. Think of this as 'cosmetic' surgery." He smiled at Maya.

Maya's expression softened and she gazed lovingly into his eyes, "Oh you. I would have loved you regardless, you idiot." Then she hugged him tightly.

"That is all we have time for tonight. Thanks for tuning into the 'State of Politics' on FNN. I am Hiro Adachi." the young fox said to the camera.

"And I am Jeo Seong. See you next time!" Hiro's co-anchor finished with his sign-off phrase of the broadcast. The off-air bell chimed, "And we're off!" the studio director said aloud. "Great show tonight."

"Well Hiro, that was a good segment. Interesting to be able to get a picture of who is already thinking of running." Jeo added, "These election seasons are starting earlier and earlier."

"It's fascinating. It seems that one cycle isn't even over and we're already talking about the next one." Hiro smiled to his colleague. "I mean, it's ONLY two and half years till the next one."

Hiro and Jeo got up and walked off the set. As he walked out Hiro stopped and thanked everyone personally as he passed them, like he always did. *"These people make this all work, without them I would be nothing,"* he thought to himself while exchanging pleasantries.

"Hey Hiro!" Max Ketterin said as Hiro was walking by. "Want to get some sushi?" Max was a great kid, bright eyed and bushy...well not bushy tailed, per se, as the young man was human and didn't have a tail. He was an intern trying to cut his teeth in production. He was green but very enthusiastic and Hiro took a liking to him.

"Not tonight, I have to do some research in the morning on next week's guests." He fist bumped Max as he was headed to his green room. "These are going to be tough people to 'debate'. Maybe next week?"

"Sure man. Have a great night," the intern said as Hiro turned to leave.

Hiro got to his dressing room and headed in but stopped to check out the hallway before closing the door behind him. *"Glad Clarissa wasn't nearby,"* he thought to himself. She was really trying hard to make something happen between them but he just wasn't interested. After his 'accident' he found himself not really attracted to human women much and especially not Clarissa. He couldn't put a finger on it, but *'maybe it's her perfume?'* Shaking his head and saying aloud, "Who knows." He certainly could smell everything about someone now. Even after six years of his better nose it still overwhelmed him a little.

His ear swiveled to the door as he heard someone walking up to it. He waited for the inevitable knock.

"Hey Hiro, may I come in?" The voice was from a younger production assistant.

"Sure Jeanine. Door's open."

She opened the door and stepped through. "A courier just now dropped off a letter for you. Strange that it came so late. It must be important." She handed it to him before excusing herself and shut the door behind her.

Sitting down on the couch, he opened the large envelope and slid the document out a little. The letter head said 'NP Legal' and was from Neville Pierce. It was addressed directly to him and not the show. "That's interesting." Now that Neville Pierce had come out of the shadows during Tyler Dresden's aerospace project press conference Hiro had taken a keen interest in the man. He was dying to score an interview with the fellow behind the world's largest, private global conglomerate.

He pulled the letter completely out of the manila envelope and set it aside. Reading out loud, "Mr. Adachi. I will be in town this week for business and I would like to formally invite you to meet with me later this week. I have been watching your career and have taken note of just how astute you are at political analysis and I am impressed. I believe that you and I have many things to offer each other. If you are interested, please reach out to my assistant at the phone number and email listed below. Regards, Neville Pierce, CEO of Pierce Industries."

Setting the letter down, Hiro sat back in the couch. "This could be a huge break. I would love to get him on the show." Mentally calculating the time zone differences, he realized it was the morning at their headquarters.

He quickly grabbed his phone and dialed the number. The conversation was brief but she had Hiro booked for lunch with Mr. Pierce on Thursday at a nearby restaurant.

***

Thursday morning came around and Hiro put on his best pinstriped suit because 'Azabu Ginza Sushi' was definitely a place that had a dress code and he really wanted to look sharp. The place wasn't in walking distance so he would have to hail a taxi to take him there.

The restaurant was in a very upscale part of downtown. As he stepped up out of the cab, he was faced with three stories of imposing glass that reflected the bustling street behind him. He pushed open the door to the restaurant and was immediately greeted by four people. As he introduced himself, they ushered him to the side and away from the busy part of the dining room to a private room.

"Mr. Pierce is expecting you." The staff member said as they opened the door for him.

As he entered, Neville Pierce got up from the chabudai he was seated behind, revealing just how large of a wolf he was. "Welcome Mr. Adachi," and he reached out to shake the young fox's hand. "My business concluded a little early so I took the liberty of ordering food for us. Please, sit down and enjoy the best sushi in the province."

Hiro looked over at the massive amount of sushi on the table and quickly estimated that it must be a thousand dollars worth. "Thank you, Mr. Pierce," the reporter said, sitting down when his host did.

After getting seated, Neville spoke, "Please, call me Neville and dig in." He motioned to the seat across from him.

Hiro admired the stainless steel chopsticks at his place setting and then plated himself some salmon. "I appreciate the invite to sit down with you. What did you have in mind today?" Hiro reached for a writing tablet he had in his jacket pocket.

"No need to take notes, this isn't an interview my friend. It's for something else." The wolf took a large chunk of a roll and popped it in his mouth. After swallowing it down, he continued speaking. "I have seen the analysis you have done on your show and I can say that your conclusions have been uncannily on the mark and I'm impressed." He popped another roll into his mouth. Neville continued, "You see, I grew up poor, disadvantaged and worked very, very hard to get to where I am at today. The world threw everything at me to keep me down. I even had to do some unpleasant things that I, frankly, am ashamed of. But I overcame my obstacles to be successful. I had lots of help along the way for sure since I couldn't do it all myself. I surrounded myself with top notch advisors and all of us built my company into what it is today."

As Neville was speaking, Hiro ate a couple pieces of the salmon he had while listening intently. *"Ooh...he is giving me some juicy info, I wish I could take notes,"* he thought.

"You see, I want all of my kind to have the same opportunities that everyone else on this planet can have and not suffer, like I did as a youth, just to survive. This is one of my top goals. You were actually a bit lucky that you didn't have to grow up a canid with all the prejudice and hatred out there. Not to downplay the trauma you must have had dealing with the accident or anything, but I think it turned out good for you in the end."

"I can only imagine. A lot of people's perceptions of me had definitely changed since the accident." Hiro really didn't want to interrupt his story, so he didn't add anything more.

"So that brings me to why I asked you here." He reached into his briefcase and handed Hiro a paper. "We want to get some more friendly faces in government around the world and I am throwing a considerable amount of capital and people at this upcoming election." He pointed at the sheet, "That is a list of congressional districts that we think are flippable. Take a look and give me your quick assessment."

Hiro was getting the sneaky suspicion that this was *indeed* an interview, just not with Mr. Pierce but being given *by* him. Hiro scanned through the list and went 'hmmmm' softly before reaching into his jacket to grab a pen. On the first pass through he immediately crossed off four of them. "I don't think you can flip these. There's just not enough support there for a canid candidate." He turned the document towards Neville and tapped at the names with a claw.

"We can run a human ally there if we need to. They don't all have
to be one of us. I also have some other tactics I can use." Neville took
a sip of some sake.

'*Us.*' Hiro never really thought of himself as one since he wasn't
natural born. "Okay, then there's probably two you might get. I'd
suggest running these people," He quickly scribbled down a couple
of names. "Now, that leaves 18 districts." He studied the list some
more before finally asking, "Three of them already have progressive
senators. Any particular reason they are listed?" Hiro pointed at them
with his pen.

"Yes. They are unfortunately ineffective and a bit too worried about
re-election. They haven't been able to foster the community support
we need and we want to get someone better in there."

"Okay, here's who I would run in those." Hiro replied as he scribbled
a couple more names. "*This is definitely a test,*" the fox thought to
himself.

The wolf leaned over to look at the list and nodded. "Good choices.
That third one is a surprise but might work." Neville looked at the
expression on the fox's face. "You're a clever fox so I'm sure you have
figured this out a while ago," he handed a glass of Saki to Hiro. "I
want to hire you. I need someone with your talents on this project."
He reached into his briefcase, pulled out a thick bound document and
handed it to Hiro.

Scanning through the booklet to understand what was being offered, he slowly closed it. It was an extremely stout offer at more
than four times what he was currently making. He tilted his head up
from the document and looked Neville in the eyes. "This sounds right
up my alley, so that's a 'yes', Mr. Pierce."

"Great!" he said very loudly. "Now what do you think of the rest of
the list?"

Grabbing the original list he started making notes next to each
incumbent. He had all the districts marked, but when he got to an
infamous district in Heartstone, he was drawing a blank. He paused
for a bit, tapping the pen on the table because he was struggling to
come up with a candidate. He reached for his sake glass, took a sip,
and then it hit him. He scribbled a name down. He knew this one
was a long shot but he thought with the right team, it could be done.
"Here, that's my quick list."

The wolf reached for the paper and studied it. "Most of these make perfect sense, good job. Now this one," he turned the paper around and pointed to one. "Do you think it can be done? This one doesn't hold any elected seat currently and is pretty young."

"Yes, yes I do. It will take a lot of hard work, top dollar spending and some great coaching but he's got a lot of popularity and charisma. Plus, he's a local celebrity."

"I can see you have a plan in your head on how to get this done. Would you be interested in being his campaign manager if I can get him to agree?" Neville asked, "You'd have to move there for a spell, but we'll take care of everything financially and get you the best team. Here," Neville reached out and slid Hiro's offer letter back over to himself, crossed off the salary and scribbled a new number. "That should really make this worthwhile to you."

Hiro mulled it over in his head for a bit. Neville had just doubled the offer. "You get him to say 'yes' and I'll do it."

Neville stood up and extended a paw. "You have a deal. I will get him, rest assured." He shook the fox's paw vigorously. "My assistant will call you tomorrow and we'll nail down the details and get everything set up."

"Speaker. Members of Congress." Senator Martin Bailey said in the microphone as he took his turn to speak. "I come to you today with a grave moral concern." The Senator panned over the crowd for effect. "We have a cancer that is growing in our world. There is a growing plague that pretends to be an altruistic enterprise in their 'so-called' help of the diseased, the amoral and depraved. They pretend to only help those in need. To assist them in 'conversion' of human being into a canines to save their drug addled, disease ridden bodies to give them a new life."

His face was turning a little red with the anger he was projecting with his words. "If GOD said it's YOUR time who are we to disagree with God's judgment?" He pressed his hands down on the podium while staring down the audience. "God himself decreed that they should pass to the great beyond and be judged on their actions in this life. WE cannot disagree with God's will."

"I also have evidence that says these centers are 'converting' people against their will. Taking them in the night from their families and making them in their likeness. Their plan is to wipe out the human race."

The senator shuffled a few note cards before continuing. "That is why today...I am introducing a bill that would make these perverted 'conversions' illegal. There will be no legal path for acknowledgment that the creature that was once a man be considered as the same being and would legally, for all time, be considered deceased."

"I cannot...WILL NOT... stand for this and will do everything in my power to stop this evil from destroying the world that was made for humanity."

***

"Ivan," Neville Piece motioned to a chair in front of the desk as he entered the private and very secure office in his home. "Please, sit down."

"What can I do for you Mr. Pierce?" Ivan queried to his employer and now genetically his surrogate father.

"I'm sure you heard about the speech and bill that Senator Bailey made yesterday." Neville reached into a drawer and pulled out a plain manila envelope and placed it on the desk.

"Yeah, that was quite a show. I was half expecting him to drop dead from a heart attack right there." Ivan added with a toothy grin.

"That would have been good but what I have here will be better." Neville pushed the envelope over to Ivan. "I have a special job for you to do." The wolf nodded down at the envelope so Ivan picked it up and turned it around in his paw. "This package needs a special delivery to our friend."

Ivan held it up towards Neville, his expression silently asking if he can take a peek inside and Neville nodded in assent. He unwrapped the string tie and slid a series of photos out into his palm and started flipping through them. "Whoa. That's some juicy stuff. When do you want this delivered?"

"Tomorrow night at 10 pm, the Senator will be on an interview with Heartstone Tonight." He grinned slyly, exposing one of his fangs. "Be in his dressing room when he gets done and deliver this to him. All you need to do is ask 'Yes or No' and call me afterwards to let me know his answer.'

***

"Good evening and welcome to Heartstone Tonight, I am Troy Alvarez. Tonight, I am joined by Senator Martin Bailey of the River City Prefecture. Welcome to the show Senator."

"Thank you, Troy."

"I wanted to ask you about the recent bill and fiery speech you gave to congress the other day. The general sentiment with the public 'is the canid population is not evil' and are generally liked or tolerated by the majority." Troy glanced down at a card in his hand. "What do you have in response to that statement?"

The Senator almost snorted, "What do I THINK? I thought that would be apparent from my speech. They are animals and not worthy of consideration. The people who support them are morally WRONG and will be judged by God in the end," he crossed his arms, putting up his guard.

"I just wanted to make sure your position was clear to the viewers out there." Troy shuffled to a new info card. "You mentioned in your speech that people are being 'converted' against their will to destroy them and destroy the human race. Do you have any evidence to back up those claims?"

"I have plenty of evidence." the senator said emphatically.

"Have you released this 'evidence'?"

"No, I have not. But you remember that boy, Brennan Clark?" he smiled. "He was 'converted' against his will as an act of political retribution."

"Yes I do. Investigations proved that the individuals were acting alone with no political affiliations, thus no 'masterminds' were behind the attack."

"Do you think Brennan wanted that? It was still an attack and shows the danger that these clinics pose to the greater human race." Martin relaxed back in his chair.

"So, this bill would retroactively strip anyone of their individual identities and force them out of society even though they followed all laws and legal precedence?" Troy looked at the senator straight in the face asking, "After seeing that young man speak after his attack, do you really think he isn't who he was before the attack?"

"No, I do not believe he is. He is now just an animal in my eyes." Senator Bailey closed his arms, signaling he was done with this inter-view.

***

Ivan arrived shortly before the interview began and knocked on the back door four times with a pause for the fifth knock. The door opened and a short ruddy haired man peeked out. The guy took a look around and waved Ivan in, shutting the door behind him.

"You want dressing room B. It's up two flights of stairs. Take a left and the back door is third on the right." the man said.

Ivan thanked him as the man hurriedly walked away and started climbing the dimly lit metal staircase. When he found the right door, he put an ear to the door to hear for any sounds. His new ears gave him amazing hearing so he was confident it was empty. He quietly opened the door, slipped inside and took up residency on a folding chair out of the view of the main door. There, he would wait out of sight for the Senator to return after his interview. The room was pretty plain with very little decor. There was a make-up desk, metal coat rack, a beat up couch and a small bathroom for the guest.

Ivan heard footsteps approaching and some muffled speech. "Yes, let me wash my face and grab my coat. I will have a word with my publicist. I had no idea what I was in for tonight." The door creaked open and the senator stepped inside and headed straight to the bathroom.

Once finished, the man came back into the room, drying his face with a towel so he didn't see Ivan sitting directly across from him. As he was wiping his face, the man realized he wasn't alone and slowly removed the towel from his face. He froze, obviously quite frightened at the hulking wolf casually seated in the chair.

"Senator, please sit down," Ivan gruffed at him as deeply as he could to make sure the man knew he was serious. After waiting for him to sit down, Ivan pulled out the envelope and handed it to him.

"What's this?" Martin looked very annoyed.

"That...is something you'll want to take a deep look at." Ivan grinned to the grinned at Martin with a nice toothy grin he had been working on.

Slowly, the man slid the photos out of the envelope, his face immediately flushed red with anger. "Who are you? What do you want? Money?"

"I am no one of consequence." Ivan smiled, "but you have a choice to make. You can pull the bill and get 'enlightenment' by simply saying 'yes', or have your life destroyed by saying 'no'. Your choice, senator."

The Senator's lips pursed in anger, "I will not be blackmailed!" He threw the pictures back at Ivan, scattering them about the room as they settled to the floor. Some landed face-up, almost mocking the senator.

Ivan stood up to reveal his true size, "I see your answer is 'no' then." Ivan started to head to the back door and turned back to to look at Senator Bailey while in the open doorway. "You keep those as a 'souvenir'." Ivan stated as the door closed behind him and headed down the stairs to hustle out of the building.

***

"We interrupt our normal broadcast tonight with breaking news. I am Troy Alvarez."

"We have just learned that Senator Martin Bailey has resigned from congress following the release of photos and witness testimony to illicit sex acts by Mr. Bailey and three different canine prostitutes."

A video of the senator flashed on the screen:

> "Effective immediately, I resign my commission as a Senator for the Prefecture of River City. I have failed in my duties and have disgraced congress and most importantly my family."

"The senator's staff has not responded to our questions," the commentator stated in a serious tone.

"*Two years.*" Brennan thought to himself. He had been mostly working for NP Legal behind the scenes to support the many legal cases on canine discrimination. He also supported drafts of congressional bill language to try and better the lives and rights of the global canine population. Overall, the growing canine minority had reached nearly 20%. It has been a tough road since there is a very entrenched, and powerful anti-canine establishment across the prefectures, going all the way up to the senate in Capitola.

He was the lead attorney on his latest assignment. He was working directly with Lev Kronovski, a senator from the River City prefect. His district has a higher than average canine population and strong public sentiments for canine equality. The high concentration of canids in River City arose due to the emergence of the region's heavy industry that required unskilled workers. Early River City industry exploited the canines, since they had no legal protections at the turn of the century and could get away with virtual slavery. He successfully convinced the senator to introduce bills limiting the restrictions that medical insurance companies can put on canids, despite their generally hardy constitutions and good health. Though the vote failed, it was close, being only two votes shy of passing.

'*BZZT!*' The phone on Brennan's desk rang. Brennan picked up the phone, "Hi Charlene." Charlene was their general office assistant.

"Good morning. Mr. Pierce called and will be in today at about 10 AM and would like to speak with you. He said it was very important. I took the liberty of booking a two hour slot for you to meet."

"Important?" Brennan though to himself. "Thank you Charlene. Let me know when he is ready for me. I'll keep working on this file in the meantime." He got really nervous, since Neville rarely met with the regular staff working on cases.

Shortly after 10 AM, Charlene rang and let him know that Neville was ready for him, so he made his way to the back where Neville's office was. He knocked and entered, "Morning Mr. Pierce."

"Brennan, have a seat." Neville waited for Brennan to sit down before continuing. "I have been reviewing your work here and it has been excellent. Your work on the health care bill with Senator Kronovski was great. It is too bad the vote failed. That is one of the many issues we have, we just don't have enough friendly support in congress." Neville leaned back in his chair, making it creak. "The opposition is just too vocal and uses fear of us to get their votes to keep their seats. It is a bit disheartening."

Brennan let his thoughts wander back to his time before his attack and the vitriol that his father constantly spewed out in congress and on the television.

"That is exactly the problem. We need more direct support in congress, we need our own reps." Neville said bluntly. "We can't rely on support from 'friendly' senators, they just can't be forceful enough, as they are still worried about their own re-elections."

"I agree. Every case that I have worked on ends up with a bill that either has no teeth, or the senators are really unwilling to go 100% in on support," Brennan nodded in agreement.

"I have met with key political scientists from around the globe and we have put together a list of key districts that are very sympathetic to the struggles that us canids go through." He clicked a screen in his desk that brought up a map of the planet. "These are the 20 districts that we think we can grab. We will have to run against some friendly allies in 3 of them, but they aren't being effective." He clicked again and 17 of them turned amber. "These are where there is a large population of canines that we can get to rally around a candidate of their own kind."

Brennan noted that his father's district in Heartstone was high-lighted. "Ooh. You think we can get my father's seat? He has been tough to dethrone for years."

Neville chuckled. "Well, the population of that district has been getting more and more progressive and our population has been slow-ly growing due to the high-tech jobs and the increasing diversity in university enrollment." He zoomed in on that district. "Canines now are nearly 40% of this district, though the entrenched money keeps pumping cash into Clark's campaign of fear, outspending opposition candidates 10-to-1."

"So, who do you think is a strong enough contender to take on my dad?" Brennan rubbed his chin with a claw thinking about it. He hasn't spent any time in his old home district since he has been out of college and working.

"You," Neville said emphatically.

"Wait...me?" Brennan sat forward in surprise.

"Yes, you." Neville leaned forward to lock eyes with the young wolf. "You are a local boy. You had widespread sympathy from the district in general after the attack that made you who you are today. Your father disowning you and your mother's subsequent divorce because of your father's rhetoric will be a huge political advantage."

"I don't know if I can handle it." Brennan looked over and out the window. "I'm not sure I am ready for that yet."

"You *can* be. His seat isn't up for another two years and we will put together a crack team to get you really camera ready." Neville sat back in his chair. "I have already started the wheels moving for a candidate for that seat, whether you choose to do this or not. What I propose is I will transfer you to our legal group in your home town. I will give you a large pay bump, so you can afford a house to establish your residency. You already have the legal chops to go toe-to-toe with your father on any law related topics. In the meantime, we will get a PR team and a campaign manager to tutor you on the politics aspects of the job."

"Well, it would be nice to be back home for sure. I do miss my hometown," the young wolf smiled at the older wolf.

"Think about it. I'll call you tomorrow to see if you're in. Otherwise, I still want to put you on the team for another candidate, but I think you are the best wolf for this job." Neville smiled. "Hope you say yes."

***

Brennan didn't get much sleep that night, as his mind was worrying away on the idea of running for his father's seat in congress. *"Could I do it? Can I really challenge my father? Will I make a good senator?"* These were all the thoughts coursing through his head.

In the morning, the soon-to-be candidate decided to give his mother a call to get her opinion. "Hello Brennan," his mother Melissa answered knowing it was her son. After her divorce, she was so ashamed of her ex-husband that she changed her last name back to her maiden name of Larson. "What has you calling me so early in the morning? What's on your mind?"

"Sorry about the early call, but I need to bounce something off you." He exhaled to relax. "I have been asked to put my hat in the ring and run for the senate."

"Oh really?" she questioned. "Any particular reason they want you to do that?"

"Yeah, they think I have the popularity and the legal chops to successfully campaign against a candidate that is growing weaker in his district." He stopped himself so he could wordsmith what he wanted to say.

"I think you can do it, if you really want it." Melissa said. Exposure to the politics in Capitola made her quite astute in political theater. "You have the sympathy vote and you certainly are charismatic. Whose seat do the poly-sci people think you can take?"

He took a deep breath, "Dad's seat."

"Ooh..." she said, realizing the importance of what was being asked of her son. "Well, you know MY opinion of your father. You have my full support and I will even join you on the campaign trail. If you beat him, I will relish that day for the rest of my life. Joseph deserves this, since he is such a bastard now and also for abandoning you."

***

Brennan had a hard time focusing on the document he was analyzing with Mr. Pierce's offer from yesterday. He started thinking about it, as he gazed out of the window, when he was snapped out of his thoughts by a knock on the door. "Come in!"

Neville Pierce stepped into the young wolf's office. "My flight doesn't leave till later, so I thought I would talk to you personally, rather than on the phone. May I sit?"

"Sure," he waited for Neville to settle, his frame almost comically large for the chair in his office. "Well, I thought about it a lot. I even ran the idea past my mother, since she still has a thumb on politics in Capitola." Brennan thought for a second before continuing. "She thinks I have a chance and has given me her full support. I will do it for all the other canids out there, but most of all, for my mother."

"Wonderful!" Neville bellowed out very loudly. "My assistants have made all the preparations already. I know this is sudden, but I will make your transfer effective immediately." The wolf laid a new packet of documents on the table. "That's all the details of the revised offer, thumb through that."

Brennan opened the packet and glanced through the bullet points, huge salary increase, movers, real estate assistance and covering closing costs on the new place. "Again, you're very generous. I will try my best to win this seat."

"I know you will do a smashing job, Brennan. I have complete faith in you." Neville stood up and held out his paw. "Congratulations, you will do great." He shook the young wolf's hand. "When you get there, we'll already have a campaign headquarters secured where your only 'real' job will be to get yourself elected." He winked at him. "You'll be 'on staff' at the local NP Legal office, but I want you to focus on getting yourself ready for the campaign and hobnobbing with the right people in the capital. Your PR manager, campaign manager and strategists are all locked in and will get in touch when you get back to Suffok, so you can get to work."

***

Brennan stepped off the private jet provided by the company to a brisk breeze, blowing across the plains in Suffok. The humid, hot wind of his hometown ruffled his cheek fur, which lifted some of the weight that was on his shoulders, since agreeing to run for a congressional seat. *This is going to be a long two years.* Brennan thought to himself, as he began walking over to the car waiting for him. "It's good to be home," the young wolf said aloud to himself.

"And I'm Zuri Mandla reporting from Dres-Tek's headquarters. Now, back to Phil in the studio."

She ended the segment for Calveras Nightly News and handed the microphone back to Jamin. "I wish I could dig up more on this new Dresden-Pierce project. I'm not sure what Pierce's angle is with all this, but there's something going on that the public isn't privy to and I am going to find out."

"Well, if anyone can dig it up, it's you." Jamin knelt down and started packing up the camera gear. "Would you like me to drop you off at your office on the way back to the studio?"

"Sure," she said, as she turned to walk with him over to the van. She popped open the passenger door and jumped in.

In the years following her accident, Zuri had found herself too well known and too recognizable to be able to do the deep investigative journalism that she really loved. Many of her good contacts had gone dark because of her fame. They were all afraid to be easily tied to leaks and wouldn't risk themselves. In the end, she took a job at CBC as a senior correspondent for the Nightly News doing mostly fluff pieces on recent events. While she was a popular figure on the program and loved by audiences, it all just didn't come close to the deep stories she used to be able to do.

The van's brakes groaned as it came to a stop. "This van isn't much better than your old car," she smirked.

"Yeah yeah, I know. Camera operators don't make as much money as you 'on-screen' personalities," he smiled. "See you tomorrow."

Zuri got out of the van next to the run down brick building and made her way up to her second floor office. Turning the lock, she opened the door and walked in. The room was largely the same as it was years ago and she liked it that way. Even though it was in a rough areas, she refused to get a new one as she had too many memories attached to this old place.

She put her bag on a side table, then walked over to the desk and flopped down in the chair. Leaning back in a big relaxing exhale and stretching out her arms she froze. On her desk was an unfamiliar laptop with an envelope with her name on it. Leaning forward she picked up the envelope and turned it over to look for more clues on the letter's origin.

Considering the stories she had uncovered over the years, she thought strongly about calling the police because this was unnerving. She squeezed the envelope to feel if there was anything inside, but it only felt like a single piece of paper. She opened a drawer and pulled out a small silver letter opener. Pausing for a little bit, she opened another drawer and pulled out a filter mask. "Just to be safe." she muttered to herself.

After donning her mask, she carefully sliced the side open and peered inside. There wasn't any powder or anything, just a single letter. As she unfolded it, it was just a typical company letterhead. She grew very interested as she started to read it. It was from Dresden-Pierce Aerospace and Exploration. The body of the letter was a brief statement. *Do you want to find out more? Open the laptop'* and it was signed by Tyler Dresden.

"*Ooh,*" she thought. "*Is this real?*" She took off her mask when she decided to open the laptop. It automatically powered up to a window that said: 'scanning' and a light scanned her face. Then, the screen changed to 'connecting' with a status bar. She waited for a minute or two before an image popped up and came into focus. The camera was pointed at an empty chair in what appeared to be a private jet. Suddenly, someone passed in front of the camera. As the person move past the camera, she got a glimpse of a tail. The canine then turned and sat down, revealing a coyote that she recognized to be Tyler Dresden himself.

"Zuri Mandla, I am so glad that you took up my offer to have this call." Tyler settled himself into his chair. "I'm sorry about getting a hold of you this way, but it is way more secure and you're always out on assignment."

"Hello Mr. Dresden," she smiled pleasantly at the screen. "Usually people call or email."

His ears flickered in amusement. "I know, I know. Please call me Tyler. I wanted to meet you in person but I needed to talk to you about this right away." He looked down for a moment and then refocused on the camera. "I know you have been trying to find out more about this new project that I have embarked on and I want to offer you an opportunity be part of it. We are building up an amazing team here at DPAE and I want someone of your skills and persona to help out."

His face subtly lit up from the side and he looked over to the right, glancing at another screen. "I have been keeping my eye on your career for a while. Before your current role as a correspondent, your work exposing corruption in the Calveras government was top-notch and I commend you for that work. Quite frankly Zuri, the network is wasting your talents. Your on-camera presence is great but your assignments have lacked any real substance and I suspect you feel the same way, yes?"

"Yes, to be perfectly honest. CBC isn't too interested in deep, tough journalism. That takes too much effort, research and," she leaned forward, "money to develop really hard hitting journalism."

"I totally get that. So here's my pitch. On the desktop of that computer is a file. It will detail everything I am offering. But in short: I want you to be the PR person for DPAE. I want YOU to be the face of the project."

She opened the file while he was talking and started scrolling through the document.

He continued, "I am focused on developing the tech and as much as I, and my ego, like to be in the spotlight I know when I am stretched too thin. I need someone like you to do this."

Zuri kept going through the offer, the money, benefits, relocation and the job description. "That is an interesting proposal Tyler." She was impressed by how much money he was offering. It was far beyond what she would have countered with. She loved Calveras, but didn't have much tie to the area aside from her mother.

"Oh, two more things," he looked down at something. "Your mother: I suspect you are very close to her from what I saw on the news after your accident. We can either relocate her as well or set up regular visits on one of my private jets. I want you to be comfortable with everything about this arrangement." he smiled pleasantly at her. "The second item is I know you have had a great working relationship with your cameraman, Jamin Baloyi, for a long, long time and I think it would be great to have him on the team as well since you work great together."

She looked back from the offer letter and to Tyler. "As long as you add language in to this offer with the details you discussed in regards to my mother, then I am in."

"Done. My assistant has already amended the document. You should see the new text at the bottom already." He leaned back into his chair to let her review the changes.

Zuri scrolled to the bottom and sure enough, there was a new section there. "Awesome, thank you. So, how do we proceed?"

"There is a section on the bottom that will allow you to digitally sign. Go ahead and do that. We'll place the other boilerplate stuff on the desktop too, NDAs, etc. Just sign those documents after you've gone through them." He looked pleased and opened his muzzle in a smile. "My team will reach out to make all the arrangements and also to your partner about his offer too. I have to drop off for more meetings but I am confident you will be absolutely thrilled with what we are doing here. Have a wonderful day!" The coyote reached over and with that, his video feed ended.

Sitting back in her chair, she started looking around her cramped, cluttered office. *"I will miss this place, though."* she thought to herself.

Part 3 – Race for the Future

Chapter 33
Data Mining

It was very late at night and Tyler leaned back in his chair to stretch, making its backrest protest with a creak. It took about six months to get the company organized and all the best people hired but now he successfully shifted to research. He spent his nights pouring over the different electronic artifacts, cataloging, documenting and generally trying to figure out their purpose. He was sure he knew what about 20 of the items did, though he still hadn't cracked what powered them up.

Tyler had one of the items partially disassembled on a test bench. He chose to start with one of the handheld communication devices that he was already familiar with. His own company had released new technology based on his clever reverse engineering of the same type of device, but his was smashed so he had only deduced how it worked from clues. He had more that quadrupled the range of his own devices and more than halved the power consumption. They also had gained a six-fold increase in wireless data transfer.

This one he was working with was actually complete. It had been found in a sealed box in one of the mountain crash sites but had no power left in its battery. The power source seemed to be a small slab of Carbon-14/Diamond crystals, layered impossibly thin. They had scanned it using the world's best scanning electron microscope so he had a pretty good idea of the composition. Tyler wondered why the power would be drained since it used beta decay of the carbon isotope and should last 'forever' in our lifespan. *"Must have been under heavy use and left on by accident when it was put away."* was the only explanation that he could think of.

Dres-Tek's super-computer, the 'Talon Intelligent Computer' or 'TIC' for short, was processing all the data and Tyler hoped it would confirm his thoughts. If it can identify what the output voltages and currents were, he just might be able to power up the device.

Tyler looked over the data scrolling past on the monitor. The status indicated '*80% complete, Time Remaining 18 hours*'. He leaned back again, this time opening his muzzle wide in a yawn. "I guess I should call it a night."

***

"64 Volts," Tyler sat down in the room next to the others on Monday morning. He muttered out loud when reading the output from the computer simulation, "Interesting number." Tyler scratched his chin with a claw contemplating it for a moment. Running that around in his head for a moment, he thought, "*Engineers typically design to nice, round numbers, if they have a choice. Makes the math easier unless physics dictates something else*".

"Octals!" he exclaimed out loud to the room causing everyone look up from their work. "Their numbering system is Octals!" He jumped up to the digital white board to write the word on it and hit the save icon. "Our aliens use eights!"

Kaitey, Darisha, Martin and Suresh got up from their desks to run over to him. They were all experts in their fields: Software, embedded systems, mathematics and electronics. They were the team that he brought in to try to hack into the artifacts. That is, if they can get them powered up.

Tyler continued, "My simulation of the artifact battery came up with 64 Volts with a 99.8% probability. That's an odd number to chose for a design. In a base 8 system, that would be 100 volts." Tyler wrote out the conversion on the screen. "Remember, all our early computers were based on eights due to binary programming." He looked over at his engineers. "If I was starting from scratch on a design, I would have used 10, 20, 30, etc. A nice round number. I bet their whole number system is eights."

"I bet you're right," Darisha added after thinking about it. She grabbed her tablet and started taking some notes.

Tyler looked over to Suresh, "Let's rig a power supply to that thing and see if that gets us anything."

***

Suresh worked carefully over the next 2 weeks to guarantee that he didn't make any mistakes. He carefully extracted the old battery while being very careful not to crack it. He didn't want to leak any radioactive Carbon-14. There were a lot of other devices based on crystal technology inside the case so that still puzzled him. After many hours of thinking, probing and diagramming he thought he had a pretty good idea of what function every component inside the device performed. He suspected that it was based on gravity waves, not typical radio frequencies. The additional crystal in the chain made him wonder if that was some sort of 'tuned' crystal to encrypt the communication. The last step in his process would be to connect jumper wires to his leads, which would allow them to power it up on the bench.

Kaitey and Darisha had added a few more sensors and probes to try to capture any data communication inside the device. The intact unit had no external ports for any sort of data connection.

"Okay Tyler," Suresh removed his magnifying visor and turned off its light. "I think we are ready. Have you reviewed my diagram?"

Tyler stepped over to his work area. He had looked over it last night, "Yes, I did. I hope you're right on this being a gravity wave communicator, not radio based. When I bench-marked pieces from one of these a few years back, I guessed it was a Terahertz communicator and that's what I implemented in the latest gen phones." He mock punched the man on the shoulder and chuckled. "If you're right, you get to claim you proved the great Tyler Dresden wrong. Let's fire this up."

Suresh closed the blast proof cabinet that the test setup was in. The whole team had just come in to witness the test. "Okay, here we go!" Suresh uttered excitedly. They both held their breath while the power supply booted. Nothing happened for a minute but then the device made a soft beep and a green light turned on. The screen started scrolling with a series of dots, lines and slashes in almost a Kanji like script.

Kaitey was watching her laptop for signs of her data sniffing sensor working. Almost immediately, her computer was receiving and recording a data stream. "We're getting something!" she exclaimed happily and kept watching the screen.

Tyler turned around to the team, "Awesome job everyone. Hopefully we can decode it!"

<u>*Chapter 34*</u>
Campaign Promises

"Man, this headache," Brennan began rubbing his muzzle between his weary eyes, his head throbbed with a borderline migraine. He had been reading too many books: 'Persuasion of Politics', 'Consistent Charisma: the key to success' and the like. None of it was terribly exciting, but very necessary for his campaign.

To keep his legal skills sharp, Brennan was still working at the law firm two to three days a week. The rest of the week he was studying political strategy books, precedent-setting court cases, doing mock debates and performing fake speeches. His skills behind the podium were getting pretty sharp but he still got tripped up occasionally when a 'reporter' asked oddly-phrased questions to get him to make a gaff.

"*Almost there,*" he thought as he moved his paws to massage his temples. It was just a couple of weeks from when Hiro was planning Brennan's big press conference announcing his candidacy. There certainly would be a lot of pundits challenging him on his experience in governing, i.e. none, so he had to be super polished, charming and unflappable when on stage. Brennan turned his wrist and looked at his watch, "I'd better get to sleep."

***

"Good morning Brennan! Ready for today?" Hiro greeted him, as he stepped through the campaign office door.

"After I get some coffee in me. Then I'll be ready." Brennan walked over to the kitchen area and poured himself a cup of black coffee. He was glad Hiro liked coffee as he brought in the best stuff. He reached over to the bag the fox had brought in that day. The slogan on the bag read: 'Made with the finest beans from San Juarez and proudly roasted in River City.' He chuckled to himself, "*River City? That's an odd place to be roasting coffee. Is it roasted with diesel fuel?*" Brennan mused to himself.

The fox walked up to Brennan and handed him a document. "Here's the latest news blurb. Seems your father is really on a tear about 'cleaning up' Suffok." Hiro smiled to himself, "With 40% of the population now canids here, Joseph Clark's rhetoric is wearing a little thin in the eyes of the district. His approval ratings are way down, so this leaves a huge opening for us."

"Yeah, I saw his speech last night. He wants to waste money on a 'task-force' to fight the 'crime' that is 'rampant'." Brennan just shook his head. "Violence carried out by his cultish followers is the only crime statistic that is up."

Hiro sat down. "Yeah, here's the latest stats." He pulled up a chart on his laptop and turned it to Brennan. "Violent crimes perpetrated against canines are up nearly 150%, while crime committed by canines is down to almost negligible levels. I'll give this to Dana to incorporate into your speeches."

***

"Welcome to Heartstone tonight, I am Troy Alvarez," the presenter squared up the blue colored papers in front of him. "Top news story tonight is local boy, football star, and victim of a brazen attack five years ago, Brennan Clark, will be giving a press conference with a big announcement. We now go live to the conference."

Brennan walked out onto the stage to a decently sized audience filled with reporters and fans. As he stepped up to the microphone, he said, "Hello everyone!" The small group of fans started clapping and cheering when he greeted them.

"I thank all of you for coming tonight. Nearly five years

ago, I was attacked by a group of individuals because of my father's hateful rhetoric," he paused while scanning over the crowd. "That attack left me a changed man. The change was very difficult for me physically. I spent months in rehabilitation learning to live with my new physique." Brennan grabbed the mic off the stand and moved off to the side of the podium. "I had to relearn how to do pretty much everything over again. Eating, bathing, etcetera. I had to adjust my speech due to the radical differences to my face. When I walked, I felt like a toddler since these legs were radically different than my human ones." He held one up slightly to emphasize his statement.

"I needed different clothes, furniture and the like." He paused while glancing over at his mother standing off to the side of the crowd. "But, most of all, I had to learn to live with the way some people started treating me, like I was diseased, like I was a monster who didn't belong among you."

"The worse of all, my father disowned me, claimed I died and that I am not his child anymore." He genuinely choked up just a little. "That hurts me to this day. I am grateful that my mother, Melissa, stood by me and treated me like her son no matter what I looked like."

"This brings me to why I am here tonight." Brennan cleared his throat before continuing, "I see what my father has been saying. I see the actions he is taking, the hatred he spouts, the fear he is trying to infuse in his followers. His rhetoric is dividing this city, this prefecture and the world."

"He is decrying, 'Crime is skyrocketing, it's all the canine's fault those dirty animals!' but in reality, crimes committed by canines in this district is down to almost zero. Though, he's right in one statistic: violent crime perpetrated by humans against canines is up over 150% and that's a non-debatable fact. That violence is a direct result of his vitriol. His manipulation is encouraging his followers to use violence against those who do not agree with him."

"My perspectives since becoming a canid have changed only a little bit. I never bought into my father's hatred, but just turned a blind eye to it. My best friend in college was a canine but I now experience the side of his life that I couldn't before. The unfathomable hatred, the inexplicable prejudice, the struggles he must have had growing up non-human. I may have been spared that hatred when I was a boy, but I now fully understand it."

"I want to change that. I will not stand by any more and be culpable with my silence." Brennan walked over to the front of the stage directly in front of the cameras. "Tonight, I am announcing that I am running for my father's seat in congress!" Brennan paused when the crowd began murmuring loudly. Once they digested what he said, many people in the crowd began to applaud.

"I know I don't have the years of experience up in Capitola that many politicians have. BUT, I know the laws inside and out. I have studied endless past legal cases and know all the precedents. I know the people and I know that I can be a force for positive change in congress. I will fight for EVERYONE, not just one species, not just one ethnic group, not just one region. Our world CAN accomplish great things for ALL denizens of the planet, not just a select few. Our government needs new blood, *A Fresh Start*."

The screen cut back to the Heartstone Tonight studio. "What a bombshell," Troy Alvarez said with a shocked look on his face. "Local boy and football hero has announced that he will take on his estranged father, Senator Clark and try to defeat him take his place in congress." Troy put down the stack of papers he was holding. "This will be an exciting election year for sure. Stay tuned to Heartstone Tonight for further developments. I am Troy Alvarez and good night."

"Good evening, I am Jordan Helmsey with UBN News. Tonight on 'Eyes on Technology', I bring you a special interview with Zuri Mandla from the Dresden-Pierce Aerospace and Exploration company." The camera zoomed out to reveal his special guest. "Thank you for joining me Miss Mandla."

"The pleasure is mine, Jordan." Zuri said pleasantly.

"First thing, let's let the viewers know a little bit about you." Jordan looked down at his notes and then to the camera, "Zuri is an award winning journalist from Calveras who has exposed countless cases of corruption in the regional government. On one of her cases, she was caught in the crossfire of a militant group, was accidentally exposed to canine blood and was transformed into the person you see before me tonight." He glanced down. "After this accident, she no longer could work undercover and joined the Calveras Nightly News as a correspondent."

Jordan paused a second before continuing, "Most recently, you joined the DPAE as their Head of Communications." He put his notes down on the coffee table and looked at his guest. "Before I get to the DPEA, do you mind if I ask you a few personal questions?"

"Sure Jordan, I rarely get to talk about myself." She flickered her ears as she smiled at the man.

"So, did you find it hard to adjust to life after your accident?" he asked sincerely.

Zuri thought for a moment, "Yes, it was difficult. It took months of physical therapy to relearn basic things. I could barely walk at the beginning." She crossed her legs to show off her multicolored legs. "Walking on my toes was really hard and took time to build up the necessary strength in my legs." She smiled at Jordan, "and bathing takes so much more time now." She laughed lightly.

"I'm sure the whole ordeal was very difficult. Do you like who you are now?" he asked with a genuine tone.

"Actually, I do. It was like being reborn." She uncrossed her legs and shifted forward. "It was like I was physically 18 years old again. I also really love my coloring, it's so darn neat." She raised her arm and rolled it around to show off the fur patterns. "If I had been given the choice in species, I would still have picked this canine type."

"That's great to hear. Imagine if you hated yourself after a traumatic experience like that. How tough would that be?" He shifted back a little bit. "Alright, so the DPEA. What made you decide to become their spokesperson?"

"When Tyler Dresden called me to invite me to join, I just couldn't say no." She sat back into the couch. "I might not be a scientist but the possibilities of their project and the potential good that can come from their discoveries was just too exciting to pass up. Tyler has put together the best team on the planet. We have the world's top scientists, technicians, astrophysicists, aerospace engineers, computer scientists and the list goes on and on."

Jordan posed a question to Zuri, "How did DPEA come into being?"

"Well, I know a lot of people don't know much about Neville Pierce. Since he was a little boy, he longed to do more than be a poor kid on the street. He has always had a keen interest in the stars, since the aliens who crashed here birthed canine-kind. He thinks of this as a way to get to know his alien ancestors better. That's pretty much what human archaeologists do, try to rediscover the past to better understand ourselves."

Zuri paused to see if Jordan was going to ask something different, but he nodded as he was listening, so she continued. "Neville approached Tyler with his idea and he jumped at the chance to restart his father's work in space exploration." She shifted forward in her seat, "We, as a planet, have sort of abandoned space exploration. I guess the public wasn't interested in having their government spend billions of dollars on space instead of fixing the problems we have here on the ground. They both decided that the only way true exploration would continue, is as a private enterprise, not beholden the political interests of the moment."

"So, what kind of exploration are you planning?" he asked.

"First thing is to develop new rockets and space vehicles that will enable more efficient exploration. Tyler's father was trying to improve rocket technology when his unfortunate accident cut his life short." She shifted in her seat a little bit before continuing, "Once we can more cost effectively get back to space, we can start to explore our solar system. Tyler has insisted all the new tech he is developing will benefit all of the world, whether through his existing companies, or through licensing deals."

"So, DPAE is not interested in getting all the profit? Seems like an odd thing for a private company to do, especially with someone like the financial giant, Neville Pierce, involved," Jordan pointed out.

"Well, of course we want to make a profit, but Tyler insists that whatever is developed will roll out to the world in one form or another." Zuri stated. "By being private, we can make the kind of decisions and choices that a publicly traded company or government institution cannot. We won't be beholden to investors that want profit now at the sacrifice of the company in three years. The DPAE is in this for the long haul. With financial backing of Neville Pierce and Tyler Dresden, we have all the financing we will need for decades."

Jordan leaped onto that last statement, "There's a lot of rumors and misinformation on just how Neville Pierce obtained all that wealth. Some say the bulk of his money came from organized crime and then by exploiting the canine population when they did not have any legal rights. Can you comment on that?"

Zuri thought about that for a second, before answering, "Well, times were different for the canine population before the civil rights movement in the 1960s and I can't speak to any endeavors he was involved in before that time. Neville and his companies have always been there in support of the canines. He started a financial company that exclusively worked to provide canines with access to money for businesses, cars and home purchases when no established banks would work with them. Neville's work helped improve the lives of the global canid population. His legal division helped usher in laws to give them equal rights. He personally helped give canines representation and a voice in congress. To this day, his legal company continues that fight."

Jordan pressed a little further, "So, you don't know anything from his business dealings before canines were given any legal standing?"

"No, anything he did before that landmark civil rights law was undocumented." Zuri's face transitioned to a serious expression. "Think about it. Before that time, anything canines did to earn money was technically illegal so you really can't fault him for working outside the laws to make a living. If you want more details, you will have to convince him come on your show to speak to those times in his life. I am not privy to that sort of personal information."

"Thank you for your candor, Zuri. I look forward to hearing more about the DPEA in the future and maybe, just maybe have a future segment with the mysterious Mr. Neville Pierce." He smiled at Zuri before turning to the camera. "That's all the time we have for tonight." He finished the show by saying, "I am Jordan Helmsey and this has been 'Eyes on Technology'. See you next time."

Chapter 36
Opposition

Senator Joseph Clark peered out from a gap in the curtain behind the stage to see his audience. The ballroom was fairly packed. There was a smattering of reporters off to the side where the press were quarantined. The reporters were mostly human with a couple of canine members of the press. Joseph scoffed, "I'll be damned if I give those animals the time of the day." The general public seated in the auditorium were all humans which made Joseph smile. "That's what this planet needs to look like."

The PA boomed, "Please welcome Senator Joseph Clark!" The audience stood up and a roar of applause erupted. Joseph stepped out of the stage and waved to his fans and purposely didn't even acknowledge the press off to the side.   When the applause started subsiding, he stepped behind the podium and placed his notes on the pedestal.

"As you know, our world is under attack," he bellowed forth with zeal. "Our world, the HUMAN world is in peril. These animals...these so-called canines want to destroy us. Do not be fooled by their kind words. Their words like 'inclusion', 'equal rights' are only a facade. They are lies to cloak their true purpose." He paused letting the audience clap. "They want to RULE the world. They want to extinguish the flame that is the human race and if they can't do that, they want to CONVERT you to their likeness with their UNETHICAL conversion treatment." More applause erupted from the audience in reaction to his words.

Joseph panned his face across the audience with a smile, "I PROMISE you I will fight them with every breath of mine to the last." He took a deep breath and then continued, "The latest attack on our God given right to this world is the monster that claims to be my dead son. That animal is NOT my son and never could be. God would never allow my son to live on within that creature. He is LYING to you, the press is lying to you, my ex-wife is lying to you. Brennan is dead. DEAD I say. That monster is a demon here to lull you into complacency to let them control us, to control YOU, to strip you of your humanity!"

Sweat was starting to form on his brow from his tirade. "I will be working until my dying breath to control, to stop their agenda to eradicate or enslave us." Flipping a page on his notes, "In the next congressional session I will be introducing several new bills."

"First, I WILL ban these illicit 'conversion' centers. People who willingly go there are selling their souls to the devil and that is why they have to be stopped. God made you human, you are made in God's image and that image is perfect. If you are dying that is God's will and we should accept that, not try to cheat it. The devil is selling you falsities and he wants to turn you from God!"

"Second, I will push for a constitutional amendment that explicitly defines what is human and what is an animal. Fangs, claws and fur are NOT human and never, EVER will be. They have NO RIGHT to exist, let alone vote." He again paused, as the audience stood and applauded.

"I am counting on everyone one of you to help STOP these animals. They cannot, WILL NOT ever govern us." Joseph paused to catch his breath, "You need to support me and the other SANE candidates across this world to keep this scourge from destroying our world!"

***

"Good evening everyone, I am Jordan Helmsey from the UBN 10 news desk," he paused for a moment, "Tonight, we bring you a special segment in our 'Politics Today' series. I am joined by esteemed political scientist Ph.D. Albert Lee from Fijiwara, Professor of Law Fletcher Davis from Suffok University in Heartstone and Hiro Adachi, campaign manager for Brennan Clark. Welcome to the show Albert, Fletcher and Hiro."

They all said their thanks to Jordan before he continued, "You all have seen the speech that Joseph Clark made the other night. Albert, what are your thoughts?"

"It was a fiery one for sure," Albert rubbed his chin. "That was definitely a calculated speech. He is trying to rile up his base by stoking their fears of the canid population. He knows that they are his key to re-election as he has no chance with anyone that is even slightly progressive. He is doubling...no tripling down on his rhetoric to energize his voters. His district is almost 40% canine at this point and leans progressive so he needs a very high turnout of his base to keep his seat."

Jordan looked over to Hiro, "Being a political pundit before heading up Brennan's campaign I am sure you have thoughts here."

"Thank you Jordan, yes, yes I do." Hiro leaned forward in his chair, "As Albert said, the district has a larger than average canine population. We also need to take into consideration the heavy focus on higher learning in this district. There are a lot of esteemed universities here so it brings in a lot of people from other regions. This district should be an overwhelming progressive district but it historically has not been. With the rhetoric of people, like Senator Clark, many of the canid population have gotten frustrated and do not vote. In fact, only 30% of canines vote. That's the key here."

Jordan looked at his third guest, "Fletcher, what are your thoughts on the speech?"

"I'll split my analysis of Senator Clark's speech by the two distinct policy propositions mentioned in the press conference. First, the bill to ban the 'Conversion Centers'. This one is mixed. The Earth Drug Agency has ruled that the treatment poses no risk, in fact reported data shows that they have a 100% success rate and no one has died from the treatment. After the treatments the patient is in perfect health. That means there is no medical or legal reason for banning them. In the eyes of the EDA, this is a voluntary cosmetic procedure."

Jordan interjected, "But that's not all the argument here, is it?"

"That's definitely the case." Fletcher agreed. "Now, on a moral and ethical front, that's where it gets a little murky. Many long-established religious institutions are against it. They think it is amoral and goes against their god's will. Ethically, many point out that individuals basically can cheat death by more than doubling their lifespans. Some feel that it's a treatment only for the rich and not widely available to everyone and that makes it a dubious treatment in their eyes."

"What about the 'accidental' conversions?" Jordan mentioned.

"Well, that really shouldn't be IN the argument, although it always gets brought up." Fletcher frowned when he said that. "By definition, it's an accident, not intentional. When someone mentions that to me, I always ask them. 'Would you rather be dead?' and the answer is overwhelmingly 'no'." The man shifted in his chair a little bit and continued, "On the argument of 'forced' conversions, that really doesn't happen. There is only one case in public record, Brennan Clark, but I will say he seems to be doing just fine for himself these days."

"If I may?" Hiro chimed in. "Let me say, I am really glad to have not been killed in that gas explosion myself. I may not look the same, but up here," he pointed to his head, "I am still the same person where it counts. Now Brennan initially was upset at the transformation but that mostly boiled down to his regret at not being able to continue his football career. Now, he sees it as a turning point in his life where he can really make a difference for everyone, not just be a celebrity on television."

Jordan chuckled and smiled at Hiro. "Nice subtle campaign message."

"Not intentional though, but I guess it came out that way," Hiro smiled with a wry grin.

"Fletcher," Jordan looked over at his other guest. "What do you think of the Senator's wish to change the constitution?"

"That is a complete bold faced campaign lie, to be honest." Fletcher uncrossed his legs, "There isn't any way you could legally claim that canines aren't 'sentient beings' and could be excluded from governance, let alone deemed animals with no rights what-so-ever." Fletcher looked over at the fox sitting next to him. "I am pretty sure Hiro here would be able to pass any 'intelligence' test we could throw at him and probably do better than 90 percent of the human population."

Albert interjected, "This is again, a strategy by Senator Clark to excite his voting block. There is no way this could pass a global vote. The constitution says that an amendment needs 65% to pass. I think you would see a large influx of canine voter registrations to prevent that. None of them want to be enslaved or turned into hunting game again. We all know from history how well that worked out for humans. Had we not done that with the feral canines, we probably wouldn't even have bipedal canines like Hiro today."

"Hiro?" Jordan posed the question to the fox.

"That is 100% hate speech. Meant to try to save his career." Hiro stated emphatically. "I don't think it will work and I bet he knows it. It's desperation."

"Well, Albert, Fletcher and Hiro, thank you for your analysis on the Senator's remarks." Jordan looked over at the camera. "That's all we have time for tonight. Watch us next time on 'Politics Today' on UBN 10. I am Jordan Helmsey. Have a good night!"

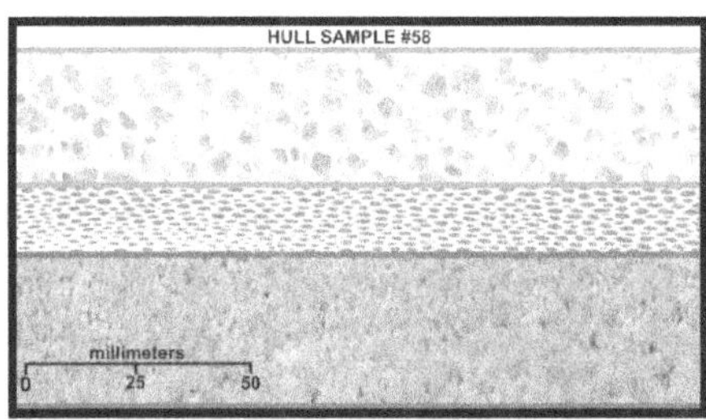

The construction inside the new Sjöberg Aerospace & Electronics Manufacturing building adjacent to the DPEA site was coming along nicely. Ingrid loudly sneezed from all of the concrete saw dust in the air. They were installing new seismic isolation foundations for the highly sensitive machinery and it was producing clouds of dust that bothered her sensitive nose. She ended her survey of the work's progress and went back to her office.

"Tyler," Ingrid got up to greet the coyote when he walked into her office. He was dressed in an obnoxiously bright floral print shirt and board shorts. He always seemed to dress very casually when he wasn't busy with outside meetings. "The machinery foundations are coming along nicely for the new machinery. Long walk down here just for a personal visit. Got something on your mind?"

He flopped down into the chair next to her desk, "Awesome. Quite frankly, I just needed to stretch my legs and thought I would drop by." Tyler leaned back and stretched his arms over his head before snapping back forward. "Oh ... hey ... I want to have you come over to our engineering office. I think our team figured out a little more of what makes up the hull material and it's way easier to show you. You have a few moments now?"

Ingrid glanced over at her laptop to check her schedule. "Yeah, I have a couple of hours. Let's go."

When the door opened from the building to the outside the heat blasted her in the face, like opening an oven door. Chuckling to herself, *"I can see why he always dresses like he does."* They jumped into a small enclosed cart and drove along the buildings until they reached the office area of DPEA.

Just to make some conversation while they walked into the building, she asked, "So, what does your team think it is?"

"Well, they analyzed it and it's something like an ultra high temp ceramic material but layered with a bunch different things. I'll let the team show you, I don't want to steal their thunder." He smirked at Ingrid as he stopped in front of another set of offices. He got out of the cart and opened the door to the engineer's room on the ground floor.

The room was a typical high tech layout, no cubicles, high ceilings, white, industrial and well lit. He led her over to the right side where a few engineers were sitting at their desks.

"This is Devin, Diego, Shanvi and Rex." Tyler introduced the four who were seated in one area. Devin and Shanyi were human, Diego was a brownish canine and Rex was a jet black canid of some sort and had one half floppy ear which gave him ridiculously cute look. "This is Ingrid Sjöberg. Show her what you have all found."

They all looked at each other trying to figure out who wanted to talk. Shanvi spoke up, "Sure." She brought up a series of photos. "What we have is a laminated composite." She brought up a closeup of the cross-section. "The outer layer is a high-temp ceramic made up of borides, carbides, nitrides and oxides of Zirconium. That's nothing special in-and-of itself. It's already been used in re-entry space vehi-cles. What's strange is its internal structure makes it more akin to a closed-cell foam. Impervious to water on the external skin, but able to conduct heat along its lattice work. This makes the ceramic layer much stronger and lighter weight that what is used today."

Shanvi clicked to another picture. "The next set of layers, is a high content nickel and chromium superalloy. Very strong, great high temp resistance, can be subjected to high pressure loading and high mechanical loads. There is a second inner layer of the same material but what is unique about the middle layer: is it has a three-dimension-al honeycomb structure." She brought up a 3D rendering of the inner structure. "This composite material ends up being one tenth the mass of the latest rocket hulls but many times stronger and thinner."

"How was this made?   Do you have any thoughts?" Ingrid asked of the four.

"I have a theory on the steel." Max, the metallurgist, spoke up. "I think the inner hulls are 3D printed and sintered segments, then welded together.   They also have 3 dimensional edges that lock together, sort of like a tongue-in-groove wood joint but better. This makes for a very light, stiff and impact resistant structure. Welding the metal is tricky due to its high temp resistance and care must be given so it doesn't crack. Devin can speak to the ceramics."

"I, um," Devin stammered a little, not wanting to talk, "I think this is also 3D printed and then fired in a kiln. That's the only way to get this structure in a ceramic and in such weird compound curves." He reached over to grab a very small chunk of salvage. "The ceramic tiles are made in a compound shape to match the curvature of the hull. They are then bonded on using a super high-temp structural adhesive that we are still trying to figure out. It makes this whole hull sandwich lightweight and nearly indestructible to most normal things a space craft would encounter."

Tyler piped up, "So Ingrid. Do you think that we can print this with current tech?"

"The latest equipment we have been making for Dres-Tek is super precise, but they are designed for making silicon chips. Maybe that can be adapted for these materials?" She reached up and flattened her ear while thinking. "Probably going to need all clean sheet designs."

Tyler looked at Ingrid as he put a paw on one of the engineer's shoulders, "Diego here ... is a high tech 3D printing expert and one hell of an engineer. We'll get him working with your manufacturing engineers to see if they can unlock it," Tyler looked from Diego to Ingrid. "Sound like a plan? In the meantime, we'll get that adhesive figured out."

<u>*Chapter 38*</u>
Campaign for the Future

"Man, just campaigning for a single district is grueling. Imagine if I was going for Prime Minister." Brennan thought to himself as he sat forward in his chair to stretch his back. He had been doing endless meetups, town halls, interviews for the primary election and he was so over it. The primaries were in a week and he had a few more interviews and a primary eve speech left to do. *"Three more months after that,"* he thought to himself.

Brennan got up out of his chair to get some blood flowing to his legs. He padded over to his open office door to lean on the frame. The campaign headquarters was a flurry of activity and he silently watched everyone working for about five minutes. There had to be fifty volunteers working directly with them and hundreds more across the district. What he loved was that his volunteer staff was nearly 50% human, which made him feel that his popularity and his message was reaching across the species divide.

He waited for a moment when he didn't see anyone on the phone. "Everyone," he said loudly with his powerful voice. The room went quiet save for the printers whirring away in the back. "Everyone. No matter the outcome of next week, whether we win or lose, I just want to let you know just how much I appreciate your help and support. This campaign would not be happening without the contributions everyone in here and out there has made. No matter how large or how small they have been, they are all important. I am nothing without all of you, thank you so much!"

The room applauded for a little while before it subsided. A phone rang and everyone got back to work.

Hiro walked up to Brennan and put a paw on his shoulder. "You're going to easily win the primary, no worries there." Hiro mocked punched the larger wolf's shoulder. "You worry too much. We got this."

"I hope so, Hiro." Brennan looked the fox in the eyes, "I hope so."

Once the campaign ramped up, Neville had sent Brennan a whole security detail. He now had four personal body guards. They were an imposing site: four large, black wolves who look like they could be a whole army by themselves. Ivan Grecov used to be Neville's personal man, but now he was acting as Chief of Security for the campaign. It hadn't been much of a problem so far. Mostly it was a few rowdy, drunk supporters of his father that thought they would cause trouble.

"Brennan," Ivan walked up to him. "Time to go."

Brennan was giving his next campaign speech on the campus of his Alma Mater, indicating that this would be a pretty easy one. The students were almost 100% behind him so this was more of a 'thank you' speech to his supporters. Ivan opened the back door to one car for Brennan and then sat in the front, next to the driver. He still wasn't used to the armored cars, security detail and kind of longed for the simpler days. Nothing was a causal trip anymore.

***

The ride over to the campus wasn't long since his headquarters was located only blocks away from the campus. The cars entered the gated, secured area near the administration building. It slowly weaved its way between the buildings to park at the back of the temporary stage the university had erected on the quadrangle. Ivan said something to his radio before he got out of the car. Ivan then visually scanned around the area before he opened the door for Brennan. The crowd erupted into applause, whistles, hoots and hollers, as he stood up out of the backseat and waved around to the mass of people gathered on campus.

Brennan made his way over to the stage, but made sure to clap hands with the people lined up along the rope as he walked by. When he reached the stairs, a staff member attached a wireless microphone to his lapel and then gave the thumbs up. If Brennan thought the crowd was loud before, it became deafening as he ascended the small stairs on to the stage.

"HELLO SUFFOK!" Brennan yelled as he raised his arms and waved to the crowd. Now that he was on the stage he could see just how many people had come out to see him. There had to be four times the number of people than students attending the university. He waved his hands at the audience in a quieting motion, "Thank you, thank you!" He waited for the volume to lower before continuing, "It seems like I was a student here just yesterday, winning the big game. The support that the students of this great institution have shown me is just amazing. I thank you with all my ..."

A gunshot rang out and a bullet struck Brennan in the left shoulder, knocking him off his feet to land on his rear. A second shot rang out as he fell, but missed him and struck the stage backdrop behind him. The crowd immediately started screaming and running, utter chaos erupting around the stage. Ivan and his crew were immediately there covering Brennan with their own bodies as a third shot rang out, striking one of the wolves in the back. They quickly pulled Brennan to his feet and ushered him off the stage in a protective circle and ran him back to the safety of the armored car.

Brennan was pushed inside the car to get him out of view. Three of the wolves piled into the car with Ivan dripping into the front passenger seat quickly talking on the radio. Quentin, Brennan's long-time personal security quickly opened a panel and yanked out a first-aid kit. He looked over the wound. "Good, it passed through." Brennan's head was spinning from the blood loss. Quentin took out a spray from the kit, popped the top off and sprayed the bullet wound. Brennan's head was spinning as he started to pass out. "Stay with me kid." Quenton said sternly. He then tightly wrapped the would with bandages to try to stop the bleeding. Quentin then pulled out a large syringe, popped its top and injected it in the shoulder near the wound. "That was a concoction of adrenaline, antibiotics and the Nano-Docs. Those will get to work on healing you right away. This is exactly what the aliens engineered them for. In a week, you will hardly be able to tell you were shot. Also, don't worry, Mahiri is okay and is being treated in the other car."

***

"Troy Alvarez with Heartstone Tonight. I have just received break-ing news from the campus of Suffok University." The screen popped up an image of Brennan speaking in front of a podium. "Brennan Clark was about to give a campaign speech to the students at his Alma Mater when a gunman attempted to assassinate him." The corner image changed to an image of a man being hauled off by police. "Local police have taken the gunman into custody, but have not released the identity of the man yet." The screen switched to a video of Brennan's security whisking him off stage. "Brennan was stuck by at least one of the three shots fired and was quickly moved to safety. His campaign and family have not issued any statements at this time.

***

Hiro sat down at the chair next to Brennan's hospital bed. "How are you feeling?"

It was the day after the shooting so he was still in pain. "Better. Thankfully they have canine blood in the banks at this hospital." Brennan was glad that his hometown had a large canid population. "Imagine if this happened in a rural town in the middle of nowhere, I would probably be dead."

"Ivan briefed me, you'll be back up to 100% in no time. Some of those rural areas might have let you die on purpose." Hiro smiled. "So, we need to get a statement out there condemning this. Anything in particular you feel you want added or should we just wordsmith it?"

"Go ahead and just have Dana write up the press release with what you think should be said. I want to heal a little more. Then, we can get back to the campaign."

"Sure thing buddy," Hiro patted the wolf's good shoulder. "I am absolutely sure you will get the primary, I have no doubt in my mind. I will be back tomorrow."

***

'*Brennan wins!*' was all over the news by midday on the province's primary day. The assassination attempt seemingly had clinched the victory early for them. The entire Reform Party had rallied around Brennan, the popular local boy who now had two major life changing attacks on him. The after-party reminded Brennan of his fraternity. Everyone was really happy, being loud and boisterous. Drinks were flowing and not a frown to be seen.

"Okay Hiro," Brennan sat down on a couch in the hotel ballroom they had rented. "You were absolutely right."

The fox joined him across the table. "We got just over 90% of the party's primary votes. I am actually surprised that it wasn't 100%. Who would not vote for you? The victim of two nearly fatal attacks that changed your life forever and a hateful father who disowned you. The book practically writes itself. You'd be rich on the movie rights alone."

"Yeah, when I started football I planned for THAT to be my whole life. Who knew that I would end up on this path?" Brennan sipped his beer. "I almost can't imagine NOT being here now. Like I was born for this."

Figuring out the fundamentals of the crystal battery tech in the alien devices had unlocked their abilities to power up a variety of the different devices they had in their collection. They had communicators, handheld weapons, computers, tools and probably the most exciting find: Large data storage devices.

Tyler had brought in a few more experts in software encryption, cryptology, data storage and machine language to try to make sense of the mountains of data they had been able to extract. One computer box in particular, was a mass storage device filled with data crystals. About 70% of the crystals in the device were fractured but they were still able to get 20 petabytes of data from the device. They still didn't know what kind of information they were able to retrieve.

"Well, we've made some headway on their written language." David Brynn sat down with a coffee cup in the chair next to Tyler to give him an update. He was a short, middle-aged man with red hair and a wizard in cryptology. "We've identified the kanji on many of the devices. That means we mostly have equivalents to function items: send, receive, device names, operations, etc. They're purely functional words so no real conversational language. Also, using your eighths numbering theory, we have confirmed that they use an octal number structure and now have symbols for all their numbers." He paused to have a sip of coffee. "Storage, on the other hand, is still encrypted. I'm hoping that once we crack that we'll get some audio and video to get beyond the basics."

Tyler leaned forward, put his elbow on the desk and rested his chin on his fist. "I sure hope we can get into that data soon. I have a team waiting to start processing it." The coyote leaned back into the chair. "How long do you think it will take?"

"The computer is still chugging away." David looked down at his tablet to view the progress. "I think by the end of the week it might crack the encryption. The computer model is starting to converge and looks to be on track to finish sometime on the weekend."

***

"I hear a lot more data might be ready next week?" Maya said, as she walked with Renata into the hanger that contained all the larger debris. They had been working with a small group to assemble what they thought was cockpit debris from a ship.

"Yeah, hopefully they'll crack it and we'll get to see some video of what our aliens looked like. That would help immensely," Renata replied as they came up to the carefully placed debris. "I hear you have met with that young wolf from Heartstone running for a senate seat. Brent, no Brennan, right?"

"Yeah, Neville asked me to also be a consultant on spiritual matters for his campaign. Help him better understand how to appeal the spiritual members of his district that aren't under his father's anti-canine spell." Maya smiled, adding, "He is surprisingly non-religious for growing up under his father's influence."

"Hmm," Renata uttered as she was looking down at the grouping of salvage in front of them. "Something just doesn't look right to me. I think we are thinking too human on how this is laid out." She scratched at one of her large ears in thought. Then, she looked around the hanger and spotted who she was looking for. She shouted across the hanger to a short fox nearby who was working on the debris team, "Minn, can you come over her for a second?"

"Sure miss Renata," the young fox came over to where they were standing.

"Let's rearrange this and put it on the floor instead of on the table." Renata pointed to a burnt-out control panel and Minn put the console on the floor for her. "Next, this thing that kind of looks like a cockpit chair," she pointed at another object. "I think that needs to be laid on its back and rotated and placed in front of the console."

"Okay. Lon!" Minn waved to a human member of the team. "Help me a sec." They both grabbed the chair, laid it down gently and spun it into place in front of the console.

"Hmm, I think that looks better." Renata knelt down onto one knee to have a ground level look at it. "I just had a random thought a moment ago. On all my expeditions, we found lots of 'thrones' for important people but they were all tailored for a human physique. Upright back with a place for our rears to sit on. We," she pointed to Maya and Minn, "were created from terrestrial canines and I thought *'What if they were more like earth dogs than us?'* and that shape of the chair looked more like a form suited for a four-legged creature." She put a hand on Minn's shoulder. "Lay down on that and pretend to operate the console with your hands."

Minn furrowed his brow in puzzled look but moved over to the couch, carefully climbed onto it and laid on his belly on top of it. He then extended his hands out to operate the console.

"See!" she exclaimed, adding, "If his rear legs were shorter and his chest was skinny like an earth dog, rather than wide like our unique physiology, he would fit perfectly. Stay there for a minute," she said to Minn and proceeded to look around the other debris. "Grab these," she pointed to a couple of wedge-like pedal contraptions. "Let's put these under his feet."

Lon and Renata pulled the items over to Minn, placed the pedals under his feet and stood back.

"That's it! That makes sense with these parts," she had an excited expression on her face. "Our aliens are quadrupeds! Let's get some pictures." Renata pulled out her phone and snapped a few different shots to capture her thoughts.

"Welcome to UBM News at 10, the Heart of Heartstone. I am Georgia Stavros. Top story tonight: Authorities have released the identity of the gunman who attempted to assassinate Brennan Clark, the recent winner of the Reform Party primary here in Heartstone."

The screen flashes to show a mugshot of a black haired man with a grizzled beard and unkept hair.

"Burk Falosian, seen here in his booking mugshot, is a member of the Humans First Coalition. The HFA is a militant hate group and as they say in their mission statement: 'their purpose is to exterminate the demons living among humanity.' They have not released any official statements on the assassination attempt, but in member's social media accounts, it is clear they are unhappy that Burk wasn't successful in his attempt on Brennan's life."

The screen switched back to Georgia at her desk.

"It is clear that the HFC has taken Brennan's popularity as a serious threat. That's all the latest information we have on the assassination attempt."

***

"Morning Ivan," Brennan said to his friend and Chief of Security as he walked down the stairs from the upstairs of his home.

Ivan put down the briefing tablet he was reading, "Morning kid. The debate request by your father's campaign was denied. They where emphatic that *'The Senator will not debate with that devil'*. I'm pretty sure he knows you will destroy him on stage."

"It makes me sad that he is so far gone. As much as I despise him these days, he still is...was?...my father." Brennan said, with a frown.

"Yeah, I feel for you kid. Never knew my father. The deadbeat left my mom and I to had to fend for myself in Dogtown. I did the best I could and so have you." He smiled at Brennan after saying that. "Oh, I need to head out of town for a few days to take care of some business for Neville." Ivan looked around at the six canines scattered around the lower floor. "I think you're in good paws. Your schedule for the next week is mostly community focused. So you've got no big speeches, just eating at random local joints and other 'meet the people' things."

"Haha," Brennan smirked. "Nothing these days is 'easy' or 'just eating'. Did Hiro book me into any good places this time around?"

"I couldn't say. My tastes are pretty basic. Give me a big steak and I am happy." Ivan smiled a big toothy grin. "That fishy sushi stuff isn't for me."

***

The car he rented was a boring large sedan, nothing like his beloved old classic he had back in Uptown. He pulled the car to the curb in front of his old bosses' place in Dogtown. As he got out he scanned around and noticed that everything just looked brighter. There were a lot nicer cars parked out on the street. Houses were freshly painted and he could see a new coffee shop down the street. "This place has changed." he thought to himself.

He walked up the short set of concrete steps as the door opened. Francisco saw him coming and opened the door for Ivan. "Well damn. I heard the rumors and couldn't believe it, but here you are. All six and half feet of you." He extended a hand out to greet him.

Ivan wrapped his massive paw around his old friend's hand, "Yeah, just slightly different now. How are things up here?"

"Come in, Dorian is expecting you." He closed the door behind them as they entered the house. "Things are really nice now. Just look at the area outside. Dorian has been able to really kick the city's revival into high gear with Pierce's financial backing. Dogtown has turned into a Hipster hangout and I kind of like it. I don't have to do a lot of nasty things to people anymore."

Ivan looked around at Dorian's place. Nothing was really different as Dorian's taste was always a bit more traditional. "Same office?" he asked.

"Yeah, same one. Dorian's up there. Security is way less tight now so there's no one sitting outside his office anymore." Francisco motioned up the stairs. "I let him know you are here."

"Thanks man." Ivan walked up the stairs and the door to Dorian's office was open.

"Ivan!" Dorian got up to come greet his old enforcer. He looked up at Ivan's face. "My, you were such a scrawny kid when we found you and now look at you." Dorian smiled, "Looks like you've been working out and put some hair on your chest. Come in, sit down."

Ivan noticed that the guest chairs were larger with open backs. While looking at the chairs, he chuckled a little bit before saying, "I see you've redecorated."

"Yeah, after going legit with Pierce's group, family, company or whatever you want to call it, My chairs were comically small for a lot of my new guests and employees." Dorian sat down into his chair. "Oh, I have something for you." He reached into his desk and brought out a gold chain. "Thor moved out of town but asked me to give this back to you if you ever got back this way."

"Oh man," Ivan picked up the chain. "I haven't thought about this in years." He tried to place it around his neck. "Hah, it's more like a choke collar and less like a chain. I'll need to get this lengthened," Ivan said as he pocketed the chain. "Thank you."

"You flew a long way, so let's get down to brass tacks." Dorian reached in and pulled out a brown envelope and handed it to Ivan. "Neville had me dig up some info on that Burk Falosian guy who tried to murder that young politician. Turns out he grew up here in the worst part of Dogtown. Somehow, he's got a very clean rap sheet but my contacts say he's a gun for hire."

Ivan opened up the envelope and started flipping through the dossier. "So, what in here is so important that Neville wanted me to get it personally?"

"The press is saying he was in that hate group, but my contacts say otherwise. The last few pages are on a different guy that is rumored be connected to Senator Clark's Chief of Staff, Robert Almirez." He waited for Ivan to get to those pages. "This other guy, Frederick Yanko, is a former special forces sniper and worked for Senator Clark's security team for a while. This Frederick was also good friend with Falosian in the army. I think there's something deeper here. I think Almirez paid Burk though this Yanko guy to assassinate the senator's son."

"This seems like something more for the police to deal with," Ivan stated bluntly.

"Yeah, but my contacts say some of the police are sympathetic to the Senator so they aren't really investigating too deep. They'll just convict him on the evidence so no connections will be made to the Senator." Dorian looked at Ivan square in the eyes. "Either you need to get some of your press people to dig into this or you may need to get access to this Burk guy directly to get the evidence. He wasn't a stupid fellow. I think they're just making him look like a crazy hate group member to keep the suspicions down. Anyone of my contacts I talked with said he was very organized and they are 100% sure he has physical evidence hiding somewhere."

"Hmm..." Ivan rubbed his chin. "I can probably feed this to some press people here but I want to try something else first. I don't want the Senator's loyalists get wind of anything so they won't have any warning." Ivan put the documents back into the envelope. "Thank you Dorian."

"Anything for my 'adopted' son," He smiled. "Now, lets go get some dinner. There are really a lot of nice restaurants nearby now."

"Steak," Ivan grinned with teeth showing. "Those politicians love to eat all this gourmet stuff. I just need a big, juicy steak right now."

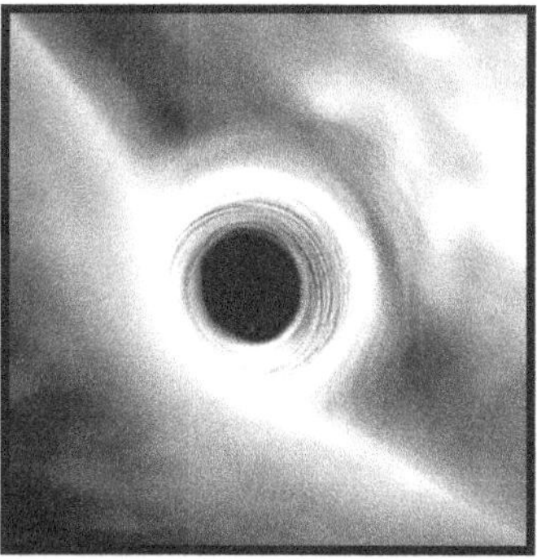

"You think this is the power reactor?" Tyler asked his chief propulsion physicist and engineer, Demitri Rusnak. They were standing on a catwalk above a large, organized debris field on the hanger floor.

"Yeah, I think we have enough of this debris to make some educated guesses." Demitri pointed to the center of the wreckage. "I believe they are using a tiny, artificial black hole to generate an electrical field. This structure here," he motioned to what seemed to be remnants of a large spheroid, "would be the containment structure. The tiny, primordial black hole would be placed in the center and held by ... I am speculating here, with some sort of magnetic or plasma containment inside the sphere. The problem with a primordial black hole is it does not spin, so it doesn't fling any useful material. To be perfectly clear, we are hand-waving a little here, as all of this is theoretical."

"I read some of the papers written on this type of reactor. If it's not producing charged particles, how is it useful to create energy?" Tyler asked him, but he had an inkling of what the man was going to tell him.

"Well, to charge up the black hole to be useful, it must be bombarded with charged particles. Once charged it will repel enough of the particles, which are flung back out at a higher state of charge and can be harvested to create energy." Demitri made a circular motion around the perimeter. "This would be the part that collects the electrons and positrons for use as an energy source."

Looking back at Tyler, Demitri continued. "Also, we can use the plasma field that the black hole produces in its accretion disk. It's electrically charged, so we might be able to gain some more energy from magnetic induction in coils." He looked back to the debris,

"There's two huge issues: One, we don't have proof that primordial black holes actually exist. Second, we need room temperature super-conductors to keep this from completely melting down."

"So, what you're telling me is we can't build this ourselves with our tech?" Tyler rubbed his chin, thinking about what was being presented to him.

"Yes, this is beyond our technical abilities now. My team of physicists are running simulations but I think this is beyond us for the foreseeable future. Shall we head back to the offices?" Demitri suggested heading back by motioning with his hand. "Without some real data from an alien scientific database I'm afraid we can't replicate this. So, we will have to focus on better versions of current rocket and spacecraft propulsion."

"Okay, so let's focus everyone on that and table this idea for the time being." Tyler said decisively, as they started walking back into the offices. "Maybe if we get lucky with the data we have managed to extract and we'll find more know-how and shortcut the century we'll need to figure it out ourselves."

Burk Falosian was being held without bail in the Suffok Regional Federal Penitentiary. Prosecutors felt that he was a flight risk with his training in the Earth Special Forces so they doubled the guard on his watch. Burk was laying on his back on his bunk in solitary just staring up at the ceiling when a baton rattled on his cell door.

"Get up Burk, you have a visitor. I'm not sure why anyone would want to see you." A tall gray wolf said in a deep, gruff voice. Another human guard was standing to the side of the larger canine with a serious look on his face.

"Go to hell, mutt." Burk growled as he got up and walked to the bars. He knew the drill and put both his hands through the bars allowing them to handcuff him.

The smaller human guard chuckled out loud as he clamped the handcuffs onto him very tightly. "They're going to fry you boy," the man said while putting on the cuffs.

The wolf opened the doors and grabbed Burk by the arm and roughly walked him down the hall. They went into the administrative part of the prison complex and was unceremoniously dumped into a chair in an interrogation room.

The room was dark save for one bright light shining on him nearly making him blind. Burk heard the door open behind him the room. A shadowy figure entered quietly and closed the door behind him. "Oh goodie, another lawyer. You mine or one for that corrupt prosecutor?"

Suddenly the chair leg was kicked from behind and out from under him, crashing him to the floor on his back. "OOF!" was all that came out of his mouth when his head slapped the concrete. His eyes slowly refocused to a giant black wolf wearing very non-descript black clothes looming over him. "Fuck you."

The wolf reached down with a massive paw to yank him up to his feet by his hair. "That's just to know who you're dealing with." The wolf kicked up the chair upright with his foot and plunked Burk back into the chair. "You see, I'm not here to dilly-dally with the courts."

"Go back to the hell you came from!" Burk spat at the dark figure.

"You need to tell me some information," and then he backhanded the man with a large furred hand. "Who paid you?"

"No one did you asshole. I did it for me and the rest of the humans." Burk retorted.

"No one? I don't believe you." The wolf leaned down to put his nose right up against his Burk's. "You are going to talk to me." He then placed his open palm on the man's face, pushed him back which caused him to fall and smack his head on the floor again.

"Damn you. I am not working for anyone!" Burk rolled off the chair and onto his side looking at the feet of his assailant.

The massive wolf reached down and wrapped a paw around his neck, squeezed and roughly pulled him to his feet. "You WILL tell me." He then picked him up by his neck and slammed his back into a nearby wall in the dark side of the room. Still holding him up in the air against his back the wolf added, "Don't worry, the cameras aren't running. They are 'down for maintenance'."

Burk's eyes widened in fright as the wolf's face curled up into a menacing toothy snarl. "I...I told you, I work for NO ONE!" He started to kick at the wolf's legs as the animal's hand closed tighter around his neck.

"Then I have no use for you." The wolf then let him drop to his feet and subsequently grabbed Burk's shoulders tightly. In a blinding motion, the wolf snarled, lunged and wrapped his teeth around the man's throat.

Feeling the teeth of the beast clamping down he screamed, "GET OFF ME YOU MONSTER!" One of the sharp teeth had just pierced the skin and a blood droplet ran down his neck.

The wolf released the pressure and pulled his face back. "I would reconsider your course of action little man." The wolf said as he grinned, showing his full set of canines to Burk. He then dragged the prisoner back to the chair and roughly set him down.

Burk's heart was beating a million miles an hour. He steeled his nerves, "Okay, I get your point. What's in it for me?"

The black figure then dusted the shoulders of the man's jumpsuit with a paw, "That's more sensible of you. You get to live. That's what I am offering."

"Why would I care? Everyone says they're going to fry me anyway. No skin off my back," Burk smirked at the beast.

Suddenly, the wolf punched him in the gut shoving the chair back two feet. "OOF!" came out of the human's mouth.

"Oops, my hand slipped," the wolf grinned right back at him. "I assure you, death by lethal injection will be better than being eaten alive and I will make sure you're alive for most of it." He emphasized his statement by licking his lips.

The wolf really looked like he might bite a chunk out of his face. "Okay, Okay. Yanko. Frederick Yanko paid me." He shakily said.

The wolf patted his cheek with an open paw, "See little man, that was easy." He stood up, towering over the seated man. "I know you are very organized and I need EVIDENCE. Where is it?"

Burk tried to match the wolf's stare, but looked down as he thought he might get punched again and the beast had a strong punch. "Dog-town. There's a storage locker on 12th street under the name Marvin De La Cruz. Everything is there."

"Thank you, I will check that out." He leaned back on the interrogation table making it creak under his weight. "To assure your silence I will only take the documents I need. The rest is safe provided you keep your trap shut. Understood?"

"Yes, completely understood." Burk said quietly.

"Silence is golden. I would hate for you to end up in the general population in the canine wing. They won't be as nice as I am. You can imagine the rest."

***

Ivan walked to an unregistered gray car down the street and drove away from the prison.   He then took out a burner phone and dialed a number. "Dorian."

"Evening Ivan, What's on your mind?" Dorian answered.

"I need a favor. Can you check out a storage locker over on 12th street under the name Marvin De La Cruz?" he asked. "I think we found the goods on our shooter."

"Sure thing Ivan," Dorian agreed. "Call you when we found it."

"One more thing. Call someone in Calveras and dig up stuff on Frederick Yanko and do it quickly. I suspect once this is out he will either be hard to find or dumped in a river."

Ivan hung up the phone, drove out of town and ditched the car in a wrecking yard.

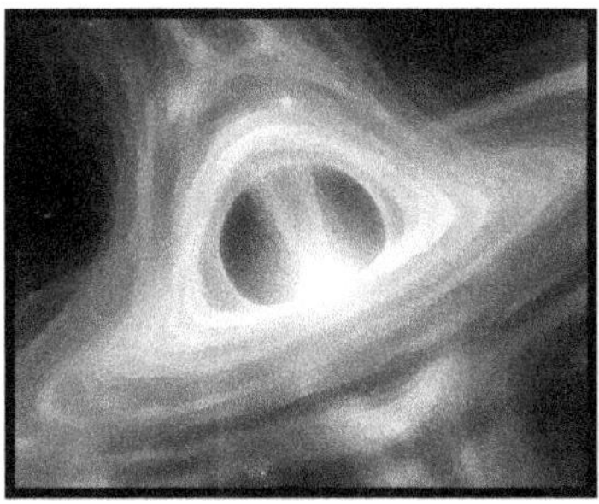

Demitri Rusnak's team was waiting for Tyler to finish a meeting so they could share their latest discovery with him. The group was mostly just milling about the conference room, chatting and drinking coffee to pass the time.

"Sorry about that folks," Tyler apologized as he came into the room along with Neville Pierce. They sat down at one side of the white conference table that ran the length of the room. "Let's get to it."

Demitri clicked a button on his tablet and walked over to the display screen. "Our team had identified two different new systems in the wreckage." He tapped his tablet to bring up a photo: a linearly arranged selection of wreckage. "First, this set of debris appears to be a subliminal ion drive. At its heart there is a fusion reactor that produces electricity specifically for this device. It's a typical ion drive that uses xenon gas so there's nothing special here, aside from the scale of the system. Our alien craft was very, very large."

Tyler spoke up, "Why do you think it has a separate fusion reactor instead of using the black hole power generator?"

"Good question. We think it has a lot to do with redundancy. This reactor is sized for the power needs of interplanetary travel, not interstellar travel. The black hole device, we believe, is for another very specific purpose." Demitri smiled before clicking to another close-up picture. "This is what we think is the fusion reactor." Then, he used his tablet pen to highlight several components. "These are very similar to the fusion reactors that we have had in service on Earth since the early 2000's. It is much more advanced than ours so we are learning a lot about the alternate materials they were using. For instance, we don't have any idea what fuel they were using. If we just swap in Deuterium/Tritium into the model, we get a reactor that puts our terrestrial reactors to shame in pure power output and in one quarter of the size."

Neville, who had been completely silent up to this point spoke up, "Can we build it?"

"Oh, we believe so. Nothing we have found in it would prevent us from making a working prototype from our technology."

"Done," Tyler interjected firmly. "You and your team work out the math and basic designs and I will get a team to commercialize it. Do you think we can engineer a smaller size for an ion drive in the size we need for the 'Ligare'?"

"Ligare?" Demitri looked at Tyler.

"Oh sorry, that's what we have named the first ship," he sat back in his chair. "It means 'to tie or bind'. It's our oath, our promise to make the world a better place."

"Ahh, thanks for clarifying." Demitri looked down at his tablet for a second. "If the space plane team's weight estimates are correct then we should be able to make one small enough to fit. It's not going to be a blazingly fast craft but I worry more about getting enough fuel up to space. We will probably have to rely on launch thrust to get us the speed we want on the way out of Earth's atmosphere to have enough fuel to get the craft back. There's no way it would be powerful enough to reach escape velocity on its own."

"Give us the specs and we'll see what they can fit," Tyler said in a positive tone. "Please, keep going."

"Thank you. Now back to the topic of the black hole power source." Demitri made a new image appear on the screen. "We don't have a lot of debris to go by but the team is convinced that their craft used what is referred to as an 'Alcubierre Drive'. If you aren't familiar with this conceptual theory, it basically uses space-time manipulation to produce faster than light travel." He clicked to a rendering. "If you compress space-time in front of the craft and simultaneously expand space-time behind it you basically create a fold of space-time and the ship is pushed forward along. Theoretically, there is no discernible acceleration due to the speed change. If you power up the drive while stationary you would be in zero gravity. The more power you have, the longer the space-time folds can be and the faster you would be moving relative to everything else."

"There are some problems with this drive," Demitri clicked to an animation. "Due to the gravity waves this drive would produce you can't run a drive anywhere near inhabited planets or anything large. You do not want to accidentally disturb a field of asteroids and bombard a planet. The gravity waves this drive produces could actually cause enormous damage to a nearby planet. In other words, it would cause gravity anomalies, earthquakes and tidal waves."

Tyler moved a hand up to rub on his chin, "After my 'accident' and the forming of this company, I have been avidly reading a lot of history of the planet to get a better understanding of our alien interlopers. I wonder if this alien ship crash was the source of the massive earthquakes that happened back in 1357? Written reports say there was a planet-wide earthquake, followed two days later by a massive explosion, fireball and a shower of meteorites."

"Very possibly. That's what the physics suggest." Demitri continued on with his previous train of thought, "Second issue is it would take immense power, hence the need for the black hole power generation. Third, when the drive is cut off you immediately drop back to the same speed you were cruising at. In theory, the area of space you're traveling in stays at the same state and is just pushed along, so there isn't any acceleration change. We just don't know the answer to this. Everyone on board could become liquefied due to a rapid change in acceleration if the occupants were subjected to it. That's a gruesome thought. You could bring the drive up really slowly and slow down slowly but I guess that would defeat the purpose of an FTL drive. You would spend so much time speeding up and slowing down. There are just a lot of unknowns to this theoretical drive."

"That sounds extremely hard to do and completely a non-starter for us with current technology." Tyler sat forward to rest his chin on his hands. "Does anyone actually have a theory on just HOW to be able to manipulate space-time?"

"No, not really. It's only been purely theoretical work but we think our aliens managed it." Demitri clicked back to the debris. "It's only a working theory at this point. This is way beyond our technical know-how."

"Interesting. I guess this gets put on the same pile as the black-hole power source, so let's focus our efforts on the improved fusion ion drive." Tyler leaned back. "Okay, thanks for the update. Keep up the great work people."

"Welcome to Heartstone Tonight, I am Troy Alvarez." The screen changed to play the short intro for the show before switching back to the presenter. "Big news tonight. A trove of documents were released to the press regarding the assassination attempt on Brennan Clark's life. This man," the camera switched to a photo of the assassin being taken into custody. "Burk Falosian, who was thought to be a member of the Humans First Coalition was not working alone."

The screen changed to a picture-in-picture of Troy and the shooter. "Documents were uncovered and released openly on the internet which links him to a greater conspiracy. Burk kept detailed accounts of his communications, financial records and bank accounts. According to his documents, he was paid a hansom sum of money to assassinate the young candidate."

"His records also indicated that Burk was working for this man." The screen swapped to a low resolution picture of a black haired man in military fatigues. "Frederick Yanko. Frederick is a former member of military special forces and has been an independent contractor since leaving the military. Burk and Frederick served in the special forces at the same time which leaves many speculating that they were friends in the service."

The screen returned to the news desk. "Only details regarding this contract were released, but experts think Burk had turned into a professional assassin and is probably linked to dozens of other murders."

Frederic Yanko has connections to Senator Joseph Clark's campaign. Yanko worked for Senator Joseph Clark as a security expert twelve years ago but was terminated for non-specified reasons. Pundits are saying this bodes poorly for Senator Clark's campaign as Yanko might still be connected to the Senator. The same pundits wonder if the Senator ordered the hit."

"We reached out to Senator Clark's office but they did not respond to our inquiry. Authorities have not released any new information on the case but say they are now looking for Frederick Yanko as a person-of-interest in this case." Troy ended his monologue.

The camera switched to a wide angle shot showing the news anchor and a guest. "Tonight, I am joined by Hiro Adachi, the campaign manager for Brennan Clark, here to find out what their campaign has to say about the new developments. Welcome to the show, Hiro."

"Thank you Troy, most pleased to be here." Hiro said while nodding at the newsman.

"So, big news uncovered today. What is the campaign's position on this?" Troy asked of his guest.

"Right now, we are in a wait-and-see mode. Until the documents can be verified as real we can only speculate." Hiro leaned back in the chair before continuing. "I can understand if the HFC is behind Brennan's attack. His popularity does not bode well for their cause across the globe. People's minds have been shifting to a more positive outlook on Canine-kind, so it has them worried."

"And if the Senator ordered it?" Troy questioned.

"The link is only superficial as this Yanko guy was loosely connected to the Senator. It would be a shocker if the Senator was found to be connected to Brennan's attempted murder." Hiro brought a hand up to rub his jaw. "With the fiery, hateful rhetoric the Senator has spouted on camera over the past few months he has riled up several extremist groups, like the HFC. I think they took that as a signal to go on the offensive. Senator Clark is too savvy a politician to head down that dark path, at least one would hope so."

***

"Augusto," Senator Clark addressed his Chief of Staff. "When I asked you to figure out how to beat Brennan, I sincerely hope you didn't take that as a request to pay someone to murder him?"

"No Joseph," Augusto Okazaki said. "You are not involved in any of this, I assure you." The Chief shifted in his chair. "We are working hard to get a statement out to spin this. We need to reassure the general public you had nothing to do with it."

The Senator's face was getting red, "You'd better get that done. Polls are dropping fast on this news," Senator Clark angrily replied.

***

Augusto hurriedly walked out of the Senator's office after being berated for 30 minutes. He was typing some info into his phone before pocketing it and pulling out a second phone. He was parked down the block and dialed a number, as he walked. "Yes, take care of it." He listened to other party for a minute before cutting them off, "DON'T give me excuses. JUST TAKE CARE OF IT!" and he angrily hung up.

He grabbed a handkerchief out of his pocket and started wiping the phone. As he reached his car, he dropped the phone by the curb. Using his heel, he crushed the phone and kicked it into the storm drain.

"WE GOT IT!" David Brynn burst into Tyler's office.

Tyler jumped as he had his head down pouring over schematics of their space plane. He settled back into his chair. "You gotta knock David, you nearly gave me a heart attack! Okay, WHAT did you get?" Tyler asked of the man.

"Computer models came back today and we have an 80% probability that we now have about 60% of the alien language decrypted." He was very excited. "At least 60% of their technical language, at any rate. Most of the data seems to be ship operations and scientific documents."

"That IS exciting!" Tyler smiled at David. "Anything else uncovered?"

"Well, now that we have some of the basics, we are scanning to see if we can pull out anything other than text. If I was traveling through space, I would be recording everything. They seem to have a metric ton of storage capacity on those crystals so there's got to be video logs, crew reports, security footage, etc. I would bet my career on it."

"Well, let's not go that far," the coyote smirked at him. "Is the computer giving you any inklings there are those types of files? I hope we get something soon, I think Maya, Renata and the team are getting a little bored sifting through the rubble."

"I think it has located the data blocks, the system just needs to process it to decode it. Then we'll have more to look at." David stated.

"Alright, keep me posted, but please knock next time!" Tyler said just before picking up a schematic again.

***

"Okay folks, sit down and let's get started." Tyler motioned for everyone to sit down. The small auditorium had about 200 people crammed into it. "First thing, this video we are going to show today is extremely confidential. David's computer models have given us the basics of the written alien language, as you already know. Last week, the models identified audio and video files and decrypted them. David. Go ahead." Tyler motioned to the screen.

"Thanks Tyler," he pushed something on his tablet and a staticky, grainy image appeared. "First thing, the data crystal that this was extracted from was pretty thoroughly shattered. The laser scanners were lucky to be able to reconstruct anything at all from it. We used a 3-dimensional recreation of the scanned crystal structure and used a computer model to 'play' the data, as the computer would be reading it from them. This video comes from what we think was a 'black box' recording device on the ship and I think you will agree with our assessment that this is the most revealing, and important, video we have decrypted so far..."

David looked over at Tyler, "Are we all ready?" The cryptologist looked around the room and everyone nodded. He noticed that Neville Pierce had quietly entered and was standing at the back of the room.

David pressed play and the video began. It was barely visible. Static, streaks and blank-outs were happening all at once. The video appeared to be taken from a cockpit recorder on board the alien craft. From what they could see from the broken up video, the operator of the ship looked like a jet-black terrestrial coyote laying on its belly operating a flight console in front of it.

The being was speaking audibly in series of whuffs, squeaks and gruffs but it was very hard to hear it over the explosions, rattles and vibrations. The camera was shuddering with more intensity as the video rolled on showing that the ship was apparently in serious trouble. They could just make out that the pilot was barely able to stay in its couch, since the craft was lurching and heaving constantly. During the five minute video it was frantically yelling over the noise of the ship the entire time. Whomever this being was, they were obviously panicked and in trouble.

In one final act the pilot looked right at the recorder, screamed something at it and smacked a glowing red button. The pilot and couch disappeared into the floor. The final clip of the video seemed to be taken from the front of the ejected pod. The shot showed a long cylindrical ship with two large rings concentric with the hull of the ship. One ring in the front was already erupting with explosions and fire, as the ship was entering the atmosphere. The video went blank, appearing to lose connection with the ship.

Everyone in the room was silent taking in what they just saw. Tyler let them think on it for a little while before stepping to the front of the room. "When I saw this video, I was as surprised as you. The alien race seems to be physically similar to our Earth born four-legged feral canines. The sheer scale of the ship pictured shows the scale of the construction they are capable of. It's quite remarkable. Any of you have any questions?" Tyler waited patiently, as he knew the team was still absorbing what they had just seem.

After a while Renata raised a hand, "Well, it seems my guess on their physiology was correct. The pilot was laying on a formed couch similar to the one found. Do we have any more video? I want to see more of these creatures at work, get a feel for them and their social structure."

David piped up, "Yes, the computer has decoded a lot. Most of it is just a time-lapse of the ship running itself. It looks like they all are in some sort of hibernation during interstellar travel. They probably travel in statis due to the length of time it takes to avoid crew boredom. We are still working through a lot. Hopefully we can link the timestamps of any active video to some of the ship data so we can see what they were doing at the time of the recording."

Tyler added to this, "Renata, on your topic of physiology, I also think their system of counting in eights is because they have four digits on each hand, unlike us, with ten." The coyote held up his hand with his finger splayed out. "They seem to have two thumbs on either side of the middle two fingers. I guess that's why they became such good tool makers."

"Are there any engineering diagrams, blueprints or advanced mathematics in the data?" Demitri Musnak asked. "My engineering team would love to find any technical data on their ship," he added.

"No, not that we have found. If the ship had full technical documents in the device we have, it was unfortunately lost to the crystal damage." Tyler responded. "That doesn't mean we won't find some. Neville's expedition group is still working on salvaging more parts from the ocean floor. Maybe we will find more data storage units. I suspect a ship that size would have a LOT of redundancy." The coyote paused for a moment. "Okay, one more question."

"The ship in that last bit of video," Lewella Price, a small astrophysicist fox spoke up. "That ship, those two large rings at the front and aft of the ship. Do you think those are the space-time warp drives?"

"That is a good question. We don't know, but it does seem to match one of the concepts that a theoretical physicist dreamed up in the 1990s. Okay people, the video we have uncovered won't be viewable on the wider company intranet yet as we are deciding whether we are releasing this publicly or not. Please send a message to David Brynn if you require watching that video for your job. We are keeping this under tight security and David will be very selective on who can view this video. We will keep everyone posted on what new things are uncovered This is an exciting day for us."

Brennan sat down on the couch with a tired 'thud' after another full day of campaigning and took a swig of bourbon that he had been nursing for the past hour. Hiro came over to sit down across from him.

"Check out this headline." Hiro handed him a tablet open to the Calveras Time website.

"Frederick Yanko Found Dead in River" Brennan read it out loud. "Remind me who this guy was?"

"Sorry, I was handling all that. I wanted you focused on the campaign and policy issues. That is the man who paid the assassin." Hiro flattened his ears at the thought of Brennan getting shot.

"OH, that man. My head's been swimming with speeches, talking points and just trying to keep on top of my daily schedule." Brennan rubbed between his eyes.

"Yeah, the article also mentions that his entire flat was burnt out. I guess someone is getting worried and really didn't want anyone to find out who paid HIM. This guy worked for your father a while ago and everyone's trying to connect the dots to your father whether that's true or not." Hiro poured himself a small glass of bourbon.

"My father might be an asshole, but it doesn't feel like he would want me dead." Brennan sunk into the couch a little. "Or am I just projecting my own feelings here?"

"Well, I wouldn't focus on that. We're polling 20 points ahead of good old dad so we should be in a good position for the last month push, which begins in ..." Hiro looked at his watch, then added, "a week from Monday."

***

"Patrick Steele of Heartstone News here in front of Senator Clark's campaign headquarters. Authorities in Calveras recovered critical data files from Frederick Yanko's apartment after he was found murdered. Yanko was identified as the man who paid Burk Falosian to assassinate the young Senate candidate Brennan Clark. Today, police in Heartstone released a statement. They said, and I quote, 'The files that we recovered from Frederick Yanko in Calveras show us that Senator Clark's campaign made several large payments to Mr. Yanko. This morning, Augusto Okazaki, Senator Clark's Chief of Staff, was arrested on first degree murder charges.' Patrick added, "At this point in time the Senator has not been indicted for this crimes."

"Okay Zuri, we're almost set." Haoqi had spent days getting ready for the recording. Last week, Tyler and Neville agreed that they should release some of the alien crash video and diverted him from his regular task of documentation. He hadn't produced any videos like this before but thankfully he had Zuri's ace cameraman, Jamin Baloyi, setting up the video feeds. Minutes later the white wolf announced, "You can get settled in on the couch."

Haoqi had set up a nice modern looking living room set to give the viewers the feeling of a casual daytime talk show. Zuri, who had already been mic'd up, positioned herself on the couch and fluffed her cheek fur.

Zuri closed her eyes for a moment thinking through the script. "Okay, I'm ready."

"Audio check," Houqi asked the gentleman over by the computer. "Zuri, give me a mic check."

"Mic, mic check," she said in a calm tone and his production assistant nodded.

"Good. Zuri, please give me a 20 second pause between each paragraph for editing space. Okay, we're rolling in 4...3...2..." Houqi nodded to her.

Zuri watched the large screen they were using for the teleprompter and began once the text started appearing.

"Hello there, I am Zuri Mandla, Vice President of Communications here at Dresden-Pierce Aerospace and Exploration Company. We, at the DPAE are dedicated to pushing the boundaries of science, technology and space exploration."

"Back in the 1970s, the Earth Aerospace Administration built and flew the world's first space plane. Over the next decade they flew about 6 missions before cost overruns, public interest and inflation caused the program to be terminated. Since then no one has taken space exploration seriously and all we have done globally is put satellites in orbit for communications."

"We founded the DPAE to pick up that fallen torch. By leap-frogging off the work that the EAA and the late Michael Dresden had accomplished, we are aiming to open up space in a more efficient and economical way."

"Over the past couple of years we have created an amazing team of engineers, scientists, metallurgists and manufacturing engineers. These teams have made astounding progress in our quest. The first prototypes of our rockets and space plane are transitioning from the virtual world to reality as I speak. Construction of the rockets are moving forward on schedule and we are looking for a late summer ignition test."

"Our first space plane, called the 'DPAE Ligare,' represents the first step of our promise to bring the world of space travel to the people of Earth. Our teams have begun physical construction of the air-frame for the ship. We have designed a plane that is about the size of a small passenger jet but will weigh about 25% of what the current crop of aircraft weigh. This will allow us to launch with much smaller rockets, lowering the cost and environmental impact of every launch."

"We are really proud of the work and progress our teams have done in such a short time. All of their accomplishments should be celebrated as feats of knowledge and determination."

"That brings me to one of the most amazing discoveries that the DPAE has made during our development of the project. During the initial research phase many of our experts were given access to the alien artifacts that were collected from around the world."

"We have learned a lot about their technology. These aliens are vastly more advanced than us. They are at least a millennia or more beyond where we are technology-wise. Many of the systems of their spacecraft use tech that has only been theorized by the world's top minds and are science fiction to us here on Earth."

"In analyzing some of the computer tech, our brilliant team was able to power up some of the artifacts and have managed to access the memory bank of one device. With help of Dres-Tek's supercomputers we have been able to decrypt some of the alien's written language. We have also found the data contained one particular video that we would like to share with the world right now."

"This video appears to be the last recording made by the spacecraft before crashing to Earth. The video we are about to show you is pretty corrupted, but it gives us a glimpse of how the Earth was changed forever by these aliens. Parental discretion is advised."

The screen cuts to the video of the alien ship in its last few minutes in space above the Earth. After playing, the screen returns to focus on Zuri.

"You can see from the video it appears the alien spacecraft was in trouble before crashing onto our planet, changing the course of our history. In reviewing this video, our experts came to the conclusion that the crash was accidental and was without malice."

"The alien pictured in the footage looks much like our terrestrial wild canines than we could have imagined. This might explain why their Nano-Docs were seemingly compatible with our wild canine's physique. We were able to extract some of the spoken alien language from the utter chaos in that video but we are unable to translate any of it. At this point, we do not have enough audio or video to do this."

"We are making this video public as it is such an important discovery and we cannot keep this secret with good conscience. We will also be releasing any new information on the alien's culture if we manage to uncover more."

"and CUT." Haoqi said. "One take, that was great Zuri! We can get to work on editing the video and release it!"

Zuri stood up and smiled, "Well, we will see how the public reacts to *that*."

***

"That video was fake, pure and simple." The traditionalist pundit, Alvin Krebbs, on the left side of the screen said bluntly. "That is totally put together to garner more support for the canine candidates that are behind in the polls. It's pure propaganda. Do we actually believe that the aliens are just like our feral canines? The timing of its release is so close to the election that it seems too convenient to me."

Ph.D. Salina Chen was sitting in the middle and spoke up, "Well, there's been a lot of alien debris dredged up across the world. And consider what the alien's nano technology did to our native canines. They must have been genetically similar enough for them to work on them. A lot of conclusive research was published on the effects of the tiny doctors on the native canine population. It seems plausible to me."

Gamba Noor seated on the right added, "I believe it. I see no reason that an aerospace company would release a fake video, let alone trying to prop up candidates. Especially so, if you consider they are a private company and do not do business with the government. The government isn't holding the purse strings."

Krebbs interrupted, "Neville Pierce's legal group has been lobbying for canine rights for YEARS and he is a partner in that company, so their motivations are suspect to me. Also, don't forget that Brennan Clark used to work for Pierce's legal group. Besides, my daughter can make better videos than that."

"Well first thing, Brennan is way up in the polls and it looks like he will have a lock on that district. Especially now that all that evidence has dropped that loosely connects his father with the attempted mur-der." Gamba retorted.

"Suspected connection," Krebbs added. "There's no proof. That's also fake. This smells of a conspiracy to discredit the Senator."

"Well, someone DID try to murder Brennan and that's NOT fake." Salina added, "His father has NOT been silent about his disdain for his son after the accidental transformation."

"I think someone in Capitola should investigate the DPAE." Krebbs boldly stated. "They are up to something. The government needs visibility into what they are doing."

***

"Jordan Helmsey at the UBN 10 News Desk. Tonight's top story: Aliens. The release of the alien crash footage from the Dresden-Pierce Aerospace and Exploration company has caused quite a stir across the Earth. Many are labeling the video as a science-fiction fantasy and are accusing the DPAE of releasing this video to help the pro-canine caucuses in this election season. Some are calling on Senate Election Oversight Committee in Capitola to investigate the company for election interference. Whether it is real or a fake, the release of the video seems to have helped the canid candidates that were lagging in the polls. Pro-canine support has grown across the districts since the release of the video. It looks like the Reform party has a chance to gain a majority in congress for the first time in history."

"Welcome to our continuing coverage of election night. I'm Troy Alvarez with Heartstone Tonight." The camera zoomed out to show Troy standing in front of a large screen with all the global congressional districts. "We will be broadcasting live until the polls close tonight. Early polling in the congressional race has shown us some interesting trends." Troy clicked a spot on the screen then continued, "These are the results from the last election. You can see the Neo-Populist party has a slim majority in congress but if you look at the polls from mid-day today," a selection of the blue districts started pulsing green. "Twenty-seven of these districts are polling towards the Reform party. This would give the Reform party control of congress for the first time in Earth's history."

Troy clicked on one district in Heartstone. "Over here in the Suffok province of the Heartstone Prefecture, it has been one of the most politically charged races in decades." Icons of Brennan and his father Joseph appeared with their polling numbers shown under them. "Brennan, the popular local boy and hero, has a commanding lead. His father's campaign has been in absolute turmoil since the attempted assassination of Brennan. The senator is not implicated in the attempt but his chief of staff, Augusto Okazaki was arrested on charges of first degree murder. The Senator's campaign has not recovered and his polling numbers have plummeted." He clicked on Brennan's icon to enlarge it. "Brennan is polling ahead by nearly 40 points and is widely expected to win this district handily."

Troy clicked and returned the overall map. "So, let's explore these other districts......"

***

"The battle was long and hard, but we have won the day! I cannot overstate how much I appreciate all of you out there who helped make this victory possible. I promise I will fight for everyone in my district and for the betterment of Earth. Thank you all for your support!" Brennan said before stepping to the side of the podium to wave 'goodbye' to the crowd. He made his way off to the secured area behind the stage at Suffok University. Since he was at the same place as the attempt on his life, security was much tighter during his speech.

"Well done Brennan! Your victory speech was flawless." Hiro reached out and took Brennan's hand with both his paws.

Brennan smirked at the fox, "This wouldn't be possible without you and the amazing team you put together. I cannot thank you enough. You're going to be my Chief of Staff, right?" Brennan smiled at his campaign manager.

"Oh, I think I could be convinced to take that job." The smaller fox nodded in agreement. "Though, I need to see what Neville needs as I am technically still on contract with him."

***

The next morning Brennan rolled out of bed still tired from the previous night. The victory party went until the wee hours of the night and he was definitely feeling hung over. He yawned as he prepared some coffee. Grabbing the mug he padded over to the couch and flopped down on his back. He opened his tablet and began scrolling through the news. Every news outlet headline was some form of "Reform Party Wins the Night", "Father Beaten by Son in Campaign of the Millennia", and so on.

Brennan was quietly sipping his coffee when the front door opened. He suddenly realized he was naked as Ivan stepped through the door and put an envelope on the table nearby. The senator-to-be quickly placed his computer tablet over his crotch to hide himself.

The wolf smirked when he saw Brennan on the couch. "I thought you would still be asleep." Ivan grabbed a towel sitting on a chair near the front door and tossed it to Brennan. "Cover up, shy-boy."

Brennan grabbed the towel and tied it around his waist as he got up. After all this time he still wasn't used to the fact that he was covered in fur and not really naked in the human sense. "What brings you by so early?"

"Oh, I am taking a shift for one of your normal security guys. His wife went into labor this morning." Ivan picked up a package he had left by the door. "Besides, how often do I get to see you naked?" The wolf chuckled before he continued, "Hiro wanted me to drop off a batch of documents for you to look at." He handed the papers to Brennan and Ivan added. "He put together a list of houses to rent in Capitola as well as some congressional orientation documents. I think there are a few houses that fit the bill as far as security is concerned. I ranked them for you."

"Thanks Ivan. Now let me enjoy my hangover in peace." Brennan smirked and laid back down on the couch.

"Sure thing boss. I'll be downstairs if you need anything." Ivan started to open the door then turned to look back at Brennan, "Oh, Hiro booked you into a celebration dinner with Neville tonight. 7:30 pm. I'll drive you there."

"Oh, that's nice. I haven't sat down with him for a while. Talk to you later Ivan." Brennan sank into the couch to enjoy his coffee, as the wolf left.

***

Ivan had dropped Brennan off at the restaurant and he went inside to the host station. "Hi, I'm Brennan Clark and I'm here to meet someone," he said to the hostess.

"Yes, Mr. Clark. Congratulations on the victory yesterday. I voted for you!" she pointed to a 'Vote For Brennan' sticker on her lapel. "Mr. Pierce is already here so please follow me."

The woman escorted him to a private room upstairs. Neville was already seated at the table enjoying a glass of whiskey and got up when Brennan entered.

Neville stood up and reached out with both hands to grasp Brennan's in a handshake, "Congratulations young man, I knew you could do it. Please sit down." Neville gestured to the chair at his table. "Do you like whiskey? I have an excellent bottle of bottle from River City Distillery, 1992 vintage."

"Sure, I'll have a glass." Brennan really didn't want liquor since he was still nursing a hangover from last night but he didn't want to be rude. They sat down and the wait staff brought in menus. Brennan quickly scanned over the menu and ordered himself a tasty looking steak.

After the server left Neville poured a glass of whiskey for Brennan and then spoke, "I am really proud of you. You've come a long way from the youngster that joined our firm five years ago. You've really come into your own."

"Thank you Neville. I really couldn't have done it without the help of Hiro and the rest of the staff." He took a sip of the whiskey before adding, "I am excited and justifiably nervous to get to work."

While they waited for their food to arrive the two made small talk: Neville asked about his mother, if he had found anyone special, thoughts on his father and how he handled the assassination attempt.

"To start, you'll be a junior senator so you'll have to work your way into committees and bill authoring." Neville glanced up at the server who brought in their food and nodded in thanks. He returned his gaze back to the young wolf. "You'll have to pay your dues."

"Yeah, Hiro briefed me." Brennan cut his steak with a knife then brought up the piece to give it a good sniff. "I'm always amazed at how much better steak smells as a canid. I never knew I was missing so much before."

The wolf chuckled, "You're not the first person to say that afterward."

"Back to the junior senator business. Hiro gave me a bunch of documents to read. I'm sure all the 'procedures' in the senate are in there." Brennan popped the steak piece into his mouth and closed his eyes in enjoyment.

"Yeah, basically you have to be in congress for a few years before getting deep into committees and introducing legislation by yourself." Neville paused to take a sip of whiskey. "Do you remember Senator Lev Kronovski who you worked with on that medical bill from a few years ago?"

"Yes, I do. Too bad we couldn't get that passed." Brennan said with a slightly sad tone to his statement.

"Well, as a junior senator, it's good to get a mentor and I have asked Lev to take you on as his junior." Neville leaned back in his chair. "Lev has always been sympathetic to canid issues and he is more than happy to do that for me."

"Oh?" Brennan asked. "That's nice of him."

"Yeah, and we spoke about reintroducing that bill at the beginning of the new term with you as a co-author." Neville added.

"Yeah, we should be able to capitalize on the new found support for canids. Strike while the iron is hot or so they say." Brennan nodded.

"Exactly. There will be a few tweaks we should make. The basic bill is good but I think we can stretch it a bit more with less compromise." Neville said.

"Agreed." Brennan stated. "I'll get in touch with Mr. Kronovski and we will work up a draft before hand."

They continued to talk about the election results in other districts, especially some of the surprising upsets while they finished up their meal. Once done, they said their 'goodbyes' and Brennan headed back home to get some duly deserved sleep.

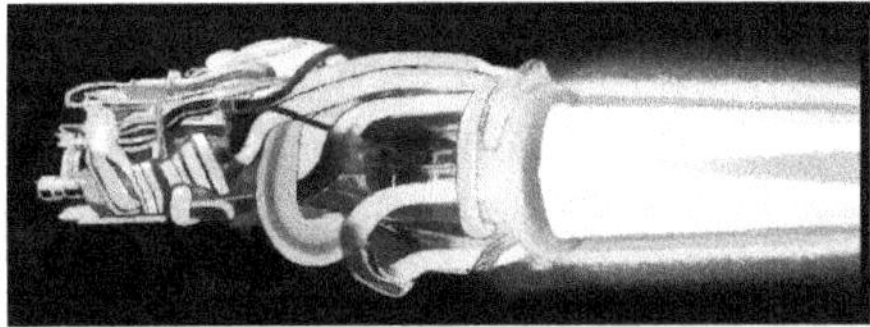

Haoqi motioned to Zuri, "We are live in 4...3...2..." and the wolf pointed to Zuri on the silent one.

"Welcome to the stream everyone, I am Zuri Mandla, head of Communications here at Dresden-Pierce Aerospace and Exploration Company. I hope everyone is as excited as we are for today's event. We will be live-streaming our first powered test of our new rocket engine, called the Goddard Minimus." Zuri was seated at a desk with the company logo on the screen behind her. "Aptly named after Robert Goddard who is widely considered to be the father of the liquid-fueled rocket. His first rocket launched way back in 1926 eschewing in the era of modern rocketry science. Goddard has 214 patents to his name and his team had launched 34 rockets in pursuit of Goddard's dream. Without his revolutionary work we would not be here today."

The stream had switched to a montage of photos of Goddard and some of his early rocket experiments during Zuri's brief history of about the man. When she finished the screen switched back to Zuri.
"The DPAE has taken the last 100 years of rocket development and brought it into the 21st century. With modern super-computing technology combined with hyper advanced material science, we have created an engine that is small, efficient, powerful and most importantly: reusable." She paused for a moment while the teleprompter caught up with her. "This engine will be the backbone of our launch and booster rockets, propelling the Ligare to outer space on its maiden voyage. The shape will look somewhat familiar to you if you watched the space shuttle launches back in the 1970's but trust me, this is way more advanced."

Haoqi, who had become the producer for these DPAE podcasts, motioned to Zuri with a thumbs-up signaling to transition.

"I am being told we are ready for the test. We will switch live to our team at the test facility." Zuri finished and the Dresden-Pierce logo appeared rotating around as if it was an art deco sign before fading into a multi-split screen, showing the team in the control center.

"Welcome to the test firing of our Goddard Minimus engine. I am Tyler Dresden, head of the DPEA. Today, marks the first step in returning our planet back to true outer space exploration." Tyler was looking directly at the camera to the virtual audience that was watching. "This engine has been designed to work directly with our space-plane launch rockets. The Ligare is going to be the lightest and highest tech spacecraft ever built on Earth. By making our craft as light as possible the engines do not need to be huge and over-sized. Our team has engineered the rocket and booster to be just large enough, hence the 'Minimus' in the name. I think we are ready. Electronics?" Tyler was doing double duty today as he was filling in for their controller, who was out due to a medical emergency.

"Control, computers ready." Konrad Singer said aloud. He was the chief computer systems engineer working on the new Goddard Minimus engine. He had come on board with the DPAE early on and was critical in upgrading the engine control computers with Dres-Tek micro-supercomputers. "Systems nominal."

"Fuel Systems, are we in the clear?"

"All green for fuel. Pressure's good, tanks purged." The propulsion engineer in charge of the fueling system was a young, brilliant female fox named Marla Johannsen. She was a recent addition to the team and was a great catch. She obtained her Ph.D. from the prestigious Miyazaki Institute of Technology in Fijiwara and joined them after a short stint at a competitor. Tyler was pretty happy having poached her for the team.

"Mechanical. Status?" Tyler asked of the Chief of Mechanical Systems, Hideo Izumi. Hideo was also from Fijiwara's MIT and an expert in mechanical integration.

"Mechanical Systems Green." Hideo answered Tyler.

Tyler looked at the panel below him, "Okay start the countdown Konrad." He had addressed Konrad Pachinko, the engine expert on the rocket team.

When the countdown reached zero the main valves of the engine opened and the engines roared to life.

"We have engine ignition. Systems nominal. Throttling up to 40%." Konrad spoke up after reviewing the initial data. He tapped a finger on his control screen and the engines increased in thrust. "We have 40%. Systems are still nominal." Konrad's control program let it burn at that state for 1 minute and then automatically throttled down the engine.

"Success!" Tyler yelled at the room and everyone watching erupted in cheers and applause.

The camera switched back to Zuri at her press desk with a picture in the corner showing the video of the engine throttling down. She turned her head to the camera and enthusiastically spoke. "Today's test firing of our new engine was successful and marks a huge milestone for all the teams here at DPAE! I personally would like to thank everyone on the staff for their hard work. We would not have reached our goal without each and every one of you. That's all we have for today. Thank all of you for tuning in today and we look forward to the next time we can show you our progress."

"And we're disconnected." Haoqi said aloud. "That was amazing! We had nearly 3 million people tuned in to watch this test. Imagine just how many we will have during an actual launch."

"That's really cool, Haoqi. I need to head over to the flight control room for the debriefing." Zuri started to walk out, "Oh, do you and Maya want to get some food later?"

"Oh yes, definitely! Text me when you're finished," he replied enthusiastically.

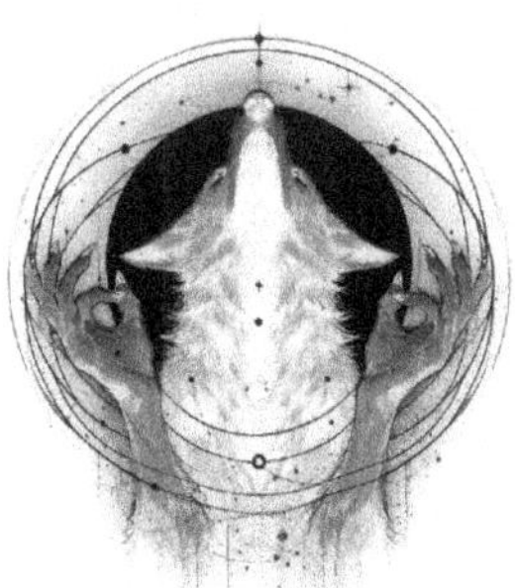

In the first two years Maya felt out of place at the DPAE. Neville had brought her on to help them decipher the alien's culture but extracting the data had proven to be an excruciatingly slow process. She wasn't technically minded and felt a bit useless around the office. Mostly she ended up counseling for the over stressed-engineering staff. Not that she was unhappy being a general councilor, but the staff wasn't generally religious so she had a hard time offering anything more than being a friendly ear. Thankfully, Neville had realized she was slightly under-utilized at the DPAE and he asked her to help out with Brennan Clark's election campaign. That gave her a much needed confidence boost. While on assignment, she had counseled the young wolf on how to appeal, but not patronize, the spiritual members of the community he was trying to represent and it seemed to have paid off.

Now that the campaign was over she was back at the DPAE to finally get to work on her original assignment: figuring out who the aliens were as a society. During the campaign the Dres-Tek computers had managed to decipher enough of the alien language that most of the videos had been translated. This let her start to review them in detail and to try to figure them out.

Maya leaned back in her chair reaching out her arms behind her in a big stretch. She looked over at Renata sitting nearby and spoke, "Most of these videos are just purely boring, automated logs of the days activities on the ship." Maya finished her stretch and sat back forward. "I am starting to understand some of their words though. Their whuffs, gruffs, squeaks and growls have a lot of subtlety to them." She chuckled out loud, "There is NO way a human could hear half of the conversation let alone speak it."

Renata added, "I'm thankful they added the subtitles in both languages. I'm beginning to recognize the characters." She held up a

claw. "I can definitely see them using their claws to write their Kanji."
Renata had an alphabet up on her laptop and it showed a series of dots,
dashes and zigzags that clearly could be easily written with a claw.

"Yeah, definitely. I hope I get to something personal soon. The
technobabble is giving me a headache." Maya smirked.

***

"Okay, I think I'm ready." Maya said as Tyler Dresden and Neville
Pierce sat down next to her. "I have gone through countless hours of
video. Once I found the personal logs I was able to target my searches
for social interactions, cultural references and historical documents."

"Once the computer pulled up my search results I was able to target
the personal logs and messages of the crew." Maya flipped to a still of
a canine alien in front of a camera. The alien's body was covered fur
was a shiny, completely jet-black color. It had a pointed muzzle, large
pointed ears and yellow eyes. "After sifting through all the boring,
routine end-of-shift logs of their work, I had the computer separate
the personal messages to family back at home. This is where things
got real exciting to me. Give me a second." Maya started rapidly
flipping through her open tabs to find the video she lost track of.

"Don't rush," Tyler smiled and put a paw on her shoulder. "Relax,
this isn't an inquisition," he could obviously see she was a bit nervous.

"Okay, this video," She hit play. "This one is a personal message
and the crew member was asking about how their child was doing
at school." She paused it at a particular point on the video with a
particular piece of subtitling. "The translation isn't complete here.
David Brynn looked at the raw footage per my request. He told me the
alien language subtitles are hard baked into this particular video and
are not from our translators. He guessed that was to prevent audio
drop out over long distances. I used the contextual clues in the rest
of this log to deduce their child is in some sort of religious or cultural
study program. There wasn't much in this video but it gave me some
words to search for in the archives."

Maya brought up about a dozen characters. "Next, I searched the
archives for references to these untranslated symbols and came up
with several different relevant document matches." She flipped to
one. "This text seems to be a guideline for living under the teachings

of...well, our analog here would be Gaia, or Mother Earth." She looked over to Tyler and Neville, "Any questions so far?"

Neville chimed in, "Not right now, please continue."

"So if the translation of this text is correct, it seems that they don't have a religion per-se. They don't worship 'gods', all-powerful beings or such. These teachings speak of respecting their world and treating it as you would yourself and others." She looked back at the text before looking back to the other two. "This is probably more like the religion, Shénmì Zōngjiào , or Shenism which coincidentally I was brought up studying at the temple. Mother Earth is to be revered and protected. No one individual is above nature."

"Now that isn't the only text that I found that contain religious references." She opened a couple of documents. "The translator program seems to think these are historical documents. These documents all refer to a 'Great Cataclysm'. It looks like their world used to have many clans. Each one with their own religions and their own distinct beliefs, philosophies and rules. It speaks of the a great purge, where one clan rained down fire upon the others to destroy their enemies, to purify their world. They eventually destroyed most of their species in the process."

Maya's eyes started tearing up and quickly looked away from the other two while adding, "From what I interpreted from these writings, I think they unleashed a nuclear war on their planet. They almost extinguished themselves ..." Her religious upbringing taught her to respect others, to listen to them and love them, despite their differences. She couldn't fathom hating someone so thoroughly that she would want them exterminated. She wiped her eyes before returning her gaze to Tyler and Neville. "They speak of themselves being spared from the Wrath of Gaia."

"Take a moment, Maya." Tyler could clearly see she was upset at the thought of a nuclear holocaust. He knew how connected Maya was to her emotions compared to a typical scientist. He always had to remind himself that she wasn't trained scientist, but a spiritualist. The saying "wearing your heart on your sleeve" popped into his mind as he paused. Tyler also believed patience was an extremely valuable virtue in life. Thus, he had a kind and gentle cadence behind his words as he tried to let her wrestle with her thoughts.

Maya took a deep breath, "No, I'm okay. I will continue." She flipped to another text. "Right here they talk about being spared from the cataclysm. So I had the archive program locate maps of their planet." She flipped to an image. "It seems they were the only clan in their southern hemisphere and they were spared from the nuclear fallout that wiped out everyone in the north."

"Looking at their planetary layout I think their clan didn't have any real enemies. Their lands were resource poor, fairly geographically isolated and not as technically advanced. So no one considered them a real threat. They were also a pacifist society so those things combined together to spare them from the devastation." She clicked to a montage of all the crew. "It looks like the genetic gene pool was pretty limited so they all look nearly identical or just homogenized after centuries. I wonder just how many actually survived their war?"

"After the war, they settled into a peaceful existence and built themselves into a technological wonder of a society. Their texts speak of no wars or conflicts after this Cataclysm." She turned back to Neville and Tyler. "That's it, in summary."

"Great work Maya," Tyler smiled. "The lessons learned here seem like something we should take to heart here on Earth."

Neville remained quiet for a minute rubbing the gray fur that was starting to take over his muzzle. "I think." he paused for a second. "I think we need to publish your findings." He looked over at Tyler, "What do you think?"

Tyler pursed his lips while he thought for moment then adding, "Yeah, I agree."

"Maya," Neville looked at her. "Haoqi did a great job with his other two books. I think you should work with him and Renata to put this into a book. I think this discovery can...should...be made public."

"Agreed." Tyler nodded. "I'll have David's team go through and 'declassify' the materials you can use and publish with."

"Oh and after the book," Neville smiled, "Plan to hit the lecture circuit. There will be a lot of people very interested in what you have discovered."

"Thank you!" Maya was getting excited. "I'll get with Renata, Haoqi and David to make preparations."

"Here I sit again. Two more years have gone by." Brennan said out loud to himself as he sat down on his couch in his home in Suffok. He took a sip of his coffee and exhaled, "I wonder..." he said out loud again as he was interrupted by a knock at the door. Brennan looked over to the door, "Come in."

The door opened and his friend, Press Secretary Hiro, walked in. Neville had suggested that Hiro take the press job, instead of the Chief of Staff role since he was so good on camera. "Good morning Brennan."

Brennan wasn't expecting Hiro this early but thought to himself, *"at least I wasn't naked on the couch this time."* He motioned over to the kitchen counter, "There's a fresh pot of coffee, if you'd like one."

"Thanks but I have already had two espressos this morning. I brought over the talking points for my interview this evening. I want to make sure we agree on what you think are your best accomplishments in your first two years as a Senator." Hiro sat down in the chair opposite Brennan after handing him a couple sheets of paper.

Brennan flipped through them quickly. "Yep, list looks good. Make sure you mention how we improved the medical bill and that it is a better bill for everyone, not just canids. I want to stress this was a joint effort between all the parties."

"Yes, definitely!" Hiro nodded. "I've got everything memorized so I should be able to field any 'surprise' questions from the interviewers. Anything special you feel we should focus on the upcoming voting reform act?"

"Nothing special that isn't already listed in the bill." Brennan brought his coffee mug to his lips and took a sip. "Just that it gives everyone an equal voice in our government by removing the anti-canine restrictions many provinces still have on the books as well as the anti-gerrymandering language. Also, please focus on the new voting technology the bill proposes and the improved security that goes along with it. I'm sure you can spin the anticipated questions about 'easily manipulated by tech companies' rhetoric."

"Understood." Hiro smiled. "This is easy after being a political pundit. I'll chew them up and spit them out." Hiro grinned with a toothy smile.

"Hah. So when are you running for an office? I can't see you being my second forever." Brennan gave Hiro a serious look.

"Oh, maybe next cycle I'll run for a prefecture senate seat. I would be CRAZY to run for a Capitola Senate seat before I had any experience in local government. I don't want to go through the hell that Brennan kid did." He winked at Brennan. "I do miss Fijiwara and I'd like to get back there." Hiro relaxed in the chair. "I really miss the night markets, plus I need to find a lovely little vixen at some point" the fox gave a sly grin when he said that. "Oh, non-sequitor. Congrats on getting onto the Global Aerospace Oversight Committee. You'll definitely get to see that shuttle launch that Dresden-Pierce is planning next year."

"Oh, I don't think Neville would let me miss it regardless of what the other committee members thought. At least now I can try to squash the opposition to their launches. Some of them are squawking 'illegal, illicit plans. The canines MUST be up to something nefarious' rhetoric. There are some bought-out...I mean deeply entrenched senators that keep trying to limit what the DPAE is doing and want to swoop in and confiscate anything alien related. They keep touting that ridiculous conspiracy that the alien video is fake and was released to sway the election." Brennan just shook his head. "There's just too much hate. Can the planet overcome this eventually? I sure hope so."

"All we can do is keep fighting." Hiro got up from his chair, "Okay, I'm off to the press conference. Enjoy your anniversary day off."

Chapter 52
Alien Revelations

"Good evening, I am Jordan Helmsey with UBN News. Tonight on 'Eyes on Technology' I bring you a special interview with co-authors of the book 'Alien Revelations', Maya Metta and Renata Alonso. This book dives into the culture of the aliens who crashed on Earth, back in 1357." The camera zoomed out to reveal his guests. "Thank you for joining me, Miss Metta and Miss Alonso."

Maya spoke first, "Thank you Jordan."

Renata added, "Thank you as well. Happy to be here."

Jordan put down his blue colored note papers on the table in front of him. "So, this is quite a book. You both work for the Dresden-Pierce Aerospace and Exploration company. Did they authorize you to write this?"

Maya looked at Renata to see who wanted to speak first. Renata motioned to Maya so she began. "Yes. The company had deciphered what they could from the alien storage devices. Renata and I were tasked with going through the content to find videos and documents that would tell us who these aliens were. After reviewing our findings, Tyler and Neville authorized us to publish our discoveries."

Jordan looked to Renata. "Renata, in the book you go into great detail on how you determined the probable physiology of the aliens before any of the videos were decrypted."

"Yes, that is accurate." Renata leaned forward. "I was looking at wreckage that seemed to be a control seat and it just didn't fit our physiology." She motioned to all three of them at the interview desk. "I just kept thinking back to my time exploring the ruins in San Juarez. Every temple always had a throne, a seat for the ruler. Along that line of thinking, all our aircraft on Earth have a pilot seat, and they always share one thing in common: a place to sit and a vertical-ish backrest. None of this fit with the debris we looked at. I had a moment of insight that the control seat must be form fit to a quadrupedal form like our native wolves. To test my theory, I asked Minn, a small fox on our team to lay down on his belly on the pilot seat. He was really confused at the request as no one had ever asked him to lay down on a pile of junk before. Once he laid down, I knew that had to be true."

"When you saw the alien crash video, how did you feel when you saw your intuition was right?" Jordan asked.

"I was ecstatic! It was so satisfying when you realize you put the puzzle pieces together correctly." Renata smiled at Jordan. "Another interesting fact about their physique: Tyler Dresden had figured out the alien numeral system was an eight based system. When we dived into the videos we realized that they had four fingers on their front hands. Imagine you are counting on your fingers: We have ten, but they have eight. So an eighths based counting system made perfect sense."

"Very intriguing findings." Jordan moved his gaze to his other guest. "So Maya, your background seems like a strange one for an aerospace company." He looked at his notes, "You grew up in Zhang-mi in Escabon in the Shénmì Zōngjiào temple and then you majored in Religious Studies. After that you were a community outreach Professor of Religious Studies at the local university. How and why did you end up joining DPAE?"

"Neville Pierce approached me. He explained they were investigating alien technology but also wanted to truly understand them as a people. He wasn't purely interested in just their technology, he was interested in *them*. He was curious about their social structure and their beliefs. He felt I would bring a fresh, non-scientific perspective that would be invaluable for the team." Maya finished that question with a pleasant smile.

"So, you were able to figure them out. Can you elaborate?" Jordan asked of her.

"Sure. During my exploration of the decrypted data, I found a couple of mentions in translations of crew log that led me to documents that actually laid out their beliefs in detail. It turns out their beliefs are really similar to the beliefs of Shenism. Respect the planet, respect others, treat others how you would treat yourself. Remarkably similar in fact. They don't have gods like many of us typically understand them." Maya stated.

"After reading the book last weekend, I found it interesting where you talk about their history. They almost destroyed themselves."

Jordan focused on Maya. "Do you think there are lessons contained in their writings we can learn from?"

Maya did a half smile. "Well, when I read those passages I was very saddened by the tragedy. Yes, these are lessons we should take to heart. If we don't curb our instincts, we too could destroy ourselves."

Jordan looked at both of them then abruptly spoke, "That's all we have time for tonight. Thank you both for joining me this evening." He then looked at the camera, "Check out the book 'Alien Revelations' by Maya Metta and Renata Alonso, available everywhere books are sold."

<u>*Chapter 53*</u>
Boosted

Tyler was sitting nearby watching the crew get ready for the full booster test. The test controller had just gave Tyler his confirmation that all systems were nominal in the rocket and they were ready to begin the test. It had taken them six months to get the remote launch facility ready for the solo launch of the booster and he had high hopes for a successful launch. Several of the subsystem tests had failed previously but his team had worked through the known problems. They were confident that the issues had been resolved. He sat in the chair with his headset on nervously bouncing his left foot in anticipation.

They had built a platform just off the coast of southern Los Diego, which was an engineering feat in-and-of itself. The circular platform was connected to the shore by a stout bridge. This allowed them to bring assemble the launch vehicle in a fully upright position then wheel it out to the platform ready for fueling. They had chosen the water launch to prevent wildfires since most of the region was a dry, scrub desert. The coastal climate kept all the vegetation nearby in a low fire risk state.

"Attention everyone. Status?" the controller asked of the teams.

"Computers, GO."

"Telemetry, GO."

"Sensors, GO."

"Fuel, GO."

"Mechanical, GO."

"Flight, GO."

"Alright." the controller keyed his command code in. "Countdown. 10 seconds."

As the clock counted down, everyone stared intently at their readouts making sure nothing fell below the minimums required for launch.

"Ignition." The controller said aloud as the rocket's engine fired to life in a huge plume of smoke and fire. The exhaust splayed out in a radial direction away from the rocket and began obscuring the platform from view. The rocket started to lift off from the launchpad as they reached full throttle. Gusts of red and yellow streaks could be seen as clouds of fuel and smoke billowed into the air. "Liftoff!" the flight engineer hollered over the radio.

As the rocket started moving, Marla Johannsen, the engineer in charge of fuel status, saw one of her readouts flash red and called into the radio, "Fuel pressure dropping below nominal."

"Fuel anomaly — do we abort?" asked the controller.

"ABORT!" Marla shouted as the readout kept dropping.

The controller slammed the large abort button on the console in front of him immediately cutting off the main engines. The rocket had reached about 1,000 meters off the pad when they cut the engines. Tyler saw a small jet of fire shoot out from one of the rocket segments just before the shutdown. That jet thrusted the rocket from its vertical trajectory twisting the rocket to a horizontal path towards the ocean. As it started to angle the rocket split open and exploded in a ball of flames and smoke, tumbling into the water.

The DPAE had started a regular live streams to talk to the public and millions of viewers had been joining in for each broadcast. These shows were bringing the company a lot of positive attention and had been invaluable in keeping up public support for their cause. Today was the first broadcast after the failed rocket test so Zuri was a bit nervous.

"Five seconds Zuri," Haoqi motioned to Zuri. "We are live in 3...2..."

"Welcome to our latest stream everyone, I am Zuri Mandla, Vice-President of Communications here at Dresden-Pierce Aerospace and Exploration company. Today we have lot of news to talk about with all you viewers out there."

"Last week during our full booster test, the test rocket experienced a malfunction in the fueling system. The team aborted the launch shortly after liftoff and the rocket was destroyed during the event. I have Tyler Dresden, the leader of the DPAE teams here in the studio with me." The live stream switched to a slightly wider view of the des, showing both Zuri and Tyler. Zuri continued, "Tyler wanted to directly speak to everyone out there about the incident." She then handed the floor over to him and the camera zoomed in closer on his face.

"Hello everyone. I wanted to speak with all you personally. As you know, we are pushing the boundaries of technology, which inevitably may have some mishaps and technical glitches along the way. During the ignition sequence a seal in the liquid fuel tank gave out. This subsequent pressure drop resulted in a fire, ultimately destroying the rocket. The team identified the leak pretty early on and aborted shortly after liftoff." Tyler sat forward and continued, "Over the past week our engineering team determined that a regulating valve failed, causing an over pressure condition in the tank which blew out the seal between rocket segments. The failure of that seal caused an external leak, resulting in fuel pressure drop and a created a small fire. As the pressure dropped the fire was able to backtrack and follow the leak back into the main tanks causing the destruction of the rocket. We have already redesigned the regulators to prevent a future occurrence of this event. We have also implemented new engineering fail safes to automatically cut off fuel when a compromise is detected. I take safety seriously and have asked the team to engineer even more redundancies into the fuel delivery system to effectively eliminate this failure mode altogether." The camera zoomed back out to show both of them in the studio.

"Thanks for that explanation Tyler." Zuri looked into the camera. "That's not all we wanted to talk about today. I am most excited to announce that the Ligare's chassis has entered the final assembly stage and is on track for our intended launch in late 2027." The screen went to a picture-in-picture showing the Ligare sitting on a cradle while workers were installing a silver, curved section of the hull. "The team is installing the protective heat shielding that will safeguard the vehicle during re-entry and protect it from space debris. The hull is constructed of all-new advanced materials inspired by alien technology. This has allowed us to design a vehicle that is the size of past space shuttles, but comes in at 1/10th the weight. Once hull construction is complete we can install the engines, fuel systems, electronics and life support systems."

The screen switched to a pulled out view showing Zuri and an-other guest. "Ingrid Sjöberg is CEO of the Sjöberg Aerospace & Electronics Manufacturing, who is the sole manufacturing partner of DPAE. Ingrid and her team have been responsible for developing the advanced manufacturing techniques used to construct the outer hull of the 'Ligare'. Can you tell us a little bit about that?"

Ingrid began, "It has definitely been a unique challenge. The many layers of the hull are built to its final shape with a new technique that we developed. We call it 'Nano-Deposition'. The machines can be tailored for many different materials and in the case of Ligare's hull, we are using both high tech steels and ceramics. I'm sure some astute viewers have probably read, we filed patents for this process last week. It uses nano-scale material deposition and sintering to produce a three-dimensional structure that is strong and lightweight, which can withstand quite a lot of abuse. The hull is then assembled using a variety of techniques from welding, structural adhesives and another SAEM patented process called 'Nano-Sintering". We devel-oped a high power, ultrasonic sintering process to join the ceramic hull pieces together while placed on the hull of the craft. This results in a barely detectable seam and weld zone strengths equal to the base material. In effect, the outer hull is basically one singular part when its finished. It also can be repaired in a vacuum with pre-built patch panels using proprietary techniques. Repairs can be easily handled by an astronaut or a repair robot."

"That's amazing work. I am sure your team was excited with the amazing results they've achieved. I would like to thank you for joining us today." Zuri then turned back to the camera and the screen switched to her. "This is a really exciting time for all of us here seeing just how fast and how amazing the craft is coming progressing. We also have begun recruiting for the team who will pilot the Ligare on its first mission. When the crew is chosen we will definitely chat with them here on this stream. That's all for today. Thank you so much for joining us, we look forward to to seeing you next time! Have a pleasant weekend everyone!"

Chapter 55

Oversight

Brennan Clark and Lev Kronovski's private jet had just touched down at the regional airport near the DPAE's launch site and were taxiing to a secure parking area at the edge of the airport. Security had really been beefed up in the area. The Humans First Coalition had made online bombing threats against the company that they viewed as run by the enemy of humanity. Online conspiracies were rampant: Mind control drugs in the atmosphere, planting space lasers to target humans, rounding up humans and banishing them to a moon prison, and so on.

Brennan and Lev were headed to the DPAE site with the rest of the Global Aerospace Oversight Committee members to view how the company was progressing. Brennan was sure two of the members were attending solely to try and invent some reason to shut them down. As transparent as the DPAE had been with their space program development, including their publishing of videos and documents related to the alien cultures, the results showed they had garnered the absolute trust of the public. Brennan felt there wouldn't be much logical reason that they could shut down the DPAE launch, though logic doesn't always apply.

Once the plane parked they descended the stairs to the waiting car below. The members of the committee had taken separate planes and were parking in different parts of the airport due to bomb threats. Brennan scanned around the runway area for other planes. It looked like their plane was the first to arrive which was good. He wanted to have a nice conversation with Neville and Tyler before the antagonistic committee members arrived. They got into the car and were shuttled over to the secured area. He was relieved that there were snipers and security everywhere as he idly rubbed the shoulder where he had been shot.

They were escorted into a large white conference room where Neville and Tyler were seated sipping on some coffee. They got up to come greet them when they entered.

"Welcome Lev and Brennan, good to see you two again." Neville reached out a paw to shake their hands.

"Welcome to the DPAE, glad you could come." Tyler also extended a paw, "Hope this is just a pleasant boondoggle for you two and not filled with some nonsense committee infighting." Tyler winked at them. "Please sit down. Coffee?"

"No thanks," Lev replied.

"No coffee, but some water would be great." Brennan added.

Tyler nodded to someone in the corner who left the room, leaving the four of them completely alone. "Neville and I are glad to have both of you here. We're excited to show the committee our progress."

Neville chimed in, "We worked out the schedule so that we have you two for about an hour before the other committee members get here." Neville poked at the desk lighting up a hidden touchscreen. "I have something to show you two since you are such trusted allies of mine. As you know, we plan to develop space technology and restart the exploration of our solar system." He clicked the keyboard and a montage of space photos appeared. "This is one of the mission goals. In orbit around the planet is all sorts of space junk. It is starting to get crowded up there with defunct satellites, rocket parts and alien space ship debris from the original crash. We want to start cleaning up the orbit to make room for an expanded space program. Globally, we have been quite sloppy with space exploration and we want to help clean it up to help future explorers. In that process we will be collecting some of the alien debris as well, but that's not really the most important thing."

Lev moved his hand to rub his chin. "Well, you have me intrigued. What IS the important thing?"

"This." Neville clicked to zoom in on a picture. "This is an intact lifepod from the alien ship. We think this is the pilot's pod that was ejected at the last second before the ship broke up in the atmosphere."

Brennan sat forward, "Really? Do you think there is a dead alien in there?"

"Maybe," Tyler replied. "It's a completely intact piece. It would be interesting to find an alien body but I'm more interested in any data left onboard. I am speculating here, but if this was the main pilot's escape pod it would have a large backup of the spacecraft's computer system on board. Imagine the knowledge that might be tucked away. Language, engineering, science, we could leap forward *centuries* in technology. The possibilities are unlimited!"

"And that's why," Neville leaned forward, "it's VERY important to keep this very secret. I really don't want to be secretive but I think this object alone merits that discretion. The technology on board could be completely benign but consider if they had schematics of advanced weaponry in those files? I have zero interest in unleashing alien weapons onto our planet by letting any military anywhere NEAR that information. I think we need to be mindful of the fact that these aliens almost destroyed themselves and it would be reckless of us to not consider we could do the same. It seems more than likely given the HFC bomb threats recently. I positively think this discovery would likely be leaked by certain members of the committee and that would bring the military swooping in. I need you two to make sure that the government is happy to basically leave us alone. There are very few people here that know of this and I trust those individuals with my life."

Brennan spoke first, "Yes, you have my promise."

"Mine too," Lev added. "I shudder when I think of advance weapons getting into the hands of extremists. It is a scary proposition. Promise me if you do find any information on advanced weaponry you will destroy it permanently?"

"That's the plan," Neville nodded to Lev.

A man entered the room and motioned to Tyler.

"It seems that we have about 30 minutes before anyone else gets here. Let's get some lunch." Tyler stood up and they all followed him to another room.

"Welcome to 'Eyes on Technology', I am Jordan Helmsey for UBN News." The screen switched to a zoomed out camera view with the logo of the DPAE. "Today the Dresden-Pierce Aerospace and Exploration company announced the flight crew for their first launch of the Space Plane, the 'DPAE Ligare'."

"The first flight will have a crew of six individuals." The screen switched to a human male with graying, rust color hair dressed in a dark blue, high altitude pressure suit. "Aturo Zavala will be the commander of the mission. He is a highly decorated, former pilot in the Earth Global Naval division and has been working in the private sector as an experimental test pilot for the past 12 years. Former officers of his have vouched for him, stating that he is an extremely competent pilot who remains cool under any kind of pressure."

"The pilot for the mission is this man:" The screen switched to a rusty-brown fox with large swaths of black fur. He was standing in a field dressed in a bright orange jump suit holding a balled-up parachute. "Akito Hattori is a 15 year veteran pilot in the Earth Global Air Defense. Akito is no stranger to risky adventures. In his down time he is a daredevil pilot performing in airshows for thousands of fans. This fox loves to fly and also performs in aerial parachuting stunt competitions. His enthusiasm for flight makes him the perfect choice for this type of risky endeavor."

The secondary image then switched to a black-haired, dark-skinned woman giving a presentation with equations and flight trajectories on the overhead screen in front of a crowed audience. "Kayra Bashar earned a Ph.D. in physics and Astro-Dynamics and the Calveras Institute of Technology. She worked for an aerospace manufacturer planning their satellite orbits and navigation after graduation. She has been tapped to fill the Navigator role for her quick thinking and efficient use of the limited resources on a satellite."

"Running the computer systems on board is Malina Salvatore." The image changed over to a small framed, curly brown-haired human female dressed in a leather jacket sitting on a motorcycle. "Malina attended the University of Suffok and graduated with a Ph.D. in Computer Science. She also minored in Electrical Engineering and Mathematics. Before joining the crew as the Computer Specialist, she worked for a computer hardware startup writing the operating system for their high performance gaming platform."

"The fifth member of the crew is Kazik Motychka." The screen switched to show a gray wolf leaning on an industrial robot. "Mission Specialist Kazik comes from the River City prefecture where he spent 12 years designing advanced robots that are now used in most auto manufacturing plants in the region. He got his Ph.D. in Robotics from the preeminent Los Diego Tech University."

"This last choice has raised some eyebrows." The screen changed to show a multicolored, but mostly black wild dog. "Garai Masango hails from Calveras. Garai has no degree from any college or university. He was the key inventor behind the latest generation of drone technology that hobbyists and the military have been using for the last 10 years. He is rumored to have been working at a DPAE competitor working on military drones but joined the DPAE about two years ago. The public has been really speculating on what his role is in this mission."

Chapter 57
Neville

(Narrator)

"Earlier this decade, Neville Pierce, the man behind the financial powerhouse known as Pierce industries revealed his face to the public for the first time in the long history of his company. Neville shocked the world revealing that he was, in fact, a canine and not a human as everyone had thought. Jean St. Claire was the public face of Pierce Industries and its subsidiaries for decades so everyone just assumed that Neville was human and was satisfied pulling the strings from behind the curtain."

"Over the decades journalists have been trying to find out more about Mr. Pierce. Speculations and rumors placed him as the founder and leader of the Uptown Crime Syndicate but no evidence has ever turned up to corroborate that rumor."

"Last month, Neville sat down with a journalist for a candid interview. It has been the only one he has ever given in his long, private career. During that interview, he revealed that he grew up extremely poor and lived on the streets after his parents were murdered. Neville didn't know his true age but he estimates he is close to 150 years old."

"He soon found himself a victim of kidnapping and was forced to work in factories as a bona fide slave to human

masters. Kept in cages, beaten, starved and worked nearly to death he managed to escape when his fellow slaves
revolted by blowing up the factory to escape. He vowed
never to be under the thumb of any master again and
struck up many partnerships with the local underworld.
Canines in the late 1800s had no real avenue for legitimate opportunities and many either lived in the wilds or
resorted to underground activities."

"For the first half of the 20th century, Neville worked
within the confines of the underworld and stayed outside
the law. He built many loyal business relationships with
the many different families and organizations in the River City prefecture. Over the years, he worked his way up
to lead the syndicate in Uptown City area.

"During the 1960s canine kind gained some legal standing during the Civil Rights Revolution. Neville took that
opportunity to take many of his ventures legitimate. His
earliest money-making opportunity was expanding his
distillery business and soon began shipping his products
worldwide. Using this new found source of income, he
started his own financial company to help other canines
establish themselves by giving them super low interest loans for homes and businesses. Most conventional
banks still wouldn't deal with canids believing that they
are an unnecessary risk to their bottom lines."

"His businesses gained momentum in the late 1970s and
a windfall of profits let him expand his reach through
acquisitions. He branched out into accounting, legal
services, biomedical and other smaller businesses that
mostly focused on the growing canine population."

"His identity reveal was timed with another historic
event. Neville partnered with the tech magnate, Tyler
Dresden to form a joint venture: the Dresden-Pierce
Aerospace and Exploration company. Their goal was to
rekindle the planet's interest in exploring our universe
using more than just telescopes. In his words, 'I am
getting old and I am not going to be around forever. I
had to do many unpleasant things for the first half of my
life and I want to make it up to the world by building a
better world ... better for everyone.' "

"Tomorrow is a landmark day in Neville Pierce's life.
The DPAE will be launching its first space plane the 'Ligare'. They have reignited the world's passion for space

and scientific exploration and captured the attention of people all over the planet. Once they have a successful launch they plan to ramp up their missions' schedule. The company recently revealed to the Global Aerospace Oversight Committee that one of their primary missions is a philanthropic one: To clean up the decades of space debris that we have left in orbit. They want to 'keep the planet tidy' for future generations."

"Will they be successful? Watch the launch tomorrow and see for yourselves."

Chapter 58
Launch Day

"Welcome esteemed scientists, journalists, members of the Global Aerospace Oversight Committee and all you space fans who came out to watch." Zuri announced as she was gazing out over a sea of people gathered outside the safe zone for the launch. "Today is a historic day for the DPAE, for the planet and for the future. We venture back into manned space missions for the first time in over forty years. Tomorrow, our children will not know there was ever a time without space exploration."

The crowd started cheering so she paused to smile and waited for them to calm down. "I am so excited to see the launch of the most advanced space vehicle ever constructed on Earth. Our space-craft weighs one-tenth of older space shuttles. Combine that with our advanced launch rockets we will be able to reach space with a fraction of the fuel it used to take. Once in space, the Ligare is equipped with a new compact fusion reactor that allowed us to engineer a new propulsion system based on Direct Fusion Drive theory. This will allow longer mission times, better maneuverability and more cost-efficient missions."

Zuri looked over at her assistant just off stage who pointed at her watch and gave her the thumbs up. "In one hour we will be launch-ing!" On cue the count down clock above her started. Simultaneously the large jumbo screens changed from the DPAE logo to a view of the Ligare on the launch pad. "In one hour, we will make history!" She started waving and walking off the stage as the crowd erupted in cheers again. Then, she jumped into a car that was waiting for her in order to return to the command center.

***

The room at the command center was absolutely packed with folks from the launch team, dignitaries and all sorts of politicians jostling to be seen by the press cameras. Neville, Brennan, Renata, Maya, Ingrid, Zuri, Hiro and Ivan had all gathered to one side just listening to the bustle going on around them. Tyler noticed the group of colleagues over to the side and walked over to them. "Are you all as excited as I am?" Tyler asked.

"Yes, I am!" Maya said almost jumping in the air.

"Now that we're all gathered here." Neville piped up, adding, "Each and everyone one of you have been instrumental in getting us to where we are today." He looked at Brennan, Hiro and Ivan. "I am absolutely thankful for what you have been able to accomplish on the legislative front. Without your hard work and perseverance we wouldn't have the respect and worldwide support we do today." Then he shifted his gaze to run across Tyler, Renata, Maya, Ingrid and Zuri, "You have accomplished everything I could imagine and more. We could not be here today without each and every one of you doing what you do best. Let's get a picture for this historic event." He waved to a photographer gesturing for him to come over their way. "Take a picture of these folks for the scrapbook." He grinned at them all and stepped behind them.

The nine of them all stood there for a moment to get their pictures taken before Tyler piped up, "Okay, time for us to get started." He then motioned for Zuri to follow.

***

After they broke up from the photo op, Zuri and Tyler made their way over to a video studio staged to look like a morning talk show. The room was brightly lit and the screen in the back was showing the animated DPAE logo. They had three comfortable looking, white leather chairs arranged around a simple round coffee table. They both sat down, Zuri on the left, Tyler in the middle with an empty chair on the right.

"Sorry I'm running a little late, I was just doing some last minute checks." Suresh Kandar said as he walked through the door and then closing it behind him. "Everything seems good." Then he took the empty chair next to Tyler.

"Alright. We're ready to begin the broadcast." Haoqi said aloud. "4, 3, 2..."

The camera was zoomed in on Zuri. "Hello everyone, thanks for joining us for a livestream of our historic launch. I'm Zuri Mandla, Vice President of Communications here at the Dresden-Pierce Aerospace and Exploration company. We have just 45 minutes before our historic launch so I thought we would talk about some of the new and exciting technology that we have created to make this mission a true success in science and engineering."

The camera switched to a view of the three of them seated. "So Tyler, what's the first new technical innovation on board the Ligare?" Zuri asked, as she turned her head towards Tyler.

Tyler leaned forward towards the camera, "First, I would like to introduce one of our principle R&D engineers. Suresh Kandar joined the DPAE very early. He came on board to work on experimental electronics and to dissect some of the alien technology. He was the one to crack this new bit of tech which will enable near real-time communication with the Ligare from flight control here. Suresh, tell us what you found."

"Thanks Tyler." Suresh looked from Tyler to the camera. "After a lot of tinkering, calculations and probing, we were able to power up one of the handheld alien devices we had acquired. Based on the components inside, I believed that it wasn't a typical radio wave transmitter and used a different technology. I was convinced that it used gravity waves with a modulating crystal for point-to-point encryption. Tyler had reverse engineered the non-functional nuclear battery inside the device and calculated the theoretical voltage the device used. I spent weeks carefully instrumenting and prepping to power up the device."

Suresh paused for a moment before he continued, "Once we had the device powered up we were able to record operational data happening inside the device. From that we were able to figure out some basic alien symbology and their data protocols. This discovery allowed us to start extracting data from a lot of the other devices we had taken apart. In a storage crystal we found schematics of the hand-held device and confirmed that is was based on gravity wave communication. The Ligare is equipped with this new communication device and allows us real time conversations and telemetry with the crew on board the ship. Ground control has a similar device that is matched to the ship's communicator. No one else can decrypt the communication without having a 'matched' crystal. This instant communication will allow us to easily send control commands and see what is going on in real time here at ground control. In fact, we can take full, real-time control of the craft from the ground in case of emergency."

Tyler spoke up after Suresh finished. "Great work on this Suresh. I would also like to thank Kaitey and Darisha, who were instrumental making this discovery. This will allow us here on Earth to easily work with the crew on board to troubleshoot any issues that might arise during the mission. We have never before had this sort of instant communication without a laser line-of-sight to the craft. It does have its limitations due to power if we were using it in a handheld device, but we have sufficient range due to integrating the device right into the core systems on the craft."

The camera moved to just focus on Zuri and Tyler. "So Tyler, there's one more interesting piece of tech your teams have developed for specifically retrieving items in orbit. Can you speak about that?" Zuri asked

"Certainly," Tyler leaned back into his chair. "As you know, one of the missions we have given ourselves is to help clean up orbiting junk. Old satellites, rocket parts, etc. Mission specialists Kazik Motychka and Garai Masango have been putting their expertise to use in developing a drone powered 'net' to capture the debris and bring it back to the cargo bay. Earth based drones use prop or jet engines, but those don't work in a vacuum. The two specialists worked with our propulsion teams to integrate small ion thrust engines." The screen then swapped to an animation as Tyler spoke. "The 'Net Capture' is comprised of multiple drones and a metal alloy 'net'. The drones start out as one unified craft upon release from the space plane. Once they reach the target they spread out to stretch out the net into its capture position. The drones then envelop the target with the net, then recombining into one craft before returning back to the Ligare with their catch. This means the main spacecraft doesn't need to get into dangerous proximity of the debris. This keeps the ship and crew at a safe distance in case something goes awry with the retrieval."

"Thanks, Tyler." Zuri looked at the camera when Haoqi signaled her. "It looks like we have about 15 minutes before liftoff. We'll send you to out to Mayura Devonshire to speak to some of the folks in the crowd who have gathered outside the safe zone to watch today's historic event while we get ready for the final countdown here in mission control."

***

The ground controller spoke into his headset and started the final countdown. "T-minus ten, nine, eight, booster and main engine ignition, five, four, three, two, one, and we have LIFTOFF!" The service tower connections rotated away just as the DPEA Ligare started moving upward off the launch pad. The entire crew at mission control were all eerily quiet as all their eyes were glued to the their screens, watching for any signs of issues as the clock started counting up.

"T-plus two minutes, approaching booster cutoff." the controller spoke calmly into his headset. "Booster cutoff. Ten seconds to separation." One could only hear the white noise of the ventilation systems as everyone was silently focused on their displays.

"We have confirmation of booster separation." Commander Aturo Zavala's voice came in on the radio. "Main rocket engine thrust nominal."

Another six minutes ticked by while the main rocket propelled the craft into the upper atmosphere. "T-plus 12 minutes and 20 seconds. Prepare for the main engine cutoff." Another ten seconds clicked by before flight control spoke, "Main engine cutoff, separation in 10 seconds."

"Main rocket separation confirmed, preparing for main craft engine ignition." Aturo replied to ground control. "Confirmation of main craft engine ignition. Burn for 1 minute 12 seconds."

The display screen in mission control updated its animation while the clock counted down the burn time.

"We have main craft engine cutoff. We are now in orbit at target speed and elevation." Aturo's voice sounded confident and happy at the same time. "Welcome back to space everyone."

Mission control erupted in applause as everyone stood up after hearing the Commander's confirmation they successfully made it to orbit.

"Well done everyone!" Tyler had grabbed a mic and shouted his congratulations into it.

Chapter 59

Mission Zero

"Welcome to 'Eyes on Technology', I am Jordan Helmsey for UBN News." The screen switched to a zoomed-out camera view with a split screen of the DPAE space plane. "Today the Dresden-Pierce Aerospace and Exploration company had a successful first launch of the Space Plane, the 'DPAE Ligare'."

"The company is reporting the flight went off without any complications. Now in orbit, the crew of the Ligare are preparing for their first retrieval mission to remove a defunct communication satellite. This kicks off a series of missions where the DPAE will be removing space junk from the skies above."

"With the successful retrieval of the satellite the Global Earth government has offered funding to the DPAE to assist in clearing the skies but the company has politely declined."

The screen switched to a press conference by Zuri Mandla, Tyler Dresden and Neville Pierce in front of the DPAE headquarters. Zuri began to address the reporters gathered in front of them.

"While we appreciate the offer of funding we politely decline to take the money from the government coffers. When we started this venture we set aside capital just to fund this sort of activity using no outside financial support. We are committed to providing this service to the world with no cost to you, the taxpayers of the world. Tyler's other company, Dres-Tek, has been just as guilty of leaving obsolete satellites in space as did many other companies. Our government's own space exploration missions of the past have left their own trail of debris floating in outer space. Our profits will be derived from the technology that we have developed for this program and will not burden the general public with additional expenses for past short shortsightedness."

The camera switched back to Jordan, "The DPAE has already starting licensing its newly developed, highly efficient, compact fusion technology around the world. The first reactor based on their design is scheduled to be online late next year in the remote region of Escabon. That reactor will be bringing much needed electricity to the underdeveloped mountainous areas of the prefecture."

***

"Congratulations everyone. The mission has been a success so far. Let's keep the successes going!" Tyler addressed the room of engineers and technicians that had gathered for a pep talk by their leadership. "Today we will be trying out the 'Net Capture' system for orbiting junk removal. If this works we should be able to clean things up with very little risk to the ship and crew." Tyler slapped his paws on the table before him, then shouting as he quickly lifted them back up, "Alright everyone, let's get to it!"

***

The crew of the Ligare gathered in the main area just behind the flight deck. They spent their first orbit checking the systems on the ship and prepping the drone packs for release. They had a total of four drone sets on board. Two of them were built in a small form factor designed to nab a small communication satellite that went dark 25 years ago. This specific satellite had never received the command to de-orbit and burn up in the atmosphere. The two remaining drone packs were vastly larger. That was for the second part of the mission which no one on board had been told any specific details.

"Okay, systems check." Commander Aturo grabbed his mission tablet and was looking at the readouts. "Bay doors?"

"System's green. Control system is in order." Malina said, then adding, "Kazik performed the mechanical check twenty minutes ago when he was back there and confirmed that all is good there."

"Drones?" Aturo readied his finger at the tablet.

"All set. Net-1 array in the launch sling." Garai answered. "Flight path is all programmed in thanks to Kayra. She tweaked the trajectory and we should now have a 30 percent margin on propellant."

"Awesome team. Let's get to it." Aturo dismissed them and they all moved to their control consoles.

Akito had already buckled himself into the pilot's seat and gave a thumbs-up to Aturo. The commander strapped himself in front of a large screened console to watch the outside activity through an array of cameras. The others were all strapped into their stations waiting the order to begin. "Everyone in place. Akito, execute phase one." Aturo uttered the mission go ahead.

"Rolling the ship, 20.2° on axis." With a short burst of attitude jets Akito expertly rolled the craft clockwise on axis, then fired another short burst of the counter jets. He stopped the ship with the bay doors facing the planet and the satellite below. Then the fox fired a retro thruster, slowing the ship's speed a tiny bit to match the speed of the satellite. "Bay doors on target, velocity nominal."

"Phase two, evacuate air from cargo." Malina pressed a control button to remove the air from the cargo bay. They all sat silently as this process would take nearly five minutes. Once the air was pumped out Malina spoke up, "Cargo evacuated. Ready for bay door opening." She pressed another control button activating the cargo doors. "Doors open and ready for phase 3."

"Executing phase 3." Kazik adjusted one control knob to better focus the surveillance camera. "Launching Net-1," Once activated the slingshot propelled the drone pack into space at a virtual crawl. They had decided to use a sling launch setup to preserve propellant on the drones for course corrections on the return trip. "Net-1 on target."

"Phase 4 active." Garai activated the automatic guidance system on the drones. The rest of the retrieval was automatic at this point unless there was problem. "Nothing much to do for a while other than watch," he nervously said, but that was mostly to comfort himself.

They all just sat silently at their consoles, remaining focused on the slow activity on screen and the readouts on the status screen. Overall, from launch to retrieval, the trip would take about 25 minutes. Five minutes there, five to unfurl the net and fifteen minutes back.

When the drone pack approached close to the satellite it fired their reverse thrusters in unison to nearly match the same speed as the satellite. After passing behind the satellite, the drones separated and slowly moved to position the net in behind the target.

Once unfurled into capture formation, the thrusters fired again to grab the satellite into the net as the drones accelerated back towards the Ligare. Once past the satellite they slowly closed back into a group, fully capturing their prey in a shiny spider's web.

On approach to the cargo bay, Net-1 fired its lateral thrusters sending the net into a very slow pirouette so it could enter the bay with the cargo first.

"Cargo entering hold. Executing Phase 5." Kazik used a joystick to reach a robotic arm to grab the package pulling it down. Once the claw had a grip on the satellite, Net-1 fired thrusters to soften the descent into the hold. "Cargo clamps engaged. Cargo secured. Ready for cargo bay doors."

When Kazik confirmed they had the satellite, they all cheered.

"Great job team!" Aturo exclaimed. "Let's get that cargo hold closed and get ready for the next one."

***

"I am Jordan Helmsey for UBN News. Welcome to another install-ment of 'Eyes on Technology'. Today the DPAE Ligare completed its first space junk retrieval mission. They successfully captured a defunct communication satellite using their new 'Net Capture' sys-tem." A sped up video of the net capturing the satellite flashed up in the corner of the screen. "They say this can efficiently capture ob-jects without serious risk to crew and spacecraft by using expendable drones, rather than risk crew members performing EVA missions. It looks to have been a complete success."

***

Tyler sat down in a private conference room and clicked a few things on the keyboard in front of him. A live video feed of the crew in the Ligare appeared. "Hello everyone and congratulations on the first capture!"

"Thank you sir!" Commander Aturo saluted Tyler from the common space on the Ligare. "I think I speak for the entire crew, but thank you for this opportunity. It's certainly one I will never forget."

"The 'thanks' are all mine. We couldn't have done it without all of you." Tyler smiled before his smile dropped into a serious expression. "Now, I bet you have been wondering what the next mission is as we haven't made any public statements about it, nor divulged anything to you. You were all chosen because you have the right skills for this mission. You must understand that this next part of the mission is top secret and has the blessing of the Earth Aerospace Administration. Secrecy is of the utmost importance, so none of this goes public until all the involved parties agree upon the time."

They sat silently for a moment before Aturo spoke. "I fully understand sir." Everyone else on camera nodded as well.

"Great! This item ..." Tyler pressed a key and a picture of the alien capsule showed up on their screen, "is the true mission of this flight. That's why Kazik and Garai has built Net-3 and Net-4 so large. We want to retrieve this. This part of the mission has always been classified as a need-to-know matter. We needed to verify whether we could manage to snag it on this mission before we tasked you with it. The team here has done the calculations and we think we have plenty of fuel to position the Ligare for the capture and have plenty to return to Earth with this prize."

"Is that about the size of a van?" Akito leaned forward to get a better look at the pod.

"Yes, good guess you sly fox. We think this artifact is an alien life boat that never made it to Earth. It has been orbiting the Earth in a super long orbit since the 1300's and we want to get it back down to Earth intact to take it apart. There is a lot we can learn from it." Tyler clicked and returned the camera to himself.

"Wait," Malina spoke up. "You said 'alien life boat'...does that mean there's an actual alien on it?"

"Who knows really. We could be totally wrong on what this pod is for. Maybe an alien is on board, maybe not. If yes, it's not going to be alive after 700 years so don't let those cheesy sci-fi movies about alien invasions spook you." Tyler smiled at his own joke. "I am transmitting all the relevant mission parameters. Kayra, you are the best astro-dynamicist at the DPAE. Please get to work reviewing the course for the Ligare and Net-3, I'm sure you can improve on both paths. Unlike the last catch this one will not be televised." Tyler winked at the crew. "Let's get this done!" Tyler grinned as he cut the video connection with the crew.

***

The crew just sat there for a bit before Aturo broke the silence. "The more I think about it, the more excited I am. Imagine if there's an alien body in there? We have all heard the stories and seen pictures of the technology that people have dug up. Heck, we wouldn't have this great spaceship without the things the engineers learned about their tech."

Malina was digging through the mission parameters on her screen. "So, once this thing is on board it says that no one goes into the cargo bay. They say it needs to be sealed, locked out and no air pumped into the cargo bay. We only get to see it through the cameras. That's kind of lame."

"Well," Akito piped up. "They probably don't want to unleash an alien virus on the crew. I'm sure its just a safety precaution."

"You're probably right Akito. Let's get on with it. Kayra, what do you think of the plotted course?" Arturo asked.

"Seems legit, there's only a few maneuvers I would tweak but they did a great job." Kayra nodded while she looked at the plots. "The maneuver will take us quite far from Earth. The object's orbit brings it between Earth and the moon and it's moving fairly fast. This is going to take about 8 days total. We'll be accelerating for a day using the Earth's gravity to leave orbit at a speed that is slightly faster than the object's speed. Next, we slow down to pick it up as we head towards outer space. Finally we then make a slingshot maneuver around the moon and head back to Earth. The only problem I can foresee is the

Perseids. Earth is passing through an annual meteor shower at this time of year. Hope we don't have an impact."

"Never in a million years would I have thought I would get to see the moon on this trip. I can see why the fuel capacity on the Ligare was as large as it is and how overpowered the engines are. I just thought they oversized it for bragging rights." Akito smiled. "This will be fun."

"Okay, let's get to it." Aturo moved to sit down in the copilot's seat. "Times wasting."

***

"Welcome to Heartstone Tonight, I am Troy Alvarez." The logo of the DPAE popped up in the corner of the screen. "Today, independent observers have noticed that the orbiting DPAE Ligare has begun accelerating, picking up a tremendous amount of speed. Many are wondering if something went wrong with the aircraft and it is accelerating out of control or if the ship is increasing its speed for a second undisclosed mission."

Our correspondent caught up with Senator Brennan Clark on the Global Aerospace Oversight Committee in Capitola.

"Senator Clark, can you comment on the activities of the DPAE Ligare's increasing speed?" as the correspondent shoved a microphone in Brennan's face.

"I am not aware of the reasons behind the change in velocity of the Ligare and if I did, I likely wouldn't be able to comment on it at this time." Brennan flatly stated as he entered the capital.

"We have also reached out to the DPAE and the EAA for comment. Neither organization has responded to our inquiry. We will keep you posted as this story develops."

***

"Commander, we're approaching the decel coordinates." Kayra said into the headset.

"Akito, ready on my mark." Aturo sat in his command chair watching the readouts in front of him. "Mark."

Akito fired the front thrusters for two minutes to slow the Ligare down. The view from the front window was blocked out by the white vapor of the propellant so they were flying using instruments only. "Speed matched to 2.7 kilometers per second. Ready for rotation." He then fired the clockwise thrusters to rotate the ship into recovery orientation. Instead of the momentary burst of thrust he was expecting, one of them fired at full thrust sending the craft into a spiraling spin. Akito slapped a button disabling the malfunctioning thruster. He worked rapidly at the stick furiously trying to correct the spin. It took him a couple of minutes to do so and got the ship into the right orientation. He looked over the readout in front of him. "Whew, that was fun. It looks like we had a damaged port thruster. Kayra, we will have to adjust future maneuvers to compensate. We are now in position but had to burn more propellant than I would have liked. I need to make a speed correction again. We'll have 15% reserve on the thrusters after this." The rear thruster burned for 2 seconds to correct the speed. "Okay, back at 2.7 KPS."

"Good work Akito," Commander Aturo stated. "Let's get this thing."

This one was going to take more than an hour to get back to the ship. The drone array was using 50 individuals in the cluster. They had navigated closer to the pod than they were in the first recovery. That made sure they had enough fuel in the Net-4 array to pull this off.

They were being very careful, so the whole recovery maneuver took an hour and twenty minutes but they were almost there. They had rotated the netted pod to face the cargo bay. The pod was heavier than expected and the drones were now out of fuel. "Velocity is higher than desired." Kazik alerted everyone. "We're going to feel this." He worked his magic with the robot arm to get a hold of the pod, but it was moving too fast and his arm bent when it gripped. The pod was still moving but thankfully still aimed at the landing cradle. The team on Earth had assured him the cargo cradle could handle the impact. He sure hoped they were right.

The ship lurched as the pod hammered down onto the cradle but thankfully the clamps immediately locked it down.

"We're locked!" Kazik bellowed in excitement. "Lock the doors. This baby is secure!"

Malina pecked at the keyboard, activating the cargo bay doors to close. "I think we got lucky. The cradle compressed during that impact otherwise the pod wouldn't have fit. It is slightly bigger than estimated." The ship made a slight groan as the doors closed and locked themselves down.

Commander Aturo spoke to the headset. "Ground control, we have the package." Then he cut off the transmission while he just stared at the pod on his monitor. "Well...break out the orange juice, we did it!"

"Huzzah!" Garai exclaimed while he put a fist in the air. "Let's get home! I'll need a nice vacation on the beach after this."

The acceleration around the moon went better than the calculations so they had a 20% margin on the fuel for the main fusion drive. Most of which would be used to slow them down at the speed they were traveling. They had two days to coast so everyone switched to a shift system to keep an eye on the ship's vitals.

***

Two days later, Akito strapped himself into his pilot's chair. Thinking to himself, "*Hopefully the missing thruster won't pose to much of a problem in orienting the ship for decel and re-entry.*" Then he spoke aloud, "Decel coordinates approaching. Strap in everyone. Executing flip maneuver." Akito used the attitude thrusters to make the ship flip smoothly to an engine forward attitude. "Ship positioned for decel. Firing in 3..2..1," he punched the fusion engines up to 80% thrust to start the decel. With the gravity assist of the moon he was going to have to run the engines for 45 minutes to slow it down to re-entry velocity.

Akito looked at his status screen and commented, "Target velocity achieved, cutting engines." The engine whine slowly died down to silence. "Okay, executing flip for re-entry." He flipped the ship back over just as smoothly as his previous one. "Maneuver complete. Ready for re-entry in 5 minutes" The pilot scanned over all the readouts and then activated the automatic re-entry protocols. Akito wouldn't be able to see anything, so the computer had been setup to handle the re-entry automatically. He also wouldn't need to land the plane himself. It wasn't really designed very well for atmospheric flight, so he would need the computers as backup if he tried to do it manually. *"Hopefully I don't have to."* Akito thought to himself.

The Ligare smoothly touched down with no drama at the DPAE airstrip just outside of Uptown City. When the six of them climbed down the exit stairs they were greeting by a large group of journalists, the entire ground control crew, politicians and other dignitaries from around the world. They got a chance to wave at the cheering crowd, before they were ushered into a waiting van and taken inside the compound.

***

"Good evening, I am Jordan Helmsey with UBN News. Tonight on 'Eyes on Technology' my guest is Zuri Mandla from the Dresden-Pierce Aerospace and Exploration company." The camera zoomed out to reveal the both of them. "Thank you for joining me, Miss Mandla."

"The pleasure is mine Jordan." Zuri said warmly.

"Congratulations on the successful mission. You must be really proud of the team there at DPAE?" Jordan asked of Zuri.

"Most certainly. The entire company has worked really hard to pull this off and I am really happy for what they have achieved. From the spacecraft engineering team, to the launch team, everyone had to contribute to pull this off. We are looking forward to many more successful flights. This is only the beginning for us." Zuri smiled. "This was such a milestone. The DPAE team took a giant leap forward in space exploration for the planet."

"I saw the images of the satellite that the DPAE Ligare brought back to earth. What will happen to it?"

Zuri leaned forward on the desk, "Well, we are donating it to Los Diego Tech for their museum. That satellite was the first digital satellite and carried hundreds of broadcast networks out to the world. It definitely earned its place in their tech museum."

Jordan leaned forward, "So, the first satellite rescue was broadcast live for the world to see. But what our viewers really want to know is this: What was the purpose of that flight around the moon? The high definition videos you released of the moon fly-by were really a pleasant surprise. Was there something else to that part of the mission?"

"Well, we were using this flight as a test of our recovery techniques as well as a performance test of the spacecraft. We designed it as a multi-purpose exploration vehicle and needed to run in-situation performance tests to see the capabilities. We also used it to find anything system performing below specifications to see what needs to be improved. The DPAE learned a ton from this flight and our engineering teams are already getting down to work on the next generation of the craft."

"Amazing work, congrats to the whole team over there and we all look forward to the next launch." Jordan looked at the camera as it zoomed in on him. "Thanks for watching tonight. I am Jordan Helmsey of UBN News and this has been 'Eyes on Technology.'"

Ivan had personally been tasked with overseeing moving the Ligare and its precious cargo inside while the celebrations happened. The team had taxied the plane inside a very secure hangar shortly after all the press photos and speeches were done. The ship had immediately been plugged into the ground computer systems to begin full diagnostics and testing before they could open the cargo bay. Out of an abundance of caution, they hooked up an air purifier to remove the cargo hold air in case something from the wreckage was leaking. Since it took a pretty good impact during retrieval it seemed like an appropriate precaution. Most of the DPAE leadership had been parading the flight crew around in a series of interviews and were currently heading to Capitola to meet with the Prime Minister and Congress. That meant they could work in peace for the next week to carefully deal with the cargo in the hold.

The battery of tests took the crew about 3 days and they were given the all-clear to unload. "Scans show the air inside is clean so let's get this unloaded." Ivan waved to the hanger crew who were standing nearby. "Let's get the satellite out first and take it to Bay 2."

Slowly the cargo bay doors opened and one of the crane operators moved the overhead gantry into place. Ivan chuckled in amusement and thought to himself, *"That hook looks like a giant redemption machine claw."* The claw was expertly dropped down around the satellite and two riggers carefully strapped it to the cargo. A quick thumbs-up and the satellite was lifted out of the Ligare and placed onto a large electric cart nearby. Two drivers whisked it away and another driver maneuvered a much larger cart into place next to the ship.

Ivan had moved to an overhead platform to monitor the retrieval from above. Glancing down at a tablet screen he looked over to the ground control supervisor who came to stand next to hime. He was a coyote named Fasile Ramirez. "Man, that pod looks pretty beat up. It's amazing it is still in one piece." The coyote just nodded in agreement. "Hope the other claw is strong enough."

The gantry operator wheeled the second crane in above the ship which was equipped with an articulated claw tailored precisely to grab the cylindrical pod. This time he went in extremely slow. In its open position the claw barely fit through the cargo doors on the top of the craft. Two other cargo handling staff members went into the plane to help guide the claw around the object.

After being inside for a little while, one member of the cargo team called on the radio. "The pod did quite a number on the landing clamps. They're pretty bent up. It will take us about an hour to free the pod. Minn, please bring the tool chest over here."

A small fox wheeled the tools near the hatch and started handing in different tools that the team was calling for. Eventually they cleared the broken clamps and had it strapped to the claw for removal.

"Okay, ready for lifting," one the workers radioed to the other crew. The cargo pad groaned as the weight of the pod was slowly pulled up. "Pause." He radioed to the gantry operator so they could make sure everything was still secured and holding. "Yeah, this pad is compressed about 150 millimeters. Took quite an impact. Okay to resume lift."

Ivan headed down from the platform he was on so he could get a better look at the pod when it was set upon the carrier. As the pod touched down on the cradle it made a loud metallic groan as it settled. Ivan walked up to it and ran a palm across it. He walked down the length of it to the front of the pod, dipping a finger in some of the many divots peppering the hull. The hull had a dull, dark gray color with a lot of carbon scoring. It was made of metal and had no ceramic shielding unlike their own ship. The windows were covered with some sort of shielding and those too, were covered in craters from meteorites. "Doesn't look like it was designed for planet-fall. This thing has taken a beating over the centuries its been out there. It's lucky to not have been hit by something larger." Ivan said not really aiming his comment to anyone in particular. "Okay, take it to Bay S-5 and let's get it hooked up."

Ivan grabbed his phone and dialed some numbers. "Tell David Brynn that the pod will be ready for his team to plug in." He listened silently for a bit. "Yeah, it's in Bay S-5 and will be there in 45 minutes. Also send down Security Team 6. We are implementing security protocol Delta-4 for that room. No one goes in without my express permission and I mean NO one."

It had been a few weeks since the historic landing and the pod was moved into a high security lab. Tyler had finally returned to the DPAE from all the press junkets they had been on. While he was out, David Brynn and his team had hooked up their computers to the pod to try to access the data storage on the pod. Thanks to the earlier decryption they had easily gained access to the memory systems on the pod. Moreover, they downloaded exobytes of information and had begun the arduous task of cataloging everything.

"Okay, let's head to the observation control room." Tyler motioned to those who he had gathered to discuss what they had found. It was a small, tight-knit group of people he could really trust. He had Maya, Renata, Ingrid, Zuri and David from the DPAE team along with key members of the Global Aerospace Oversight Committee. Representing the GAOC, Senator Brennan Clark was in attendance along with his Press Secretary Hiro Atsuko. Neville Pierce was also present, which was not surprising, since he was the architect of this whole mission.

Ivan met them at the entrance to the secure section of the DPAE. "Follow me," said Ivan. As they walked down the hall, they would see different teams dressed in full body, white clean suits entering different secure doors. Ivan reached a door, pulled out a badge and scanned for entry. The wolf then leaned forward to the retinal scanner to scan his eye. The light on the panel turned green and the door lock clicked, signaling it was unlocked. He turned to everyone following him, "We will not be going into the chamber, so you will not need special protections, like the teams you see walking around." Ivan then held the door open to let everyone file in.

Once inside, the lights automatically increased in brightness, revealing a couple tiers of tables and chairs aimed at an opaque window, like in an auditorium. Ivan waved to the seats and said, "Please, take a seat." Then, he moved to a console positioned to the right of the window.

Tyler moved to the floor in front of the group. "So, I will remind you that what you see here is considered highly classified both here at the DPAE and to the GAOC and the military." He nodded to Ivan who pressed a key on the control panel, triggering the glass to turn fully transparent revealing the pod they had retrieved. "So, some of you know this but the Ligare had a secondary and very important mission. The mission was to retrieve this artifact." The screen started to overlay some computer graphics outlining the pod and putting up the vitals on the screen. "This...is the pilot's escape pod that ejected at the last minute before the alien spacecraft exploded. It was in an elongated orbit around Earth since the mid-thirteen hundreds."

Brennan stood up and moved to the window to get a better look. Turning to Tyler. "So in that alien crash video, this is the vehicle that took that last parting shot?" he questioned.

"Yes, it was. The alien ship, the "Wandering Mist", managed to be in contact with this pod for a short amount of time and that's why it was in that video." Tyler turned to look at the pod through the window. "This pod represents the largest, most intact piece of alien technology ever found. I am amazed that it's in this great a condition after being out there for over 650 years."

"Wait," Maya piped up. "Pilot's escape pod? Does that mean the alien's body is still on board?"

Tyler looked over to Maya. "The short answer is yes but I'll get to that in a moment." The coyote's gaze wandered to the craft and then returned it back to the group. "David and his team have been able to access the storage device on the pod. There's a massive amount of data stored on it. So much so we had to quickly build a new data storage room for all the information. Their ship was an exploration and science vessel tasked with exploring unknown planets. We are confident that this pod contained a complete backup of the main ship's storage. Unlike the fractured systems we previously had, this one completely intact. David's group has determined that it's a complete repository of their science and culture. It's like a backup of their society so they would have all the information needed to establish new colonies. The data dump contains everything: theoretical work, genetic engineering, medical science, construction techniques and full design schematics of every bit of their technology. That includes the full design of the 'Wandering Mist' and its FTL technology. The information from this ship will change everything on Earth as we know it."

Everyone just sat there silently taking in the gravity of what Tyler just said to them.

After a little while, Maya stood up to walk down to the front to the viewing window. "That brings me back to my earlier question: What about the pilot?"

"Yes Maya, the pilot is in there." Tyler motioned to Ivan who keyed another button.   The screen opaqued, then the computer drew a multicolored wire-frame drawing of the capsule. Notations slowly appeared labeling the systems and vitals on the pod. In the middle of the pod the computer identified the pilot's area. "This is the layout of the systems on the pod. The pilot is contained in a sub-capsule in the middle."

Ivan then clicked the touch screen which enlarged the pilot's capsule and started displaying the vitals of that system.

Renata stood up to join them in staring at the pilot's container schematic. She pointed at all the statistics scrolling by. "What does this all mean?"

"The pilot's capsule is a life-pod. It's a hibernation chamber and its systems are working within specifications. The pilot is..." Tyler paused for a second to look at each of them and then stated emphatically. "*alive.*"

⟡